LORD OF SILVER ASHES

ROWAN BLOOD VOLUME TWO

KELLEN GRAVES

CONTENTS

PRONOUNCIATION GUIDE (FICTIONAL & INSPIRED)

AILIR (FICTIONAL) *EYE-LEER*

ASCHE (FICTIONAL) *ASH*

AON-ADHARCACH (SCOTTISH-GAELIC) *OON ER-KACH*

BEANNIGHE (IRISH-GAELIC) *BAN-NEE*

BEANTIGHE (IRISH-GAELIC) *BAN-TEE*

CONNACHT (IRISH-GAELIC) *CON-AH-KT*

CLYMEUS (FICTIONAL, GREEK INSPO) *CLAI-MAY-US*

CYLVAN (FICTIONAL) *SIL-VAN*

DERDRIU (IRISH-GAELIC) *DER-DRU*

EIAS (FICTIONAL) *EYE-USS*

ELLUIN (FICTIONAL) *ELL-OO-IN*

GAEILGE (IRISH-GAELIC) *GWEL-GAH*

GEIS *(IRISH-GAELIC) GESH*

SHAMHRADHÁIN (IRISH-GAELIC) *SHAM-RA-DIEN*

SÍDHE (IRISH-GAELIC) *SHEE*

TUATHA DÉ DANANN (IRISH-GAELIC) *TOO-HA DE DAN-AN*

TITLE REFERENCE (FICTIONAL)

HE/SHE/THEY

LORD/LADY/GENTLE

KING/QUEEN/DANAE

PRINCE/PRINCESS/DAURAE

It was sorrows were foretold, but great joys were my share always; yet it is a cold place I must go to be with you, Naisi; and it's cold your arms will be this night that were warm about my neck so often. . . .

It's a pitiful thing to be talking out when your ears are shut to me. It's a pitiful thing, Conchubor, you have done this night in Emain; yet a thing will be a joy and triumph to the ends of life and time.

Deirdre of the Sorrows
JM Synge, 1910

1

THE GHOST

There were lies in every myth.

Humans claimed Persephone ate four pomegranate seeds; the fey claimed three.

There were only three children of Lir painted on the ceiling of Morrígan's Grand Library; humans told stories of four.

The Greeks claimed there to be three Fates; but according to the smuggled book in Saffron's lap, high fey knew four, one for each season, for each time of day. Morning, day, evening, night—no different from their Courts of Expectation.

In human myths, heroes overcame adversity through learned wit and cleverness.

The fey tapped into power already existing inside of them. High fey bowed to fates already decided, where the hero's tribulations came through learning to accept a pre-determined end. They might earn divine mercy to change their fate by being the strongest, smartest, most beautiful, purest creature to walk amongst others, though the chance to change fate only ever came to those born into lives already brimming with indulgence. There was no mercy to spare for imperfect, simple, lesser creatures. Their fates were sealed.

Saffron found a way to burn that book, specifically, in the

little fireplace in his attic bedroom—but not before tearing out any blank chapter pages for the growing collection of paper for a new sketchbook.

Through the round window, overcast light festered from the sunset's nightly dance, leaving the world gray and mundane. Tapping rain on the window anchored him in reality, having greeted him as he awoke from the same recurring nightmare he rarely found relief from.

Reading in the barn. Losing his way back to Cottage Wicklow. Wandering in the woods for hours and hours, sun never rising, never crossing a familiar path, only to be attacked and pinned by a putrid beast, teeth sinking into his throat before he could scream—and just like every other night, Saffron jolted awake drenched in sweat and shaking. Just like every other night, he managed to gulp back the scream pinned in his throat by the silver collar around his windpipe. He always woke up choking, suffocating beneath silver hands encircling his neck and refusing any sound louder than a gasp. Drowning beneath pooling spit and bile until the grip finally loosened, and he could swallow it back.

From there, every waking ritual was the same. Searching the room for signs of unwelcome visitors, he found the string over the latch of the window unsnapped; the charcoal dust at the foot of the door remained undisturbed except by pixie hands; the desk chair remained propped beneath the knob in lieu of a working lock. No one had bothered to disturb him while he slept the day away—again. The reassurance was as much a comfort as it was like pinching fingernails reminding him how easy it was to be forgotten.

He'd gone almost two weeks without hearing another living voice within reach, including his own. The only words he overheard came through the floorboards, the open window, or, only once, when one fey lord forced his way inside before Saffron knocked him unconscious.

Saffron never realized how easy it was to wither away in silence.

Danann House had some residual noises—scuttering mice under the floorboards and in the walls. The muffled, ticking clock from Cylvan's suite below. The muted whistle of wind on the other side of the round window that never sealed all the way closed. The owl finches in the ceiling rafters that constantly argued with Saffron's three pixie companions. The occasional, quiet whispers he'd long since attributed to the ghosts of the house.

But the sounds he'd grown accustomed to in the attic of Danann House were so very, very different from the constant noise of Beantighe Village. Cottage Wicklow. Fern Room.

He missed the sound of Letty's snoring. How Berry and Fleece would whisper to one another all night, as if they really thought they spoke softly enough to go unheard. How Hollow always tried to move carefully when he arrived back from his night-shift, but his heavy footsteps always made the board right inside the door squeak beneath his weight.

Saffron missed the passive sounds of the woods right on the other side of the iron fence and rowan trees. He missed crows pecking at the garden until Baba Yaga raced out to screech at them to leave. In Danann House's attic, despite still being within reach of the trees, he only sometimes overheard sunsingers in the distance. As if they kept a wide berth from the gardens, the apple orchard, and any wild trees that framed the yard. Crows pecked at the fruits and vegetables growing in the back greenery, but they never stayed long enough to demonstrate real interest, as if even those foods were rotten and tasted as bitter as the air in the house.

But it wasn't just the silence—it was the pure isolation that chilled Saffron down to his bones, to the point he wondered if that was how ghosts became nothing but cool gusts of air.

Beantighes were used to veiling their demeanors. Many even preferred it, sought comfort in hiding away, in disappearing into anonymity and keeping their faces for themselves. Saffron had been one of them—but he never knew how it would feel to be veiled entirely from the rest of the world. Not just his face, but every single part of him that proved himself alive. Locked away in the attic of Danann House where he seemingly ceased to exist, without a voice, without a soul, without a being. Just a residual spirit passing between his room, the washroom, the walls, the study.

Sometimes, late at night, he wandered the parlor. The kitchen. The corridors between rooms, finding every secret place and forgotten corner. But never for long. Danann House and all her nooks didn't belong to him—there were other ghosts who had been there much longer, who slept in the adjoining attic rooms and sometimes wept with their own ancient loneliness. Perhaps the only reason they hadn't noticed him as something different was because, more often than not, his misery joined their chorus once the house fell silent.

Perhaps he felt it more intensely that evening, and the three evenings prior, because there had been no difference between *silence* and *sound*. In the first week, he'd gotten so used to laying on his back on the floor and listening to Cylvan in the suite below him. Pacing. Drinking. Playing his violin for hours and hours and hours, sometimes wailing the strings long into the morning. All those times he listened to Cylvan weep, or scream, or argue with Taran—all the times he overheard multiple voices making love on the sheets, only to be commanded out again with no warning—all the times Saffron heard furniture break, listening to gusts of wind tear through the room and out the windows—had helped him feel alive. Because only something living could experience agony so deep in their bones, they splintered and crumbled until left sobbing in tandem.

But Cylvan and Taran had gone somewhere. For three days, the house had been empty, except for the occasional knock on his door and tray of food left on the floor of the other side. Since then, Saffron resorted to sleeping during the day in the silence, as he couldn't handle the thought he'd actually been forgotten about entirely. It was normal for silence to come at night. He enjoyed the silence at night; he was terrified of silence that came during the day.

Pushing sweaty hair from his eyes, Saffron slipped into the routine he'd established early in a pathetic attempt to find solace in loneliness. He made the bed with perfection. He pulled the desk chair from under the doorknob, grabbing the hours-old food off the ground on the other side and leaving it on the desk before washing up in the bathroom across the hall. He scrubbed his sleeping clothes in the sink, and left them to dry on the line in the corner.

He bypassed the charcoal dust on the floor inside his room, not having much left after scattering it almost every night from the start. He used to sweep it up again in the morning and apply it again before going to sleep—but he was quickly running low of the charcoal stolen from the cold hearth in the parlor. There had been a boisterous party the night before the house fell totally silent, so perhaps Saffron could find more…

Except to harvest more charcoal, it would mean leaving his room. Leaving the attic. And something about facing the potential of having been left behind, would be exactly the push he needed to break apart entirely. What if he went downstairs and found all the furniture gone? Layered with dust, not unlike before Cylvan transferred to Morrigan in the first place? What if the Aon-adharcach suite was empty of the prince's things, his party clothes, his myriad of lip colors and eye shadows, his bath oils, his lotions and perfumes? What if Saffron had truly—been forgotten?

He didn't want to know. So he stayed in his room, and kept to the routine.

He dressed in the black blouse, slacks, and shoes, though left the veil folded at the foot of his bed.

He broke up bits of stale bread for the owl finches nesting in the rafters.

He offered pieces of pressed sugar to Dewdrop, Goldie, and

Apple, the pixies who shared the nest with the birds when they weren't sleeping in Saffron's hair.

He checked the pitiful good luck altar on the narrow shelf by the window, where a constant candle burned surrounded by pixie gifts and pieces of paper with his friends' names written. Specifically, his Fern roommates, whose noise he missed the most out of anyone. Hollow, Letty, Fleece, Baba Yaga. That morning, the candle sank within an inch of its life, and Saffron used the existing flame to light a new one before scraping dripped wax from the shelf and floor, wadding it up into a recycled shape around a thread of knotted cloth. Another reason he wouldn't have to leave the attic until someone came for him, or he heard signs of life down below.

Finally, he snuck into the adjacent room, kneeling in the corner and pulling up one of the loose floorboards with a subtle clatter of old wood. One by one, he removed every book he'd managed to steal from the house's study and didn't wish to burn, though there weren't many, as he'd learned quickly his chance of finding anything actually useful on those shelves was slim. Still, he'd managed to snipe a reference guide to wild fey, and even an instructional text on calligraphy and handwriting. His messy lettering had greatly improved in the past few weeks, at least. He couldn't wait to show Cylvan.

A lump formed in his throat. He removed the final book hidden amongst the corn husk and cotton insulation—the book of human Greek Myths left by Cylvan, himself, outside the window of Adelard's office. Tucked far down into the gap of the spine, the prince's family ring was lodged safely as well, though the bulky shape made it impossible to lay the book flat and open. It was even beginning to push through the spine between pages, and Saffron anticipated the day it finally emerged like a spring flower breaking through permafrost. Right amidst the story of Icarus and his wax wings, which Saffron had read at least a hundred times since becoming an attic ghost.

Returning to the bedroom, he shoved the desk chair under

the doorknob again, and dragged the writing desk closer to the bed. Sitting cross-legged, he opened the book of calligraphy to practice his alphabet, sighing loudly as he was forced to witness the notes he'd recorded previously. It started as random thoughts, but soon those grew too miserable to copy down, so he resorted to transcribing anything he happened to hear through the floor, the open window, during parties or late night gatherings. Filling every margin, gap between chapters, empty space between chapters, like an obsessive journalist frantically scribbling every lick of gossip he heard whispered.

Matt-hild had to drop out becase her family can no longer aford the tuishion(?)

Did you here about E-nic? They still have'nt come back from Hesper.

I herd some-one spotted the rowan spirit in the woods the other night.

Oh? I heard that too! Has any-one seen the wolf along with it? The headmistress said their're one and the same.

I don't think any-one has seen the wolf. I herd it was only a myth.

I herd the rowan spirit was just a beantighe causing a stir.

I herd it was a true wild spirit who glammored itself to look like a beantighe.

Either way, the headmistress goes mad when ever she hears it mentioned, but will reward you with enough merits to take a day off if you tell her...

It was strange to overhear chatter about himself—especially

when he, the rowan spirit, hadn't set foot outside Danann House in weeks. Sometimes he feared one of his friends had taken on the red veil in his stead, in some misguided attempt to avenge him. Or, perhaps the one student was correct, and a wild thing simply wanted in on all the fun. Perhaps they only imagined it. Perhaps sightings were falsified for Elluin's reward. Either way—Morrígan was stained with gossip about the spirit, the wolf, the head-mistress, which had been Saffron's intention all along. To know it continued even after he vanished was something bittersweet. At least attention had been drawn away from Cylvan, like Saffron hoped.

When he could no longer focus, Saffron pinched the bridge of his nose, and instead bent over the book of myths. Just wishing to disappear. Just wishing to coax the night to pass faster, so that he might lie down and close his eyes again as soon as light returned. He didn't even have the rhythmic rain to keep him company once the sun fully set, and he was reduced to strumming fingers and tapping the nib of his quill in order to keep it together in the silence.

Fuck. He hated the silence. His mind always focused on every little noise outside the window, through the floor, on the other side of the door. Despite knowing he was alone. Despite knowing there was no reason for anyone to come. His mind still searched for any sign of life in the house, anything that might be able to acknowledge him, too—but that was a lost cause. It was a painful thing to want. Saffron learned quickly, to want to be found was nearly enough to break his will entirely—and there were more important things at stake.

If he was obedient, if he played by the rules, if he stayed on Taran's good side, no other beantighes would have to die. Saffron could rest assured they were safe, morning and night and every-where in between.

And with his two weeks swiftly coming to a close, he would eventually, hopefully, be allowed to leave the house again. Even if it was in search of the wild fairy fruits meant to drug Cylvan into a forced proposal—at least Saffron knew he would be close to Cylvan when it happened. So that even if he found the fruits, he would be able to make sure they never went anywhere close to the prince.

So that even if he never found the fruits, he could be there to ensure Taran didn't try anything else.

All the while—he would continue to scour the house's study for anything that could help. He would figure out a way out of the house at night, while everyone else slept, and he would write messages to Baba Yaga asking for his books and arid reference notes. He would be able to cross campus in the dark and return to the Grand Library, and continue where he and Cylvan left off. He'd been so close to a breakthrough in charming the fern ring for Cylvan—he might only need a few more hours with helpful words in his hands.

Saffron only had to be obedient. Timid. Silent. Well-behaved.

Silent. Restrained. Disgraced; the basic requirements of being a beantighe.

Saffron was, if anything else, good at being a beantighe.

2

—

THE OMEN

Ink dripped from the end of Saffron's stolen quill, leaving black marks amidst the words on the page below him. It blotted out a long, meandering description of the wings of Icarus and Daedalus, who, on the next page, would take off into the sky to escape imprisonment—only for the son to tumble right back to the earth.

Candlelight reflected off one of the silver cuffs on Saffron's wrist, carved into two overlapping hands. So many times, he'd wondered if it was the same cuff Cylvan wore to imprison him in Danann House, too. Locked in his fate, just like he'd been locked in the house. Just like Saffron had been locked in the house after him.

His eyes flickered to the window. He should have been asleep as soon as the sun rose, but he brimmed with restlessness. According to the marks on the desk, that day was the end of his two weeks.

Exhaling through his nose, Saffron returned the quill to the page. He underlined the familiar word *hubris*, before trailing toward the margin.

This is certainly the thing that makes you so disagreeable, he wrote, referencing the first time he heard that word in Cylvan's suite on Imbolc.

Soon, Saffron would show Cylvan his own annotations. The notes Saffron left in improved handwriting, text occasionally blurred with loosed tears as he wallowed in his own loneliness. Just trying to find a single thing to hold himself together, finding comfort in the words of fantastical tales just like he once did with Derdriu, Naoise, Niamh, Oisín.

Nibbling at what remained of dinner, Saffron absentmindedly drew the silhouette of what he imagined the wax wings to look like in a gap between words. Dewdrop, hovering over his shoulder, waved the pen away, reclining on the page as if the inked wings were theirs. Saffron smiled to himself, offering it a piece of breadcrust, which was snatched away without the pixie so much as sitting up.

Something bumped at the end of the corridor, and Saffron's eyes flickered upward. A sound, the thing his subconscious mind sought out despite his pleas for respite.

He tried not to think about it too much. He returned to the pages. He read another line—and another sound came, that time making the floor vibrate. Saffron sat up, glancing toward the door. His heart pounded. Was Cylvan finally back home? He swore he heard voices somewhere in the distance. He slowly closed the book. The chair beneath the knob jolted as a knock came on the door, and Saffron nearly leapt from where he sat.

He wasn't used to being summoned, as his dinner was usually left in silence. It was the first time anyone had intentionally tried to get his attention, to intentionally see and speak to him—and Saffron almost thought he'd only imagined it.

But the knock came again, slightly more impatient that time, and Saffron's instincts kicked in. Hurrying to cork the ink and sweep his books under the bed, he shoved the desk away and jumped to his feet. Pulling the chair away from the knob, he opened it just enough to brace for whoever stood on the other side—and he didn't know whether to be frightened or relieved to find Taran mac Delbaith meeting his eyes.

"Beantighe," he said with a faux smile. "You took so long to answer, I thought perhaps you'd died."

Saffron frowned. He straightened up, glad he was dressed as primly as he could be in the blouse and slacks.

"Let's talk," Taran said, nodding in request to step into the room. Saffron moved out of the way, not having much of a choice.

Taran stepped inside—the first time he had since trapping Saffron there—and regarded the room. In another time and place, Saffron might have even considered the space to be *quaint*—but those were not normal circumstances. The faded wallpaper on the walls did nothing but slouch inward at night, the ceiling did nothing but sink as he tried to close his eyes to sleep, reaching within an inch of his mouth and making it hard to breathe.

Taran finally turned around. He steepled his fingers politely over his chest, then put on a matching smile that made goose-bumps race down Saffron's arms.

"The prince and I have been away in Avren," he said, as if Saffron hadn't already noticed and suffered through every horrible, silent moment. Saffron just nodded. "While we were there, I had plenty of opportunity to think about things, including the details of our geis. I've come to the conclusion... I would like to release you from our deal."

Saffron stared at him for a long time; long enough for his ears to ring. The words didn't comprehend for an eternity, but when they did, Saffron barely felt them. He must have imagined it. Was this just another dream? But he and Taran remained in that silence for a long, long, long time, enough for the world to turn upside down then rightside up again beneath Saffron's feet.

All the while, Taran never looked away, searching Saffron's expression. As if—expecting something other than pure, silent disbelief.

"I am no longer in need of wild fairy fruits," he finally went on. "Nor do I have any more reason to ask beantighes for them. As such, I've decided to let you go."

Saffron still couldn't react.

"Because of what you know, however, you cannot remain on Morrígan's campus," Taran went on, and Saffron sensed the slightest hint of frustration as Taran still didn't get the reaction he wanted. What had he been expecting, jumps for joy? Howls of relief? "Kaelar has agreed to formalize his patronage and transfer you to his family estate in the Fall Court—"

Saffron jumped slightly, instinctively taking a step forward and cutting Taran off. He tugged at his silver collar, demanding for it to be removed so that he might speak. Taran shook his head.

"I'm releasing you from our geis, beantighe; I do not even care to kill you. You should be thanking me. You will live a peaceful life with your new patron-fey."

No—those were false words. Perhaps Taran wasn't killing him outright, but he was sending him to the other side of Alfidel to work under Kaelar. He didn't remove the collar or the cuffs, either, and Saffron suspected that was on purpose. The ringing in his ears turned to steam, and then pounding thumps. His mind could only race, trying to figure out any reason why. Why, why, why.

Either Taran still sought the fruits, but simply realized doing so with Saffron would be too much of a complication—

Or he'd found another way to get what he wanted out of Cylvan.

Even if Taran willingly released Saffron back to Beantighe Village; even if he willingly released Saffron back to Luvon in Amber Valley, instead—Saffron would still refuse to go so easily. Not when those words were so haunting.

But he knew better than to show Taran anything other than polite gratitude. He forced a blank smile onto his face, knowing the fey lord wouldn't care enough to notice how empty and skeptical it was. He bowed slightly in thanks, before motioning to his small wardrobe of things, as if to ask, *"when should I be ready to go?"*

"We're having a welcome party in the house tonight; you will leave tomorrow afternoon after you finish cleaning up after it. Kaelar will take you to the edge of Morrígan, where you will take a horse to Connacht and board a ship. There will be a ticket waiting for you, to take you to the Fall Court."

More alarms, like banging drums in the back of Saffron's mind. Why not leave that night? Why allow him to travel alone? Why would Kaelar only accompany him to the edge of Morrígan? Why give Saffron any amount of unchaperoned time on the road at all, when it would be so easy for him to flee in the opposite direction...?

Ah. Unless that was exactly what Taran hoped would happen. He wished for Saffron to disappear, didn't he?

No, Taran would not simply allow Saffron to disappear, without any trace, without any knowing of where he'd gone. Saffron suddenly wondered if he was ever meant to make it to Connacht at all.

Perhaps Taran meant to summon his beast back, to claim one last beantighe life, to place one more sin on Cylvan's back? Why not, if it would only benefit him?

Either way, Saffron knew better than to go anywhere with anyone the following morning, or anytime before then. But Taran wouldn't allow him to stay, either, and it wasn't like Saffron could leave the house on his own whim in secret because of the cuffs trapping him. He would have to figure a reason to stay, something even Taran wouldn't be able to refuse—but without the ability to speak, without knowing what else Taran planned to use instead of the fruits, what was Saffron supposed to do?

Still—Saffron nodded. He smiled again in thanks for the opportunity to be released, but didn't shake Taran's hand when it was offered. He pretended not to notice. He turned to take stock of his few belongings, like the air-headed human servant Taran always thought him to be. When the fey lord rolled his eyes and finally left, Saffron could only sink to the edge of the bed and wrap his arms around himself in anxiety.

What the fuck was he supposed to do? Clearly, Taran never actually held Saffron in any esteem at all. Perhaps he never even considered Saffron to be useful in searching for the fruits in the first place.

Perhaps—he'd purposefully meant to hide Saffron away while doing whatever else he wanted outside. Knowing Saffron was locked up, silent, unable to meddle any longer. To have Cylvan all to himself, to lie about whatever he wanted, to do whatever he wanted...

Saffron clutched the front of his shirt, closing his eyes.

Had Taran already found the fruits? Had Taran bypassed the agreement of their geis entirely, and asked Hollow or someone else to go find them while Saffron waited patiently and obediently in Danann House? Had they found the fruits in Saffron's wake? Had more people died while he thought he'd protected them?

Or—did Taran actually have another means of getting what he wanted from Cylvan, without need of the fruits at all? But, Arrow had said it, themself—

There are only two ways to compel a high fey; with their true name, or with wild fairy fruits.

Unless Taran had somehow gotten a hold of Cylvan's true name... what else could Taran possibly use to push Cylvan into the mold designed to control him?

Below the floor, voices came through the slats between the wood. Saffron once obsessively listened to every word, memorizing the sound of Cylvan's voice, imagining what he must be doing, who he was with, what kind of a mood he was in—but that time, it was easy to hear.

Cylvan sounded—happy. Cheerful. He spoke with more ease than Saffron had heard in a while, enough that chills raced down his spine as he almost couldn't believe it was really him. He almost refused to listen at all, terrified that there was something else going on—but then another voice joined, and Saffron went quiet to listen.

"I think it's great you've finally chosen a title, Asche. 'Daurae' suits you."

"What if I change my mind later, though?" The second voice responded, and Cylvan chuckled.

"You can always change it, whenever you want. Even I cycled through daurae, princess, *and* prince *before finally settling on one. It doesn't actually mean anything."*

"Mother said it's from old tradition, right? Why even bother anymore?"

"Gods know. When you usurp me for the throne, you can change it."

"Ha, ha. You know I hate that joke."

Saffron bit his lip. Unable to resist, he lowered himself to the floor on his knees, claiming his normal position of lying on his back and closing his eyes to listen. To disappear into the sound of Cylvan's voice, especially that time when it was so... content.

"Ugh—you're really going to make me sleep in the dusty guest room downstairs?" Daurae Asche complained, followed by what sounded like a body *fwumping* to the bed. *"That's not fair at all. I think you should sleep downstairs while I get the suite."*

"How exactly is that fair?" Cylvan asked playfully. *"I'm the oldest, of course I get the biggest and best room."*

"Since when did the oldest get the best of anything?"

"Ah, right, I almost forgot—I'm also the smartest, the strongest, the prettiest, and the favorite."

"Are not! Tross told me so, himself."

"Tross is playing favorites with his kids, now, is he? Interesting how that works the second he has one from his own family line."

"Joke's on you, because Fírche isn't his favorite, either. It's Néah."

"... Shut up, is it really? Hasn't she and Nem been spending all their time with mother, lately?"

"She convinced mother to wear something red at the last family

dinner. You know father has been trying to do that for years. He's run out of ideas for black lace on black silk with black buttons..."

"But now he can use red."

"Yes."

"I'll believe it when I see it," Cylvan laughed. *"The only red Naoill has ever worn was the blood of their enemies."*

"Néah did imply there was something about a bear involved..."

"... Danu's mound, I really am missing out on all the family gossip, aren't I? At least now you get to miss it all with me in this miserable place."

"Miserable? I think Morrigan is nice. Taran was telling me all about the history in the carriage."

"Yes, because Taran only cares about decorum and old traditions as much as the rest of the conservative bores attending here..."

Siblings. It was one of Cylvan's siblings, brought all the way from Avren. Did something really happen while they were gone...?

Was there any chance—Cylvan had already proposed to Taran while they were in Avren? Was that why family suddenly traveled with him?

Could it have happened, already?

Saffron jolted to his feet a little too fast, and the voices below went silent.

"What was that?" Asche asked, and Saffron's heart stopped.

"Probably just a ghost," Cylvan answered after a moment of consideration. *"Get used to it, Asche—there are plenty of spirits wandering Morrigan's campus."*

"Oh—like the rowan spirit, right? Do you think I'll see it while I'm here?"

"... How do you know about that?"

"Everyone was talking about it at school... they said there was a rowan spirit at Morrigan who was threatening students with wolves..."

"... No, I don't think you'll see the rowan spirit while you're here. He's... long gone."

No. No—Saffron wasn't gone.

And he wouldn't be anytime soon, even if Taran tried to force him.

Saffron was very much alive. He'd been waiting patiently for the moment he could be with Cylvan again to prove it, too—and he wasn't going to let all of his misery, his loneliness, his soul-devouring guilt go to waste without at least letting Cylvan know he'd never left his side in all that time. Not once. Not one fucking time.

Turning to the mirror on the wall, Saffron met his eyes—and decided.

If Taran wouldn't do it, Saffron would simply resurrect himself for Cylvan to witness.

3

THE REBIRTH

Proserpina's silver cuffs kept Saffron from leaving the walls of Danann House, but they did not contain him within the walls of the attic. Perhaps Taran didn't realize that; perhaps Taran truly never thought that far ahead when it came to creatures he considered to be lesser than him. But Saffron was not someone to underestimate. He was not someone to revoke a deal on. He was not someone to never spare a second thought to.

Saffron donned the black blouse, veil, slacks, and boots of a prim and proper beantighe servant. He stood for an hour, gazing out the window in waiting, so as not to wrinkle anything. He watched through the round glass as string lights illuminated the gardens below, then slowly filled with chattering voices, moving bodies, the sound and smell of alcohol and music and a fete not unlike the last one he crashed in search of Prince Cylvan.

I was waiting for something to come and break up this boring fete.

Saffron fiddled with the prince's family ring on his finger, pulled from the spine of his book of myths. He would use it as proof that he was himself; a real, living thing, wearing Cylvan's crest. Gifted by Cylvan, himself; something not even Taran knew about. Not something Taran could ever recreate or falsify or manipulate his way out of.

As far as Cylvan knew, Saffron was arrested and taken to Avren for execution, just like Taran told him two weeks prior. But, as far as Cylvan would also find out that very night—Saffron had returned, and had been wearing his ring the entire time he was away.

Perhaps the ring had even been the thing to save his life. Perhaps it was the only thing Saffron protected while under arrest, even when his memories were stripped, as a reminder of someone who must have cared for him before being taken away.

Perhaps the ring was the reason he, as a newly memory-stripped beantighe, knew to seek Prince Cylvan out once returning to Morrígan because, surely, after regaining consciousness with no memory left, Saffron was so curious why he'd been given something so beautiful and rare and intimate...

His fantasies ran wild—but no matter how it played out, Taran wouldn't get what he wanted. Saffron would not leave Danann House without one other person knowing he was still alive. One other person—who once gave Saffron his ring, and swore to patronize him. Swore to protect him. Who screamed with such agony once told of Saffron's supposed fate.

Gazing down at the ring, Saffron squeezed it, then closed his eyes and steeled his nerves.

Taran would learn that night—to never underestimate Saffron, ever again.

IT WAS LIKE WANDERING BACK IN TIME. BACK TO THE first time he entered Danann House to prepare every room for the Imbolc fete that would come, having just escaped a trick played by a wild thing in the yarrow field. That time, he'd worn white. He'd had that first book of myths tucked into the back of his waistband. He'd just walked as Bríghde the night prior, and collected the wishes of every person in Beantighe Village. He was only hours from meeting Prince Cylvan, realizing who he really was. Making their geis in the Aon-adharcach suite.

Hours from—finding Arrow. From learning about the wolf.

Back then, he'd been so naïve to what he was walking into. He had no idea what would come of his geis, his insistence, his little games with the Night Prince of Alfidel, their secret time spent together in the Grand Library—but all the same, if Saffron could go back, he wouldn't do anything differently. He even clung desperately to what remained of that naïveté for himself, refusing to allow people like Taran mac Delbaith to strip it away from him.

Saffron left the attic in search of a raven who thought he'd lost his treasure. Who, Saffron hoped, upon seeing him again—would do anything to keep him. Would refuse to allow Taran to send him away. Even if Saffron couldn't tell Cylvan everything, even if he would still willingly keep his geis with Taran under the protection of performing a useful task, he hoped Cylvan had once cared for him enough to protect him one more time. Saffron only needed one more favor from his prince, and then he would gladly carry every burden from Cylvan's back until their own geis was realized.

Stepping into the kitchen from the servants' stairs, it was the first time Saffron found himself surrounded by so much movement, heat, noise, chatter, in weeks, and it all crashed into him at once like an ocean wave demolishing a withered dock. Nearly pummeling him into nothing but splinters, body and bones weary from disuse and inactivity while hiding in the ceiling. But his black veil was a gentle boon against the onslaught, and he was able to hold his breath long enough to gather his nerves again.

It helped that hardly anyone turned to look at him when he emerged in the kitchen, and those who did, didn't have enough interest to keep staring. Perhaps wearing all black helped him blend into the walls, the low light of the candle sconces, better than if he wore ghostly white like normal. They knew he was a beantighe, but didn't know what kind. They knew he was a beantighe—but didn't know what to do with him. So they simply didn't.

He had to reassure himself of those reasons, so as to not tumble into the growing pit of fear that he'd simply ceased to exist, after all.

Saffron made sure to move carefully through the crowd—like rotten boards of a dock on the tide—while keeping acutely aware of anyone who might recognize him, even from a distance. Kaelar, Taran, Magnin, Eias—any of them would see and know exactly who he was, what to do with him. Despite the throng of people making Saffron's skin itch and bubble, it at least offered a natural shield from anyone who might have spotted him, otherwise.

The kitchen crested in and out with people helping themselves to snacks and drinks, more cakes and fruits and buffets of indulgence stretching into the parlor, as well as out the back doors onto the terrace. Further down into the gardens, plots and fruit vines had been haphazardly torn away to make room for a bonfire in the center of the grass, and Saffron silently cursed every single one of them for ruining the only pretty sight he had out the back window. There would be a crater of charred wood and burnt greenery once they were finished—though it would be ironic if they accidentally burned down Danann House in the process. Then what would Taran do?

Standing at the edge of the terrace doors, Saffron scanned the crowd, though most of them blurred together in the dark or from unrecognizability. He did, however, spot Kaelar at the far edge near the apple trees, teasing Eias about something that was impossible to hear. Something about it made Saffron curious, gazing down at his cuffs, knowing Kaelar owned the silver hands-and-dagger ring that controlled them and set their boundary. It had never worked while he was away from the house, before, but— Saffron extended a hand through the door, heart fluttering when it passed without restriction. He wouldn't question it.

"Excuse me," a voice came from behind, and Saffron instinctively disregarded it, never having been spoken to so politely before—but then something touched his shoulder, and he glanced around quickly. Behind him stood a stunning face of familiarity that was, at the same time, completely strange to him. He must have pulled an expression visible through the dark chiffon, because the stranger frowned and pouted their lips.

"Excuse me," they insisted, waiting only long enough for Saffron to step back in order to pass. They didn't go very far, though, taking a sharp left to claim one of the terrace benches overlooking the gardens. It allowed Saffron a chance to observe them a moment longer, finally realizing who they resembled upon fully seeing the shape of their black horns.

That must have been Daurae Asche. With long blonde hair, crystalline-citrine eyes, and black horns carved into vines that matched their older brother's. Younger than Saffron expected, Daurae Asche was probably in their early teens going by human standards. They had the same slender figure as their older brother, though the sharp edges of their features were softened somewhat by a roundness in their cheeks and shoulders. Saffron wondered why they weren't engaging in the same debauchery as everyone else, knowing high fey practically started drinking the day they could speak a full sentence, but then noticed how they appeared more interested in the Tuatha dé Danann Family crest they beaded in an embroidery hoop than anything having to do with the party. Saffron chuckled despite himself, then got an idea, glancing down at his ring.

Not wanting to appear like he approached for that reason alone, Saffron grabbed a wine bottle from the kitchen, popping the cork with all the ease Luvon ever instilled in him. Bypassing every fey guest who immediately extended their glass for a refill, Saffron made his way out the back door. He paused only to bow and offer a silent greeting to the daurae, offering to refill their wine glass—only then realizing they didn't have one. A tingle of panic made his thoughts scramble, but Asche was as observant as Saffron could have only dreamed, noticing the ring on Saffron's finger. Raising their eyebrows slightly, they glanced up at him.

"Did you come from Avren with us?" They asked in confusion. "I don't remember bringing any handservants... oh, did my father send you? Can I see your face?"

Saffron pulled the veil off with ease, though kept his eyes low like a respectful beantighe should. Despite the ring, he put on all the airs of someone who had no idea what Asche was talking about, before pretending like he just then noticed the beadwork spread over Asche's lap. Making a face of timid curiosity, he let his eyes linger on the design, before glancing at the ring on his finger. The mysterious ring that was his only connection to the past after his memories were taken—according to his role to play.

Taking the bait, Asche claimed Saffron's hand to glance a little bit closer.

"Oh..." They said with continued confusion, tilting their head slightly and brushing a thumb over the face of the gold carving. "This is... Cylvan's ring. Where did you get it?"

Saffron demurely pulled his hand into his chest, trying to look as innocent as possible. Asche, who clearly hadn't been taken as a fool by anyone in their entire life, gazed up at him like he was the most interesting thing to happen all night.

"Let's go ask him," they said. "Maybe he forgot you were here?"

Saffron nodded, then was surprised when Asche took his hand like a child leading a stuffed animal.

Stumbling along behind them, it was more difficult to keep his eyes out for anyone who might be watching, especially when he already knew Kaelar and Eias were on the other side of the yard. Saffron pulled down his veil again, just in case—but all of those anxieties fell away the moment Cylvan came into view alongside the bonfire.

Clearly dressed for the fete, Cylvan wore high-waisted, damask-embroidered pants. A billowy black shirt draped open over his chest, revealing the smooth column of his throat and collarbones. His hair draped long and loose in perfect, inky waves, and silver liner accentuated the shape of his eyes. All of him, every last detail, every miniscule stitch of his outfit, his face, his entire being, gripped Saffron by the throat, making it hard to breathe.

But—it was more than his clothes. It was carved horns Saffron had once recreated in his sketchbook; sharp nails Saffron once played with; a mole under his eye that Saffron brushed a thumb over so many times. It was the mouth Saffron still fantasized about kissing, which once spoke his name so gently. *Beantighe. Saffron. Púca.*

But that same mouth, illuminated in the orange glow of the bonfire, was lip-locked with a pretty blonde fey, practically devouring one another where they sat in the grass by the fire. Saffron plummeted into instant, misplaced jealousy, fighting the urge to tear away from Asche's hand to rip the high fey from his prince's grasp and throw them in the fire. No, no, *no*—Saffron had to be naïve, timid, demure, uncaring, aloof, *fuck*—

Cylvan's hand not tangled up in his partner's hair held a sloshing bottle of wine, and in the light of the flames, Saffron could tell it was already halfway empty. It explained the prince's sloppy movements, the way his eyes hung heavy every time he cracked them open to peer at his partner. Every time he did, his expression wrinkled slightly, as if wishing it was someone else. Anyone else.

Saffron just focused on breathing. On being... empty. Polite. A blank slate. No memories, no recollections of the handsome person in front of him, even as badly as he wished—he was the one suffocating beneath Cylvan's mouth, instead of the stranger who vaguely resembled him.

If Saffron intended on maintaining his deal with Taran once Cylvan got involved and ensured Saffron stayed in Danann House, he would have to lead, from the beginning, with the idea he was the unthreaded, memory-stripped, ignorant little beantighe he and Taran once discussed, long ago. There would be no undoing it if he played himself too well, if Cylvan learned he was actually entirely in one piece. If Saffron kept up the ruse of his unthreading from the very start, Taran may be easier convinced to keep him alive in the house. Saffron hoped that to be the case, anyway.

He would die on the road to Connacht in the morning, otherwise.

Asche called for Cylvan's attention amidst the passionate act with the other fey, and Cylvan drunkenly rolled his head back, searching the darkness before scowling upon eyes landing on his sibling. As he pulled away, his fey partner kissed down his neck, hands creeping lower and making Cylvan exhale sharply. Saffron flushed hotter than the bonfire.

"What do you want me to do with your beantighe?" Asche asked.

"My what?" Cylvan grunted, before snapping at the fey lord on his lap, shoving them away as the person just smiled and licked their lips.

"Your beanti—!"

Eias suddenly, almost frantically, emerged from the darkness. They commanded Cylvan's attention—and arms hooked around Saffron's middle from behind, yanking him off his feet. All within that brief moment where Cylvan turned at the sound of his name, just long enough for Kaelar to burst from the shadows, himself, and bodily heave Saffron away faster than he could fight back.

Saffron dropped the wine and kicked his legs, thrashing back and forth and cursing as much as his choker would allow. Behind him, the fete faded slightly as he was carried to the far edge of the yard, holding his breath as Kaelar unexpectedly lifted him over the outer fence. He pulled Saffron back upon his feet hitting the ground on the other side, though, keeping him in place just long enough to whisper.

"You were supposed to wait until tomorrow," Kaelar breathed into his ear, and Saffron shuddered. "A little too excited, huh? I'm upset. I was hoping to get a little more time with you, but—seems you're eager to get going. I'll go let Taran know to meet you, alright?"

Saffron jolted, making the fence clatter as he rammed into it.

Attempting to claw himself free of Kaelar's arm, Kaelar commanded *restraint* on Saffron's cuffs, and they clacked together.

"You know the rules of moonhunting, don't you, beantighe?" Kaelar grunted as Saffron reeled back with a gasp and fought harder.

Moonhunting—compelling beantighes into the woods only to chase them down for fun. Fey played it with night-shift workers more than anyone else, but even Saffron had been snatched from campus after the sun went down. He'd always managed to navigate back to Cottage Wicklow simply because he knew the woods well enough—but he wouldn't be able to do that, again. And by Kaelar's threat, all of Saffron's fears were confirmed—he'd never meant to make it to Connacht in the morning. He was never meant to go to the Fall Court. He was meant to die on the road, to disappear into nothing but a true ghost.

But since he'd left confinement early—he would die that night in the woods, instead. Before Cylvan had ever seen him. Just like Taran originally wanted.

Cold terror grazed Saffron's skin as Kaelar's breath cascaded over it from behind. A finger pointed in the corner of his eye, indicating the bright, waxing crescent moon smiling lopsided in return. Grinning for any myriad of reasons—but for Saffron, it was an immediate teller of how close they'd come to Ostara.

How close they'd come before it all fell apart.

"Follow the moon."

Compelling enchantment washed through him, balming the anxiety and panic in an artificial, nauseating blanket, like a quilt he knew to be infested with insects. It coated his muscles, laid claim to his thoughts, reduced his agency to nothing but cotton fluff enamored with the glowing goddess overhead. He offered Kaelar a small, calm smile, as if thanking the fey lord for the opportunity—before his body moved on its own, and he walked without restraint into the dark trees.

4

THE SPIRIT

It was bittersweet for his first escape into the woods, unchaperoned and unchained, though burdened with chasing down the tilted moon that never came closer. That beguiling grin summoned Saffron farther, all while he blinked up at her with a drunken smile of his own, as if she were only playing coy. He would reach her, soon. Soon. Soon. He just had to keep walking. Eventually he would catch up, and then she would help him find his way back home, no matter how far into the wilderness he wandered.

Crickets chirped amidst wafting, encouraging voices in every direction, belonging to shimmery things in the distance, shadowy things up closer. More than once, a cold breath of something caressed the back of his neck—but the enchantment wouldn't allow him to turn and look. Not that he wanted to, the moon was the loveliest thing he'd ever seen. To avert his eyes for even a moment would surely break his heart. No wonder so many people went missing while moonhunting—they made the mistake of pulling their eyes away, only to instantly drop dead from loneliness. But he wouldn't make that mistake. He'd known nothing but loneliness for two weeks—the moon was finally offering him comfort, companionship, maybe even a soft touch on his skin. He wouldn't lose that chance.

But the longer he followed, the more his nerves realized they could think for themselves again. The more he felt the fresh air, the more he felt the increased thrumming of his heart. Step by step, Kaelar's command wore off. Like washing clay skin in a downpour, it sloughed off him in a trail on his heels—until he was fully revealed, relieved of the weight, and he could gasp in a panic.

Saffron twisted around too quickly, losing his footing and hitting the earth with his wrists still bound in the silver. The forest fell silent. He heard only his breath, the sound of his heart in his ears. If he strained hard enough, he swore he could also hear the laughter and excitement from the fete far off in the distance—but that could have been anything. That could have been any fey revel, anywhere within the trees. God knew—there were worse things in the woods to stumble across.

Gulping, Saffron returned slowly to his feet, fighting to pick useful thoughts from the panicked cacophony clanging around in his skull. If he just... walked straight ahead, with the velvet moon constantly over his shoulder, he would be able to find his way back. He only had to follow his shadow, when he could see it through a clearing in the canopy. Straight ahead. With the size of the bonfire burning, he should be able to find it again it no time. In no time, and then he could finally approach Cylvan without interruption—

Something crunched to his left, and he turned, blood striking like cold metal as giggling shapes returned to the shadows. Attempting to swallow back pre-vomit, Saffron turned his tongue over between his cheeks. He sought out the moon again, but didn't let his eyes linger, afraid any residual enchantment might surge again in his blood. He put her at his back. He clenched his bound fists in front of him.

Scampering feet and ringing giggles circled the entire time he walked, and Saffron struggled to maintain his composure, let alone his course. But he knew, whatever it was stalking him—if he bolted, they would take chase. He had to be calm. He had to be a ghost. He had to be something incorporeal, silent, unnoticed, unwitnessed—

"I thought I recognized you," a slurring voice made Saffron whirl around, finding a fey lord illuminated by the moon from behind. He held a bottle of wine from Danann House, smiling unevenly like he'd wandered out on his own and hadn't expected a meal to be served up right at his feet.

Saffron took a slight step back as his mind raced, but the encroacher never pulled his eyes away. He took another swallow from the bottle, before speaking again.

"You're the seelie prince's little beantighe pet, aren't you? You knelt in front of him at that party a few weeks ago before racing into the woods. Ah... ha, into the woods. That's where we are now."

Saffron habitually opened his mouth to deny it, only to halt with a squeeze of his silver choker. The fey lord took his silence as confirmation, and smirked.

"I thought so. Where is the Night Prince now?"

Saffron took another step back. His shoulder touched the nearest tree, and he wondered how fast he could turn and disappear into the shadows—but then another weight shifted in the bushes alongside them, and the fey grinned toward it.

"Is that you, your highness? I'm sorry to interrupt your little game. What is this, some kind of foreplay between you and your—"

A blood red blur lunged from the bushes, slamming into the fey lord with a heavy crunch. Rolling to a halt in the mud, the fey shrieked in alarm, and Saffron's knees gave out beneath him in tandem. Collapsing to the forest floor, his heart leapt into his throat the moment he laid eyes on red smoke trailing in the breeze.

That red veil—Saffron recognized it. He would recognize that rowan-drenched chiffon in an instant, even in the dark of the woods. Thrown out the same day he was given the disgraced black veil to wear in replacement—and reclaimed by something else wanting to don the rowan spirit mantle. No wonder the rumors were still alive and spreading—he was witnessing the spirit for himself.

He didn't have a chance to question it further, before the red spirit buckled forward, burying teeth into the fey lord's neck.

Saffron couldn't hold back his scream, a moment of it peeling out before the choker cut him off. Slamming backward into the tree, he gasped as the wild thing tore a bite clean out of the shrieking lord, who swore and thrashed and clutched at the wound. He nearly shoved it away, only for an aged hand to grip his wrist, the other hovering over his chest, fingers curling as if stealing something unseen.

"*Glyndwr,*" the veil-thief said, and chills kissed Saffron's skin when he realized, he knew that voice from somewhere. But there wasn't a chance to search his memory as the fey lord's mouth dropped open, and then he screamed again, throwing himself back and forth in a new, frothing panic. But the attacking creature lost interest as quickly as it came, rising back to its feet, then shoved out of the way by the fey lord tearing off into the woods with shrieks for help.

Saffron thought he'd gone unnoticed, until the veiled person turned slowly to him. He couldn't see her face, but the moon glowed through the veil, silhouetting her head—and he saw the slightest hint of a round ear within strands of wiry hair.

"Rowan spirit," her voice scraped like branches against the side of Cottage Wicklow. Saffron gulped, then barely nodded, wondering how she ever knew he was the first one to don that red mantle. The woman grinned, barely visible through the chiffon. "Are you searching with me?"

Gulping, the lump in Saffron's throat prickled with thorns.

"The wolf king," she rattled when he didn't answer, pointing after the fey lord sprinting away. "He's close by. But not that one."

Wolf king. Saffron attempted to swallow again. No—King Clymeus had been gone for centuries, no longer stalking humans for Queen Proserpina, no longer killing or displacing them through the veil on her command. The only wolf stalking Morrígan was Taran mac Delbaith—and Saffron wondered if that crone had simply realized the irony like he once had.

Perhaps she heard Saffron despite not a word leaving his mouth. Instead of asking again, she gazed down at the hand still gripping whatever it was she took from the fey lord, unfurling her fingers. Something only she could see drifted off into the sky as she watched it go.

"Come soon," she went on. "I'm tired of delivering on my own. I need to rest."

Saffron nodded, willing to agree to anything so long as it kept her from chomping the flesh off his shoulder—just like his reoccurring dreams with the wolf. To his relief, she smiled and nodded, then disappeared back into the trees as silently as she'd arrived.

The rowan spirit people claimed to be seeing in the woods— was definitely a wild thing.

5
____

THE FURY

When Saffron finally found the strength to get back to his feet, the forest erupted with sounds. Screams ricocheted off the trees, tearing through the darkness so quick and so devouring that his knees buckled beneath him and he sank back to the ground to cover his ears as the cuffs finally separated.

"Clarkaus was attacked! Call the headmistress!"

"It was the rowan spirit! Look there—there he is, in the trees!"

"The wolf must be nearby! I can see its shadow!"

"The rowan spirit is back! That means the wolf has returned!"

"Do you think...!"

Saffron's heart slammed. He leapt back to his feet like a bolting deer—but his muscles remained locked in place. Pressing his hands harder against his ears, he attempted to block out the accusations before they found him, inundated with *no, no, no*—it wasn't him, they couldn't think that, they couldn't declare it. He was obedient. He was behaving. He hadn't done anything wrong, he'd only left the attic to save his own life, he still intended on working within the rules of his deal with Taran—

Something hot scattered against the back of his head. Lurching, Saffron fell on his stomach before twisting around and scrambling backward. A short scream escaped him—but the beast crouched in the shadows didn't move. He didn't have to. Saffron could see him, his pointed ears, wiry fur, yellow eyes. Seeing him, questioning him, accusing him—

"I—!" He attempted, and the collar tightened in turn with Taran's snapping teeth. The animal took one step from the foliage —but someone from the fete suddenly stumbled from the shadows with a sharp, drunken laugh, tripping over Saffron and falling flat on their face. Upon lifting their head, they looked directly where Taran hunched in the dark—and shrieked.

Saffron took his chance, pushing himself to his feet and running.

Low-hanging branches whipped his face, clawed at his hair, ripped at his clothes—like a pale hand reaching to clutch his sleeve and offer one last warning before giving way to the overcast sky. *The wolf, the lord, the prince.*

Saffron shouldn't run, he should have stayed right where he was and begged for forgiveness—but those thoughts stood no chance against the erupting panic claiming his mind, his bones, forcing him to fear for his life. To taste blood in his mouth, to feel hot blood on his chest, his arms, choking on it as Arrow's ringing voice begged Saffron's name from the undergrowth. A small taste of what Taran meant to do to him if caught, whether it be that night, or in the morning, or—

"Saffron!"

Something wild shouted Saffron's name, but Saffron barely slowed his pace. Snapping his head to search, there was nothing. There was only the sound of his gasping breath, the voices of ghosts, the distant noise of fey entering the woods from the house to search for the rowan spirit, to search for him, to search for the wolf, to blame him, to blame Cylvan, to ruin everything, when Saffron had only wanted a chance to stay with his raven—

Splashing through a creek, Saffron tried to make sense of his frenzied thoughts, barely perceiving his surroundings, where his feet landed, how his hands grappled trees and foliage for balance, burying into a carpet of moss on a fallen tree to leap over it—only to slam on his back on the other side, struck by a sudden blast of wind. Hitting the earth, he threw his arms over his head as the force tore through trees in every direction, ripping branches from trunks and downing wood giants in the distance. It blanketed him in leaves and branches and debris, and when the power finally trailed off again in a breath, the forest went silent. No more howling fey. No more chasing feet. No more crickets or birds or any signs of life at all, except for Saffron's trembling breaths, struggling to find purchase on any inhale offered to him.

Saffron lifted his head with a small sound. Felled branches and twigs slid off his back, and he startled when one bounced off a nearby rock with too loud a noise. He glanced up ahead, then over his shoulder, heart slamming in his ears and filling his throat—but there was nothing. Only darkness. Stillness.

He forced himself to the balls of his feet, then upright, though remained partially hunched. He couldn't hear anything over the pounding of his head. He only saw destruction, forest floor carpeted in broken branches and patches of torn leaves like the aftermath of a summer storm. He no longer smelled the rotten fur of the wolf, either—though even breathing in deep gasps of fresh forest air didn't matter. His lungs didn't want it. His lungs wished to suffocate, out of fear of being found.

Something crunched right ahead of him, though he couldn't see it in the dark. Saffron stumbled backward, turning to run again—but a compelling voice came from the shadows, first.

"Be still."

Saffron drew up short, every muscle going rigid. Not unlike when he followed the moon, movement came behind him, but couldn't turn to look. Footsteps approached, and then paused. They were heavy, dragging slightly as if the owner walked for the first time in days. As if they weren't sure why they were there, or what they would do once they circled around Saffron and regarded his face—

Cylvan was expressionless as he stepped into view, and stayed that way for a long time. He looked Saffron up and down, every part of him, from his tree-ripped blouse to his sap-sticky hair, scratched face, heavy shoulders from the effort. Saffron wanted to scream; Saffron wanted to cry; Saffron wanted to embrace him; Saffron wanted to tell him to *run,* knowing Taran's wolf was somewhere nearby—but he could do none of those things. Not with Cylvan's enchantment still containing him like a warm blanket. It was a wonder his heart didn't stop with the rest of him, though the way it strained at the sight of his prince up so close, it might as well have.

Cylvan's face suddenly twisted in fury, and he grabbed Saffron by the front of the blouse. Slammed against the nearest tree, Saffron gasped as the air was knocked out of him, but barely had any other chance to react as a clawed hand planted over his mouth.

"Who is it? Hm?" Cylvan asked with a wild, enraged smile. "Is that you, Kaelar, you walking shit? Magnin? Eias? Some other prick who wishes to test me? I'll have you know—wearing that face is the fastest way to get every one of your ribs broken, then pulled out one by one through your mouth. Still want to pretend?"

Saffron stared with wide eyes, on the verge of cowering as his knees went weak. He raised his eyebrows, attempting to shake his head, but winced as Cylvan's hand pressed harder against his lips, crushing them into his teeth.

"You are not nearly as afraid as you should be," Cylvan promised, leaning closer and sending bolts of ice down Saffron's spine. Saffron clambered for the wrist pinning him. The second he touched Cylvan's arm, though, more pressure crushed his jaw, and he cried out beneath the weight.

But then Cylvan saw his family ring on Saffron's finger. His breath caught—then started, then shuddered. He barked a cold laugh, grabbing Saffron's hand and pressing into it.

"So this is what Asche saw," he said, voice shrill as Saffron gasped while his finger was bent backward. Cylvan—was drunk.

He was blind with rage, thinking Saffron was a high fey glamoured using his face, thinking Saffron was some sort of prank. Saffron should have known Cylvan wouldn't believe he'd suddenly arrived back in Danann House, without warning, without explanation, not after two weeks of believing Saffron was dead—

Saffron's finger snapped beneath Cylvan's strength. He bit back a scream, slumping to his knees as Cylvan finally released him and stepped back.

Saffron clutched his hand to his chest, trembling all over, but managed to lift his eyes to meet Cylvan's in the dark. Cylvan wore a familiar expression—one of hatred. Disdain. It reminded him of that first moment they saw one another as they truly were, without the airs of false identity. A prince and a beantighe, on the front steps of Danann House on Imbolc.

Cylvan, that person Saffron cared for as much as his friends in Beantighe Village—looked down on him with nothing but loathing.

Except that time, Saffron knew it wasn't real. Cylvan directed that fury at someone he thought to be playing a trick. He didn't hate Saffron that much, he only hated anyone who reminded him of Saffron that much. Saffron might almost be relieved, had the pain in his hand, sparking up his arm and into his jaw, not hurt so fucking much.

"Cylvan! Prince Cylvan! Oh, fuck!" Magnin of all people tumbled suddenly from the undergrowth. Cylvan barely turned to look. "Ah, your highness—you caught him! Thank you, what good news—you can go back to the party, I will deal with—"

"Who is he?" Cylvan asked flatly. "I want to know, so that I may send funeral flowers to the right family. After I break his neck, that is."

Magnin threw his hands up before Cylvan could act on that threat.

"Wait!" He shouted, and Cylvan barely restrained himself. Saffron's heart pounded, knowing he was truly one flinch from actually dying. How ironic, to die at the hand of the person he was trying to protect—how ironic, to die that night despite everything he tried to do to make it otherwise. "It's... that is... he's..."

"It's who he looks like."

Goosebumps spread over Saffron's body, going still as if he'd been enchanted for a second time. Taran emerged from the trees alongside Magnin, though even Magnin looked surprised. Taran didn't acknowledge him, just held eyes with Cylvan, who scoffed and prepared to argue—

"He's the beantighe I saved you from, Cylvan. I went looking for him while we were in Avren," he interrupted before Cylvan could start. "I had him transferred to Connacht, where Kaelar brought him to Morrígan. They were meant to leave for the Fall Court in the morning. You were never meant to see him at all."

Cylvan's posture didn't move—but perhaps that was more frightening. Saffron couldn't see his expression as he faced Taran, but he sensed tendrils of wind emerging from where Cylvan's feet met the earth. They stretched long, cascading over Saffron like incorporeal snakes wishing to feel every inch of him.

"You... told me he'd been executed," Cylvan finally responded, voice even.

"I also said I would confirm if that were the case."

"You told me—!"

A gust of wind burst from Cylvan's body, knocking Saffron back. He covered his head as branches overhead creaked and whipped against the wall of air, more leaves and dead twigs raining down on the circle of people. Taran was the only other person who didn't move, just putting his hands up slightly in defense. As if Cylvan was something wild, something to be frightened of if not kept under control.

"You have nothing to worry about," Taran said in a cool voice. "He can't hurt you again. I made sure of that, as well."

"What?" Cylvan croaked.

"That beantighe doesn't remember anything from Imbolc to

now. He has no idea who you are, let alone what he did to you. He will travel to the Fall Court with Kaelar in the morning—"

But Cylvan's head suddenly snapped around, searching where Saffron cowered in the dirt. Saffron met his eyes as intensely as he could—and finally, he witnessed a slight break in Cylvan's harsh demeanor. A crack in his armor. A thin line of confusion, uncertainty. Saffron had to resist leaping to his feet.

"No," Cylvan's voice barely came. His eyes stayed on Saffron, shaking his head slightly. The shock, the disbelief, was clearly heavy on his shoulders. Saffron shook his head slightly in return, begging Cylvan to understand. To forgive him. One day, at least —to forgive him.

"Magnin, take Cylvan back to the party," Taran said calmly, next. "I'll take care of the beantighe."

Saffron's heart jumped, knowing what that meant, already smelling wet fur and the stench of breath—and he leapt to his feet, taking shelter behind Cylvan in the center. He had to resist throwing his arms around Cylvan entirely, but took handfuls of Cylvan's tunic, gazing past him at Taran. Just an innocent, frightened beantighe.

Taran glared at him, nostrils flaring. Saffron responded with something of the same.

Cylvan's heart under Saffron's ear pounded. His hands shook as they found Saffron's back. At first, they merely flattened over Saffron's shoulders—but then they suddenly took handfuls of Saffron's shirt, and another gale of wind tore out from where he stood. It careened through the foliage encircling them, and Saffron swore his feet lifted off the ground an inch—

Taran suddenly called out: "Cylvan, think of Asche!"

The wind died in an instant, but Cylvan's hands didn't pull away from where they gripped Saffron. Instead, they held him harder—as if attempting to keep himself grounded, rather than securing Saffron to fly away. Cylvan's eyes were back on Taran again, wide, but empty. Taran held them with his own gaze, hands still up. He nodded slightly.

"Let's go back to the party," he urged calmly. "Come on, all of us. The beantighe as well."

"He cannot go to the Fall Court," Cylvan answered, fingers tightening on the back of Saffron's shirt. There was a sudden sort of clarity to his voice—one of someone seeking survival, and knowing exactly what to say to earn it. Even from an opponent like Taran mac Delbaith. "Who knows what threads remain that he could use against me, Taran. Even unweaving—"

"None of that matters, Cylvan," Taran tried to assure him. "He cannot speak. His tongue is gone."

Cylvan's voice cracked. He gulped, clenching his jaw, balling his hands into shaking fists, before continuing as if uninterrupted.

"He can read and write, Taran. There may be other things that could come back to haunt us. We must keep him close until—"

Cylvan's mouth went dry. It dangled open slightly in uncertainty.

"Until—Ostara, at least. It'll be too risky to let him leave our sight before then."

Taran nodded evenly. His eyes flickered to Saffron, then back to Cylvan, in the most minute of movements.

"You're right," he answered. "Let's talk about it in the morning, shall we? The beantighe can stay in the servants' quarters, tonight."

"Good," Cylvan whispered. He still didn't glance back down to Saffron, but his movements were stiff, as if fighting to keep Saffron as close to his body as possible. Saffron allowed him, memorizing every sensation for as long as he could. He followed as Cylvan turned toward Magnin, who jumped when acknowledged. "I may have hurt the beantighe's hand. Can you heal it?"

"A-a hand? Of course, your highness. That's no trouble at all. Come on, beantighe..." Magnin put an arm out, but subtly sought Taran's approval, first. When Taran didn't say anything to dissuade it, Saffron pulled away from Cylvan, hurrying for

Magnin's reach before any wolves could tear through and devour him.

He threw one final glance back to Cylvan as he went—but Cylvan was looking at Taran, again. Saffron didn't hear what they said, but vividly recognized the deep cracks returning to Cylvan's demeanor.

6

THE MIRE

S affron wandered through the darkness with Magnin for what felt like an eternity, before they finally broke through the trees and faced a dimly-lit Danann House on the other side. It was a night and day difference from the fete Saffron left—the people were gone, the bonfire was still and cold, the air smelled of churned soil and burnt wood. It made Saffron's nose sting; it made his stomach turn over, knowing it was because of whatever thrust of wind Cylvan released upon realizing...

Saffron gazed down at his hand, broken finger throbbing and swelling with heat as if stolen from what the bonfire once was. Gritting his teeth and biting back tears, he wiggled the ring from the injured finger before Magnin or anyone else saw, not wanting to risk losing it. It might still be his only way of proving himself to Cylvan once all the excitement died down—and once Taran finished telling Cylvan what Saffron assumed would be plenty of honeyed lies where they were left in the clearing.

Approaching the house in silence, candlelight wisps wandered through the kitchen on the other side of the back doors. Inside, the gentle, if not impatient, voice of Eias came from where they and Daurae Asche clustered in the pantry.

"I don't know if we have any lavender tea, your highness. I can make earl grey, instead?"

"That's not what I asked for…"

"Right…" Eias sighed, but then glanced to where Magnin and Saffron entered through the doors. They stiffened, glancing at Asche before stepping into the main area and speaking in a whisper.

"Everything alright?"

Magnin nodded, closing the door behind them with a faint *click*. "I'm taking the beantighe upstairs to heal his hand. Where's Kaelar?"

"He took Lord Clarkaus to the healer."

"That's good," Magnin muttered in relief, as if there was a part of him hoping he wouldn't be responsible for that injury, too. "Did you ever figure out what happened?"

"He said something jumped out of the bushes and attacked him… probably just some wild fey, right?"

For some reason, Eias glanced at Saffron as they said it, and Saffron stiffened. He nodded, thinking back to that old crone who donned his red veil, but quickly pushed the memory away as he didn't want to think of the implications. Someone else had seen Taran as the wolf, too—surely rumors of the rowan spirit and its beastly companion would be alive and flourishing again in the morning. He didn't know whether to be bitterly thrilled or apprehensive.

"Hey! That's the beantighe from earlier," Asche smiled brightly from behind Eias, and Saffron couldn't help but smile slightly back. He wasn't totally sure why, Daurae Asche was just naturally refreshing. Cylvan had once described them as Alfidel's favorite golden child, the one who resembled King Ailir, the exact opposite of the icy first born. Saffron thought he understood after finally meeting them. "Do you know where to find lavender tea, beantighe?"

"No," Eias and Magnin both said in tandem, before Magnin cleared his throat and nudged Saffron forward.

"I actually have to take the beantighe upstairs for bed, your highness. Perhaps he can find your tea, tomorrow."

Asche pouted, huffed, and flipped their hair. It might as well have been a call for Magnin's head by the way Magnin's breath strained, but all the same, he urged Saffron forward a few more steps. Saffron obeyed, moving for the servants' stairs without meeting anyone else's eyes.

MAGNIN TALKED TO HIMSELF WHILE WORKING, AND IT reminded Saffron of the previous time he'd sat in that same chair with Saffron on the edge of his bed while healing magic happened. Saffron still didn't understand how it worked, where it fit into the family tree of opulence and charms, but was too tired to try and puzzle it out, that time. The fey lord had previously healed Saffron's broken wrist, the bite marks around his shoulder, and other various scrapes and scratches and fractures from the events leading up to Saffron's geis with Taran, but that night, Saffron's finger was the only part of him addressed.

As he was finishing up, footsteps approached on the other side of the doorway. Saffron braced himself, hoping it was only Eias—but then Taran stepped through, meeting Saffron's eyes with a look that made Saffron's heart swell into his throat. Still, he didn't look away, keeping the fey lord's eyes until Taran finally glanced away long enough to light a stick of floral tobacco and take a long drag.

"Don't let me interrupt," he said as Magnin lifted his head, too. Below them, Saffron recognized the slight sound of movement in the prince's suite. So faint that neither Magnin nor Taran even flinched, perhaps not knowing the Aon-adharcach suite's silencing spell only worked through upright walls.

Magnin finished his work, and Saffron curled his stiff finger when prompted. A sharp pang bolted up the underside of his arm, making him flinch, but the bones were at least back in place. Magnin was satisfied enough with that result, returning his bottle of thick healing pomade and curled treebark that'd wrapped around Saffron's finger. Saffron rubbed the sore digit with a quiet sigh as Magnin stepped away—only for Taran to suddenly step forward, grabbing Saffron by the front of his shirt and striking him across the cheek.

Tumbling backward with wide eyes, Saffron clutched his cheek and stared at Taran in shock, even Magnin having gone still. Taran didn't say anything at first, just loomed over Saffron, staring at him, before finally sinking to a knee on the bed to blow smoke into Saffron's face.

"You get your wish," he whispered. "You'll stay right where you are as the house-beantighe, when you aren't hunting for my fruits. You have until Ostara to bring them to me, according to our previous agreement. But, my previous warning also remains. If I sense even a flicker of familiarity returning between you and the prince, I won't hesitate to kill you and leave your body at the gates of Beantighe Village as a warning. You'll play by my rules, you'll bow to my stipulations, you'll do everything and anything I say. If I don't still find you useful every morning that comes—I won't hesitate to let you loose into the woods for whatever beast to come and tear you apart. Understand?"

Saffron nodded, removing his hand from his cheek, knowing it was likely bright red with how it warmed and tingled. He made sure to meet Taran's eyes directly. He wiped any uncertainty, hesitation, fear from his expression.

That was exactly what he wanted—and for Taran to give it to him with so many words thick with irritation and resentment, was deliciously satisfying.

Saffron attempted to sleep. He closed his eyes and laid on his back, forcing his breaths in and out—but something bumped at the end of the corridor, and his eyes snapped back open again. His heart pounded in his ears like it always did, washing out any sounds that would come, next. Was Taran rescinding his offer once more? To kill Saffron in his bed while the rest of the house slept?

It was long, dragging motions. It was heavy feet. It was scratching knobs as they turned under a hand, and doors creaking open. It was—quiet, gasping, sobbing breaths. It was Saffron's name spoken in anguish.

The spirit of someone Saffron knew.

Rising to his feet slowly, Saffron lit a candle with shaking hands. He soundlessly pulled the chair from under the knob, then pulled the door open to gaze into the dark hallway outside. Silence answered him—and then a raspy breath in the distance. Breathing hard and fast, interspersed with broken words whispered unintelligibly.

Saffron sought the source of the sound, a part of him already knowing before finding him—Prince Cylvan, slumped to one knee at the far end of the hallway, draped in darkness and only visible as Saffron approached with his pinprick of candlelight. Cylvan's head lolled side to side with drunkenness, moaning more pained words between begging Saffron's name—and Saffron almost lost his will to continue. He almost broke into a thousand pieces right there, scattering across the floor, offerings for Cylvan to use to replace where he had his own chips and gaps forming beneath the weight of the same person who buckled Saffron over. Two ghosts within an inch of their lives, crushed beneath the weight of Taran mac Delbaith.

But—Saffron wouldn't break. He wouldn't bend. He would be the thing Cylvan needed for support, no matter how badly it hurt. That was what he promised.

Crouching to the balls of his feet, Saffron moved slowly, so as to not startle the weeping spirit bent over on the floor. Cylvan, who was more intoxicated than Saffron had ever seen him; who lifted red, swollen eyes as Saffron tucked hair from his face, but showed no recognition upon meeting Saffron's gaze. As if—that wasn't the first time Cylvan thought he saw Saffron kneeling in front of him.

As if, just as Saffron dreamed of Cylvan, Cylvan dreamed of Saffron in their time apart. Dreams riddled with guilt, regret, shame, misery. And despite Saffron right in front of him, alive and once again within reach—Cylvan was still too broken, interred too deeply in the mire to recognize it.

"Púca," he croaked, attempting to lift a hand to touch Saffron's face, but it sank heavily back to his lap. "I'm sorry, I'm sorry, I'm sorry..."

Saffron managed to smile weakly, though the corners of his mouth lifted and ripped the seams of his heart in his chest, like a puppet on a string. It hurt worse to nod slightly in reassurance, next—because the way Cylvan smiled blurrily in reply was almost too much for Saffron to bear. He had to close his eyes, gulping back the thorny lump in his throat before risking another breath. Saffron had to get his prince back to bed, before they both grew too incorporeal to touch one another ever again.

Keeping the candlestick in one hand, Saffron offered Cylvan the other, and carefully pulled the drunk sídhe prince back to his feet. Cylvan sank heavily against him, nearly toppling both of them through the nearest open door, but Saffron braced his legs and managed to half-carry, half-drag Cylvan back to the attic door. Then down the stairs, one at a time. He finally helped Cylvan through the third-floor panel in the wainscoting, where Cylvan stumbled before collapsing as if the rug had been pulled out from under him. Saffron hated seeing him so out of it. So unlike himself. He should have been laughing every time his feet tangled together. Grinning, teasing, howling in amusement. But the Cylvan who struggled to remain upright, even with Saffron's help—clearly drank to forget, even once the party was gone.

Back on their feet, Saffron carefully led Cylvan to his bedroom door. He pushed it open, setting the candle on the first flat surface within reach, making it easier to carry the sagging prince to his bed. Cylvan lost his footing near the edge, spilling flat on his stomach over the black silk sheets with a groan and more mumbled sounds. Saffron managed to untangle himself from under Cylvan's dead weight—and for the first time, released a little laugh of disbelief.

Puffing hair from his eyes, he took a hand of Cylvan's shoulders, next, rolling him onto his back like a ragdoll filled with sand and clay. Cylvan obeyed, though each limb sagged in the wake of every movement. Saffron couldn't help but chuckle again, and then—Cylvan did, too, as if in reaction to hearing Saffron's. The sound made Saffron's cheeks flush, butterfly sprites swelling in his chest. That sound—was so lovely. Even if it came from a place of darkness, a place seeped through with alcohol, enough to feel nothing, Saffron liked hearing it. It meant, despite the strange and sudden circumstances, Cylvan felt... comfortable. Numb enough to the pain of the earlier evening to recall how it felt to laugh. Even just a little bit.

Saffron finally settled Cylvan on his back, but had to lift a curtain of black hair from his face as it draped like a twisted blanket. Cylvan puffed and spit strands from his lips, attempting to claw them away with his nails but missing his mouth and just scratching blankly at his cheek. His eyes remained half-lidded and hazy as Saffron worked over him like Baba Yaga used to work over beantighes who drank too much at seasonal celebrations.

Once he was righted and safe, Saffron nearly left him, worried someone might come into the suite suddenly and misunderstand —but his heart twisted too tightly the moment he even pulled his hands away. He'd spent too many nights knowing Cylvan slept fully clothed from whatever fete he stumbled home from, never making any noise to imply he undressed at all. Tripping over his own feet, partially without his body, collapsing into bed for a restless night... alone. With no one there to see him. Help him. Care for him. No one—within reach.

Gazing down at him, at his broken prince who continued to mumble under his breath, somehow still perfect despite also so very disheveled—Saffron knew, he wouldn't be able to sleep knowing he'd turned his back on Cylvan when the chance to offer even such a small comfort was so easily within reach.

Saffron wanted to offer comfort. Saffron wanted to take care of him. Saffron wanted nothing more than to prove what he once promised that same night Cylvan offered him patronage.

I will stay with you—so that you may always know there is at least one person who cares for you.

Saffron knelt to the floor. He took one of Cylvan's feet, bracing it on his shoulder and working down the laces of the heeled boot. Pulling it off, he couldn't stop another tiny smile of amusement when Cylvan sighed in relief.

Setting it aside, he addressed the next one. He pulled off Cylvan's socks, then couldn't resist leaving a barely-existent kiss on the inside of his ankle bone where the stiff leather had rubbed and left a sore spot.

Next, Saffron rifled through the dresser on the wall, pulling out a clean pair of wool leggings from the bottom of one. In the process of seeking out a nightshirt in the standing wardrobe, Saffron stumbled unexpectedly across the gold jewelry box that once housed Cylvan's family ring—and curiosity got the better of him, cracking it open. He nearly dropped it, hands going stiff as his heart stopped in tandem.

Saffron's library ring was right inside, tied off in a little bag containing familiar quartz pieces unearthed by his own hands from the edge of Quartz Creek. Quartz pieces—once offered to Cylvan like payment for access to the library, in Saffron's feverish haze.

Saffron bit his lip, then gently dumped the contents into his palm. The library ring tumbled out with the glassy crystal points, and his heart squeezed somehow tighter. He already knew Cylvan had kept the crystal pieces, but the last time Saffron saw them, they were still coated in mud. Between then and that moment, the prince had meticulously washed every single point, until they were nothing but shine.

Closing his eyes, Saffron caressed the crystals closely, wishing to imbue them with protective magic. As much as a beantighe like him could, anyway. Then, he regarded the library ring, familiar to the touch despite looking no different from any others on campus. A realization struck him, something he'd already known and mulled over an infinite number of times when days and nights in the attic passed too slowly, as the changing moon reminded him how they crept ever-closer to Ostara with every passing hour.

If Saffron could find a way to escape Danann House, to come and go as he pleased, whether that be negating the cuffs or stealing the hands-and-dagger ring from Kaelar—he would be able to travel to the Grand Library at night and continue what he and Cylvan started. He would need the library ring to get inside.

Saffron squeezed the treasures in his hand again, that time wishing he could soak up every pleasant, thrilling, happy memory that once encircled them. For a long moment he stood there, fighting off, then inviting, then pushing away, then accepting the tide of memories that washed in, until his fingers tingled from the pressure. Finally, he released his breath, cracking open his eyes and returning every trinket except the ring to the bag, and then the box. He slid the gold circlet onto the same finger he once wore it, closing his eyes again and letting that sensation warm him from the inside out.

Closing the wardrobe, he tossed the leggings and nightshirt over one shoulder and returned to his half-living prince on the bed. Cylvan had somehow rolled back onto his stomach while Saffron was distracted, groaning and complaining as Saffron forced him back again. Saffron just bit back more timid laughter, smiling when Cylvan's heavy eyes opened and searched for him in the darkness.

"Hm..." he grumbled as Saffron undid the infinite line of small buttons down his beautiful black doublet. "Are you here to bed me, my lord?"

Saffron flushed, biting his lip and shaking his head. Cylvan groaned again, rolling his eyes and attempting once more to turn onto his side, only to be brought back again by Saffron's hands.

"You... smell like him," Cylvan went on, hardly speaking the words at all. "You... must sleep with me. Cover my pillows. He's faded too much."

Saffron's hands shook. He might be sick.

All he could do was nod, knowing it didn't actually matter what he promised or didn't promise, as Cylvan would definitely not remember a moment of it again in the morning.

When the doublet was open, Saffron carefully coaxed Cylvan out of it, one arm at a time. He undid the collar button of his undertunic, next, pulling it off and revealing his naked chest underneath. But—it wasn't like the last time, when Cylvan undressed fast and rough in a moment of passion. Saffron spent that moment, instead, searching for bruises. Searching for aches and pains that didn't belong. He was relieved to find Cylvan unharmed where no one else could see.

Pulling his prince upright, Cylvan slumped against him with more slurred, whining complaints, but Saffron was used to dressing drunkards like him and Hollow after enjoying a party too much. Admittedly it was a pain in the ass to thread Cylvan's horns through the collar of the nightshirt, but he somehow managed, and Cylvan collapsed back to the bed in a plume of hair and more sullen complaints. At one point, he suddenly groaned loudly and bolted upright—and Saffron barely grabbed a nearby wastebasket for him to vomit into, before collapsing back to the bed with a long and loud sigh. Saffron was used to that, too.

Stripping off Cylvan's pants, Saffron left the prince's under-garments intact, covering them with the comfortable leggings. When he wasn't sighing and whining, Cylvan continued mumbling slurred words to himself, occasionally trembling with breath, sometimes grabbing Saffron's arm as if he felt like he was falling. Every time he did, Saffron paused and gave him time to recompose his balance, before carefully moving on with preparing him for bed.

Heaving Cylvan upward into the pillows, Saffron chuckled as he fought to tug the duvet and blankets out from under Cylvan's heavy, boneless body. He loosely braided Cylvan's hair so it would stop tangling with every movement, then claimed a wet hand towel from the bathroom and, with the strength of a moth's wings, wiped away all of Cylvan's eyeshadow. The color on his cheeks. The pigment on his lips. Carefully, deftly, gently enough that Cylvan's eyelashes fluttered closed—and never lifted open again. Soft enough that, when Saffron had finished, his prince's breaths came in low and deep, as if sinking into a sweet, safe place the moment someone pulled off all his baubles and jewelry and clothes from the day.

That should have been the point Saffron excused himself. Saffron should have risen back to his feet and left through the door, down the corridor, back through the wall, and back to his own room right overhead. But—Cylvan's hand reached out for him the second he moved, and Saffron settled back again in uncertainty.

"You... didn't forget me," he murmured in sleep, and Saffron turned to ice. He bit back a rush of emotion, closing his eyes and shaking his head. An offered truth that Cylvan wouldn't see, wouldn't recall in the morning. "Tell me... you remember me, Saffron... please..."

Cylvan's brows furrowed, and Saffron instinctively touched a hand to his cheek. The prince's expression softened again in an instant, head rolling to the side to press his nose into the curve of Saffron's palm.

"I'm sorry... I'm sorry... I never... told you how sorry I was..."

Saffron hunched forward slightly more, pressing his hand to his chest as he thought his heart might never start again. He clutched where the returned library ring sat on his finger, stiff alongside the digit Magnin had just finished healing. It all made it hard to breathe, too many emotions crowding the back of his throat and blocking his airway.

When he did crack open his eyes again, he saw only Cylvan's peaceful expression in the darkness. Wiped clean of the makeup and facade, lying bare and vulnerable right in front of him. Cylvan was—right in front of him. Saffron could reach out and touch him. Saffron could see him, feel him, take care of him. It was enough to bring his heavy heart back to life with a flutter of relief, and he couldn't stop himself from rising carefully to his feet, placing a whispered kiss to Cylvan's forehead.

I never forgot you, he offered without a voice. *I remember you, Cylvan, and I'll explain everything as soon as I can. Until then...*

Saffron trailed the slightest touch over Cylvan's brow, brushing loose hairs away from his eyes.

Until then, I swear, I'll keep you safe.

7

THE BREAKFAST

*S*affron *usually avoided the woods once the sun went down, but there was one small clearing made safe in agreement with the trees. He followed the path only he knew through the thick ferns and grass and stopped at the edge of the well-used burn clearing.*

That night—there was something waiting for him.

He raised his eyebrows as a blackbird perched at the head of the stone circle chirped, then tilted its head in curiosity.

"Hello, blackbird."

"Saffron," it croaked in return, and Saffron smiled. He dug around in his pockets for a piece of charcoal, flipping open to a page of the book in his hands.

"Can you speak again?" He asked.

"Saffron, Saffron," it repeated two more times, and Saffron sketched its shape on the page. Something about its eyes shimmered, like pieces of rock crystal. Like amethyst, illuminated in the moonlight.

"Your eyes... remind me of someone," he whispered. "Have we met before?"

"We've met," the bird warbled. Saffron lifted his eyes, suddenly finding a person standing in its place. He gasped and tumbled back-

ward, instantly buried in darkness, beneath hot breaths and the smell of pine and gardenia.

"You remember me, don't you?" The shadow begged, taking Saffron's face—and kissing him. Saffron's mouth opened, breathing the stranger in, then allowing their lips to crescendo against one another. A tongue slid between his teeth to taste him deeper.

"You remember me, don't you?" They asked again, and Saffron whimpered as hands found his waist, burying sharp nails into his flesh through his shirt. He dropped the book, the charcoals, taking fistfuls of the person's cloak as his legs were gently coaxed open.

"Please, Saffron—" They pleaded. A wind picked up in the trees, rushing in every direction and making branches snap, leaves cascading down over where they lay in the grass. "You remember me, don't you?"

"I—" Saffron's voice shook. The shadow's mouth claimed the words before he could speak them, as if terrified to hear the answer either way.

"Why did you let the wolf kill beantighes?"

Saffron's eyes snapped open—but the stranger just shoved him back into the dirt.

"Why would you let me take the blame? Even after everything I told you—you would still let me take the blame?"

"No—" Saffron attempted, but he didn't—he had no idea what they were talking about—

"Did you care for me?" They begged, and Saffron's heart drummed. Finally, he threw his hands up, taking the person's face —but he didn't recognize who he held. Tawny skin, green-gold eyes, shoulder-length brunette hair. They smiled viciously, as if hoping he'd do exactly that.

"Why did you let the wolf kill beantighes, Saffron?" Taran asked through the splitting smile—and something crunched behind them. Saffron's head snapped around, only for teeth to sink into the side of his neck, ripping flesh clean from bone before he could scream.

. . .

Knock, knock, knock.

Saffron woke to the chair beneath the doorknob tumbling and hitting the floor. He lunged out of bed with a rush of adrenaline, but Kaelar was already shoving his way inside. He held a tower of apparel boxes in his arms, throwing them on the bed before even checking to see if it was empty.

"Taran wants us in the woods today," the fey lord said upon finally spotting Saffron rooted at the opposite end of the room. "... but you have to make everyone breakfast, first."

Fuck your breakfast, the bitter thought shoved its way to the front of Saffron's mind, quickly followed by a rush of panic when he fully comprehended what Kaelar had just said. Into the woods, already? He didn't know whether to be relieved—or immediately apprehensive, considering what happened in the woods the night prior. A small part of him suddenly worried Taran somehow knew about Saffron's tucking Cylvan into bed, too, intending to lure him into the woods to his death, after all—but he swallowed it back. He had to be on guard, but he couldn't continue thinking everything was a trap. Otherwise, Taran might see that as the new *'thing Saffron wanted,'* and graciously grant him that wish, as well.

"These are your traveling clothes," Kaelar went on, motioning vaguely to the pile on the bed. "They're gifts from Lord Taran. Ah... and one from me."

Smiling, Kaelar placed a lacquered box on the desk and tapped it with his fingers. "I'll give you some privacy, but don't take too long. I look forward to seeing you wearing it."

Even once Kaelar left, Saffron remained with his back pressed into the wall until his heart finally slowed enough to think straight. His movements were stiff, but he approached the wood box like it was something that would sting him. He scooped it into his hand before putting it off any longer.

Except the moment he opened it, he wished he hadn't.

A gaudy, sparkling opal ring stared back at him, nestled in black silk. But while the color of it surprised him, first, it was the hatchmarks carved around the edge that made his heart stop entirely. A new patron ring, likely to replace Luvon's that was taken from him early in his time as a ghost. Fuck—all Saffron hoped was that no one had said anything to Luvon. As far as he was concerned, his transition to patronage under Kaelar was only for show. It would only be for a few weeks, and Luvon wouldn't ever find out.

Saffron snapped it back shut. He threw it at the wall, and the box cracked in two, spilling across the floor. He glared at it, before running hands down his face and focusing on inhaling. His heart refused to slow, but he had no choice except to go on with the morning. It was, like Taran said the night before, exactly what Saffron had caused such a scene for, anyway.

Box after apparel box, Saffron uncovered eclectic choices for regular day-wear, let alone *traveling clothes*. Had any fey lord in that house *traveled* before, in any way that wasn't by horse or carriage? Suede and cotton leggings, corduroy cinch pants, linen tunics, silk shirts, vests, decorative corset tops, thick socks, pretty shawls and knitted sweaters, and a pair of stiff leather boots clearly meant more for walking down the street than endeavoring in the woods... and every piece, perfectly tailored to silhouette Saffron's shape. Made from quality fabrics. Clearly costing more than Saffron probably made in a year's worth of wages. Probably purchased before Taran first changed his mind about ending their geis.

He cursed himself for being so surprised. The day after Saffron became the house ghost, Taran sent him to the campus baths after curfew where he was soaked and scrubbed raw. His hair was cut, acne pricked and healed with thick tonics, tan lines faded with magic cream. Even his teeth were whitened, all because Taran insisted on immaculacy even with the spirits in the attic. Saffron had received specific guidelines about his appearance that he was expected to uphold as a servant of Danann House—and to think those expectations wouldn't extend to literally *hiking through the woods*, perhaps he was more naïve than he originally thought.

Stripping down, Saffron pulled on the first things grabbed from a pile on the bed, careful not to squish any pixie insurgents drawn in by the fancy fabrics. Suede leggings, a high-collared linen shirt, a black vest, thick socks, and—god help him—brand new leather boots, stiffer than the silver cuffs on his wrists. *Fuck*, they were going to devour his feet alive.

Draping a fringed shawl over his shoulders, he then scowled while shoving Kaelar's patron ring on last, ignoring any further commentary from the opinionated pixie cluster. He then forced himself to enjoy the briefest thrill of exiting his room for a second day in a row. That time, at least, with permission.

Breakfast. They wanted *breakfast.* Frustration festered in Saffron's gut all the way down the stairs, until he emerged into the kitchen and had to pause at the sight of peaceful sunlight filtering through the terrace doors. A view he'd only seen through the cramped attic window for two weeks, finally wide open in front of him.

He couldn't help but sigh, begrudgingly acknowledging the genuine flutter of his heart.

He could finally move forward. No more hiding in the attic. No more playing dead. No more just a ghost.

Saffron was alive. He clung to that small reassurance, mentally reiterating what he needed to do, next. Survive—and learn.

Smashing coffee beans into a useable grind, Saffron scoured his memory for something simple he could cook with the kitchen's limited ingredients, eventually settling on potato cakes, black pudding, eggs, ham, sausage, and soda bread.

More sunbeams peeked through gray clouds as he finished setting four places at the breakfast table—Cylvan, Asche, Taran, Kaelar—and he was just pouring fresh coffee into the carafe when light rain speckled the windows and caught his attention.

Perhaps it still wasn't under ideal circumstances, but—he would walk into the Agate Wood that morning. Prepared, dressed better than when he was forced to go moonhunting the night before. Even though Kaelar would be with him, even though he was expected to find the fruits meant to control Prince Cylvan... he would still, finally, be stepping foot back into the place he loved the most. With its fresh soil, soft breeze, gurgling creeks, squeaking voices of sparkling creatures.

Saffron wished he still had his sketchbook. He wished he had his voice to greet the rainbow things he hoped were waiting for him, the wildlife, even that bloody crone from the night prior. He hadn't realized how much he would miss disappearing into the trees, all by himself, with no one there to follow, or watch, or make demands—not until he was forced to sit alone in the attic, with only the open window to offer him a glimpse.

Unable to resist, Saffron pulled open one of the dining room terrace doors, leaning out as much as his silver cuffs would allow. Closing his eyes, he breathed in the fresh air, the smell of early morning, listening as sunsingers announced the daylight. In the sun, the sprinkling rain was like glitter tumbling from the heavens, ringing off the windows and copper gutters. The chorus made Saffron's heart flutter again, and he released a quiet sigh of reprieve from Danann House.

"Why is it so cold down here?"

Jumping, Saffron turned quickly, meeting eyes with Cylvan through the entryway. He looked surprised, for some reason, as if not expecting to find Saffron setting their table. It made Saffron wonder how much of the night before Cylvan recalled, especially their drunken back and forth in the Aon-adharcach suite.

It wasn't actually Cylvan who spoke, Saffron realized as Daurae Asche appeared alongside their brother. Raising their eyebrows at the in-progress breakfast, their nose wrinkled in a way that reminded him of new beantighe recruits when they realized what their own breakfasts were going to be going forward.

"I thought we ate breakfast in the dining hall?" Asche went

on, and Saffron's instincts finally kicked in. He offered a bow, not expecting how his face went hot at the sight of Cylvan in his Morrígan uniform like it was truly just another day. Asche wore a matching ensemble barely out of the box, though their skirt was cinched poorly in the back as if it hadn't been tailored properly. He suddenly wondered if their visit hadn't been totally planned, rushing to find a uniform to wear without time to adjust the proportions. Either way, the daurae clearly thought Saffron was appreciating their appearance, because they popped out a hip with a smug expression.

"We could," Cylvan finally answered, "but Taran is trying to be a good host. Go on, sit down."

"I thought you said this was *your* house," Asche muttered, and Cylvan narrowed his eyes.

Closing the terrace door, Saffron kept his gaze averted while hurrying back into the kitchen to gather the dishes waiting to be eaten. Plating them as nicely as he could, his fingers trembled the whole time, as if one shared look with the prince was enough to turn his body to crumbling snow.

Saffron served them without a word. Cylvan offered a polite, simple *"thank you,"* while Asche poked at their eggs with a golden fork. He allowed himself to silently appreciate the way Cylvan looked in the morning light, wearing a soft rose-gold shadow over his eyes and a golden clip shaped like a bundle of ferns in his hair. There wasn't a single part of him that showed any remnants of his drunken night prior, not even bags under his eyes or the wince of a headache against the sun. A cloud of pine and gardenia perfume overtook him while leaning over the prince's shoulder, making his breath catch.

But then, Saffron noticed how Cylvan's eyes never fully left him, either, even while he performed the most mundane tasks. Filling glasses with orange juice, setting out cream and sugar, replacing napkins, offering warm maple syrup and seasonings...

"Why are you dressed like a tavern maid?" Asche asked as Saffron poured more coffee, making him instantly self-conscious.

He spilled a drop on the tablecloth in the process, exhaling through his nose before *accidentally* knocking Asche's fork to the floor the next time he passed. Cylvan prepared his own sarcastic reply—but went silent just as Saffron came to a quick halt in the doorway, blocked by Kaelar who smiled. The fey lord's eyes appraised him up and down, before nodding.

"Lucky me," he said, laughing when Saffron glared at him before shoving by to get more coffee. Kaelar lumbered into the dining room to claim his own seat at the table, immediately sinking into a long exclamation about how much he enjoyed all the excitement of the fete the night before, how thrilled he was to be keeping his new servant in Danann House, how everyone would be *so jealous* of his pretty silken-beantighe, how nice it would be to have something soft and obedient to warm his bed at night...

Saffron returned to refill coffee, only stopping when a slender hand extended and touched his arm. The slightest, most minuscule contact, but Saffron might as well have been clawed to the bone. Cylvan remained a beacon of pure composure. It even edged on disinterest, a complete shift from the night before when Cylvan slumped drunkenly to his knees outside of Saffron's attic room and begged for his forgiveness. In any other circumstance it might have upset him, but Saffron could feel Kaelar's eyes from across the table as well as he was sure Cylvan could.

"Next time it brews too long, don't just add more water to dilute it," the prince suggested, and Saffron nodded awkwardly. He nearly bowed his head in apology, too, but paused when Cylvan's eyes lifted to meet his with a handsome smile. "I know beantighes are expertly trained in brewing coffee, so this is rather unacceptable. I'll let it slide since it's only your first day."

The words themselves were critical, but Cylvan's voice was smooth as silk. Saffron thought about how the Prince Cylvan he first met would have scoffed and chewed him out. A show of such patience was abnormal for him to extend to a beantighe assumed to be unthreaded of any familiar recollection. But even under the impression that Saffron saw him as a stranger—Cylvan still spoke to him with calm respect. It almost edged on *kind*, as if... still wishing to make a good first impression on the beantighe he assumed didn't know him, or only knew of him because of the family ring he had from before his memories were taken. He really must not have remembered anything from the night before, and Saffron was both relieved and slightly disappointed.

He just nodded again, while Asche proceeded to agree with their brother and make a far-bigger deal out of the mistake. Cylvan said nothing else, sipping his brew before spreading jam over a piece of soda bread.

Saffron tried to ignore Kaelar's continued leering, infuriated gaze as he moved to leave the dining room—but he couldn't ignore the sudden drench of searing hot coffee across his face and arm. He lurched and dropped the carafe with a gasp, where it shattered across the floor. Blinking through the shock, he grit his teeth, then met Kaelar's eyes, who stood smirking with an empty cup extended.

"I agree with his highness," he said. "Don't let it happen again."

Saffron knew Kaelar didn't give a shit about the coffee. No—he gave a shit about someone else circumventing his authority as Saffron's new patron-master, even if that person was someone of royalty. And perhaps Kaelar thought being drenched in boiling liquid would be intimidating enough to force Saffron into submission—but Saffron had had worse thrown at him in almost ten years of working at Morrígan.

So—he smiled. Wiped himself off. He bowed politely. He didn't react at all.

But Cylvan did, grabbing his own cup and flinging it over Kaelar's lap. Saffron covered his mouth as Kaelar shrieked and leapt to his feet, Asche erupting into laughter as Cylvan stood with a flip of his hair.

"Asche, help the beantighe clean up the glass."

"*What?*" Asche whined, but Cylvan was already leaving the

table. He paused in front of Saffron on his way out, but Saffron couldn't meet his eyes, shaking his head when asked if he was hurt. Kaelar then shoved past Cylvan into the kitchen, and Taran finally arrived to ask *what the fuck was going on.*

"Good morning, Taran," came Cylvan's overly-sweet reply, pulling Taran in and pressing a kiss to his cheek. Even Taran looked a little surprised, before glancing in question at Saffron, who just bowed his head and hurried away.

SAFFRON WAS ELBOW-DEEP IN WASHING DISHES WHEN Kaelar approached from behind, pressing Saffron into the counter and coyly asking if he was ready to go, as if the confrontation at breakfast never happened at all. Saffron feigned dramatic surprise, throwing a bowl of water directly into the fey lord's face and making him splutter, stepping back and cursing as he'd just finished changing his clothes from the first time he'd been assaulted with coffee.

Taran approached next, interrupting the storm of insults Kaelar prepared to unleash.

"We're going into Hesper after class today, so we won't be home until dinner," he started, with no intention of pausing. "Kaelar, you and the beantighe should be back by early afternoon. Beantighe, finish unpacking our luggage and prepare four bedrooms for Kaelar, Magnin, Eias, and Daurae Asche, who will live here moving forward. Their belongings should be transferred while you're out. Dinner will also be delivered this evening, so prepare it for when we get back." He paused for just a moment, looking Saffron up and down before leaning in slightly. "Do not let Prince Cylvan see you leave. Wait until after we're already gone."

He pinched the shoulder of Saffron's shirt, still damp and stained with coffee.

"Change into your black uniform and veil the moment you get home, and wash the stains out of this. In the future, I expect you to be veiled while preparing breakfast, as well. You will only wear casual clothes while wandering the woods. Understand?"

Saffron frowned, but didn't let it hang for too long. He nodded, then frowned as Taran still wasn't done. That time, though, he leaned in closer.

"Make sure you are back before sundown, at the very latest," he breathed. "Your friend Hollow will be taking your place in house chores while you're away. If you're not back by the time he's excused... well. Use your imagination."

Saffron could only stare at him, but Taran didn't meet his eyes again. Satisfied with his threat, he finally left the kitchen for the parlor, where Cylvan and Asche hovered. Asche immediately initiated excited conversation with Taran while Cylvan's eyes lingered into the kitchen, but Saffron barely noticed. The world turned nauseatingly beneath his feet.

He should have known Taran hadn't forgotten about Hollow. Perhaps Saffron had manifested that with all of his anxieties, too.

He just—had to focus.

Hollow wasn't in danger, yet. He wouldn't be in danger so long as Saffron returned with plenty of time to spare.

Taran even admitted they wouldn't be in the house all day.

Hollow wasn't in danger. Yet.

Saffron... just... had to focus.

Finishing the dishes from breakfast, he and Kaelar waited ten unbearable minutes past the front door latching shut before Kaelar left through the back to retrieve a horse. As soon as he was alone, Saffron closed his eyes and rubbed the back of his neck, mind racing and ears ringing, attempting to force down every new fear placed on him just since waking up. Kaelar's patron ring, his strange dynamic with Cylvan, going into the woods, and now Hollow—

Perhaps that was why he didn't notice when someone suddenly rushed into the kitchen, grabbing his arm and spinning him around.

Caged against the counter, Saffron missed the first part of

Cylvan's hurried words, growing even more alarmed when a cold hand suddenly grabbed his—and pulled it to touch different parts of Cylvan's body.

"Here, here, here, and here," Cylvan said in a single breath, pulling Saffron's hand into his throat, the middle of his stomach, the side of his stomach, even brushing between his legs. Saffron's face erupted into flames, before realizing what Cylvan was doing —he was demonstrating all the places on the body to strike and disarm; Hollow had once offered Saffron the same advice a long time ago. Saffron made the mistake of meeting the intensity of Cylvan's eyes, and the prince's jaw was clenched hard enough to pop a tendon. He added with finality:

"If Kaelar—no, if *anyone* tries anything with you, beat the shit out of them. I know you can. I will vouch for you. Do you understand? Taran despises pathetic, perverted shows of dominance, and Kaelar knows it."

Saffron stared as his heart pounded, finally managing a single nod. Cylvan paused for only a second longer, holding Saffron's gaze, before offering a tiny nod of his own and leaving without another word. Gone in an instant, so quickly that Saffron questioned if it actually happened at all.

8

THE WOODS

Saffron stood in a daze on the path between the house garden and the apple orchard. He regarded the hand that had brushed Cylvan's neck, his stomach, ghosted between his legs. Cylvan's grasp had been firm, but nowhere near as wild as the night before when accusing Saffron of wearing a glamour in the woods. His grasp that morning had been commanding—but somehow, at the same time... thoughtful. Intentional. Full of restraint. As if Cylvan's only two options had been showing Saffron how to defend himself, or following Kaelar to the stables to break his arms, and choosing the first was a test of his self-control.

But then Kaelar emerged on the back of a horse at the far end of the yard, and Saffron saw the way he wiped his nose on the back of his hand. How his hair was a mess and his face was flushed, as if rosy with blood. There was a small tear in the shoulder seam of his doublet.

Saffron's heart thumped. He tightened his hand into a fist, then closed his eyes.

I will vouch for you.

Kaelar attempted to put hands on Saffron early in his time in the attic, coming to the house drunk in the middle of the night and shoving his way inside while Saffron was sleeping. Saffron fought back, and Kaelar was knocked unconscious after Saffron shoved him hard enough against the doorframe. Cylvan had been away at a fete, but all the noise got the attention of Taran, who arrived to find Saffron hyperventilating, catatonic, on the floor across from where Kaelar lay with blood gushing from his head. Taran calmly asked what happened, then saw the tear in Saffron's shirt. Scowling, he said nothing else, dragging Kaelar away without any further acknowledgement.

That was when Saffron started propping his door shut with the chair. Day and night. Even though it would do nothing against anyone determined to get inside, it would at least alert him with all the noise.

It was why any sound on the other side of the door left Saffron wide awake in apprehension. Straining his ears, eyes unblinking, listening for the sound of the knob rattling. For footsteps in the corridor. For the scraping of the chair's feet on the floorboards.

Nothing else in that vein had happened since, and Saffron just assumed Kaelar found someone else to harass—but he suddenly wondered if it was actually for the reason Cylvan said. *Taran despises pathetic, perverted shows of dominance, and Kaelar knows it.*

Saffron knew from his own experiences that Kaelar never thought twice about assaulting someone, harassing them, bullying them, attacking them—and Saffron had to wonder exactly what it was Kaelar had been promised to make him so willing and wanting to stay on Taran's good side.

In fact—Saffron wondered what *all* of them had been promised. Kaelar, Eias, Magnin—even Headmistress Elluin.

Smiling bitterly, Saffron adjusted the coffee-stained shawl over his shoulders as Kaelar approached. Trotting up, the sable horse bumped its snout against Saffron's face, eliciting an unexpected smile from him. But then Kaelar offered a hand to pull Saffron into the saddle, and Saffron's expression sank back into a frown.

"Come on," Kaelar attempted a handsome expression, but Saffron just saw the swelling of his cheek and a hint of blood in one of his nostrils. He'd definitely been punched. "If we go by foot, we definitely won't be back in time for dinner."

Saffron's frown remained, tempted to yank Kaelar straight off the horse and into the mud. Instead, he resentfully took the offered hand to pull himself into the saddle, smoothly avoiding Kaelar's chosen place between his hips and kicking a leg behind so they sat back to back. Kaelar huffed in annoyance, but defeatedly pulled the leading reins toward the path along the apple trees, then into the woods.

The sweet perfume of greenery. Soil. Rain from the day before. The smell of growing sun, which Hollow had always argued wasn't a thing. But sunlight smelled like freshly dried cotton sheets. Warm pine sap. The banks of the creek. Flower tea. Golden honey. Early spring-morning sunshine was even sharper, biting the nose without being painful. Dew and new budding growth and loamy earth seduced him like velvet drenched parchment that would melt at the touch of a hand.

Ah—Saffron closed his eyes and experienced it all at once. He allowed every sound, smell, sensation to puncture his skin, seeping into his pores to cleanse the tacky, thick coating of Danann House lacquer and dust that painfully stiffened his insides. He silently hummed along with the chorus of sunsinger songs, not realizing exactly how far his attic bedroom was until he heard the cheerful birds so close again.

A morning breeze brushed his cheeks like a lonely lover, tickling the fringes of his silk-embroidered shawl. It kissed the bare skin of his neck where he obsessively upkept his proper haircut, perhaps wondering when and how and why he was suddenly so well-done and so well-dressed. His silver cuffs were chilled to ice, turning his wrists and fingers pink; it made him glance curiously to where Kaelar grasped the horse's reins. He spotted the silver hands-and-dagger companion ring that allowed Saffron to escape the house's invisible cage. If he could just take it for himself...

"We'll start where Taran previously left off. Where that one last beantighe described," Kaelar's voice came and went over the sounds of the forest, and Saffron tried to ignore the stab of irritation he felt with every word. The way the breeze picked up as Kaelar spoke made him wonder if the Agate Wood felt the same.

He spent the morning imagining all the ways he could dump Kaelar over a rocky cliff, lose him in the creek, perhaps feed him alive to hungry flower sprites, then puzzled every possible explanation that might get him out of facing any consequences upon returning alone to Danann House. Oh, was that wild old woman wearing Saffron's red veil still crunching around nearby? Was she still hungry? Saffron couldn't promise Kaelar tasted any better than rotten fish floating belly-up in standing water, but the crone didn't have to know that. She could take a sinking bite out of his neck before deciding for herself. Who was Saffron to withhold a potential meal?

The fantasized maimings festered more gruesome as it was clear Kaelar had exactly zero experience navigating any terrain that wasn't paved cobblestone streets. More than once, he walked them straight into a low-hanging branch, coaxed the animal over an entire fallen tree, cursed when the horse lost its footing and flapped its lips in complaint. Every time Saffron scraped against a tree or got smacked in the face with a fist of leaves, he made sure to wipe leftover sap directly onto Kaelar's back under the guise of regaining his balance.

When he couldn't take it anymore, Saffron kicked a leg over the saddle—ramming Kaelar in the back of the head in the process —and hopped to the ground. Snagging the reins for himself, he guided the horse back to an actual walkable path through the bushes and long grass, and the animal showed gratitude by munching on his hair.

The problem was, as soon as he took the reins, he also claimed the lead—and Saffron had no idea what he was doing. Where he was going. One thought persisted that morning just as it did the very first time Arrow mentioned wild fairy fruits in the woods, and that was how, despite Saffron's familiarity with the forest, never once did he ever cross any wild pink fruits in all his years exploring. Surely he would have noticed if he had, since the color *pink* was only natural on pixies and flowers. Not fruits. Not like the ones high fey enjoyed at parties, anyway. Surely he would have noticed if there were any in his path.

Where they grew, how they grew, in what kind of environment they grew... Did they even look like strawberries or blueberries or whatever else he knew was normally served at fetes? Were they even *pink* like party fruits at all? Perhaps they were blue? Purple? Green? Perhaps they didn't even resemble garden fruits Saffron was familiar with?

Perhaps they didn't exist at all?

The racing thoughts quieted as he suddenly recalled something Arrow had said the night they died, when asking for Saffron's help outside of Danann House.

I think I found them, but can't get to them...

Was there a reason they needed Saffron's help, specifically? Arrow was bulky, burly, strong like Hollow, though on the shorter side—did they need someone with a smaller frame to reach them? Someone who could wiggle into some cramped place they were too broad for?

Between two trees? A narrow cave? Down in a hole? Arrow wasn't afraid of much, either, so it wasn't like they would ask because they were too frightened to explore someplace, themself...

Saffron's stride slowed as he wracked his brain. What was it Hollow said that night Taran made the request of him?

He said he needs fairy fruits for the wolf.

He said he's been able to keep it away from campus, but not from Beantighe Village, which is why it's been attacking us instead.

If he gives it wild fruits, he can compel it into submission...

"Find something, beantighe?" Kaelar asked. Saffron didn't react, just wavered before claiming the pace forward again. Deeper into the woods, farther from Danann House. Kaelar said that general area was the last place Taran searched. The farthest place Cloth had searched...

He said... they're behind an iron gate in the woods. In some old ruins.

Saffron's pace halted again. He lifted his eyes to search every direction as those specific words stood out. Which beantighe first gave Taran that clue? Arrow hadn't mentioned it while beseeching Saffron; Cloth hadn't mentioned it while being carried away; only Hollow suggested it. Did Taran always have that idea, or had someone seen something and told him? If it was true, it made sense why Taran couldn't find the fruits, himself. Why he couldn't reach them, himself, and needed a human's help. If the fruits were behind an iron gate, it might have been too painful for him to cross. Was that what Arrow meant when they said they knew where the fruits were, but couldn't reach them? Because they couldn't get through the iron gate?

Saffron scoffed. Not only had he never seen any wild fairy fruits during his own explorations of the Agate Wood—he'd never seen *ruins*, either, let alone a gate big enough to keep the likes of Taran mac Delbaith out.

Something caught Saffron's eye, and his head snapped in the direction of swarming colors. He recognized a cloud of flower sprites attempting to overtake a streak of sky blue feathers zipping in and out of the trees, moving faster than Saffron could keep up. Even the horse stood distracted by the sweeping movements— only for another blur to race from the trees.

The color of blood, it launched off the grassy earth, and Kaelar only had a second to scream before he was bodied from the saddle and slammed to the ground on the other side.

The horse reeled, yanking its reins from Saffron's hand like a whip cutting through air. Saffron snapped away before it sliced his palm in half, stumbling out of the way before he was trampled. There was no time to chase after the startled animal, spinning and watching Kaelar throw a defensive arm across the rowan-veiled woman's neck. He barely pinned her away as she hissed, spitting and baring her teeth. The same teeth that tore flesh and muscle from the fey lord outside the fete the night before. As if she heard Saffron's plea on the morning wind.

He hesitated just a moment too long—overcome with want to see Kaelar ripped apart—allowing a second shadow to burst from the trees and hook him around the neck to the ground. Thrusting his hands out, Saffron grabbed the attacker's wrist moments before they pressed a knife to his throat—and then they locked eyes, both going still in shared disbelief.

"S-Saffron?" The woman questioned. Her warm brown skin was dotted with freckles, eyes like honey with tight, warm-blonde curls swirling like a cloud around her face. Her face—Saffron knew that face, but the shock of seeing it so close made his unspeakable words jumble together.

Sunbeam? He finally gaped. Sunbeam—who went missing around the same time Cloth did. Who Berry died searching for. Whose name had gotten lost amongst the carnage, who even Saffron had forgotten about, realizing as much with a twist of his heart. But—it was definitely her, crushing him beneath her weight, still donning the knife. Why was she with the bloody rowan crone?

Sunbeam remained on top of him, glancing over her shoulder where the wild woman continued accosting the fey lord in the dirt.

"What are you...? With a high fey?"

Saffron stiffly motioned that he couldn't speak to answer, and Sunbeam's eyes trailed on his patron ring that caught the light and sparkled over her face. Returning a stubborn frown of her own, she still didn't roll off him, instead grabbing his cheeks until his lips puckered open and she could peek inside his mouth. Witnessing his tongue clearly furthered her frustration, questions piling behind her eyes like bees arriving to dust her warm irises into honeycomb.

"Did he..." She started, before furrowing her brows. "Lord Taran. Did he ask you to find fairy fruits?"

Saffron's lips parted in uncertainty, before grimacing. Sunbeam's pretty face twisted up in resentment, just as the red-veiled woman suddenly erupted.

"Broderic!" She cried, and Kaelar howled again while fighting to shove her off. "Your name is *Broderic! Be still, Broderic*, you goddamn dog!"

Kaelar's thrashing came to a startling end. Lying prone, the fey lord stared blankly at the sky as the old woman clambered off of him; even after returning to her feet, he remained catatonic in the dirt.

"Not him," the woman announced on approach, smiling with yellow teeth and looking rather pleased with herself. "Not the wolf king."

Wolf king. Saffron couldn't keep the alarm off his face, and the woman noticed, pointing at him and grinning.

"You're the one I met last night!"

"Last night!" Sunbeam exclaimed in question, glancing at Saffron and then snapping her head to the old woman. "You left the ruins? Did you run out of washing again?"

The ruins—! Saffron writhed beneath Sunbeam, but she was busy scolding the woman like an overbearing parent.

"I sensed him suddenly, I had to go searching." The woman frowned, squaring her shoulders. "Not even washing could distract me from his presence, Sunny."

Sunbeam rolled her eyes with a frown, then turned back to Saffron in exasperation. Finally getting to her feet, she pulled him upright with her.

"You should get out of here," she said matter-of-factly. "Don't get wrapped up with Lord Taran, Saffron. I don't know what he offered you, but he's never told an honest truth in his life."

Saffron frowned, shaking his head and tugging the cuff of his sleeve to show the silver bracelet underneath. She scowled instantly, shaking her head and calling him a *dumbass* under her breath. But the old woman's eyes went wide, lumbering closer and taking his arm to shove the sleeve higher. Her hands then traveled all over his torso, and Saffron just smiled awkwardly, worried any quick movements would leave him in the same state as Kaelar a few yards away. He tried to get Sunbeam's attention again, wanting to ask what she meant when she mentioned the ruins—

"*Yama!*" Sunbeam suddenly snapped, and Saffron nearly leapt out of his skin. "Stop messing around!"

A trilling song answered, and the bright blue wren evading sprite hands fluttered up to land in Sunbeam's curly hair. Saffron tilted his head in question, but then the old woman hooked a finger over the collar of his shirt, pulling it down to reveal the silver choker underneath.

"Ah!" She exclaimed. "The queen's devices! Opulent silver! Come this way, rowan spirit!"

Before Saffron could do anything else, the woman gripped his wrist and tugged him into the trees. Tripping over his feet, he attempted to protest, then searched for Sunbeam to help, but found her following behind as calmly as ever. She even looked a little curious, as if the woman's exclamation meant something to her, too.

Stomping through the undergrowth, Saffron's wrist ached by the time he gave up fighting back, resolved to being eaten alive or whatever the woman intended to do with him. But not much further into the unknown, the trees thinned, then parted entirely, and Saffron was pulled onto an overgrown path he'd never seen in all his years exploring.

Glancing up and down the long clearing, Saffron recognized undeniable dips of wheel-ruts carved into the ground. Though long reclaimed by a thick carpet of grass and ferns, he was sure the place they stood had once crawled with wagons and carriages.

Farther down the old road, an impossible amount of mist coagulated thicker than smoke from wet logs. It festered against an unnatural edge as if contained by an invisible wall, reaching into the sky before dissolving into the morning light. Something told him it wasn't there on accident; it also appeared to be exactly where the woman intended to take him.

Saffron's curiosity heightened as they passed a wooden signpost standing on the side of the old road; devoured by the ages, only just clinging to life, the words carved into the front were barely legible.

✝ LAKE ELATHA.

✢ CONNACHT.

⚴ WEST MORRÍGAN.

Φ HAMLET.

His eyes locked on the scrawling hatchmarks at the bottom, clearly added by hand much later than the first directions. Unnaturally placed, just like the wall of mist. Just like the old woman wearing his red veil. Just like the abandoned road. Just like the beantighe everyone thought missing and killed by the same wolf that took the others.

He'd never heard of the campus being referred to as *West Morrígan*. But he knew *Lake Elatha*, he knew *Connacht*. He even had a general idea of where they stood in the Agate Wood—so why had he never stumbled across that place on his own?

Towed to the edge of the mist curling like smoky fingers, the instant they crossed through, the air shifted. It drenched Saffron in dry water, suppressed the movement of his blood, brought everything on his skin to a standstill. It left him breathless, the final gasp of his lungs ringing in his ears, surrounded by incorporeal cotton that flooded him and everything else with a heartbeat in the trees.

Unnatural.

The old woman finally halted, then turned to him expectantly. Even her footsteps in the overgrown grass seemed to echo, like yarn dragged through a pinhole. Saffron raised his eyebrows in question.

"Do not hesitate," she prompted. "Speak now that the queen cannot repress you."

"... Huh?" He muttered, before another ringing gasp hitched from his lungs, hands flying to his mouth. "I-I'm—! I can—?!"

The choker shuddered as he did, tightening just slightly, but not enough to fully cut him off. Saffron clutched at it, staring at the woman with wide eyes, before turning to stare at Sunbeam, too, who remained curious. The crone then huffed in annoyance, popping her hand on the side of Saffron's head. He yelped, smacking it away. Something about it reminded him of Baba Yaga.

"Speak! You wear Queen Proserpina's silver, so where are they hiding her king? Where did they take you to perform your trials, rowan spirit? Are there others there, too?"

"Wh-what? I don't... I don't know anything about King Clymeus," he insisted as genuinely as he could, though a part of him suddenly worried the old woman had no idea where she was, let alone in what period of history she stood. King Clymeus was long gone, as was Proserpina. He quickly added: "There's a Sídhe fey nearby who can change into a wolf, though, so maybe that's what you're sensing?"

"That's what I keep trying to tell her," Sunbeam finally spoke. "She doesn't believe me."

"Can't you feel him!" The woman insisted, grasping Sunbeam's arm and shaking her impatiently. Sunbeam just looked exasperated, so the woman grabbed Saffron again. "Can't you taste him on the air! Are you a rowan witch or not! Surely I am not the only one with any sense left!"

Saffron nearly jumped out of his skin at the sound of Kaelar's horse crunching hesitantly into the mist, whirling and grabbing the horse's reins before breathlessly apologizing for startling it again.

"Shit," he groaned, turning to Sunbeam. "I have to get back."

"Wait, you're *going back*?" She argued, grabbing the horse's opposite rein to keep Saffron where he was. "What the *hell* is wrong with you?"

Saffron blinked. "The—the what? The '*hell*'?"

"The—*oh*, nevermind. You don't have to go back, Saffron, I can show you how to get to Beantighe Village from here."

"No!" He stumbled away as Sunbeam tried to grab him, thinking of what Taran said that morning about Hollow. His heart thudded in anxiety. "It's... it's complicated. I have to go back. But—I'll be in the woods again, soon. Can we... can we meet again later?"

He glanced deeper into the mist, biting his lip, biting back the rush of additional questions he wished to ask.

Are these the ruins? Is there an iron gate nearby? Why are you here? Why don't you go back to Beantighe Village? Why are you with this wild crone? What—the 'hell'—is going on?

Sunbeam watched him for a good minute, her own curious bees bumbling around in her eyes. Then she glanced to where the old woman had wandered off in annoyance, hardly more than a red smudge in the mist.

"*Fine,*" she answered on a stubborn huff of breath. "But only so I can make sure you're alright. When will you be back?"

"I'm... not sure." Saffron smiled apologetically as Sunbeam's frown grew in frustration. "Maybe tomorrow, or the day after that... It'll probably be around the same time in the morning, though, so..."

"Will you have Lord Kaelar with you again?"

Saffron glanced to the horse, who tugged on the reins in an attempt to pull him away.

"I think so, unfortunately."

"Damn, alright... Just don't tell anyone about this place, alright? Especially not Lord Taran." She must have seen the instant rush of a thousand questions behind Saffron's eyes, putting her hands up in defense. "I'll wait in that spot every morning for the next week, until you can come again. After a week, if you don't come—you'll be on your own. Sorry. Erm... can you find your way back, for now?"

"Yes, I think so." Saffron wanted to ask *why. Why. Why.*

Why. Why!—and the curiosity would eat him alive until he could return.

Sunbeam nodded again, watching as Saffron pulled himself into the horse's saddle. Her hand snapped out to grab the leather rein before he could pull away.

"Can I ask you something first? It's about... it's about Berry."

"Oh..." Saffron trailed off, biting his lip and patting the horse's neck as the animal snorted impatiently. "Berry... got lost in the woods after you went missing, and... he was..."

Saffron swallowed back the needles forming a painful web in his throat, trying to keep the words down. He pushed away the mental images of Taran dragging a motionless Berry out of the trees, painting a streak of blood across the road. His voice trembled when he concluded, though couldn't meet Sunbeam's eyes.

"Berry was killed outside of Beantighe Village. I'm sorry."

Sunbeam let out a weary sigh, shaking her head. She released the horse's rein again.

"You don't have to apologize... God, that dolt..." Running a hand back through her tight curls, she closed her eyes for a moment, then offered Saffron a gentle smile. Something about her voice was newly patient. "I'll wait in that spot every morning until you come again, Saffron. We can talk more, then."

"Alright..." Saffron trailed off, suddenly resistant to leaving at all. But Kaelar wouldn't wait as soon as the old woman's enchantment wore off. Taran wouldn't be understanding, no matter what excuse Saffron made. And knowing Hollow was vulnerable in Danann House...

"One more thing, actually," Sunbeam punctured Saffron's rising panic. "Ah, earlier you mentioned 'a Sídhe fey who could change into a wolf.' I assumed you were referring to Lord Taran, but you should know—he actually only controls it. The wolf, I mean. He tells some people it's the prince behind it all, but it's actually him."

"Oh..." Saffron smiled awkwardly, papping the stirrups against the horse as it shifted and spluttered its lips. "Actually...

I've seen it. I know he's the one changing. Um, we can talk about it more next time—"

"Are you sure you didn't just imagine it?"

Saffron frowned. Annoyance flared in his chest.

"Yes. I know it's him."

Despite the insistence, Sunbeam still didn't look convinced. She just kept smiling like she thought Saffron's assertion was endearing.

"I'm being honest!" He snapped.

"I'm not trying to start a fight, Saffron." She put her hands up. "I just don't want any more rumors to spread. And honestly, Taran couldn't change into the wolf even if he wanted to."

"What?" Saffron argued. "What could possibly make you say that?"

"It's just..." Sunbeam suddenly looked unsure, clearly tempted to cut the conversation short and flee. Perhaps she knew Saffron would chase her down into the mist, because she continued, anyway. "Taran mac Delbaith... is ashen. He's not capable of opulence. No one in his family is, ever since the fall of Proserpina..."

Saffron stared at her for a long time. A sarcastic smile peaked the corner of his mouth, waiting for her to drop the punchline or laugh or at the very least exhale through her nose in amusement. But she never did. She just watched him watching her, before sighing and averting her eyes.

"Let's talk more next time. Get back to Kaelar safely, alright?"

She disappeared into the mist before Saffron could protest further. Straight through the white wall in the direction the old woman went.

Saffron stared even after Sunbeam was long gone. His body grew heavy—as if those parting words sliced him open, allowing thick mist to flood between his ribs.

9

———

THE MARKINGS

Kaelar was already on his feet and stumbling through the trees like a drunkard by the time Saffron caught up to him. Panicked, pale, muttering frantically, he shrieked when the horse crunched up behind him. Had he been carrying his rapier, he might have sliced the animal across the snout.

Returning to Danann House, Kaelar rushed through the gardens to the back terrace, leaving Saffron to take care of the horse. He silently cursed the fey lord, wanting nothing more than to make sure Hollow was alright, but still trudged off toward the house stables. The isolation did nothing to balm his own frenzied mental cloud clanging around in his skull like bells.

Taran mac Delbaith is ashen. He's not capable of opulence.

No one in his family is, ever since the fall of Proserpina…

To imply the mac Delbaiths *used* to be opulent, and that their opulence had been *lost* or *taken from them* at the fall of Proserpina… Saffron scoffed. If that were true, why had he never heard such a thing before? Not even a whisper, even though the mac Delbaiths were one of the Sídhe families explained to him by Cylvan? Taran, the Sídhe lord, who even wore a citrine ring like Cylvan and Asche to keep his extra magic at bay?

Scoff. *Scoff.* How could Sunbeam insist something so outrageous with a straight face?

In the stables, Saffron unbuckled the leather straps from the horse's belly, then heaved the saddle to a hook on the wall. The whole time, he grumbled under his breath as much as the choker would allow, though it didn't help him feel any less annoyed.

Ashen. He could vividly remember the conversation with Cylvan in the Grand Library when he first learned that word. It had been while discussing Queen Proserpina, King Clymeus, a little bit about their Night Court. That was right before Cylvan explained the purpose of his citrine ring, then demonstrated his wind magic, lifting Saffron in his arms to caress Derdriu's face on the ceiling...

Surely, Cylvan would have said something back then if Taran was ashen. Saffron even distinctly remembered him mentioning how there were two Sídhe lords on campus, of which he was one.

Glancing down at the reclaimed library ring on his finger, its shine in the light through the stable window helped Saffron's blood pressure relax. Tucked into the curve of his new patron ring, he could at least thank Kaelar for giving something so ugly no one would ever look closer and see what was hidden beneath. His next trick would be stealing the hands-and-dagger ring that controlled his cuffs—and then he could put the library ring to use again.

Closing his eyes, Saffron furled his hand into a soft fist and inhaled a long breath. He pushed away every racing thought, every cannibalistic wonder eating him from the inside out. He was back at Danann House. He had to focus. He couldn't show any sign that anything happened in the woods outside of the old woman's attack. That was just a random event. It wasn't anything. There was no reason to be suspicious.

Hurrying from the stables, Saffron turned his focus to Hollow—but Danann House was completely silent when he entered through the back door. Even Kaelar was gone. Only the clock in the parlor ticked with life.

Swallowing back the disappointment, Saffron had to assume his friend had already been excused for the day, since he and Kaelar arrived home early. The alternative might have made him sick.

The pain of hiking in brand new leather boots made itself known as Saffron dragged himself to the attic, just wanting to change into his black blouse and veil and return to being a ghost. Undoing the shoelaces, he couldn't hold back the tiny gasp as he was sure a few pieces of skin peeled off his feet with their removal. It was a bad sign that he could feel his heartbeat in his toes. At least his uniform boots were well-broken enough to stretch around his quickly-swelling arches, though he didn't bother stripping off the socks as he changed, worried a wave of blood would drip out of the cotton.

Returning to the kitchen, he stood in the doorway upon spotting an unfamiliar box suddenly sitting near the back entrance. Inside, he found a myriad of brown-paper wrapped parcels of ingredients, as well as a few handwritten recipe cards in an accompanying envelope. *Salmon, potatoes, stuffed onions, broiled mushrooms...* enough dishes to make Saffron's whole world spin. Was he really...? Just him, by himself? When his feet were rawer than the cold fish wrapped in paper? Groaning, he pressed the cards to his forehead with a sigh of defeat—but then someone cleared their throat behind him, and Saffron jumped to look.

It had only been two weeks, but Hollow looked at Saffron like he'd been gone a century. With wide eyes, he searched every inch of Saffron as if second guessing what he saw. Had Eias and Magnin's voices not come from the parlor, he might have even said something in greeting or alarm.

Saffron straightened up with an expression of forced calm, clenching his jaw to keep all the other emotions at bay. He offered his friend a tiny nod, full of infinite words and apologies and feelings he wished he could express. Hollow nodded back, as if he understood. As if someone had already warned him to be on his best behavior, and he finally understood why once laying eyes on his friend who was not, in fact, dead.

Not being able to react to seeing his friend for the first time in weeks was almost as painful as hearing Cylvan's voice through the floorboards every day. Close, but out of reach. Lest they both be in danger.

From there—they would have to work side by side in silence, just like any other day with chore assignments. At least that sprinkle of normalcy was offered at all; Saffron could be grateful for that much, for the time being. Just like with Cylvan, there would be a chance to explain everything to Hollow one day, too. Saffron swore it.

HOLLOW HANDLED MOST OF THE HEAVY-LIFTING OF moving furniture and luggage into Danann House, things belonging to Eias, Magnin, and Kaelar who would be transferring from their dorms. Most likely to help Taran keep an eye on Saffron, just like how Eias and Magnin hovered while he and Hollow worked together. Saffron was reminded of his question earlier that morning, wondering what exactly it was each high fey was promised in order to do whatever Taran asked. Perhaps by living so closely with them, Saffron would be able to find out.

Whenever Hollow and Saffron crossed paths, they made eye contact, but otherwise didn't pass any messages. They both clearly knew it was too risky to try, and simply acknowledged one another every time they had a chance in the same room. Occasionally, Hollow would step in to help with meal prep, and Saffron would address smaller tasks in the bedrooms, every time resisting the urge to embrace one another. Even when perceived to be alone.

Eventually, though, they developed a means of communicating without speaking, without ever breaking the façade of two servants cooking or tidying up. Most beantighes could, a result of being veiled and having to work in silence most of their days together.

Saffron showed Hollow his hands, all of his fingers and fingernails where they were supposed to be. Thank goodness Magnin already healed his broken finger from the night before.

Saffron smiled with his teeth, to show they were all intact and regularly brushed.

He tasted a spoonful of sauce, before adding more salt with emphasis, to prove he still had a tongue.

Meanwhile, Hollow offered reassurances of everyone whose name he could characterize through things within reach. He took a head of lettuce, patting it in appreciation, before rolling it toward the cold fish on a cutting board and pretending to make them kiss. Letty and Nimue. Saffron snorted in laughter, pretending like he'd inhaled some flour to cover it up.

Blade was sharp like the kitchen knives. Silk, Fleece, and Quilt were all accounted for like the blankets in the laundry. Splinter was obnoxious and clingy, but that was normal, too. Feather was floaty and careless like the feather of a messenger raven, like always.

Saffron was tried to figure out a means of discussing Baba Yaga, but lacked any chicken feet like the ones she wore around her neck. He hoped she was doing as well as the rest of them.

All the while, forced to silently sound out more words than he was proud of from the recipe cards, Saffron occasionally resorted to making up his own steps when he couldn't figure out what exactly the instructions wanted. Luckily, he'd worked in the campus kitchens, in Beantighe Village, in Luvon's estate enough times to have at least baseline cooking knowledge to work from. He could fake his way through anything else, and Hollow was always there to help him. It was even then that Hollow hinted at having learned how to read a little bit while Saffron was away, and Saffron wished more than ever to ask every question swelling inside his head. All of them combined with those reserved for

Sunbeam would soon make his skull pop like a swollen mushroom.

Smoked salmon garnished with pickled fennel seed; spreading linens on the beds. Potatoes à la crème; wiping down bathroom counters. Stuffed onions with gravy and lemon juice; dusting off the dressers, mantles, and quickly mopping the wood floors. Steamed sea-kale, broiled mushrooms with coarse salt, white asparagus soup; unfolding wardrobes and organizing them as well as he could. Iced gingerbread for dessert; evicting any pixies who followed into each room and busied themselves with shiny trinkets they could find.

Their combined chores devoured the remainder of the day, as well as the remainder of the skin on Saffron's feet. Hollow was finally excused when Taran, Cylvan, and Asche returned at the start of dinner, and he left without acknowledging Saffron at all. Saffron overheard Eias tell Taran there was nothing suspicious between their interactions, either. It was a bittersweet compliment. And—Saffron hated how he hoped to see Hollow again soon, despite the circumstances under which it would happen.

As the dining room eventually filled with the voices of the fey residents of Danann House, Saffron transferred each dish to an appropriate serving plate. Setting them around the table, he was both self-conscious and annoyed at how they all appeared surprised at his ability to make a decent meal. They glanced to one another in silent question, as if to ask whether or not Saffron was capable of poisoning them. *Yes, absolutely*—but only on purpose. Nothing in front of any golden-spoon fey would make them sick purely by accident.

When the initial hesitance faded and normal conversation sparked, Saffron disappeared into the motions of serving around the table. Between every refilled glass, replaced utensil, introduction of the next course, he eavesdropped without being obvious, watched how each member of the table interacted with one another. Like witnessing wild fey in the woods, Saffron once again wished he had his sketchbook to jot down observation notes.

Eias and Magnin sat alongside one another on one side of the table. Across from them, Asche made enthusiastic conversation with Taran, while Prince Cylvan sat at the head. Kaelar was the only one missing, but Saffron considered it a blessing.

Just like at breakfast, the prince was the first and only person to audibly compliment every dish Saffron settled in front of him. Saffron bit back a smile, bowing in modest thanks while his heart flipped in excitement. What else could he do to earn more compliments from the raven at the head of dinner? To provide him even the slightest comforts in what he offered?

There weren't enough leftovers to bother plating for himself, so Saffron accepted his lot and filled the sink to soak pots and pans. He recalled bread and cheese in the fridge, at least. Maybe he could find an egg or two. A part of him wasn't hungry, feet throbbing too hot, muscles aching too stiffly, mind spinning too fast and making it hard to know which way was up.

Scrubbing pans with a broomcorn brush, washing with foaming soda ash, drying with a linen towel, the movements were as familiar as the day's earlier chores had been while traveling between cleaning up and addressing final requests from the dining room. Perhaps they were even a little *too* simple, allowing Saffron's mind to wander from Sunbeam to the bloody crone, Hollow to Baba Yaga, Letty to Nimue, King Clymeus to Taran, Asche to Prince Cylvan...

Bringing himself back, Saffron focused on the movements of his hands. How the water from the faucet smelled like Quartz Creek, wondering if perhaps it was. Surely the stuffy high fey of Danann House wouldn't drink water straight from the source like beantighes in Cottage Wicklow, though. Did they use charcoal filters in the walls? Perhaps magic to fight off worms and stomach bugs? Saffron couldn't resist smirking at the thought of Lord Kaelar shitting himself dehydrated after one gulp of creek water...

But as he reached to turn the faucet, something scrawled around the pipe in the wall caught Saffron's attention. Leaning closer, he had to squint in the low light of the flickering sconces, thinking at first the marks were just a trick of the eye. But the closer he went, the sooner he realized—he recognized those markings. They resembled the same arid hatchmarks Baba used on her teacup saucers, the arid markings he saw on the signpost outside the old crone's wall of mist. Even grabbing the nearby candle and holding it close, Saffron was sure of it, and his heart skipped as he brushed fingers over the ancient lines.

Their placement told him they must have some sort of effect on the water from the faucet—or perhaps used to, as the circle was cracked in a myriad of places around the rim. Didn't arid circles require physical touch to do their magic? What was it Baba Yaga called it, *deliverance?* Even the bloody crone mentioned something about *deliverance* the first night they met, and how she was tired of 'giving it all by herself'...

Someone called out for more wine, and Saffron nearly dropped his candle. He hurried for the cellar stairs right outside the back door, barely within reach of the silver cuffs. Perhaps only because it was on his mind, or perhaps because the light of his candle illuminated it just right—Saffron found himself face-to-face with additional markings carved into the architrave at the bottom of the steps. Equally aged, equally dilapidated from the passage of time—but undeniably arid marks.

He hadn't spent much time wondering about the human servants who worked in Danann House before him; he'd even avoided their ghosts during his time trapped in the attic.

Apparently they were eager to introduce themselves.

WITH AS MUCH DISCRETION AS POSSIBLE WHILE Danann House's residents finished dinner, Saffron scribbled any arid marks he could find onto some of the brown paper used to wrap herbs. Around the faucet and over the wine cellar came first —but then there were more on the floorboards under the stove. On the inner frame of the back door. He had no idea what they said, but amidst uncovering another and another, he had ideas.

Perhaps those under the stove kept things from burning. Around the faucet was to clean the water, or maybe to heat it. The one over the cellar might have protected against humidity, or maybe temperature changes that would ruin centuries of precious wine. Ah—or perhaps they lured wild clurichauns to come protect the cellar and its offerings?

Rummaging around in the food pantry, Saffron chased out a handful of mice and sprites making homes in cracker jars and gutted loaves of bread, eventually unearthing a dusty recipe box filled with a myriad of handwritten cards inside. Recipes for cakes, roasts, brunch snacks, drinks—and on the bottom of the box, another line of arid markings.

Eias and Magnin eventually went to bed, while Cylvan, Asche, and Taran left for a fete on the other side of campus. Once the house fell silent as a tomb, Saffron scoured the dining room. There was one over the entryway from the kitchen. One at the top of the terrace window. One beneath the lip of the table. Two in the seams of the chairs at the heads of the table, including where the prince sat. Saffron hoped it was a friendly spell, at least, even if too old to work any longer. The thought of Cylvan unknowingly within reach of potentially harmful magic made Saffron's insides twist up, just channeling the anxiety into more reason to expedite his pursuit of arid knowledge.

He was in the middle of transcribing a particularly complex circular spell under the prep table when a sound rang out from the dark house, and he went still. *Knock, knock, knock.*

Lifting his head, he glanced toward the back doors, but there was nothing on the other side. Pausing to listen a moment longer, he assumed he'd only imagined it, but the sound came again. *Knock, knock, knock.*

Frowning, he got to his feet. Claiming his candle, he moved into the parlor, and then the front corridor, where he spotted shadows looming outside the front door. He considered ignoring them again, but worried they'd seen his light, or thought maybe it was Cylvan and the others too drunk to get inside. He would answer it as politely as he could. Like a good house-beantighe.

But upon opening the door—those waiting on the other side were the last faces he expected. Headmistress Elluin and her assistant, Silver, smiled at him in the low lantern light of the front step.

"Hello, rowan spirit," Elluin greeted with a wild smile. "I was hoping to find you here."

Saffron instinctively stepped back, fully intending on slamming the door shut and racing to the attic—but a restraining command came from behind the visitors, and Saffron's cuffs crashed together. His candle tumbled to the floor, rolling until Kaelar bent through the door to claim it for himself.

"Why don't you brew us some tea?" He said, meeting Saffron's eyes before blowing out the flame.

10

THE ACCUSATION

Kaelar made friendly conversation with the headmistress as Saffron prepared a tea tray in the kitchen. His hands shook the entire time.

Saffron bowed as he carried the offering into the parlor. His ears rang. Setting it on the table between the couches, he attempted to step away again, but Kaelar took his hand and pulled him onto the couch. Then—he removed his patron ring from Saffron's finger.

Saffron held his breath. He adjusted himself, sitting up straight but avoiding eye-contact. The fire in the hearth starkly illuminated Elluin from behind, seated on the couch while Silver stood at her back. Saffron's most basic instincts writhed in apprehension.

"I truly thought the wolf had taken you, beantighe," Elluin started with a smile, claiming and sipping her tea. "Of course, I never *really* thought you to be a spirit, either. We have wards protecting against that all over campus."

Sure you do. Saffron's instinct was to be sarcastic, even silently. He fought to keep his expression blank, wanting to act as nothing more than the unthreaded beantighe he was supposed to be— though Elluin's comment made him realize, she must not know he'd apparently had his memory threads taken. He curled his hands into fists on his knees as the headmistress settled her cup to the saucer.

"Master Kaelar told me you cannot speak. Is that true?"

Master Kaelar almost made Saffron vomit. Even Elluin seemed to know better than to compliment his ugly patron ring, though.

"Did they really cut out your tongue?"

Saffron nodded. He adjusted his hands to mimic the way Elluin held hers on her lap, noticing how her hands shifted as soon as he did. He matched her next posture, and she wrinkled her nose before changing it again. He followed suit until her mouth twitched like it was full of bees.

"I will not linger, beantighe. I assume *someone* in this house meant to keep you a secret; and they might have, had your patron master not been the second student attacked on my campus in so many days. Imagine my surprise when he described his assailant as a wild old woman with human ears, wearing a red rowan veil..."

She sipped her tea again. Saffron waited for her to continue, having no patience for the headmistress' dramatic pause. She smiled at him over the rim of her cup.

"Naturally, my first thought went to the henmother of Cottage Wicklow."

Saffron's mouth dropped open. It was clearly the reaction Elluin hoped for, grinning and fanning herself with her hand.

"Seeing as I also received reports of the wolf wandering the wood during the time of the first attack, just last night... it also occurred to me how obvious the connection between the two of them is."

She trailed off again—and, again, Saffron gave her exactly what she wanted, despite his best attempts to keep the emotion off his face.

"As of an hour ago, I've arrested Cottage Wicklow's henmother, Nora Everhart, beantighe name Hearth, on the grounds of attacking two Morrígan students, as well as performing arid magic to summon a beast from the woods."

Saffron nearly lunged to his feet, but Kaelar was prepared, compelling *restraint* again without even pulling his mouth from the edge of his cup. Saffron sank back into the cushions, clenching his bound hands into fists as Elluin continued with her shit-eating grin.

"I understand your surprise, beantighe. That's actually why I'm here." She patted her mouth with a napkin, before biting into a sliced apple glazed with caramel. "You see, as easy as it would be to find Nora guilty of summoning the wolf, herself... I'm reminded of that beantighe who died on the road a few weeks ago. The one *'killed by the wolf.'* You all tried to save him by performing an arid spell... ah, my mistake. *You* tried to save him, all by yourself. That's what you claimed in Cottage Wicklow, wasn't it?"

She gazed at him, pausing again and chewing in consideration. Saffron's knuckles went white against the strain he held them on his knees.

"Considering how you once confessed to practicing taboo magic, and how you have a history of wearing the red veil, yourself... it does worry me that I may have arrested the wrong person. As such, I wish to provide you an opportunity to take her place."

Saffron leapt to his feet in agreement, but Kaelar's hand found his waistband and yanked him back down again. Elluin helped herself to another apple slice.

"I expected that reaction, of course—but unfortunately, I am devoted to finding the truth, and only the truth. The last thing I want is to arrest you in Nora's place, only to later learn, for example, that you're not actually arid at all."

Her eyes flickered intensely back to Saffron, before crunching the apple between her teeth like bone.

"I am offering the opportunity to prove yourself skilled enough in arid magic to do everything your henmother has been accused of. Specifically, summoning a wolf exactly like the one seen in the Agate Wood. Only then will I believe Nora Everhart is innocent, and that there is no connection between her, the wolf, and the wild woman."

She never pulled her eyes away. Could she tell how Saffron stopped breathing? How his heart swelled three times its size, sharp with barbs and tearing him apart from the inside?

How? He mouthed. She grinned wider.

"You'll undergo five trials of aridity established by Queen Proserpina during her Night Court," she said, and Saffron's heart skipped. Hadn't the old crone said something about *trials* earlier that day? "You must prove you are not only passively arid, but can perform arid magic at will; with summoning the wolf as your final test. Otherwise, I will force your henmother to perform the trials, instead... and I have very good reason to believe she will reveal herself with each one."

Saffron grit his teeth. Did Elluin already know Baba Yaga practiced arid magic? What about the other henmothers, too? Was she really so mad to formulate this entire arrangement just to force Saffron's hand? For what reason?

"But not only her," she went on, claiming another sip of tea. She paused again for an unbearable amount of time. "Due to her elevated status overseeing so many beantighes, and since you were accompanied by every henmother that day I walked in on your wicked acts... I will also have no choice but to request a full investigation into every resident of Beantighe Village. Every single beantighe contracted with Morrígan Academy will be investigated, and at the very least, tried with conspiracy."

Even Kaelar smirked with a sarcastic exhale of breath. It was loud like a crossbow firing, as Saffron's entire world went silent. His skin suddenly felt hot. His thoughts boiled. He had to be suddenly buried in flames. There was no other way to explain the sudden, excruciating pain of being devoured, overtaking every inch of his existence.

When? He mouthed.

"On my request," Elluin replied coyly.

When? He insisted, and the desperation almost broke through. Elluin kept smiling, taking time to finish the tea in her cup.

"I have no reason to provide a scheduled date and time, just like when your arid ancestors performed the trials for themselves," she finally answered, then sat forward, removing a small glass bottle and knife from the inside of her jacket. "I will summon you the moment I see fit, or request your patron to perform an examination in my stead. Be grateful—the only reason I do not throw you in detention now is because Master Kaelar requested you remain in the house to continue your duties."

From the bottle, she poured an opalescent oil into the bottom of an empty teacup. Meanwhile, Silver took the dagger and handed it to Kaelar, who claimed Saffron's bound hands and pressed the blade into the palm of one of them. Saffron barely felt it, just watching Kaelar with suspicion. Kaelar, who knew Taran was the wolf. Who had admitted to wandering the wood right alongside the beast, knowing very well what was going on. Did Elluin truly still not know Taran was the wolf, himself?

Extending Saffron's hands over Elluin's empty cup, Kaelar squeezed the fresh wound until a small puddle of blood pooled in the bottom. The fey lord then filled it to the brim with fresh tea.

Handed the cup shimmering with silvery oils, Saffron smeared crimson from his palm around the outside. Across from him, Elluin hooked a finger through the loop of the cup flavored with his blood. Cylvan once told him about how old myths claimed high fey had silver blood, and Saffron assumed the exchange had to be some sort of ritual for making a deal with one another.

Sipping simultaneously, Saffron tasted bitterness on the surface of his drink, but otherwise swallowed it back without expression. Elluin watched him with bright eyes, as if expecting once again for him to react, but he remained composed. She sipped her own tea, next, before returning it to the saucer.

"Pour the tea down your front," she compelled suddenly, and

Saffron dumped it without a chance to brace himself. He hissed in discomfort, and Elluin snorted with laughter, before patting her mouth with a napkin again and rising to her feet. Silver followed, and then Kaelar, who grabbed Saffron by the back of the collar to shove him into a bow of goodbye. The moment Elluin turned her back, Saffron yanked himself away to escape.

In the attic washroom, he shoved fingers down his throat. Puking over and over again, he didn't stop until it tinged pink with blood.

11

THE TEA

Prove you are not only passively arid, but can perform arid magic at will.

Otherwise, I will force your henmother to perform them. But not only her—

Every single beantighe contracted with Morrigan Academy will be investigated and tried with conspiracy.

Only nightmares. Saffron might have grasped at a total of two hours of sleep—but they were restless, painful, and stung with tears every time he woke up gasping and choking on bile pooled at the back of his throat. All he could do was nervously fidget with Cylvan's family ring, finding comfort in its familiar shape and feel, a reminder that there was still someone he could turn to if he needed it. But—

Passively arid. Perform it at will.

Summon the wolf.

If he couldn't—everyone in Beantighe Village would be tried with conspiracy. Saffron knew what that meant without having to ask. Cylvan had once expressed something about what happened to people found to be practicing taboo magic, after all. In the Aon-adharcach suite, that night Saffron presented his idea for charming the fern ring with an arid circle like Baba's teacups.

Even just having them drawn in your book—if anyone found you with them, they would execute you on the spot, and investigate every single person you've ever spoken to.

Ah—that meant Cylvan, too. Elluin would certainly find a way to investigate Prince Cylvan, too, if Saffron failed. And then Luvon. And Adelard. And...

If he thought about it too long, he lost the ability to breathe. He could only scream into his pillow until the choker cut him off, praying it was muffled enough to not pass through the floorboards into Cylvan's suite below him. That burden was Saffron's alone to bear. He didn't need Cylvan to overhear and claim it for himself.

WITHOUT THE TASK OF SEARCHING THE WOODS THAT day, distraction came in the form of searching Danann House for more arid markings.

It was easier with all residents gone for morning and afternoon classes, but Saffron still had to keep his ears perked as individuals occasionally stopped by at random for something to eat, to grab a book from their room, to sleep between lectures. Saffron found time to search in those windows where he was left alone, and framed the acts as a beantighe doing simple house chores in case he was ever caught off guard.

Eias' suite was overrun with oddities Saffron realized must have come from the human world, a few of which he even recalled unpacking while caught in the elusive dance with Hollow. A device with a curly horn on top and a rotating knob on the side; a blocky machine stuffed with paper and decorated with lettered buttons like teeth; even something Saffron recognized as a kick-pedal sewing machine, though not recently used.

There were carvings under the work desk and above the latch on one of the windows.

Asche's guest room was exactly like their brother's suite, stuffed full of expensive clothing, fancy shoes, jewelry, and makeup. But more than that, there were *crafts,* just like the one Saffron witnessed them embroidering during the fete. Shimmering palettes of glass beads and a variety of embroidery thread, a dress form half-draped in shiny fabric adorned with hand-sewn designs, every single tool shaped like golden cranes down to the scissors. In addition to the craftswork, an apothecary cabinet weighed down one of the desks, drawers filled with scattered crystals, herbs, rattling bottles of moon water, soil labeled with words like *"Avren—new graveyard, Samhain"* and *"Lake Corsecca—clay, Winter Solstice."*

Saffron found carvings inside their fireplace.

Magnin's room was secured tight. Saffron resorted to crouching on a knee and peeking through the keyhole, blurrily finding the walls plastered with posters, desks stacked high with books, even catching the scent of something burning—but despite the initial panic, he saw no flames, and none appeared when he checked back again an hour later.

When Taran's room was equally locked, Saffron scoured Kaelar's room last. He swept through as quickly as he could, knowing the sun was setting and everyone would be arriving back home again, soon.

Even in such a short amount of time, Kaelar's suite had been reduced to chaos. Clothes piled the floor, surrounded by random pieces of leather armor, stiff boots, a collection of rapiers, and other assortments of weapons both for display and active use. Saffron used one of the ridiculous blades to snap the cord of the shiniest crossbow, just to spite him.

Just before he left, something caught his attention in the fey lord's jewelry box—a silver brooch shaped like the symbol Saffron recognized for ☖*Opulentology* according to the tome in the Grand Library, round with circles at three points on the top and bottom. It was framed by a secondary triangle on the outside, and Saffron couldn't help but appreciate the shine, turning it over in his hands before realizing there were words carved around the edge.

May Danu bless... our silver-blooded roots... May her fire...

return iron to the mounds... he mouthed, furrowing his brows as the first words specifically were familiar, but he couldn't recall where from.

"Find something interesting?"

The brooch clattered from Saffron's hands, snapping around just as Kaelar stepped into the room with an expression like he didn't know whether to be annoyed or amused. He dropped his schoolbag by the door, closing it behind him.

"Is there something specific you're looking for, my little arid witch?" He asked, and Saffron quickly gathered the brooch and tucked it back into the box. Kaelar had clearly seen him rifling around inside, but Saffron still offered a polite bow, before attempting to hurry past.

But Kaelar grabbed his arm, walking him back until Saffron bumped his shoulders against the wall. He offered Kaelar an apologetic smile, shaking his head and glancing back at the door as voices came from the other side. Kaelar either didn't notice, or didn't care, because his eyes remained on Saffron, mouth finally splitting into an exasperated grin.

"You know," he said tightly. "Any other day, I would have brushed this off. I might have even demanded a favor in exchange for my forgiveness—but unfortunately for you, I'm in a terrible fucking mood, and I just don't think I have it in me. What if I use this opportunity to put you on trial, hm? Since you failed your first two."

Saffron raised his eyebrows in confusion—*two?* When had he—?

He attempted to wrench away, but Kaelar tightened his grip and shoved Saffron against the wall again.

"You agreed to do whatever it took, right?" Kaelar leaned close, pressing his weight into Saffron's arm crossed over his chest and crushing his ribs. "Don't look so frightened—if you're really arid like you claim, it'll be a piece of cake. Why don't I show you?"

Pulled from the wall, Saffron instinctively yanked back—but

Kaelar moved quickly, twisting Saffron's arm behind his back and commanding *restraint*. Urged forward, Saffron buried his heels into the shiny wood floor, but his shoes only squeaked against the lacquer.

"You know... if I were to leave you here, how long until someone came looking? Or do you think every single person in Danann House—wouldn't even notice you missing, until your corpse began to stink?"

Saffron slammed backward. Kaelar grunted, then laughed, then shoved Saffron forward again, toward his dark closet.

"And the prince would turn to me and say, *remember when that ugly little thing used to make us dinner? Whatever happened to it?*"

A knock came at the door, and Saffron took his chance to bend his knee, ramming his heel into Kaelar's shin. Kaelar cursed and buckled, but released Saffron's hands, allowing Saffron to race to the door. On the other side, Magnin looked surprised to find Saffron rushing out—but Saffron hurried by before he could say or do anything.

DINNER CAME AND WENT IN A DAZE, PREPARATIONS AND serving and cleaning up passing in a blur as Danann House residents shared in conversation and had too much wine to drink. Once they left again, Saffron could only think to go back to exactly what he'd spent the earlier parts of the day doing—searching for arid markings around the first floor. There was no chance of him sleeping soundly, anyway. Might as well make himself useful.

But while he craned his neck under the sink in the kitchen hours later, Saffron distinctly heard someone coming down the main stairs and circling through the parlor. He frantically puffed out his candle, ducking behind the table and begging his heart to stop pounding so loudly.

A candlestick bobbed around the corner into the kitchen,

heading straight for the cupboard. Already considering his escape route, Saffron moved to flee—but then wet sniffling harmonized with the dragging feet, and Saffron's plan fizzled. Straightening up slightly, Daurae Asche came into focus, rifling through the shelves with one hand as the other maintained a trembling grasp on their candle. With long blonde hair pulled back, their eyes were puffy and red, cheeks wet with tears. Saffron's heart skipped.

His internal battle waged for exactly half a second longer, groaning silently and pinching the bridge of his nose. If he hurried by without doing anything, he would lie awake all night cursing himself for being so cruel and callous. *Damnit.*

Folding and tucking the brown paper covered with arid markings into his back pocket, Saffron puffed hair from his eyes and rose back to his feet. From the cupboard, a miserable song of weeping continued, squeezing his empathy in a chokehold.

"Where is it? Damnit... Godsdamnit..."

Dry herbs scattered to the floor, and Saffron groaned for another reason. He'd just finished cleaning and organizing inside, and the little blonde boggart was actively undoing all of that work.

Saffron approached the pantry door, and Asche yelped, flipping a tin of dry tea leaves in surprise. Saffron swore he heard the daurae's heart pounding against the cramped walls, aromatic particles raining down over both of them. The daurae flamed bright red in embarrassment, then rushed for an escape, but Saffron grabbed the back of their nightshirt, first. He suddenly recalled the night he and Magnin returned from Saffron's stint moonhunting.

Lavender tea. Wasn't that what they and Eias had been looking for? Asche clawed and tugged on Saffron's grip like a bird caught in a trap, but Saffron just scooted the disrupted tins out of the way in search. Far in the back, hidden by the daurae's own searching hands, Saffron pulled out the tea in question. Asche's golden eyes skimmed the word *"Lavender"* on the front, before narrowing in mistrust. Something about it made Saffron laugh, recognizing the family resemblance instantly.

Presenting the tin with more insistence, Asche's fight for freedom eventually relaxed. They sniffled again despite attempts to keep it down, quickly wiping their nose on a sleeve before turning away with a pout. Saffron just adjusted his grip and tugged the daurae to the prep table, pulling out one of the wooden stools and patting it in invitation. Asche hesitated, shifting their weight back and forth, before huffing again and acquiescing.

Heating water in a copper kettle, Saffron sensed the daurae's eyes digging into his back the entire time he prepared a porcelain teacup and scooped lavender leaves while waiting for a boil. More familiar movements. It reminded him of making tea for Letty or Hollow or Fleece when they were sick, soaking wild herbs offered by Silk, pouring it into a cup perched on one of Baba's chipped arid saucers. Without thinking, Saffron trailed a finger around the rim of the flawless Danann House porcelain in comparison, nearly having each magic circle memorized. *Sleep.* Or perhaps *fright?*

"Taran really made you the house-beantighe? After everything you did?" Asche interrupted the ritual, tone more condescending than Saffron expected it to be, considering their relatively light-hearted first meeting. The specific accusation, though, told him exactly why there'd been a change of heart. Taran must have shared the same lies with Asche that he once told to Cylvan, lies about who Saffron was, what he'd done. *"Hello?* Did you hear me, *beantighe?* Ah—you know you're named after extinct wild fey? Isn't that embarrassing for you?"

Saffron was well aware of the origins of *beantighe,* though he wondered if the daurae knew it started as a tongue-in-cheek insult for human servants, too, before evolving into an accepted occupational term. It didn't actually matter—Asche was just trying to be tough.

Instead of implying any of that, Saffron just offered a mischievous over-the-shoulder smile, making Asche stiffen. He recognized the daurae's unpracticed confidence right away, attempting to be authoritative but not sure where the line was between *intimidating* and *mean*. It was more endearing than they would have liked to know, and reminded Saffron of when Caetho first became an elevated-beantighe, even earning her real name, but couldn't ever figure out how to bark orders like Merith did.

"Are you really the beantighe who drugged my brother?" Asche went on accusatorily, and that time Saffron hesitated. Glancing over his shoulder again, he met shining topaz eyes in the dark, perhaps giving Asche exactly the reaction they wanted. Even though it didn't matter, Saffron still turned slightly more and shook his head.

"What..." Asche spoke too soon, clearly not with enough planned. They considered it a moment longer. "What's it like... to have all your memory threads pulled out?"

They sounded almost embarrassed to ask, catching Saffron off guard as it was a total shift from their previous tone. Still, Saffron knew that was probably a rude thing to ask. He reached across the table, grabbing a single golden hair from the daurae's head and plucking it. Asche barked, swatting Saffron's hand away, though their eyes went wide. Saffron actually had no idea, he'd never actually witnessed or met anyone who'd had memory threads removed, but clearly Asche hadn't, either.

Chuckling, Saffron bit back continued amusement as Asche scoffed and turned to storm off—but then the kettle squealed, and they timidly reclaimed their seat.

Saffron removed the copper pot before it could wake the whole house. He poured a steaming brew for the bratty daurae who wrinkled their nose and turned the cup by the handle to face them. Shifting where they sat, something in Asche's expression grew embarrassed again. Saffron waited patiently.

"Um... is there milk?" They finally requested. Saffron grabbed a glass jar from the icebox and set it on the table.

"... What about sugar?"

Scooping sugars pressed like leaves from their jar, Saffron offered a small pile on a crystal plate. Asche took the companion prongs and dunked three, before pouring enough milk to turn the drink nearly white as summer clouds. Then they took a sip, frowning and returning it to the saucer. Their skinny fingers turned the cup to and fro in consideration, barely hooking around the loop.

"It's... not as good as at home..." They mumbled, clearly more of a melancholy personal acknowledgement than a criticism of Saffron's work. The daurae's chin wrinkled, eyes welling up in a way that tugged at Saffron's heart, and he bit his lip while tapping fingers on the table in consideration. Hearing Baba's advice in his head, he reclaimed the cup and dumped it down the sink.

"Hey!" Asche snapped, nearly leaping across the table. "Stupid beantighe, what was that for!"

But Saffron held up a hand for them to wait. Scooping more leaves into the cup, Saffron then dumped the water in the kettle, replacing it with milk. As it heated, he searched the pantry for new ingredients, waiting the entire time for Asche to snap about something else. But they never did, only watched in silence.

A spoon of maple syrup, always suggested by Baba Yaga. A scatter of fresh honeysuckle, which was Letty's preference over sugar. A few blueberries softened beneath Saffron's hand, Hollow's favorite wild snack. Finally, Saffron poured Fleece's chosen steamed milk over the concoction, stirring until the thick syrup dissolved and left only lavender leaves and honeysuckle floating like the surface of a spring pond. A gift for the daurae, from Cottage Wicklow's Fern Room.

Presenting it, Asche was skeptical, sitting up straight and wrinkling their nose again. They sniffed, then risked a sip, then paused, before sipping more. Then some more, until the cup was half-empty.

"Thank you," they said quietly, gazing thoughtfully into the cup. Saffron smiled to himself, offering a few more blueberries as the first offerings were swallowed right away.

"Aschewing?" A voice came from the dark parlor, both Saffron and the daurae jolting in surprise. But while Asche groaned like they'd been caught in a trap, Saffron lost all breath in his lungs as Cylvan warily entered the kitchen. "What are you doing awake? Aren't you auditing an early lecture with Eias tomorrow?"

Instinctively, Saffron stepped back from the table, turning his eyes down and bowing in greeting. Cylvan didn't say anything else, Asche breaking the silence while Saffron hoped Cylvan couldn't hear how hard his heart drummed.

"Taste this," they offered, and Cylvan wrinkled his nose in the exact same way his sibling had. Hooking a finger through the stem, he sniffed, then took a tiny taste. Then another. Then another, until Asche snapped at him, sweeping the cup back into their own possession. "It's good, isn't it? The beantighe made it for me."

Saffron smiled awkwardly as two pairs of pretty, crystalline eyes appraised him. He nodded again, then turned this way and that, not sure what to do with himself. It made him suddenly self-conscious about the veil dangling from the buttons on his shoulders, not to mention whether or not he smelled like sweat, if his hair was a mess from cleaning all afternoon, if there were any stains on his blouse from preparing dinner...

"The beantighe has a name." Came Cylvan's answer, though something about his expression looked like he regretted the words as soon as he said them. "It's... Saffron."

Saffron wasn't prepared for how striking it would be to hear his name spoken so gently. It made him forget what he'd been so worried about, every thought overtaken by the repeating sound of it in Cylvan's voice. All he could do was hurriedly turn back to the stove, just for a chance to compose himself before he looked foolish.

"Did you have another nightmare?" Cylvan went on behind him, followed by the sound of another stool being pulled out. "What about?"

Asche grumbled, before sighing when Cylvan encouraged them to speak up.

"I accidentally burned father's design room. He was very angry."

"O-ohhh..." Cylvan chuckled. "Were you practicing with Master Cairns before I visited Avren? She was a gift for getting my wind under control. I no longer start thunderstorms inside when I get angry. Eh, unless I'm ready for the party to end and for everyone to get out, at least."

Asche huffed and mumbled something else, followed by a pause before Cylvan responded: "It's fine. It's not like *the beantighe* can tell anyone."

Saffron glanced over his shoulder, meeting both Prince Cylvan and Daurae Asche's eyes again. Cylvan wore a sly smile that time, while Asche looked skeptical, and all Saffron could do was smile politely and turn back around.

"... Where exactly am I supposed to practice *here?*" Asche argued, maintaining their hushed volume. "What if I scorch all the apple trees? My fire is still too unpredictable..."

"That would be hilarious," Cylvan teased. "Perhaps then Danu would lift her curse from me, like father always jokes."

But Asche wasn't amused, and Cylvan's teasing trailed off. Saffron glanced back once more, witnessing something secret between the siblings—a moment of quiet intimacy, Asche clearly fighting back emotions butterflied open by the simple conversation, while Cylvan flattened a hand against their back in comfort. It summoned Saffron's racing heart to slow, as if not wanting to interrupt.

"I know you wanted to trial Morrígan for advanced classes, but... is that... the real reason you were so insistent on coming?" Cylvan went on in a quiet voice. "Or are you scared of...?"

More silence. Saffron took an opportunity to offer Cylvan his own cup of maple-lavender milk tea, and the content, gracious smile that lifted the corners of the prince's mouth made pixies dance in Saffron's stomach.

He was... so *close*. Cylvan was right there, right in front of him, in a way entirely different from the first night when Saffron carried him to bed. Within reach, after what felt like an eternity of waiting, without the wall of prying eyes that dampened every other brief interaction before it. Without the wall of inebriation that would erase Saffron's existence again by morning. With his hair braided long over one shoulder, wearing a baggy tunic with a wide collar, untucked from his leggings, barefoot. Casual. Comfortable. Demonstrating, without knowing it, a new sense of ease even in Danann House, despite everything that had happened before.

It reminded Saffron of the night they danced together in the Aon-adharcach suite. The night Cylvan teasingly questioned Saffron's ideas about charming patron rings. The night they kissed, and vanished into one another between his dark sheets...

Saffron's face went hot. He flipped back around to clean up.

"... No," Asche finally muttered. "I don't want to talk about it anymore."

"Why not? If you don't learn—"

"Because all you ever do is scold me!" They exclaimed, the sudden slice of their voice even catching Saffron off guard. "Not all of us get such pretty, elegant magic as *wind, alright?*"

"Oh, come on—" Cylvan laughed lightly, but Asche pushed away from the table. Cylvan said their name, attempting to call them back, but Asche was already hurrying into the darkness without another word. Cylvan sighed dramatically, strumming sharp nails against the table before returning to his drink. Saffron felt the exact moment eyes landed on his back.

"They didn't say anything rude to you, did they?"

Saffron couldn't bring himself to meet Cylvan's eyes, especially not without an additional buffer there. Not while they were alone, when it would be impossible to maintain his composure. To keep his distance from the tempting cliff calling out to him, whistling pleas from depths he still couldn't perceive.

He thought about Cylvan's face the night of the fete, upon

hearing Taran's confirmation that Saffron was real. That look of surprise, like the world had sucked out from under him. He thought about when he found Cylvan on his knees in the attic corridor only hours later, mumbling apologies for everything Saffron knew and didn't know at the same time.

He gazed down at the prince's ring still on his finger from that morning, hating how it newly reminded him of Elluin's accusation from the night before since becoming the token Saffron fidgeted with when nervous. He'd once thought of how he could use that ring to prove himself real. To prove himself actual. As a means of finding and reconnecting with Cylvan, even silently. An unthreaded beantighe, seeking the origin of the ring on his finger, not knowing how he got it or where it came from, only that it must have been given to him by someone important...

Saffron... needed Cylvan's help. He desperately needed Cylvan's help, especially with Elluin's threat. But how was he supposed to do that, when Taran's equally terrifying warning rang in his head every time he considered approaching that cliff and gazing over the edge?

To peer over the side and answer the beguiling cries, without anyone suspecting he'd moved closer at all? Safely, secretly, so that even Taran wouldn't be able to tell. So that Saffron didn't nearly burst at the seams every time he met Cylvan's eyes, all while expected to pretend like such clawing fingers were nothing at all. He felt nothing at all.

God—how could he have been so arrogant to think he could pretend, even for a moment, that Cylvan was a stranger? That even if Saffron's threads had genuinely been taken, he wouldn't instantaneously gravitate back toward the raven who once treasured him, who gave him such an important token of patronage and care and affection?

Did Saffron really think himself better than Icarus, who lasted hardly a moment in the sky before sweeping toward the loving sun right within reach? Cylvan, his raven, his sun, who might melt Saffron's waxen wings—but whose touch would make the plummeting descent worth it? Whose rays of light might illuminate exactly what he needed in order to protect the people he loved from those who wished to use them as bargaining chips?

The clink of porcelain returning to a saucer came from Saffron's back, followed by the stool shifting as Cylvan got to his feet. Saffron hadn't reacted, hadn't responded to Cylvan's question at all, so it made sense for the prince to politely excuse himself. Gripping the edge of the counter, Saffron physically denied himself the temptation of turning to watch Cylvan go, though a selfish part wanted any last taste he could get.

When the kitchen fell silent, he released a shuddering breath, hunching over the sink in misery. But he'd survived the sun's ambrosial warmth one more night, like forcing a cloud to swallow any light he might have taken for himself. Saffron's waxen wings would remain intact one more night—even if it meant he went to bed cold as ice.

He just... couldn't be impulsive. There might be a way to get Cylvan's help, but—Saffron had to be intentional about it. He had to think of his own life. He had to think of Hollow. And now Baba Yaga, too, and everyone else in Beantighe Village.

Fuck.

Digging into his back pocket, Saffron pulled out the paper scribbled with arid markings. Flattening the page against the counter, he scowled at it, forcing his agitated frustration into something useful, like deciding where to go from there...

Cylvan cleared his throat.

Slamming the kettle with his hand, hot milk drenched the counter as Saffron reeled back. He instantly scrambled for the page again, prepared to shove it in his mouth and swallow it whole if it meant—

"What do you have?" Cylvan asked. His words were tight, like he'd just been punched in the stomach. "What is that, beantighe?"

Time slowed around them. Saffron should have looked away, should have played dumb—but Cylvan's presence commanded every inch of his soul.

Icarus' sun emerged from behind the clouds. Saffron's wax wings slumped. The first drips of melt slithered between fibrous feathers, gathered individually by hand during his two weeks of imprisonment.

Saffron could deny the sun once.

But not twice.

12

THE AGREEMENT

I don't know. The lie formed so easily—

"Where did you get it?" Cylvan inserted before Saffron's implied syllables could finish.

Saffron's mouth dangled open in uncertainty, before closing again slowly. *Bang, bang, bang,* the knocking against his ribcage grew louder. Faster. The sweet warmth of Cylvan's sun tickled the wings on his back. How close could he get before it became dangerous? Surely, just hovering within reach would be fine...?

Saffron could hardly hear his own thoughts, except those shrieking like beansidhes about how warm and welcoming and lovely the celestial light was.

He glanced down at the page in his hand.

He shouldn't. It wasn't safe. It was too dangerous to tangle with Cylvan already, after only stepping back into the light a few days prior—

But—Cylvan was right there, in front of him. Again. Offering him one more chance to say, to do anything at all. Would Saffron get another chance, or would this be the last time? If Saffron refused him entirely, would Cylvan ever look at Saffron that way again?

He... didn't even have to tell Cylvan everything.

Saffron could still maintain his secrets, carry Cylvan's burdens, while at the same time...

Two people—one who could perform arid magic, but needed help gathering resources.

The other, who could gather resources, but couldn't perform it...

Saffron needed Cylvan's help. He knew that, already—but he didn't know how to ask for it, without the rest of his already-unsteady tower of risk collapsing beneath him.

He would have to make a choice. He might not get the opportunity again.

He already knew what he wanted, more than anything else, but his hesitation lied in how easily the chance was presented in front of him. How clearly that burning sun illuminated him, beautiful and tempting and warm. But nothing could be so simple, so easy... right?

Apprehensively tracing fingers along the edge of the page, Saffron waited only one more moment before carefully flattening the creased paper against his leg. He met Cylvan's eyes, and his hands made the decision before the rest of him. Controlled by his racing heart, desperate to fly as close to Cylvan as he possibly could, never having anticipated how cold the world was without him.

Saffron forwent everything he'd learned about improving his handwriting over the previous two weeks. He wrote a painful lie on the back of the brown page, in shaking hand:

I have had it since I can re-member.

Cylvan read the words. He read them again. And again. And again. Then he took the paper carefully, and held it closer to his face. His soft lips hung parted, and Saffron disappeared into the sight of them. Into every detail of Cylvan's features, memorizing every single one in the darkness so that he might have something comforting to think about while falling asleep.

"This is..." Cylvan's voice cracked, and he cleared his throat. "This is taboo magic, beantighe. You can't let anyone see you with it. Let me... let me take it, I'll take care of it for you..."

Saffron grabbed Cylvan's arm. Cylvan went stiff, holding the page away protectively as if it was the most precious thing in his life. Then his eyes flickered to the Tuatha dé Danann ring Saffron wore, and goosebumps kissed Saffron's skin.

"That ring," Cylvan said weakly. "Where did you... Do you know where it came from?"

Saffron bit his lip, then pointed back to the page. *Same answer.*

Keeping one hand on Cylvan's arm, Saffron recalled the role he'd created when deciding he would resurrect himself in front of Cylvan to save his own life. The act, the script.

He grabbed one of the nearby recipe cards next, scribbling out:

Dorae Ash said the ring belonged to you. Is it true?

Cylvan read the words. He met Saffron's eyes, searching every inch of his face in silence. He glanced down at the arid markings again, then the ring, before shaking his head in disbelief.

"You... truly do not remember anything?" He asked. There were layers to that question, and Saffron heard what Cylvan really meant. *You truly do not remember me?*

He bit his lip, returning to the recipe card.

Did I steal it from you?

"No," Cylvan responded instantly, surprising Saffron when his opposite hand suddenly grasped where the ring sat on Saffron's fingers. "No, I... I gave it to you."

Saffron summoned the unthreaded-beantighe inside of him, and put on a smile of relief. Thankfully—Cylvan smiled slightly, too. Saffron pointed at the brown paper with the markings, next, then wrote:

You know what those are?

Cylvan's gaze returned to the markings, frowning, then biting his lip, then closing his eyes. He folded up the paper, and to Saffron's surprise, handed it back to him. Saffron swore he witnessed the exact conflict burn behind Cylvan's eyes, before he rubbed the back of his head and motioned to the page again.

"Can you keep a secret?" He asked, voice hoarse like he still wasn't sure. Saffron silently begged that he would take a step toward that cliff, too, where Saffron would stand right alongside him. Where they might peer over the side, together. "Although technically it is your own, I suppose."

Saffron nodded. Cylvan paused again, before glancing around the kitchen, into the dark parlor, then pulling Saffron suddenly into the cramped pantry. He closed the door behind them, and Saffron's pounding heart stopped as his face was only a few inches from Cylvan's, chests barely brushing against one another.

"Before your memories were taken, you and I... we were dabbling in this kind of magic." Cylvan tapped the paper in the darkness. "I don't know what these marks mean since you also stole all of my reference books, but... you must have left this page in your pocket for a reason... protected it, even, while you were in Avren... all the way up until..."

His words petered off, before taking Saffron's hand again. He squeezed the ring on his finger, then pulled it close to his body in thought. Saffron held his breath, spreading his fingers over Cylvan's chest and feeling how his heart raced, too.

"This ring, too..." He whispered. "You must have protected this ring, too, knowing it would... lead you back to me, even once you forgot. As someone who could help you. And watch over you."

Saffron nodded, perhaps a little too enthusiastically. Yes, yes,

yes—he would always come back. Cylvan could always count on Saffron to come back to him, no matter what happened—

"And these markings, they must be important. Perhaps even meant for me..." Cylvan went on in a low voice. "And... I would like to learn what they mean."

Saffron touched Cylvan's chest again, before, in the smallest slant of light through the pantry door, he wrote a few more words on the recipe card:

You will help me figure them out?

Cylvan met Saffron's eyes with a sharp intensity, and nodded. A streak of low light came through the crack in the door, casting his indigo irises in a line of silver, just like when they once knelt cramped in his wardrobe on Imbolc. Illuminated by a line of fire-light, hiding from Taran. Moments before making their geis.

"Yes," Cylvan reiterated in a low whisper. "But... we will... have to be careful. We can't let the others think we're anything more than master and servant. You will have to be on your best behavior, just as I am. And... you have to do everything I say, without question. You will have to trust me."

There was clearly something else Cylvan wished to add, but instead bit his tongue and touched the page again.

"It took me some digging to get the reference books the first time, but I will find more. In the meantime, don't let anyone see you with this, alright?"

Saffron nodded, wishing he could mention how he was almost positive Cylvan's books were actually in his bag with his sketchbook back in Beantighe Village. But—a beantighe with no memories wouldn't know that.

Still, as Cylvan moved to leave, Saffron grabbed his arm again. He didn't know why—his hand flashed out on his own—but he quickly added a final, endearingly naïve request to the recipe card as Cylvan watched:

Your name is Lord Silven, correct?

Just like Saffron hoped, Cylvan smirked, taking the card for himself.

"My name... is Prince Cylvan... dé Tuatha... dé Danann," he corrected, writing every part in swirling letters. "And your name is... beantighe."

Saffron laughed quietly, not expecting it, and Cylvan smiled as if pleased to hear the sound. Saffron knew Cylvan already knew his name, of course, but he still took the pencil back. He wrote *Saffron* directly beneath the prince's lovely penmanship. A part of him just wanted to see them next to one another.

"Right," Cylvan humored. "*Saffron,* like the flower. It... suits you."

Saffron didn't know how long they stood there in the dim light smiling at one another, and for a moment, he believed Cylvan suddenly saw and understood everything Saffron was keeping from him—but then the prince cleared his throat again, nodding and stepping from the pantry.

"Goodnight, beantighe," he said like any other respectable master fey. "Be sure to finish tidying up before you go to bed."

Saffron bit back another laugh, offering a polite bow in acknowledgement. But when he lifted his head again, Cylvan was suddenly back in close, and Saffron's breath caught.

"Don't forget," he whispered. "Everything I say, without question."

Saffron met Cylvan's eyes, biting his tongue. The smile Cylvan offered in response was enough to nearly stop his heart, before Cylvan finally nodded and excused himself.

Saffron was left alone in the silent kitchen, and all he could think was—he wished they would have shared the kiss of forming a geis.

13

THE AMETHYST

Saffron finished cleaning up after dinner. But upon returning to the attic with a few hours to spare before sunrise, his window hung ajar, while squeaking arguments and sparkling tussles skittered along the floor loud enough he heard it at the end of the corridor. Hissing through his teeth in an attempt to keep the pixies quiet, Saffron chased them around the room, cursing silently as whatever they held clattered like a rock against every uneven edge of the floorboards. When they accidentally bumped the desk chair and knocked it over, he was sure it would wake Cylvan down below, and Saffron resorted to ripping the quilt from the bed to flatten them in a strategic net-throw.

Bundling the squeaking protestors like swarming bees, he dumped them on the bed, only for whatever they fought over to tumble to the floor one more time and roll under. Cursing the creatures further, he dropped to his knees and searched before they could take chase all over again

Sweeping his arm around in the darkness, Saffron's fingers bumped against the object of interest—but also trailed over the undeniable texture of something carved into the wood. It made Saffron's breath catch, raising his eyebrows and jerking his head under the bedframe, before scrambling to light a candle because it was too dark to see clearly.

Illuminated in the glow, still partially hidden as it scrawled all the way to the wall, Saffron's eyes traced around carved arches, hatchmarks, unfamiliar runes decorating the outline. Slamming his head against the bedframe, he pulled away with watering eyes, barely managing to tuck the candle on the desk before grabbing the foot of the bed and scooting it as quietly as he could away from the wall.

Sure enough, carved into the floor beneath where he slept, an arid circle as wide as the bed was. Clearly as old as all the others in the house, there were some markings too worn away to see, but others remained stark as ever. Grabbing his piece of brown paper, he quickly drew every detail he could make out.

As much as he wished to continue observing every inch, the last thing he wanted was for Kaelar or someone else to burst in and see what he was doing. So Saffron scooted the bed back carefully, propped the desk chair under the doorknob, then searched the floor for the thing that riled the pixies up in the first place.

Pinching the shiny, delicate silver chain off the floor, Saffron lifted the necklace in reach of his candle. Soft candlelight illuminated the oval pendant from the other side, and he tilted his head in appreciation.

Amethyst. Faceted into illuminated infinity, encircled by a simple but elegant band of silver matching the chain. From the loop, a crescent moon dangled as added embellishment.

Where did you steal this from? He mouthed at the creatures emerging from under the blanket like they'd just been caught in a rockslide.

Had some pixie snipe grabbed it when no one was looking? If anyone found it in his room, he would definitely be accused of theft. His heart thumped in instant apprehension, until a slight breeze curled through the open window and fluttered an envelope on the windowsill. He hadn't noticed it in all the excitement, tilting his head and claiming it to tear open.

I HAVE HAD THESE TRINKETS FOR SOME TIME. THEY COME IN PAIRS. WHEN YOU TOUCH ONE STONE, ITS TWIN BURNS WARM.

LET'S USE THEM DURING OUR AGREEMENT, TO ENSURE THE OTHER PERSON IS ALWAYS ACCOUNTED FOR.

✳ AS THE BEANTIGHE-FLOWER.

☾ AS THE MASTER-FEY.

–PRINCE MASTER CYLVAN DÉ TUATHA DÉ DANANN.

Saffron's heart pounded, biting back a smile and touching the moon charm. At first, he wondered if Cylvan had made a mistake, giving him the wrong one—but then realized, Saffron was meant to keep the moon by his heart on purpose. To keep Cylvan by his heart, as Cylvan would keep him. His face went warm, smiling brighter and hurrying to the dingy mirror on the wall. Clasping the necklace around his neck, he stared at it the whole time in his reflection. A gift from Cylvan, his moon, his Night Prince. *To ensure the other person is always accounted for.*

Taking the precious stone in his hand again, he closed his eyes and pressed it to his lips, silently whispering a pitiful prayer of thanks to Ériu. His heart thumped faster as not another moment passed before the stone bloomed with warmth just like the note claimed, and Saffron jumped backward in surprise. Then— Cylvan was awake below him, wasn't he? Holding the matching pendant? Did he feel Saffron's warmth, too?

Squeezing his eyes closed again, Saffron returned the amethyst to his lips, swearing that, soon, they wouldn't have to rely on stones to take care of one another. To account for one another.

They would feel one another's warmth, skin against skin.

14

THE MIST

The sound of violin wove through the floorboards, summoning Saffron from a restless, short-lived sleep. He stared at the ceiling while listening to the notes, wondering if they were the remnants of a dream—but the longer they sang, the more he realized, it was real. It made his heart race, then dance; that was the first time he'd heard such a cheerful song from his prince's violin in weeks.

Sitting up, the amethyst pendant slid down his chest and caught on the chain around his neck. Saffron smiled to himself, pausing to squeeze it—and the music below petered off, before warmth responded in his hand. He nearly fell out of bed in a rush of embarrassment, and swore he heard a ghostly chuckle emerge through the floor in reply.

To be in such an elated mood after spending so much time in his mire of loneliness, Saffron knew better than to let it seep into every part of him. Especially in Danann House, anything found radiating warmth was quickly grabbed and drained.

But then, there was one moment during breakfast where he and the prince made eye contact, and Saffron let the amethyst dangle from his shirt while leaning over to pour his coffee. Cylvan made a little sound of acknowledgement, touching the necklace and complimenting it under his breath—and Saffron knew it would be impossible to ever leave the warmth of that sun, ever again. Even just to pretend.

The repeated memory made Saffron shiver slightly in joy while preparing to enter the woods, even as he met Hollow's eyes as he arrived for the day. They exchanged a subtle nod, and Saffron offered an additional silent promise that he would *be back soon.*

Donning a jewel-red cloak, he lifted the hood to protect his ears from the rainy morning chill while waiting for Kaelar to bring the horse around. When he did, the fey lord didn't attempt to coax Saffron to join him in the saddle, and Saffron was only slightly surprised. The feeling was quickly overtaken with relief.

Upon claiming the reins, however, Saffron noticed the way Kaelar held one hand on the pommel of his rapier. Precisely at the ready to defend against bloodthirsty old crones. He couldn't help but smirk, shaking his head when Kaelar snapped, *"What are you looking at?"*

Broderic. The old woman had compelled him after announcing the name *Broderic,* and Saffron considered something he hadn't had a chance to mull over, yet. Was that Kaelar's *true name,* taken from him? The word she exclaimed in the woods the night of Saffron's moonhunting, too—that had been the fey student's true name as well, hadn't it? Perhaps Saffron could lure Taran into the woods for her to perform the same trick, and Saffron could finish his geis much sooner than planned. Until then, he would just have to keep Kaelar's in the back of his mind for whenever he was able to speak again.

Recalling the path to where he'd met Sunbeam the first time, the journey remained silent as Saffron was lost in thought and Kaelar searched for threats in every direction. All the while, warmth bloomed between Saffron's fingers as he stroked his thumb over the amethyst pendant, resisting the urge to smile every time he thought about Cylvan fiddling with its twin simultaneously. Was he in class? Sitting in a lecture? Was he in the middle of a conversation with someone, sending Saffron signals that he was still within reach? Did it mean as much to Cylvan as it did to him to be able to touch again while being so far apart?

Saffron would end up spoiled rotten soon enough. He would fly too close to the sun, wings melting off his back, tumbling back to the hard and unwelcoming earth. But at the same time—it was realistic for his act, wasn't it? Even an unthreaded beantighe would fall for the handsome, lovely Prince Cylvan dé Tuatha dé Danann. He hadn't been able to resist Cylvan's charm the first time they met, how could he be expected to do it a hypothetical second time? He bit back a conspiratorial giggle.

A different breath of excitement prickled Saffron's blood as he recognized thin tendrils of mist threading between the leaves like water, knowing they were close to the meeting place. He anticipated the sight of Sunbeam at any moment, but as they kept walking without any sign of her, he grew anxious. When they emerged all the way onto the overgrown road, Saffron's heart even thudded in disappointment, until he noticed a little blue wren perched on the aged signpost.

"Let's go this other way," Kaelar snapped when Saffron took a step toward the bird, pulling back on the reins Saffron held. "The fog is too thick in that direction."

His tone was apprehensive, but coated in an attempt to exert authority—not unlike Daurae Asche demonstrating unpracticed confidence the night before. But Saffron wasn't about to turn away, not when Sunbeam might be waiting in the thick mist with answers to Saffron's merciless questions.

He put on his prettiest, most innocent smile, tugging encouragingly on the reins. As if to say, *I'm so curious, Lord Kaelar, but I can't go in alone. I need a brave high fey with a big sword to follow me, in case something jumps out. Surely a little fog doesn't frighten someone as scary and intimidating as you...*

Kaelar cleared his throat. The horse shifted forward on its feet, nibbling on Saffron's hair.

"F-fine," he finally said, puffing out his chest to look more intimidating. "But only so we can mark this area off our search."

Saffron returned the awed, appreciative smile of a beantighe swooning at a lord's courage, and Kaelar straightened up slightly more. Then he drew his sword, perhaps to imply he would protect Saffron from whatever dangers may lie within the cloud, but Saffron knew it was actually just to quell his own nerves.

Into the fog, Saffron sensed the moment his choker's magic drowned beneath whatever was in the air. He would have to be careful not to say anything in front of Kaelar, but the fact it happened again that morning meant it hadn't only been a fluke the first time. Perhaps if he could bottle the magic up, somehow, he could figure out a way to use it on the walls of Danann House in order to come and go as he pleased. It made his eyes instinctively flicker to Kaelar's hands, wondering if he wore the silver hands-and-dagger ring that drew the boundary of the silver cuffs —but leather gloves concealed Kaelar's fingers, and Saffron turned away with a pout.

Trees on either side of the road blurred into hardly more than cracked, bulging shadows in the thick cover. The air tasted like metal before a lightning storm. Even the morning birds had gone silent, only the sound of Saffron's breath, his feet, the horse's hooves crunching through the grass and dirt coming from any direction.

In the mostly-obscured distance, something emerged from the earth like a guard of narrow, fire-splintered trees—and Saffron realized with a small breath, it was a gate. A wrought-iron gate, made with dark spires lining like sentries not unlike the smaller one that encircled Beantighe Village. Saffron also recognized red rowan trees blurred by the fog, and his heart flipped again and again. Were those the ruins?

Kaelar let out a sharp breath, pulling back on the horse as if sensing the ironick berries and breaking out in hives.

"This is far enough," he announced. "Go on, start looking."

But Saffron heard only Hollow's voice from the night Taran

asked him to find wild fruits.

Behind an iron gate in the woods. In some old ruins.

His breath caught, staring down at his finger where the library ring hid beneath his patron ring. *Old ruins. Behind a gate. West Morrigan.* Were the ruins just... an abandoned wing of Morrigan Academy?

"Step back, beantighe," Kaelar snapped, reeling on the horse once more. "Or we're going back to Danann House. *Now.*"

Saffron frowned, stubbornly tugging the reins forward. He wasn't about to return to Danann House right away and let Taran know what they'd found, not when he hadn't gotten a chance to meet with Sunbeam, yet—but then Kaelar slashed his sword in a swinging arch.

The blade sliced through the back of Saffron's hand, and he snapped free of the reins, hissing as blood splattered the horse's coat. Clutching his bleeding knuckles, Saffron stumbled backward as Kaelar kicked himself from the saddle, landing in the grass and rushing with a hand outstretched—

"Sleep, Broderic!"

The fey lord's eyes rolled back, and then he slumped, buckling face-first into the grass like a ragdoll. Saffron might have laughed had he not been so caught off guard.

Sunbeam emerged from the side of the road, clearly annoyed while Saffron grappled for the horse's reins before it bolted.

"Let it crush his head like a pumpkin," she encouraged, referring to the horse's pounding hooves. "Would anyone miss him?"

"That's... complicated," Saffron answered nervously, voice a little hoarse as he still wasn't used to the sudden ability to speak. He managed to calm the animal's panic, petting its velvety nose before glancing back at Sunbeam who grabbed Kaelar's arm to drag him off to the side. "Um... thanks."

"You know his name now, too. Use it next time."

"I didn't want him to know I could speak."

"... Fair enough."

Following to where she dumped Kaelar beneath a rowan tree,

Saffron found a patch of grass for the horse to nibble, tying the reins off to a low branch. He heeled Kaelar's shoulder as he passed, then helped himself to the silk kerchief around the fey lord's neck to wrap over the blood oozing from the back of his hand. Saffron nearly turned to leave without another thought—before pausing and gazing down at his cuffs. Curiosity struck him, and he took a moment to search under Kaelar's gloves for the silver hands-and-dagger ring that would allow him to leave Danann House on his own—only to be disappointed, as even Kaelar was smarter than to wear it right on his finger.

"He'll be out for at least a few hours," Sunbeam went on, eyeing Saffron's wound but not saying anything. "That should be enough time to show you around."

"And answer my questions."

She matched his smirk. "Of course. You look like there's already something on your mind."

"Well... now I'm just wondering how that old woman took his true name?" He asked, glancing one last time at the floppy high fey in the mud.

"I don't really know how it works, but this lump is not the first high fey to have a name tangled up by the beannighe's hands." Sunbeam prodded Kaelar with her boot for good measure. "They always recover just fine."

"Oh..." Saffron considered, only slightly disappointed, before following close as Sunbeam returned to the mist. "The old woman isn't going to kill Kaelar while we're gone, is she? I kind of need him to make it home safely so I don't have any more trouble with Taran... Wait, did you call her a *beannighe?*"

"She won't bother him," Sunbeam promised, leading along the edge of the road, within reach of the trees that grew thicker than Saffron had seen anywhere else in the Agate Wood. But perhaps more unsettling—was the silence of it all. Not even birds, or babbling streams, or a morning breeze crackled through the mist. As if the atmosphere numbed every living thing into silence. Only Sunbeam's voice joined him on the journey, though he continuously worried the thoughts in his head were loud enough for her to hear. "I killed a deer the other day; soaked a bunch of rags in its blood and scattered them around the area. Her nature is to wash bloody clothes in the creek, after all. It keeps her out of trouble. Hence the nickname, *beannighe*."

"But she has human ears, doesn't she? Beannighes are wild fey."

"Who knows." Sunbeam shook her head. "I don't actually know *what* or *who* she is, but if it works to distract her, so be it. I think she's the only reason students aren't wandering around in the ruins, anyway, and I need her to keep it up just a while longer."

"The ruins..." Saffron reiterated, and couldn't help but smile. Extending a hand once they passed through the line of rowan trees and reached the outer fence, his fingers strummed along the bars as they followed it away from the road. It reminded him of how Letty always did the same along the edges of Beantighe Village.

Pausing at a particularly gnarled tree, Sunbeam pressed her fingers to one of the fence posts, counting six down the line. Grabbing the seventh, she wiggled it until it clanged loose, scooting it aside before slipping through. Saffron followed with an excited flutter of his heart.

Whether or not wild fairy fruits were shrouded on the other side, Saffron would drag out the hunt as long as he could. Burning time away, taking as much as he could for himself, using it to learn what he needed to fulfill his first geis with Prince Cylvan. As far as he knew, if *West Morrigan* really was an abandoned wing of campus, perhaps there might even be discarded books to help him. Even if there weren't—it didn't matter. He had someone back in Danann House to watch over him. To provide what he needed, without question.

Saffron's hand encircled the amethyst pendant again, like a promise made without words. Somewhere on the other side of the trees, a raven responded with blooming warmth.

15

THE RUINS

The verdant growth was even thicker on the opposite side of the fence. Even as the fog thinned, allowing for overcast light to filter through, the silence remained unwavering. Saffron almost felt bad to break it, but impatient words were filling his mouth.

"So... you're *alive*."

Sunbeam laughed. Ducking beneath a low branch, she held it out of Saffron's way to pass under. "Yes, I am indeed alive. I assume by your surprise, and by Taran asking you for the fruits, though, um... that Cloth didn't make it...?"

She said it solemnly, as if already coming to terms after their first conversation, but still clinging to a pinch of hope. Saffron bit his lip, but nodded.

"I'm sorry."

"Anyone else?" She continued. "You mentioned Berry last time..."

Saffron thought quietly about Berry again. Berry, who died looking for the exact person Saffron navigated the woods with that morning, who clearly knew what she was doing. Perhaps even better than Saffron did, considering her knowing steps, the knives on her belt, the worn leather of her boots, how she moved with ease between the trees and brambles like a stag who'd walked the same path a thousand times. There wasn't even sap on her dark cotton shirt, or scrapes on the back of her hands from whipping leaves and rough bark. Her hair was pulled into a thick braid dangling from the nape of her neck, a scarf wrapped around her head to keep the front pieces under control. She didn't particularly *look* like a person who'd been living in the woods for weeks—but at the same time, gave off every air of someone who'd been born there. More and more, Saffron accepted perhaps Sunbeam had never been *lost* at all.

"Taran also asked Hollow," he finally answered, voice flat as he hated every reminder. "But I stepped in and offered to look, myself, in order to protect him. I should have done it much sooner, but..."

Sunbeam shook her head, but didn't say anything else. Saffron's eyes lingered on her strong back as they hiked up a rocky knoll to the top.

"I never intended on staying in Beantighe Village long," she went on with her own explanation. "In a lot of ways, it was just a place for me to sleep at night. When Taran asked Cloth to search for fairy fruits, I saw it as my opportunity to also slip away and be forgotten."

"Did you want to escape your patron-fey, or something?"

She smiled mischievously over her shoulder. "I don't have a patron-fey. *Sunbeam of Finnian* is a fake name we used on my working contract."

"Wait—is your name not really *Sunbeam*, either? Why would you ever contract to work at Morrígan if you don't...?"

Sunbeam's lips pursed into something sly, but at the same time, strangely bitter. She shook her head, watching her own feet tromp through thick weeds and over roots.

"You say your circumstances with Taran and Kaelar are *complicated*," she finally muttered. "Let's just say, I know how that feels."

Saffron sensed her unwillingness to explain more, which

summoned an unexpected surge of irritation in his chest. He attempted for exactly one moment to bite it back.

"People were really worried about you, you know. Someone even asked about you when I posed as the rowan spirit!" He exclaimed, attempting to grab the back of her shirt, only to be pecked by a sudden blue wren that squeaked insults. "And Berry! He—!"

"I *am* upset about Berry," Sunbeam insisted, but Saffron just puffed up more. "But he and I were just fooling around. He knew I wasn't looking for anything more than that, and I told him over and over again I wouldn't be around for long. If he decided to come looking for me—"

"Are you saying it's his own fault he died?"

Sunbeam faced him that time. Saffron nearly bumped into her chest, taking a quick step back as her venomous look caught him off guard.

"Don't even *think* about placing blame for *any* death on *anyone* except Taran mac Delbaith, Saffron. Not on me, not on Berry, not even on yourself. Do you understand? I will not humor you or your attitude."

Saffron stood in an embarrassed daze for a moment, blinking a few times before hurrying to catch up as Sunbeam kept walking. He spluttered out an apology, but she just shook her head and sighed.

"It doesn't matter. We're almost there."

The trees thinned in front of them, and Saffron forgot what he was so embarrassed about. Woodland growth burst wide open into a massive clearing, the suddenness of it nearly sweeping him into the sky. In the center, still some distance away—buildings. At least, the cloaked suggestion of them, blurred beneath oppressive rain that had grown heavier while they were protected by the trees. They loomed like crumbling titans, sagging from age and wet earth sinking beneath stone walls, metal spires, spider webbing glass windows.

"Is this...?" He started, then forgot what he meant to say while hurrying to catch up.

Following a worn path through the long grass, Saffron kept on her heels, eventually emerging onto an overgrown cobblestone walkway he assumed stretched all the way to the front gate where they'd left Kaelar off the road.

"I'm not completely sure what this place is, yet," Sunbeam offered to Saffron's question lost on the returning breeze. "Some abandoned part of Morrígan Academy—but I assume you've already figured that out."

Approaching the first pair of withering structures on either side of the walkway, more shadows like tombstones spotted down the way. Perhaps only slightly smaller than Morrígan's main campus, the groaning stone remains were home to at least a hundred crows, ravens, magpies. A herd of deer grazed on the rain-soaked grass, carefully munching around clusters of moon-flowers nestled within the other rich overgrowth. There must have been some other less obvious way inside, though considering the size of the clearing alone, Saffron didn't want to even try and fathom the enormity of the fence around the perimeter.

Suffocating the pathway, weatherworn pillars stood upright or toppled in piles, and it was obvious the place had been desolate longer than Saffron had imagined. But other than clear degradation from age —he couldn't pick out anything that might hint at reason to abandon it. The architectural design, even the layout of the ruined buildings, resembled those of Morrígan's main campus. As if they'd been built simultaneously, not one abandoned in favor of some place newer.

The buildings still fully intact could be counted on two hands, everything else long collapsed into gritty piles of rubble carpeted in lichen and thick clusters of ferns. Cracked, dislodged pathway stones donned even more moss and sprouted mush-rooms beneath where Saffron walked, and he was careful not to smash any under his boots.

The lack of pixies, sprites, even indiscriminate glittering

clouds stood out to him as much as the peaceful silence did. No longer was the air stuffed with numbing cotton, muffling every living thing—but there was still something missing. Something Saffron couldn't put his finger on, something innate and intangible suddenly stripped away. But strangely, with it gone, he felt like he could breathe better than ever before.

"Is this where you've been staying? After leaving Beantighe Village," he asked after avoiding the temptation of a sprawling bed of wild marijuana behind a skeletal wall. "Why leave at all? This place isn't nearly as welcoming."

"There's something I'm looking for, too. I think it might be here, after Cloth told me what the wolf wanted."

"... You mean, wild fairy fruits?"

"Um... sort of, actually. I'm not interested in the fruits, themselves, but rather, something that comes with them. Cloth said that Taran thought they might be in some old ruins... which I took as another cue to leave Beantighe Village and look for myself."

Saffron frowned. "Wait—there *are* fruits here?"

"Some, yes—but I've only seen a few scattered around. I think there might be more in one of these buildings I can't get into, but I've been trying to figure out other ways before I pay Merith a surprise visit in the assignment office."

Saffron nearly asked how beantighe access rings would help—before realizing, if West Morrígan truly was an extension of the main campus, and if they were built around the same time... even if one wing was abandoned, it made sense that *any* Morrígan access ring might still be effective to get through remaining barriers...

He glanced down at his hand, where the library ring shined a little too dramatically in such low light.

"You know, I actually..." he trailed off, before smiling to himself. "I actually have a library ring, if that's one of the buildings you need to get into."

Sunbeam's eyes sparkled, snatching Saffron's hand before glancing in every direction and taking off down a branching path.

She admitted not knowing if any remaining buildings were the library, specifically, but it wouldn't hurt to try. Saffron didn't mind the extra searching it took, appreciating every chance to simply explore the area—until he spotted one of the rogue clusters of wild fairy fruits Sunbeam mentioned, and his mouth went dry. He pretended like he didn't see it, just hurrying to catch up to his hunting partner again.

More deer, squirrels, mice skittered through the wet grass around them, Saffron crouching on the balls of his feet as a wobbly fawn sniffed in his direction. At least an hour had passed since beginning the search for buildings still locked behind access barriers, and his already-tired feet were beginning to throb—but then, through the mist on the other side of a lush courtyard, a bittersweetly familiar silhouette stood out. He called out to Sunbeam, but didn't wait before crossing the wet grass where deer grazed.

It was a mirrored image of Morrígan's Grand Library, down to the columns, the stones steps, the overflowing flowerbeds within the perimeter fence. Though while the Grand Library on campus was a picture of pruned perfection, its twin burst at the seams with verdant tendrils and moss anywhere there was room. It soaked the humid air with perfumes of wet soil and wild buds, and Saffron appreciated every detail for as long as it took Sunbeam to reach him. All the while, goosebumps flushed down his arms beneath the cloak. It made him homesick in a strange way, missing the nights he spent amongst the books, nights spent quietly with the prince, existing with and without one another as if it was the most natural thing in the world.

Climbing the cracked stone stairs with Sunbeam on his heels, Saffron paused again in front of the rain-warped door. He recalled how it felt the first time Cylvan entrusted him with a library ring of his own, worried it wouldn't work upon touching the knob. That same apprehension knotted his heart as he reached for the familiar hold in front of him—but the ring twinged, just like it was meant to. It made him jump, glancing briefly back at Sunbeam, then unlatching the thumb-press and pushing open the door.

A wave of hot, prickling air crashed like opening the door of an oven. Throwing up a hand, Saffron flinched against the unexpected inferno, blinking through the sparkling buzz that surged into his lungs. Once he managed to crack open his eyes—his stomach dropped hard enough to choke him.

A meadow of shimmering pink fruits quilted the floor of the front atrium, flurries of glittering specks filling the air like hallucinogenic pollen. Reeking thickly of hot sugar and mint, Saffron held his breath in an instant, terrified of what might happen if he inhaled even a glimmer.

Wild fairy fruits.

16

THE BRIDGE

Saffron lunged to slam the door shut, but Sunbeam raced past him. He grappled for her shirt, terrified to let her anywhere near them, but she whirled and grinned, grabbing his arm and attempting to pull him inside. Saffron just dug his heels, begging her to *let go!*

"Those are—! It's dangerous! Who knows—!"

"I don't care about them!" She laughed, as if already drunk on the floating glitter. "Come on!"

"No! Sunbeam, wait—!" Saffron attempted, but she let him go, taking off into the fruits without slowing down. He had to resist turning on heel and sprinting in the opposite direction, burying fingernails into the warped wood molding of the doorway until they nearly cracked under the pressure. There were just—*so many.* He never expected there to be *so many,* enough to change the temperature in the room, the smell of the air—

Watching Sunbeam navigate through the thickest plots up the winged staircase to the second floor, Saffron just thought about Cylvan. All the nights he'd climbed the same stairs on the main campus next to him, sitting together at the tables, studying alongside one another. Those precious moments Saffron would keep forever. That person Saffron would face nightmares to protect, who he promised to keep safe—

In front of him was a nightmare, like nothing he imagined when agreeing to search for wild fruits—but he had to know. He had to know how far they spread. He had to know exactly how many there were, how much danger Cylvan was in if Taran ever found them. If Saffron could just see how far they reached into the library, he could figure out what he needed to destroy each one. Every last one, before Taran ever found out about them at all.

Sucking in a deep breath, Saffron stiffly pulled his fingers away from the edge of the door. His heart pounded hard enough to make his whole body tremble, but he managed to claim a step inside. Then one more.

Blush-colored strawberries, blueberries, and raspberries grew within tangled messes of dark blue-green leaves all around him, swallowing his feet to the ankles like piles of snakes bundling into one another. Plump bumblebees bounced between the fruits and little white flowers speckled throughout the thick growth, wings and bodies dusted with similar fairy magic that made their yellow stripes sunset-orange. Around the walls, scattered apple trees burst through the floorboards with purple-tinged leaves and pink fruit hanging heavy from the branches.

After overcoming the initial shock, freckles of curiosity infected Saffron's anxiety. He even crouched down on the balls of his feet and, while still too hesitant to touch anything, leaned closer to examine the colors, the shapes, how they differed from artificially-drugged counterparts.

While dusted fairy fruits at high fey parties were pink like vivid azaleas, natural fruits were subtler, more of a warm golden-pink, instead. After accidentally stepping on one, he also noted that, similar to dusted fruits, only the external skin was affected— visibly, at least. He wondered if peeling a rose-pink apple and only eating the flesh would be the same as taking a bite out of it whole. He wasn't about to try; the thought of being tricked into eating a wild fruit with the skin peeled off even made him wheeze slightly.

Saffron made it to the top of the stairs, and his attention turned to the shelves standing in lines just like those of the Grand Library. But upon skimming the cubbies, he was disappointed to find them all completely empty. Even the directory tomes were missing, though he spotted empty pedestals where they might have sat. Gazing up at the ceiling, he was further disappointed when only generic landscape murals swept within the empty spaces, depicting rising, midday, and setting suns, one in each section.

In the third and farthest section, Saffron discovered Sunbeam again, who hissed at him to be careful. Kneeling over the floor, she had a hand splayed out over something carved directly into the wood. Saffron's eyes followed the curve of it, all the way around and back again. A circle the size of the parlor in Danann House, where no fairy fruits dared to grow. The arching shape reminded Saffron of the one embossed beneath his bed, though the markings were clearly different.

Crouching down next to her, he touched the circle, too, tracing a few of the closest lines.

"This is... arid magic, right?" He asked, and Sunbeam tossed him a surprised look.

"You know about feda markings?" She smiled, and he vaguely recalled that word. "How?"

"It's... sort of a long story, I guess..." Saffron cleared his throat self-consciously. "I, um... I actually tried to save Berry using an arid spell in Beantighe Village... I even ate the rowan berries and drew the circle in charcoal, and everything..."

He blinked, fighting the urge to sink into that bitter memory, followed by the poisonous companion of the thought of Baba Yaga sitting in confinement due to that exact moment, too. Sunbeam just kept watching him in curiosity.

"Seems you're full of surprises, Saffron."

Dragging her hand flat along the portion of circle in front of her, she didn't take her eyes from him.

"Can you read the markings on this epithet?"

Epithet. Henmother Salma used that word in Wicklow's kitchen. Still, Saffron shook his head.

"I only drew what Baba Yaga told me. I used to have a page with the alphabet written down, but nothing translated directly into Alvish, so I couldn't read it anyway..."

"That's because Alvish is a fey language." Sunbeam grinned. "Why would human magic use a fey language in its spells?"

Saffron raised his eyebrows.

"What language is it, then?"

Sunbeam turned back to the markings, caressing them once more.

"Feda markings, specifically, are associated with a human language called *Gaeilge,* and are part of a bigger written system called *Arid-Ogham*. But there are hundreds of other ways to practice arid magic, you know. Different languages, different epithets, different writing systems. There are spoken systems, too. They all perform similar tasks, but in their own ways, stemming from various cultural roots."

Saffron's heart thumped excitedly, leaning in closer.

"Really?" He asked in a breath. "There's more than just these circles? With the hatchmarks?"

"Of course!" Sunbeam threw her hands out. "On the other side of the veil, humans are as diverse as wild fey, you know? In language, culture, and magic. Oh, *so many* kinds of magic, it would blow you away."

"How..." Saffron asked, unable to resist the tiny smile lifting the corner of his mouth. "How do you know?"

Sunbeam grinned, and it reminded him of how Nimue once smiled before revealing her biggest secret of once being human.

"Remember when I said *things were complicated?*" She let the words linger for dramatic effect. "Well—I'm not originally from this side of the veil at all. I said I was only here temporarily, because I'm trying to find my way back home."

She patted the floor again.

"And this is going to help me."

"Help you?" Saffron turned back to the carving. "How?"

"This epithet is used to open the veil."

Saffron froze, as if Sunbeam's words alone would summon the floor to sink beneath them, devouring them whole—but Sunbeam shook her head, poking through his cocoon of panic.

"Don't worry, it's not going to open on its own. I need someone to bridge with me from the other side, first."

Saffron gulped. He timidly touched the tips of his fingers to the carving again, even though they trembled. It was different from the one time he'd passed through the veil with Luvon, where they hiked to a small town in the snowy mountains, where someone had built a secret room around a tear in the veil to pass through. Luvon had so many friends who had so many spots hidden from potential eyes, all around Alfidel—but Saffron suddenly wondered if any of them used arid veil circles like the one Sunbeam fawned over.

"How can you tell it's a veil spot? Can you read the marks?"

She motioned behind them with her head, then waited for Saffron to figure it out for himself.

"The berries?" He asked, recalling what she said about wild fairy fruits being companions to whatever she was looking for. "The veil... turns the berries pink?"

"That's right." She said it in an endeared way, like Cylvan used to when Saffron solved a puzzle on his own. It made him flush. "By the size of the growth here, too, I imagine it was open for a *looooooong* time."

Saffron pulled his hands back, holding them safely between his chest and bent legs, no longer wanting to get too close. He wanted to ask why anyone would open the veil in the middle of a campus library—before wondering if that was the reason Morrigan abandoned the west wing in the first place. Perhaps the tear grew too large, too difficult to handle, so they moved until it aged and closed on its own? Or—it technically wasn't a tear at all, was it? Sunbeam implied the feda markings meant it was intentional...

"How do you get someone to bridge with you from the other side?" Saffron asked, next. "How would they know where you are?"

"Ah," Sunbeam got to her feet, brushing herself off before whistling three notes down the length of the nave. Her blue wren, Yama, came flying, landing in a fluff on her shoulder. "Little things like pixies travel in and out of the veil naturally, because they're so small. These birds—they're called fairy wrens—are the same. Humans have been using them to pass messages back and forth for centuries."

Saffron rose to his feet as well, fighting the urge to reach out and pet the little bird.

"Ready to go visit Chandry again, Yama?" Sunbeam asked, digging into a pouch on her belt and producing a miniscule scroll already sealed with a drop of wax. Tying the rolled note to the bird's leg, Saffron's eyes followed as the blue speck lifted off and disappeared through one of the high, broken windows. His heart thundered again.

"Should we—um—go?" He croaked. "Just in case..."

"The veil isn't going to tear open, Saffron, I told you that already," Sunbeam brushed him off, then rubbed the back of her neck while gazing at the circle again. "Time moves differently here than in the human world. Yama has to actually find and pass through a natural tear, first, anyway. Even if he was able to squeeze through right away, and Chandry responded right after... for her, even five minutes is at least fifteen for me. It's going to take a lot more planning, not to mention figuring out how to align the maps... fuck."

She vanished into her own mental calculations, rubbing a thumb against her chin in thought. Saffron just watched, unable to stop his heart from racing. He'd never known any reason to want to go back to the human world; it was the whole reason he'd made the geis with Cylvan to start with. But Sunbeam's words made his soul dance, made the little creature of curiosity living in his chest buzz its wings like a hummingbird.

"Where did you learn all of this?" He asked.

Sunbeam met his eyes again, but only for a split second. After averting her gaze once more, she crouched over the veil carving as if her reason was tiresome.

"I can't tell you that much, I'm sorry," she whispered. "For your own sake. And mine."

Saffron bit his lip. He took a slight step toward her. He almost insisted, unsure if he could carry the burden of curiosity much longer—but then he recognized that look in Sunbeam's eyes. That look of silent exhaustion, worry, constant internal warring over whether or not everything she did was worth the suffering, while still determined to continue forward no matter what.

He'd witnessed that same face every morning in the attic mirror, reflected back at him.

He kept the curious bird in his chest. He glanced back down the length of the library, perceiving the empty shelves again. A new thought persisted as Sunbeam went to work behind him.

Even if he was able to get the arid alphabet reference back from Beantighe Village, or Prince Cylvan provided a new one, it wouldn't matter, because Saffron didn't know enough about the human language *Gaeilge*. The overwhelming thought made his breath catch, but at the same time—after so long spent scrambling for a solid place to hook his focus, to be handed such a clear invitation, to be handed a clear path to share with Cylvan—made Saffron hungry for more.

Whether it be the geis, Elluin's trials, summoning Taran to show his wolf form, then proving Baba innocent...

Saffron simply had to learn everything there was about arid magic, until he could summon it from his hands to shield the people he cared about most.

17

THE CRYPT

Journeying down each corridor of shelves, Saffron's candle was older than he was, though worked just as well against the dim, overcast light. Skimming for any possible book forgotten in the dust, he even ascended creaking ladders to peek into higher places, but every time came up empty. A part of him didn't mind—the distraction was a welcome boon on the flames eating up the inside of his mind, carrying the weight of everything Sunbeam had told him.

Fairy fruits grow where the veil is open.

The feda marks around this circle are meant to open the veil.

Time moves differently here than in the human world...

So distracted by the shelves, Saffron didn't watch his feet within a particularly thick patch of fruits and leaves, and a crunch beneath his boot sent him reeling back with a yelp. His heart sank at the thought of crushing a mouse—but he was met with gaping eye sockets, instead.

A round skull, collapsed inward where his foot mashed it.

He screamed, throwing a hand over his mouth to stifle it from echoing off the rafters. From a distance, Sunbeam called out to ask if he was alright, and he could only croak out a response.

Holding out his candle slightly, it shook with the sudden

fright. Buried deep beneath the fairy-stained plantlife, Saffron then made out weather-worn vertebrae, ribs like cracked branches, hip bones, femur bones. He thought he might be sick, turning quickly to leave—only to crush something else under heel.

Leaping sideways, he lost balance in the ankle-twisting undergrowth, tumbling onto scattered pebbles hidden amongst the fruits. No—not pebbles. Fingers. Teeth.

Scrambling, he reclaimed his candle still bright on the ground, surrounding leaves too fresh to burn. He offered a whispered, wheezing apology, making direct eye contact with the empty sockets of the person whose toes he'd just kicked around. He sought the buckled eye-holes of the head he'd cracked like an egg, too, offering another nervous apology and a slight bow.

"Wh-why are you all here?" He asked in uncertainty, wondering why there would be scattered fey bones left to the elements like that. Were they victims of the veil that shuttered the campus?

Something heavy thunked below his feet, emanating from the ground floor. He yelped and jumped, and Sunbeam called out again, that time sounding a little more exasperated.

"Have you looked around the bottom floor, yet?" He answered.

"No~ why don't you do it for me?"

The thought of going anywhere by himself made Saffron's skin crawl—but Kaelar was probably still asleep by the road. He hadn't seen anything wilder than mice or deer within the ruins. There were only tumbling stones to startle him.

... Definitely.

Emboldening himself, Saffron brushed himself off, and headed down the nave to the stairs. Descending into the front vestibule, nothing appeared newly disturbed, and he swallowed back more nerves before moving silently into the lower corridor.

Darker shadows greeted him, windows overgrown with plantlife and turning the air a crisp, greenish color. Scouring every passing shelf as he wandered down the length, there was nothing to find, just like above. He nearly turned back at the opposite end, until something crunched underfoot.

Beneath his boot, another bone-pebble was smashed into dust.

A breath tickled the back of his neck. He whirled, expecting to find Sunbeam sneaking up from behind—but there was no one. Not even a sound, except his own startled gasp.

"Hello?" He called, voice stark in the silence. "Sunbeam? Erm —beannighe, ma'am, is that you? L-Lord Kaelar...?"

Something hissed at the mention of a high fey's name, and Saffron turned so fast his candle snuffed. Cursing, he frantically dug around in his pocket for the box of matches Sunbeam gave him, but stopped short when, the moment he was drenched in low light, a shifting, misty glow caught in the corner of his eye.

The candle tumbled from his hand at the sight of an incorporeal figure pacing outside the door at the end of the corridor. It didn't offer Saffron a glance.

Back and forth, back and forth, it walked. There was no way to tell the exact color of their long locs, downcast eyes, or clothing by how translucent they were, but Saffron could almost make out the details of what they wore—and it resembled Morrígan's uniform.

Especially in the last weeks, Saffron was more than familiar with the concept of ghosts, or spirits, or *taibhsean*, as Baba Yaga sometimes called them. He knew how Baba responded whenever something unexplained made a mess of Wicklow's attic, or trashed the barn overnight, always without any sign of a wild fey having been the cause. Even when they screeched and threw buckets and left claw marks on the floor, she and the other henmothers always spoke with respect, with comforting words, making offerings of protection and safety and understanding. Those taibhsean were different from the weeping ghosts of Danann House, but were spirits, all the same.

In that moment, despite his experience navigating the ghosts of Danann House—Saffron didn't know what to do at the sight of one so visible, right in front of him. He only watched it pace for a long time, back and forth, back and forth, before they suddenly faded back into the shadows.

He almost called out, anxiety subsiding and making way for curiosity—but a wave of inexplicable grief suddenly clutched his heart, his lungs, flooding his eyes with tears before he realized what was happening. Grief with no origin, grief as ghostly as the figure pacing back and forth. Grief given to him by someone unseen, shared for him to know.

Wiping his wet cheeks, Saffron approached where he'd seen them. The air was cold in their wake, and Saffron hovered his hand through the cloud, searching until his fingers kissed the wooden door in the wall. It rattled with the contact, a faint scent of smoke emerging from the wood—and then, through the crack along the floor, a dim orange glow grew and highlighted the toes of his boots.

He took a step back, blinking a few times in case he only imagined it, but it was just bright enough to cast a shadow from his legs. Sunbeam must have come down to find him from another way, perhaps a hidden set of stairs. He almost called out, but stopped when voices emerged like bubbling sap through the wood, first.

Frantic, frenzied voices. Hissing at one another to *be quiet, turn out that light, check the barricade on the door.* Saffron held his breath when the light at his feet snuffed. Taking another step back, he almost turned and ran, only pausing when someone asked, *"How did a fey get past the iron gate?"*

"I'm..." Saffron spoke in uncertainty. The moment it left his tongue, silence rushed in as if air swept from the room. He swallowed back the nervous lump in his throat, knowing curiosity would be the death of him in the end. "I'm not a fey. I'm—I'm human. Who are you?"

A long moment passed, before the slightest whisper emerged through the wood.

"Prove yourself."

Saffron straightened. "What?"

"Prove yourself human. Who guards the underworld?"

"I..." Saffron trailed off. That could have been anyone, according to all the myths he'd ever read. Danu, Ériu, Arawn, Beli, Macha, Badb...? Though technically many fey didn't use the word *underworld*, they referred to the afterlife as "the mounds," or a plethora of other things depending on the region or the myth...

But Saffron reconsidered the question. *Prove yourself human.* Why would they ask something a high fey could answer easily? It reminded him of what Sunbeam said about arid magic—*why would human spells use fey language?*

"Um..."

Would it matter which myth he answered with, so long as it was a human one?

"... Cerberus? The three-headed dog. Um, from Greek mythology, specifically..." Saffron's uncertainty grew the longer no one responded—until the latch clicked, and the door creaked inward.

Saffron hesitated before extending a hand, expecting to find a group of sentries huddled on the other side—but there was only darkness.

"Hello?" He called, voice cascading down a staircase spiraling into the depths beneath the library. Back in the mind to turn and walk away, he spotted a gallery of half-used candles on a little stone inlet, first.

Reaching for one, it ignited the second his fingers touched. He dropped it with a yelp of surprise, heart thudding in rhythm with every clunk of the stick tumbling down the stairs into the darkness. When it finally bounced out of range, he gulped, but risked another. Despite being prepared that time, he still jumped when it flickered to life just like the first.

"What the fuck..." He whispered, examining the rest of the sticks on the stone lip. Picking up an extra, that time the spark made his heart flutter in intrigue. He grabbed a third for good luck, bundling them in his hand with enough light to see exactly how they worked.

Carved at the bottom, around the circumference, feda hatch-marks were engraved in the wax. It was arid magic.

More questions concerning the fate of Morrígan's west campus pricked at every inch of him, gazing down the winding stairs. Biting his lip, he offered a quiet prayer to Ériu, and took the first step.

The spiral carried him further than he knew possible, until he could see his breath in the low candlelight. He thought about the underworld as he went, preparing to cross the vicious three-headed dog at the bottom. Did any stories ever explain how to get past the beast in one piece? Or was he descending into that other Greek place that wasn't quite the underworld, but where medi-ocre people like him went, instead? He couldn't recall its specific name, something like *"fields of ass..."*

Saffron recognized the moment his foot hit the bottom, echoing in every direction like a dry-fired bowstring. Lifting his candle bouquet in a feeble attempt to gather his bearings, he found only polished stone along the floor, wide columns inter-spersed with groin vaults blooming out from their heads like flower petals interweaving with one another. It resembled the stone crypts of Luvon's winery, and Saffron tried to nestle into that relief. He'd spent plenty of time in that similar stone dungeon back in the Winter Court, checking bottles for cracks and swollen corks like a clurichaun, himself. Luvon's cellars were not nearly as expansive as those where Saffron stood, though.

Still, he couldn't help but shiver at how quiet it was. Empty. Lifeless. Despite all those voices behind the door, despite responding to them directly...

Spotting a sconce on the wall, Saffron stood on his toes to light the wide pillar candle pasted to the stone lip with its own melted wax. While it didn't illuminate much more in front of him, at least he could wander a little further without having to worry about losing track of his way out.

"Hello?" He attempted again, coughing into the crook of his arm as dusty air stuck to the inside of his throat.

No one answered, and he was forced to walk a little farther. And farther, and farther, constantly checking over his shoulder to ensure he remained within sight of the sconce he left burning. When he found another one on the way, he paused and lit that one, too.

A little farther. A little farther. The darkness, the cold, the pure silence remained, except for his own controlled breaths and echoing footsteps. In the light of his candles, more and more dust kicked up the further he traveled.

His footprints remained the only ones to be seen. The fragile coating on the floor sat undisturbed like freshly fallen snow in every other direction.

When something new finally appeared in the reach of his candle, he gasped and jumped, heart nearly launching out of his ass as he thought he'd walked straight into a catacomb—but then realized what he thought were coffins were actually lines of shelving. They mimicked the layout of the empty library overhead, and Saffron approached in silence.

Expecting to find more empty shadows, his candlelight instead caught words printed on spines, and he nearly shrieked. Rushing forward, he wiped a hand down the first row within reach. It didn't matter that more thick dust turned into clay in his chest, his mouth dangled open as he saw every word.

History of Educational Statutes in Alfidel and Through the Veil.

An Introduction to Oralcry and Courts of Expectation.

Open Veils: Dangerous Tears or Natural Occurrences?

Down the line, he read every title until they all jumbled together, then looped back around to absorb all of those on the neighboring shelf. He paused just long enough to shine light on a placard at the end, wiping away more dust for clarity.

▽ *HIS;01, Original School Documentation and Establishment Information.*

Gazing up the length of the room to the neighboring shelves, he addressed the placard on the end of the next one. Then the one on the opposite side of the aisle.

⚬ HIS;06, History of Morning, Day, Evening, and Night Courts Since the First Discovery of Veil Intermittence.

⚬ HIS;02, History of Aos Sídhe Family and Opulent Lineage...

His mouth practically watered, grabbing the first book he could, surprised at the sound of a metal chain dragging on the shelf and leashing the book to its place. Only allowed enough room to pull it out, Saffron didn't care, overwhelmed with the thrill of just holding something so ancient.

The book groaned, spine cracking for the first time in what Saffron could only guess had been centuries, though his excitement fizzled the moment he realized he didn't know the language written inside. Still, he flipped through what he had, before returning it to the shelf and grabbing the next. Then the next, and the next, and the next, until his neck hurt from hunching.

It wasn't until he was three more sections down the shelves that he finally found pages scrawled in familiar, though admittedly outdated, Alvish, tugging on the chain and having to resist the urge to snap it.

Elder Futhark and the Well of Urd;

Theology and Magic, Intersections and Philosophy;

Sumerian Cuneiform: First Language, First Magic;

Language and the Veil: Ancient Systems For Maintaining Handshakes;

Creation Myths: What Do They Tell Us About Ancient Aridity?...

The last title caught his attention, and Saffron scurried to the end of the row, wiping down the section label. Unlike the others, it was fully handwritten.

⚬ HIS;016: History, Origins, Basics, & Mastery of Aridology; rescued from Morrigan Academy's Kyteler School of Aridology (above). Section made taboo in Night of the Veiled Bitch, Spring, Wheel 2...

"Morrigan Academy's... Kyteler School of Aridology... above," Saffron whispered, lifting his eyes to see if there was anything else at the top of the sign, or perhaps written across the top edge of the shelf, but found nothing. He almost sighed in defeat and returned to the shelf—before stopping short. Staring at the ceiling again, it glowed dim in his candlelight.

Above. Rescued from... Morrigan Academy's Kyteler School of Aridology... above.

"Oh... my god," He croaked—and a disembodied breath blew out his candle.

Another wave of emotion crashed—another wave that didn't belong to him. It pulled him down into the depths of its current, demanding to be felt. Knocked backward, Saffron smashed into the bookshelf, sending it tumbling with a deafening echo off the stone vaulting.

Hunching on the balls of his feet, he pinned hands against his ears as he was surrounded suddenly by screams, echoing off the walls but somehow existing only in his head. Grief that wasn't his, but he still somehow knew. Grief born of those whose voices he heard, but never saw. Whose ghastly forms paced the bottom floor of the library. Whose skulls, vertebrae, fingers he'd smashed with inconsiderate steps. He knew without introduction—he felt every single ounce of grief as if he'd been there. They made sure of that. The human spirits trapped on that unhallowed ground, anchored to the soil by spilled blood and scattered bones. They forced him to watch. They begged for him to understand—

Rushing books by the armful. Dumping them in scattered piles wherever there was room. Racing back up the stairs, pushing past peers who did the same. As many as they could, while fire grew thicker and made it hard to breathe. He's here. He's right outside. Can't you smell him? The king—the wolf king is right outside the gate. Hurry, we have to hurry, they can't keep the veil open much longer—No. Close it. Don't let the king through. He will kill every one of us, no matter which side we're on—

Saffron tore out of the vision, falling backward with a gasp, a shuddering heave of his chest. Tears spilled over his eyes, heart racing as if he'd been one of those sprinting up and down the stairs. The king, the wolf king—

The ghosts, the bones—

A school of Aridology—

Hunching forward, Saffron crossed his arms over his face, but couldn't scream.

Morrigan's west campus—had been for humans.

18

THE BURIAL

Saffron didn't have it in him to make conversation upon returning to the surface. To pretend like he hadn't witnessed what he did. There was still too much to process, too much numbness in his bones to speak at all. He could barely sink back into the memory without his breath hitching, so he did what he could to just push them away for the time being.

Insisting on finding his way back to the road on his own, explaining he wanted to know how to get in and out without help, Saffron was grateful for Sunbeam's dedication to the veil carving on the floor. Otherwise, she would have seen his wet cheeks with residual tears still spilling. She would have seen his dirty hands and dusty hair. She would have seen where he clawed at his neck when he couldn't force the anguish to vocalize, feeling like the silver was choking him. No, Sunbeam didn't need to see any of that. He just wished her luck, promising return again soon, before hurrying out the door into the rain.

He nearly lost his way after crossing through the fence, but then swore he spotted the shadow of the beannighe tromping through the undergrowth. Following, he never caught up, but did manage to find the road again. Silently thanking her, he kept his eyes down the rest of the way. He didn't want to know if more ghosts roamed the fog, just clinging to his amethyst pendant the entire time in an attempt to scrape up any comfort he could.

Saffron knew they'd left Kaelar beneath a rowan tree, and he headed for the nearest crimson blur. But upon approaching, he realized—that redness in the mist wasn't rowan trees at all. The color did not stem from ironick berries, but rather, a shocking swathe of bright red strings tangled and woven throughout like bloody spiderwebs. Devouring branches and suffocating the leaves, a braided cradle of threads even reached across the overgrown road, knitting tree after tree together down the line and disappearing into the fog. Something about it summoned more hot tears to spill from his eyes, taking a few careful steps back before hurrying away as if he hadn't noticed at all.

Kaelar was still facedown in the mud when Saffron finally found him. Saffron shook him awake, and the fey lord's eyes groggily opened. Squinting in every direction, he jolted suddenly to his feet with a bark of warning, but Saffron just untied the reins of the horse and pulled it in the direction of the road. He ignored Kaelar's demands the entire way, every shouted word muffled by dust and cotton still clogging his ears and mouth.

As they went, Kaelar's fantasies spun circles. He blamed the horse for bucking him off, clearly hitting his head on a rock. From his perspective, Saffron even sat there and waited all afternoon for him to come around again. Or perhaps they'd been attacked, after all, and left for dead. Perhaps someone had poisoned him, and he'd only just come-to.

Saffron didn't respond a single time, just nodding and avoiding eye contact.

But as they arrived at Danann House, something slammed against the back of Saffron's head, and the ground rushed up to meet him. Saffron attempted to push himself up again—only to be grabbed by the back of the collar in Kaelar's shaking hand.

"I don't know what you did to me," he said, voice cracking in paranoia. "But I'm going to figure it out."

Saffron spit dirt from between his teeth, attempting to roll over and shove Kaelar away—but his head hit the hard ground, and his eyes went dark.

"BURIED ALIVE. GOOD LUCK, WITCH."

Saffron came-to right as Kaelar dropped something closed over him. A key clicked in a lock, and Saffron instinctively slammed his hands out with a grunt, only to collide with something hard and flat above him.

He stared at the dark nothingness, fighting to piece together any recollection, any ounce of understanding of what was happening, seemingly cut off from the rest of the world without knowing how. His hands extended again in confusion, spreading over the solid mass overhead.

Buried...?

He inhaled sharply. Adrenaline surged through his heart. It reeled back on his muscles like cold elastic, and he rammed his shoulder into the hard lid once more. But the narrow space didn't allow for enough room to make it meaningful, and he bounced back to the bottom of the cramped space. Throwing his hands out, he found walls on either side of him, tight enough that he couldn't fully unbend his elbows. His legs were equally bundled up into one another, unable to stretch without colliding with another wall, either.

Buried alive—was Saffron in a coffin? Was in the the ground? He fought to maintain any composure possible, groping every inch of the interior once more before his fingers caught on something cold and metallic. A keyhole, in the center of the side panel.

Saffron was in a luggage trunk.

The relief of at least not being fully entombed beneath the earth lasted only a moment, especially once his limbs began to throb and ache from the tight, awkward angle he was pinned. His lungs went tight and itched as he inhaled dust from the trunk's wallpaper interior, and he strained to twist onto his side to tear fingernails at every edge and crease he could grope, desperate for any kind of give he could bury fingers through to let himself out. The entire time, he cursed Kaelar with warts, boils, splitting skin, rotten teeth, holes in his lungs.

But the longer it took Saffron to search, the more aware he grew of how there was no laughter, no conversation, no footsteps at all on the other side of the darkness. His heart throbbed as one more horrific thought struck him.

If he didn't escape before sunset, if he didn't emerge and return to the land of the living and show Taran he'd come back to the house when he was supposed to—

What would happen to Hollow?

Saffron's body surged, slamming against the lid again with wide eyes. His mouth dangled open in gagged alarm, inundated with the thought of what might happen if he didn't get out in time. It took him in a chokehold, slithering down his throat to squeeze his lungs, his heart, pulling back on his spine.

What the fuck—was he supposed to do?

Was this the trial Kaelar teased after finding Saffron in his room the day before?

What the fuck was he supposed to *do?* How the fuck—was this supposed to prove him arid?

And if he couldn't figure it out—

Hollow would—

How—

What was he supposed to do?

"Cy—!" He gasped, but the choker tightened. Saffron's heart drummed loud and fast against his ribs.

"Cyl—!" He attempted again, cut off once more and slamming his feet against the lid of the trunk, even though it bowed his spine and ribs. "Cylv—!!"

The collar squeezed tighter. Saffron's heart swelled in growing fear, tightening his airway further, making it harder to breathe. But despite the threat of choking, Saffron couldn't stop the heaving gasps, couldn't stop the words from surging through his mouth, clawing past the impending suffocation—

"Cylvan—!" He screamed as loud as the squeezing hands would let him, slamming his fists against the lid, choking as the collar tightened further in punishment. *"P-plea—!"*

Please!

He scraped at the paper lining again, dug his nails into the keyhole, thrashed his entire body in an attempt to break the lock or turn the trunk on its side—

Kaelar had imprisoned him. Kaelar had actually—

He attempted to shout Cylvan's name again, pushing through the choker as sobs chased the syllables. Again and again and again, shrieking and kicking and slamming his fists, begging to be let out, begging for someone to hear him, to come, to open the lid—until the collar tightened enough that he could barely breathe or sob at all, only allowed gasps tiny enough not to suffocate. The world spun as he was choked, slowly, endlessly, every sob wracking his chest like a stabbing blade.

He clawed at the silver collar with dull nails, but knew it was useless. He'd learned early on that no matter what he did, he couldn't force it or the cuffs away. Not with his hands, a bent fork, a knife, a pair of scissor, a slamming door, or flame. As if the internal prongs perpetually tasting his blood made him the only person who couldn't.

He had to show Taran he was back at the house. He had to prove he came back. Hollow was still there, if Saffron didn't appear to set him free, Taran would—

Hollow would—

Saffron was supposed to protect him. Saffron was the only thing standing between Taran and his friends, between Taran and Prince Cylvan. He was the only thing standing between Elluin and Baba Yaga, Elluin and all of Beantighe Village. How could his efforts, his misery, his loneliness, all go to waste so soon after he'd only just been given his life back?

Saffron screamed again, slamming his fists again and again against the lid, until his knuckles split and blood gushed down the backs of his hands. He clawed at the paper and wood until his nails broke and tore away. He slammed his body back and forth until littered in bruises and aching joints.

Every sob was met with choking. Every shaking breath, every whimper, every silent plea, the collar around his throat tightened and cut him off, sometimes squeezing so intensely that spit backed up in his throat and dripped out of his nose. It was a form of torture he never knew possible—to be released from the tightening grip, only to fear it again the moment he had the courage to take another breath. To die slowly, painfully, one clench at a time—then released. To return to reality, to the dark of the box full of dust and filling with his guttering exhales. To be reunited with his lungs, only to drown in the heavy air of sinking oxygen. Soon, it wouldn't matter which took him first, the choker, or the poison spilling from his mouth—Saffron was going to die. And no one would find him, not even when the stench of his body filled Kaelar's suite. It had sat alone, untouched, unvisited for a century before Saffron himself cleaned it out for someone to live in again. Saffron would die, and rot, and wither into dust before anyone even lifted their head to ask whatever happened to him.

Buried alive.

Saffron understood—how all the spirits trapped in the crypt felt when no one came looking for them again, either.

19

THE DAEMONS

Light lingered then faded through the keyhole, and Saffron tracked the hours by the creeping numbness up his body. His toes, his ankles, his calves, his knees, a numbness that devoured all feeling except pain. Stiff, frozen pain, like glass left outside in winter. Every twitch of muscle soon became unbearable, rendering him silent and lifeless on his back. His breaths came in low, shuddering, though the choker still throbbed in an out as if all of the vocalizations had made it more sensitive than ever. Every swallow of spit, of bile, of blood that dripped from his oxygen-deprived brain through his nose, into his mouth—only made him choke again. Again. Again, until he knew exactly how it felt to be buried before he was ready.

The only thing that kept him from fading entirely—was the occasional flicker of warmth down his shirt. Was it blood? Was it sweat? Perhaps that was the place his ghost decided to push through his skin to curl up into the air like smoke. He never reached for it, not wanting to give it any ideas. Any clues about how to escape. Despite the pain—Saffron wasn't ready to die, yet. Not when there was still so much to do.

Something scraped against the lid of the trunk—then paused. Then scraped slightly more—then paused, but that time with a whisper on the other side. Every movement made the box shudder, though it did nothing to wake Saffron up. A part of him was sure he only imagined it.

A scrape, a shudder, a pause, a whisper; again and again, until something kissed the ground outside. Next—a click of the lock. The subtle squeak of an old latch. The *thunk* of wooden lips parting. It was too dark to see the lid move—but Saffron felt it. A rush of cold wind, a crashing wave of fresh air that made a pathetic, shuddering whimper escape his lips.

"Oh, shit!" A familiar voice hissed, but it wasn't Asche's hands that flew inside, digging under Saffron's sore body to exhume him. Like Demeter digging Persephone from the underworld.

Pulled from the trunk's embrace, Saffron's limbs unfurled like petals after a cold night. Pain shot up his spine in a sudden bolt, and he convulsed, attempting to bite back a scream. It instead rippled out of his lungs between pained gasps, clawing at Cylvan's arms that carefully pulled Saffron onto his lap.

"Is he alright?" Asche asked, before nervously joking: "Hey, beantighe—shhh, you'll wake up the guard..."

"Be quiet, Asche," Cylvan hissed, but his voice cracked. A gentle hand pushed sweat-soaked hair from Saffron's forehead, gently commanding him to breathe, to relax. Saffron's hand flew up to grip Cylvan's wrist, eyes still wide and wild as the fresh air made every inch of his body light up like candles.

"It's alright, beantighe." Cylvan continued to pet his hair. "Kaelar is going to pay for a cruel prank like this."

Saffron clawed at Cylvan's shirt, eyes wide as he fought to speak, to form Hollow's name on his mouth in pleading desperation—and Cylvan smiled warmly in reassurance, nodding slightly.

"Hollow is alright," he promised. "He returned to Beantighe Village a few hours ago."

Saffron's entire body shook as relief crushed him like piling soil, slumping into Cylvan's arms as pathetic sobs bubbled out of him. Cylvan's hand trailed up and down Saffron's back, before gently urging him to lift his head again. Saffron obeyed, sniffling before finally glancing at Cylvan, then at Asche, then at the trunk. Asche grinned like they read his mind.

"Don't tell—but I have tracking charms everywhere," they bragged, flipping a piece of hair over one shoulder then touching Saffron's amethyst pendant. "When you didn't show up for dinner, I thought I'd check. Cylvan's twin led us right to you."

Saffron stared at them—and would have broken down into hysterical laughter had Cylvan not pressed a hand over his mouth.

"Kaelar is asleep in his bed," he said flatly. "So you have to leave quietly. I want both of you out of here so you don't witness what I'm going to do to him."

Asche smacked Cylvan on the shoulder. "I'm the one who found the beantighe, let me do it!"

"No, no, no, Asche—this is personal. And I've known Kaelar longer than you have; it's a long time coming. You'll have your own chance again later, I'm sure."

"*Ugh,*" Asche groaned, throwing their head back before putting a hand out for Saffron to take. Saffron did, albeit hesitantly, and was pulled to his feet. His legs trembled beneath him like a newborn fawn, and he would have crushed the daurae beneath buckling knees had Cylvan's hands not caught him, first.

"I've got you," he whispered, hands lingering on Saffron's shoulders before pulling away again in uncertainty. He cleared his throat, looking at Asche again. "Asche—why don't you make the beantighe some tea? I'll be down to join you soon enough."

SAFFRON ENDED UP BREWING THE SAME LAVENDER MILK tea as the first night, but he didn't mind. The motions were familiar and therapeutic. He even plated a few snacks to eat when, according to Asche, they and Cylvan went without dinner when Saffron didn't arrive to cook. Kaelar apparently told them Saffron was sick from eating a random mushroom in the woods, and they might not see him for the next few days. Jackass.

Sitting on the floor of the house study, Saffron nursed a bottle of wine as Asche never seemed to lose interest in whatever they talked about.

There were, apparently, at least two-hundred forms of tracking charms known by experts, and Asche provided an admittedly riveting exposé on the relationships between charms, wild fey opulence, high fey opulence, and Sídhe fey opulence, all while sucking down tea and helping themself to the finger sandwiches Saffron made.

According to them, charms were a form of naturally occurring magic, and could be captured and assigned depending on the combination of ingredients and the circumstances in which they became, well, *charmed*. A necklace dipped in sap from a juvenile sleeping willow would, naturally, cause the wearer to fall asleep. A doorknob interlaid with crystal chips grown in terrariums overflowing with truth-weeds would ensure anyone who entered the room was eager to spill any truth prompted of them. Even the amethyst pendants, of which Saffron quickly realized Cylvan hadn't owned for *quite some time* like he originally claimed, were two parts of a single bonded amethyst root broken at midnight on an equinox, locking in their relationship to one another... or something. God, Asche talked fast.

Anything could be combined to create anything else—but the science of efficacy, temperament, extent, lifespan, and nuance came down to specific formulas that were sometimes so detail-specific, they even required specific moon cycles, days of the year, menstrual calendars, inebriation of the charmer and charmee, a person's level of education to determine full effects, what kind of wild fey the object in question had come into contact with... it explained the apothecary cabinet in Asche's bedroom, at least.

Saffron was glad for the wine he stole from the cellar. A rebellious clurichaun taking what he felt was due to him. His thoughts swirled every time Asche spoke, but at least with a little bit of a buzz, the daurae's words were amusing rather than headache-inducing. Especially when Saffron drunkenly wrote, *can I see onne of the charmes you hid in the house?* and Asche laughed in his face.

His next request was a little more vengeful: *will you make me a charme that will make kaylar pyuke every time he gets a boner?*

Asche considered it for a long time, before intrigue draped their expression and they hopped to their feet to immediately scour the shelves. Saffron laughed, secretly knowing there would be nothing helpful for them to find, or else he already would have. He took another drink from the wine, wobbling a little bit on his balance when he leaned back too far. It wasn't his first time getting drunk in the study, technically—though hopefully that night wouldn't end with him crying pitifully into the bottle.

Initiating his own hunt, Saffron already knew the Danann House library lacked anything related to *arid magic*—including related trials, language, and anything else that could have been helpful in any way—so instead, he focused on a topic a little broader, a little more likely. The history of Morrígan Academy, as a start. If he was lucky, he may even stumble over a mention of the abandoned *west campus*, specifically, though a part of him wasn't so sure he actually wanted to know. He'd seen enough to *know*, hadn't he? He was just drunk enough to try, anyway.

The pixies joined him by knocking books to the floor and squealing with laughter every time he hissed at them to be quiet. When he snapped at one just a little too harshly, it even huffed and fluttered away, leaving him mad at himself and feeling guilty. Then jealous, because he realized it went and made friends with Asche, instead, and the others soon followed. Saffron had never been cut so deeply.

An hour passed in silence before the door at the far end of the study suddenly rattled. Saffron snuffed his light and ducked on instinct, blushing in embarrassment when Asche threw him a look of question. Saffron just avoided their eyes, searching for another match as Prince Cylvan poked his head in. Holding a candle of his own, the prince smiled mischievously when he and Saffron met eyes, and Saffron was only a little bit disappointed that he wasn't drenched in Kaelar's blood.

"I've come to laud you all with tales of my triumphs," Cylvan announced, closing the door behind him. "The evil has been defeated. And buried. Lucky for us, there was already a hungry coffin waiting for him. I only hope he waits until morning before screaming to be let out."

Saffron surprised himself with a tiny laugh, not expecting the sight of Cylvan to immediately numb every throbbing ache in his body. As if drawn by the sound, Cylvan approached with a bright smile, and Saffron lost himself in every detail he hadn't seen in the moments following his own exhumation.

Cylvan was barefoot, with silk pants cinched at the waist and a baggy top tucked into the band. His hair dangled loosely over his shoulders and down his back, and Saffron had to keep his gaze from lingering on the bare skin beneath the wide collar of his blouse. His collarbones, the dips between his muscles, the tendons in his shoulders, a single dark freckle on the side of his neck... Saffron swore he could even see small bumps of the jewelry in Cylvan's nipples beneath the fabric, and his face went hotter than ever.

"Looks like you and the daurae have been enjoying yourselves," Cylvan commented upon seeing the bottle in Saffron's hand.

Saffron flushed, but held it out in offering. He knew he was definitely drunk by how the sight of Cylvan tipping his head back, elongating his neck, throat bobbing with every swallow, a trail of wine escaping out of the corner of his mouth, made Saffron's skin light up with heat. He just stared at the prince in an overheated daze when the bottle was handed back again. Thank god for Asche, who called and demanded Cylvan's attention less than a moment later. The second Cylvan turned his back, Saffron glugged the rest of the wine away in a single breath. He would need it, anyway.

20

THE FIRST CLASS

Saffron liked watching the siblings interact. Every movement was doused with sarcasm, with the intent of teasing one another, like how Cylvan made fun of Asche's height and Asche used Cylvan's hair like a leash to pull him in another direction—but at the same time, there was a clear harmony to their movements. Sarcastic, but ultimately genuine. Asche always got the book they asked for when it was too high to reach. Cylvan always expressed genuine interest in whatever Asche wanted to show him—even if a few times, in the middle of it, the prince sought out Saffron watching from the corner and smirked.

When Asche was finally sedated with a thick book on one of the middle couches, Cylvan returned to where Saffron sat cross-legged on the floor in the far corner. It was his instinct to be small, to try and go unnoticed, as if a part of him was still wary of being spotted somewhere he wasn't supposed to be. But Cylvan found him with ease, just like he always did.

"How are you feeling, beantighe?" He asked, claiming a seat on the floor next to Saffron with a cup of lavender tea in his hand. Saffron nodded timidly as Cylvan crossed his legs, sipping at his drink and complimenting it under his breath. His eyes flickered across every inch of Saffron's body in search of his own answer, pausing on the silk bandage wrapped around his bloody knuckles, then to the place where Saffron didn't wear the Tuatha dé Danann ring, that day. He clearly wished to say something else, but instead just leaned over to see what book Saffron held open on his lap. Saffron extended it slightly to offer a better view.

"*A Comprehensive History of Morrigan Academy*, blegh. What are you reading that for? Even I didn't when it was assigned to me for homework a hundred years ago."

Saffron laughed quietly, shaking his head. He didn't know how to answer, so he just shrugged, and went back to the words in front of him. They were, admittedly, dry and tasteless—but Saffron wasn't reading to learn, he was reading to *search*. He only wanted to find one single mention of *aridity* or *Kyteler* amongst the ocean of letters, anything else was negligible.

Cylvan realized Saffron meant to actually sit and study in silence, but that didn't stop him from sighing loudly. Hunching forward and resting his chin against a hand. Touching Saffron's other chosen books, lifting the hard covers and dropping them again and again with a little puff of air every time. It reminded Saffron of when they used to sit in the Grand Library with one another—and he had to bite back the swirling amusement in his heart. His raven wanted attention, but was ever too proud to ask for it.

When Cylvan finally sighed loud enough for Asche to shout at him to *shut the fuck up*, Saffron laughed and put his hand out. Touching Cylvan's arm, he offered the prince the attention he wanted by closing the book and pointing at it intentionally, then at Cylvan. When Cylvan didn't understand, Saffron pursed his lips, getting to his feet to search the writing desk where he knew he'd find paper, ink, and a quill.

Do you have any similar books in your personell library?

Cylvan grinned in a way that was an answer of its own, but still played coy. Saffron should have known better.

Rather than responding out loud, he took the quill and wrote his reply.

WHAT IS IT YOU'RE TRYING TO FIND?

Saffron considered a response for a long time, working through every possibility with his role to play in mind. Why would an unthreaded beantighe want to read about Morrígan's history?

I want to know more about Danann House.

Cylvan pulled a dramatic face of disgust, and Saffron had to resist laughing and revealing how he was a giant liar. Still, Cylvan seemed eager to play along, or maybe just to flaunt his own collection of books, because he flipped his hair and rose to his feet.

"Let me see what I can do for you, little flower."

Saffron's face burned bright red, and all he could do was nod in thanks as Cylvan left the study to search.

CYLVAN RETURNED NOT MUCH LATER, SINKING BACK TO his original place on the floor and tucking the book in his hands into Saffron's lap.

"I haven't had a chance to even open it myself, yet—I wouldn't say the subject matter calls to me—but this is a first edition *History of Queen Morrígan Academies of the Four Seasonal Courts*, from before Proserpina's purge. You'll find all of the school's dirty little secrets inside, unlike that other court-washed bullshit. Everything they ever wanted to hide."

Oh—Saffron could have kissed him. Had he not already sobered up so much, he might have. Instead, he just grinned, squeezing Cylvan's hand in appreciation before flipping to the first chapter of the section titled *Spring Court*. Upon reading the introductory line alone, his heart thumped, and then stopped.

Founded in the Day Court of Danae Portia, descendant of Night Queen Morrígan. Dedicated to the study of both Opulent and Arid magicks...

Even Cylvan went quiet alongside him, though he leaned in slightly to get a better look. Their candles flickered together with every disrupting breath, but nothing else moved for what felt like an eternity.

"That's..." Cylvan finally whispered, and Saffron jumped like he'd forgotten he wasn't alone. He instinctively pulled the book away from Cylvan's grasp, not expecting the emotions that flooded him, making his pulse blink around his vision. Filling his ears with the sound of crackling fire, collapsing wooden beams...

Shaking his head, Saffron read the words again. Then he turned back to the table of contents, searching for a chapter header that might offer a little more that just those words. Under *Spring Court*, his fingers eventually paused on one specific line: *Kyteler School of Arid Magic.*

The ancient spine crackled as Saffron split the center pages apart. His hands shook as he was immediately met with a full-page sketch labeled *Kyteler School First Class.*

There, right in front of him—

Round human ears. Black neck ribbons punctuated with brooches of houses labeled Freyja, Athena, and Hermes. Dark Morrígan coats donning the school crest, though showing their age with long tailcoats, wide sleeves, center-buttons of old fashion styles...

Saffron stopped breathing entirely, and Cylvan extended a hand, placing it on Saffron's and gently pulling it away.

"It's alright," he said. "I'm—I'm sorry. I didn't know... I never even imagined Morrígan to have an arid class... Do you want me to take it back?"

Saffron stared at him, unsettled by the ease of those words. How the page in front of them was something surprising, unsettling for him, too—but it was as easy as closing the book to stop thinking about it.

Prince Cylvan dé Tuatha dé Danann—Saffron's raven.

But also—Prince Cylvan dé Tuatha dé Danann, descendant of Queen Proserpina, first born and in line to become the next king, beneficiary of everything that came from purging humans from Alfidel, no matter his own personal feelings on the subject.

Saffron shook his head. He hooked fingers over the edges of the book protectively. Cylvan hesitated, then nodded, pulling his hand away again. Saffron returned to the page, bending close to memorize every single face he could.

CYLVAN MUST HAS SENSED THE CHANGE IN THE AIR, because he eventually patted Saffron on the leg, then found something else to keep his attention in the study. Still, Saffron noticed out of the corner of his eye every time the prince glanced over to check on the silent human curled up tight in the corner. But as far as Saffron knew, Cylvan was worlds away.

He read every word in the chapter, and any other mention anywhere else he could find it. Most of the academic language went over his head, or described things he already knew. He returned repeatedly to the portrait of the Kyteler School's first class, and Saffron had to close his eyes and take deep breaths every time he imagined the faces of people he knew in them. Whether they were the faces of people in Beantighe Village, or in his visions of the school being burned to the ground, he didn't know—but both came crashing to a head when one face out of all of them refused to leave him alone. Even after he skimmed the next chapter, and the next, and the next, one of those young faces wouldn't leave him alone.

When he finally realized why, he stared at it for a long time, biting back tears as his hands shook.

With long blonde hair woven into two plaits over her shoulders; round cheeks; round eyes; ears that stood out distinctively from her head—

It was—Baba Yaga. Nora Everhart. A student of Kyteler School's first class.

A high-pitched noise filled his ears. He closed his eyes, before rubbing the backs of his hands as he swore he felt the heat of flames boiling his skin. Hotter than fete bonfires. Hotter than spilled coffee. Hotter than the kiss of a rapier. Hotter than the heat of sinking into a slow, choking death in the confines of the trunk in Kaelar's closet.

The light of his candle warped, swelling brighter and tinged with vivid pigments as if staring into the sun. He couldn't stop shaking. Couldn't inhale a solid breath, lest he choke on his own smoke-infested vomit—

"Saffron," Cylvan's voice was gentle, and a hand gently touched his shoulder. It pulled Saffron back from the brink, somehow—except when he snapped to meet Cylvan's eyes, he only saw pointed ears. Perfect skin. Flawless features. All things attributed to someone—who'd never known a day of labor. Bone-deep exhaustion. Stacked bruises. Criss-crossing cuts that would age into scars. Long nights scrubbing dishes. Lying awake, wondering if the chair propped under the door would be enough to keep predators out. Did the students burned beneath King Clymeus' final assault spend the nights leading up to it lying awake, too? Listening? Waiting? Knowing it was inevitable, just like Saffron did every night he swore something moved in the corridor outside his room? Cylvan had come for him while slowly suffocating in the trunk—but would he be there every other time?

Saffron opened his mouth to speak, never hating the silver choker more than in that moment. He wished to explain. He could see it on Cylvan's face, confused why Saffron looked at him with such a mix of disdain and heartbreak.

They used to teach us. They used to write about us in history books. I might have even been able to enroll, too, had I come a few centuries earlier. Life might have been easier. Life might have been fair.

But there was more to it than that, illustrated clearly by the presence of Baba Yaga in the image. Things he already knew some about, things Baba Yaga resisted speaking of in detail but couldn't keep completely secret, things even Luvon changed the subject about whenever asked about why he still made deals for changeling children.

After arid schools closed, when human magic became taboo, after Clymeus and Proserpina purged as much as they wished from all of Alfidel—Baba Yaga and every other remaining human were turned into the first beantighes. Long before changeling children became common, bringing them through the veil to act as servants.

All those spirits still trapped in the ruins—had they survived, they would have become beantighes, too. They would have been killed, or forced into servitude, but they still refused to escape through the open veil until every important book they could carry was rushed into the crypt.

Human students—who had been attending classes. Practicing their rightful human magic. Reading and writing and collaborating, offered opportunities right alongside their high fey counterparts—high fey who were allowed to continue as normal, even as their human peers were hunted and ripped away, or ripped apart. Even as their human peers were turned into the same beantighe servants who veiled their faces and mopped their floors.

Baba Yaga went to school in Alfidel; she went to the Kyteler School of Arid Magic. Saffron always knew Professor Adelard attended school in Alfidel, too, and suddenly wondered if it was also in aridology. But Adelard earned an anti-aging ring early in Proserpina's rule, graduating just in time to not be hunted down, providing value as an educator even as a human. That anti-aging ring was the reason he still passed as someone so young despite being centuries old. But despite being close to the same age, Baba only earned her own ring when she became a henmother. Perhaps

—because normal beantighes didn't get anti-aging rings. Normal beantighes had no value in being kept around. Baba Yaga had simply missed her chance while she was young, only earning it again later when she proved herself useful in the long term—

Saffron slammed the pages shut. Biting hard on his tongue, he forced back another wave of emotion, gripping the book tight before pressing his face into the front cover in a fight to maintain any amount of composure at all. Cylvan's hand touched his back, and Saffron shuddered with a small, agonized sound.

"I'm sorry, Saffron," Cylvan just repeated, as if he didn't fully understand what he meant to apologize for, just wishing to offer comfort. He probably thought Saffron was only just learning about Proserpina and Clymeus, as someone who was unthreaded. Saffron was only just learning that arid magic was human magic, period.

Saffron would have to carry the burden of his actual nightmare by himself, trapped in a lie he fostered to protect the people he cared about from Taran.

He just saw the faces of the students. The first class. He saw his henmother, who once trusted him to perform the same taboo magic on Berry. Who never stopped using arid circles on teacups when her beantighe-chicks were ill from the misery of servitude, even though discovery would have resulted in her arrest and execution. Exactly what Saffron was trying to save her from, after all that time, as Elluin used her to get Saffron's attention.

Baba Yaga deserved to live. She deserved to practice her magic. She deserved everything the fey had ever taken from her. But not just her—every human who broke beneath the burden of high fey control, deserved to live peacefully.

That peace would never come if people like Taran mac Delbaith continued to rise into power.

21

THE THREADS

The backs of Saffron's eyes burned from exhaustion. He wasn't sure how late he remained in the study with Cylvan and Asche, wavering in and out of wakefulness between bouts of miserable gasps and tears, all of it finally going silent as he stared at the ribbed ceiling in silent consideration. The whole time, Asche slept on the couch, surrounded by their books. Soundly. Safely. Without any worries at all. Saffron had to clench his fists to keep from screaming.

Once the self-pity wore off, it made room for anger eager to flood his limbs. Anger that made his fingers twitch, made his jaw clench, made a different sort of tears fill his eyes. Cylvan must have been able to sense it, because he didn't hover. He busied himself with pretending to scour the shelves, occasionally bringing something he thought Saffron might be interested in. Passing by where Saffron was prone and silent on the couch, to check if he was still awake. Eventually, he dug an old bottle of alcohol out from a hidden cabinet by the fireplace, and Saffron gulped back as much as he could in gratitude. It numbed the rage melting his insides just enough to resist burning the house down.

Eventually managing a few hours of sleep in his actual bed,

Saffron rose with the morning sun and pulled on his black uniform and veil. There were actual chores to be done that day.

Sweeping, mopping, wiping down counters and mantles and windowsills, chasing dust-wisps from the vents, cleaning the charred remains out of the fireplace and oven, gathering laundry from the rooms to leave in pick-up bags out the side door. It was then Saffron wondered if anyone knew he was the beantighe working in Danann House, which had previously been unstaffed —but the trains of thought made his anxiety spike, so he pushed them away.

It was while he was gathering laundry from Kaelar's room that he heard screaming and banging coming from the closet. God—he nearly walked away. He nearly pretended he heard nothing. But a dead body in the house would raise suspicion, and Saffron had been doing so well keeping Taran off his scent, all things considered.

He shoved the heavy box off the trunk lid, then turned the key in the lock and walked back out. He heard Kaelar erupt from inside with a crash and a gasp, tumbling to the floor and dry-heaving. Saffron bit back a satisfied smile, disappearing before he was spotted as the one who released him.

MAGNIN'S ROOM REMAINED LOCKED AGAIN THAT morning, which made Saffron instinctively check Taran's door as well—but he wasn't expecting the latch to slip, door creaking inward. Immediately, he leapt back, searching up and down the corridor to see if anyone had noticed, but he was as alone as he had been the rest of the morning, even Kaelar having dressed quickly for class and leaving in a rush.

Biting his lip, Saffron knew there wasn't any reason to scour Taran's room except to be nosy—but then he recalled what started the events on the night of the fete in the first place. *I am no longer in need of wild fairy fruits. I've decided to let you go.* Saffron still didn't know what that meant, what else Taran had planned—

and he wondered if there would be any clues in the fey lord's bedroom.

Slipping silently inside, a part of him expected Taran's space to be spotless, but Saffron was met with organized clutter. The duvet and pillows were bundled and draped over the mattress, charred logs spilling out of the fireplace over the area rug, old homework assignments scattered on the desk. Even one of the curtains had fallen from its rod over a window—or perhaps it had been torn down—only to be wadded up and stuffed between the wall and a dresser overflowing onto the floor. Precariously stacked books claimed a majority of floor space, reminding Saffron somewhat of Professor Adelard's office. More loose papers and paintings missing frames were pinned over the fireplace and work desk, others rolled up and tucked into a box in the corner. Saffron swore there was even a pile of bones sitting on a rug between the hearth and the desk, surrounded by tools he wasn't about to examine any closer.

He couldn't help but recall Sunbeam's accusation again —*Taran mac Delbaith is ashen.* It made him scoff, stepping farther inside with self-reassurance that there was nothing to fear.

Because the room had clearly meant to be locked, Saffron resisted straightening the bedsheets, kicking the overturned corner of the rug back into place, even watching his feet in the scattered fireplace ashes in order to avoid leaving footprints. He nearly made it through the entire room without finding anything of interest—before the brief sight of what he swore to be arid markings caught his eye, and his heart leapt into his throat.

Carved into the base mattress beam of Taran's bed, hardly bigger than Saffron's thumb was long, worn hatchmarks were evident in the wood. Removing the paper from his back pocket, he noted the markings with the others—and then noticed more arching lines on the floorboards under the bed, not unlike those in his own room in the attic.

Crouching further, he managed to make out a few handlengths of the markings before they disappeared too far into the shadows—but more unexpectedly, there was a single object in the center of it. He couldn't resist.

Retrieving the wooden box, he bit his lip. He pressed a thumb against the front edge of the lid, carefully pushing it open with a tiny squeak from the old hinges. Inside, four knotted red threads fought for space in the cramped basin, like abandoned craft projects stolen from Asche's collection. Were they gifts from the daurae? Saffron didn't know whether to laugh or scoff at that—but just before he closed the lid again, he was reminded of the sight on the edge of the ruins' mist. Those tangled red threads in the trees, a canopy of bloody crimson netting...

Gently brushing the top knot, Saffron appreciated the elegant shape of it, woven like the embroidery on one of Cylvan's doublets. But then he swore the bundle trembled beneath his touch, and he quickly pulled away.

Releasing a small breath, he closed the box in order to tuck it back into place, but paused again.

Why would Taran have red strings resembling those outside the Kyteler ruins? And why would he keep them in a box surrounded by arid markings, clearly hidden under his bed, meant to go unseen...?

Saffron pulled the box back onto his lap again. Something tickled the back of his thoughts. He wanted to know what exactly it was about a handful of knotted threads... that was so important for someone like Taran mac Delbaith to hide.

22

———

THE VISITOR

Saffron served dinner to the Danann House residents without any change in pace or pattern, nodding in gratitude when Cylvan complimented the fried trout and raspberry compote. He was, however, surprised when Eias and Asche complimented it, too, unable to help the warmth spreading across his cheeks.

Once everyone retired to their rooms for the night, Saffron indulged in a long bath to wash away old dirt and sweat—but also to avoid what was waiting for him in his room. Four woven memory knots stolen from Taran's box, replaced with matching bundles from Asche's embroidery collection. Just in case the fey lord sensed beantighe hands rifling around in his things and went looking.

He wanted to know what they were, why Taran hid them in a box encircled in arid markings, and... why they seemed to resemble those in the trees around the Kyteler ruins. Perhaps it was only Saffron searching for connections that didn't exist, but he was at a point of desperation for anything. Any forward momentum. Even if every act was on a whim.

Drying off, rubbing the towel through his hair last, he pulled on wool hosen and a high-collared shirt before sitting cross-legged on the bed. He would have preferred to sit at the desk, but as always, the chair was indisposed beneath the doorknob.

Hunched over crossed legs, Saffron skimmed the Kyteler chapter from Cylvan's book again, in search of anything useful he might have missed. Meanwhile, his hands worked through an additional pile of books lining the wall, absentmindedly flipping through each and tearing out pages blank enough to add to his growing pile of sketchbook filler-paper. It remained a tedious process, but a familiar one, and the rain on the other side of the window almost tricked him into thinking he was back in the barn doing the same in the old loft. At least in Danann House, a single rogue wind probably wouldn't topple the entire place.

A strong gust shook the glass from the outside, as if taking him up on that challenge—and then a more purposeful knock suddenly came, and Saffron nearly hit the ceiling in surprise. He choked at the sight of a shadow on the other side of the window, scrambling for his candle to blow it out as if he hadn't already been seen. The dark visitor just knocked again, then playfully scraped their sharp nails down the glass. It was then Saffron recognized the silhouette of horns, as well as drifting strands of long wavy hair, and he let out a shaky breath of realization.

Lighting the candle again, Saffron crawled from his nest of gutted textbooks. He reached the window and popped the latch, not expecting the storm to nearly slam it out of his hands. Cylvan laughed on the other side, but didn't try to force his way inside right away, swaying back and forth with one hand propped against the upper frame. He wore a dreamy expression, eyes half-lidded with cheeks flushed. His perfect lips then puckered into a coy smile, and the sight made Saffron's insides flutter.

"HellooOOoo, my pretty little beantighe-flower," Cylvan cooed, words slurring enough that Saffron understood in an instant. His dear raven prince was drunk. At least that time he seemed to be in a cheerful mood. "I came to check on you... and to bring you gifts. But you have to invite me in, according to the rules."

The rules? Saffron couldn't help but smile, and Cylvan nodded. He leaned in slightly more, tendrils of hair spilling over his shoulders, spotted with leaves and twigs from the wind. From his shoulder, a leather bag flapped in greeting.

"The rules of the wilds," he said in a low, tantalizing voice. Saffron forgot how to breathe, momentarily enchanted by Cylvan's handsome face like any other helpless human would have been. "So let me in, so that I might ravish y—"

Losing his grip, Cylvan tumbled forward, crashing into Saffron and sending them both flat to the floor. Cylvan grunted, but Saffron burst out laughing, only to throw a hand against his mouth as his choker protested and squeezed the sound off.

Cylvan attempted to apologize, but in the process of righting himself, accidentally hooked a nail under the edge of Saffron's nightshirt, sloppily pushing it up to reveal his bare stomach. It made Saffron squeak in embarrassment, trying to shove it back into place, only to accidentally knock Cylvan's hand away and summon him crashing down again.

"Oh, gods, I swear—I'm not trying anything," Cylvan groaned in frustration, fighting one more time to find his balance. *"Fuck*—beantighe moonshine doesn't fuck around. Is this how you feel eating fairy fruits? I swear my bones are—boiled eggs."

Saffron put his hands out to help, grinning as he fought off more rolling laughter. Cylvan loomed over him for a moment longer, as if he was the one suddenly enchanted by Saffron's face. That only made Saffron blush more.

As much as Saffron wished for Cylvan to stay right where he was... he patted him on the shoulder, sitting up slowly to ease the drunken prince upright. Cylvan followed, but still collapsed against the wall beneath the window as the world clearly wobbled beneath him. Pixies wasted no time burrowing into his dark hair, then diving into the bag on his shoulder to search for things to steal.

"Careful with those," he grunted, flicking one pixie away with a trail of glitter like a shooting star. "They'll bite your nipples off."

Saffron chuckled, nearly putting his hand out to touch Cylvan's chest in tease—but he stopped himself last second, quickly snapping his hand back again. Cylvan grinned, grabbing the collar of his dark shirt and pulling it open to show, anyway. Gold jewelry poked into view, and Saffron erupted hotter, planting his hands against his cheeks before scrambling to cover Cylvan up again. Cylvan laughed, before apologizing and wiggling in order to straighten back up.

"I have some things that belong to you... as well as some extra moonshine, thanks to Hollow."

Hollow? Saffron mouthed, sitting on his knees in rekindled curiosity. Cylvan nodded, attempting to pull the bag off over his head, but the strap tangled in his hair and horns. Saffron sat forward, unhooking the stubborn loop and pretending he didn't notice how Cylvan's hands cupped his waist in an excuse to keep him balanced. Saffron wasn't the one struggling to remain upright.

"Erm... imagine my surprise... when I came home for lunch yesterday afternoon, and you were gone, but then I found Hollow throwing away all my lipsticks while pretending to tidy my bathroom..." Cylvan went on with a weary smile. Saffron snorted. "We... we made conversation—and by that I mean, he threatened to kill me unless I answered his questions, pretty ballsy considering I'm a prince, and he's just a... *scoff*, anyway—and then you were trying to say his name after I pulled you from Kaelar's trunk, and I realized... I wanted to know... what was going on. So after dinner tonight, I visited Beantighe Village to chat with him more..."

Saffron stared at him in surprise. Cylvan nodded in uncertainty, then nudged the leather bag in Saffron's direction. Saffron realized with a rush of excitement, he recognized it. It was his own.

Burying his hand inside in an instant, he gasped upon pulling out his sketchbook, then again at Cylvan's notes, even finding the wooden box of charcoals Cylvan had once gifted him on the edge of the nymph lake. At the very bottom, he also found a bottle of moonshine already half gone—and then a book he didn't recognize. Upon opening it to the first page, his stomach flipped.

Queen Morrigan Academy, Spring Court;
Kyteler School of Arid Magicks and Theology
First Class
This Grimoire Belongs To:
♡ Nora Everhart ♡

"Ah… Hollow told me… Baba Yaga has not been back to Cottage Wicklow for a few days," Cylvan said as Saffron flipped through the pages. He paused, eyes flickering up to meet Cylvan's. "And that, apparently… Headmistress Elluin has accused her of performing witchcraft."

Saffron's thrill sank into guilt, and he slumped back onto his knees. To be so excited suddenly tasted bitter, turning his blood to sap. Cylvan noticed, putting his hands up and waving them around to bring Saffron's attention back.

"I know where Elluin is keeping your henmother," the prince went on in reassurance. Saffron's anxiety only quelled slightly. "I actually took Hollow to see her. Erm, admittedly it was after we both had a few drinks, and we were feeling a little dangerous, but… she is safe, Saffron. Oh, she… told me to tell you that I am very handsome and nice, by the way. And tall."

Saffron croaked a laugh. Cylvan's lips hovered in a hesitant smile as he considered his next words. Before speaking them, he slouched slightly as if they were heavy.

"You might not understand because you can't remember, but… Elluin has a… a grudge against me. She thinks I… Well, maybe the details don't matter. But you got wrapped up in the middle of it, and now… even now, I worry there is still a part of her who thinks… ah, there was this wolf people kept saying was killing beantighes, and I think this might all be related to that, but… I don't… I don't know…"

He shook his head. Saffron instinctively touched Cylvan's knee, wanting nothing more than to assure him it wasn't his fault —but, like always, he could only silently look. Closing his mouth again, his chin wrinkled in frustration. Cylvan brushed his thumb along Saffron's bottom lip, as if detesting how Saffron held it back.

"I'm sorry, Saffron," he said. "But I meant it, when I offered to help. I made sure your henmother was alright, and that your friends were alright, and then I got everything I thought you might need. I wish there was more I could do, but for now..." He touched the front of the grimoire. "Baba Yaga says she doesn't remember everything written in here, but that if I could find where she put it... there might be something that can help you. She said she hid it away centuries ago, but... magic doesn't age and wither like the rest of us..."

Cylvan trailed off as Saffron pulled the book against his chest, trying to feel Baba Yaga's intention within in. Then he stretched out an arm and wrapped it around Cylvan, pulling him into a close embrace. With every word of thanks and appreciation and devotion he couldn't speak. Cylvan's arms encompassed him in return, pulling him closer, until the old book was pinned between them. Cylvan pressed his nose into Saffron's hair, breathing him in silently, running a hand up and down the back of his neck.

"After we figure out what you were trying to do with the markings on that note," he breathed, hot against Saffron's skin, "we can confront Elluin. We'll rescue your henmother, and anyone else Elluin threatened. I'll do anything I can to help, so just... I don't know, just... just let me focus on them. You have enough to worry about. And I know you don't have any reason to trust me, I know I'm only a stranger, but... I swore to protect you, once, and I intend to keep that promise, even if you don't remember..."

Saffron disappeared into the shape of Cylvan's shoulders, broad enough that he felt like he could disappear entirely. That was what Saffron wanted—to be small enough to disappear, especially into the arms of someone he trusted. Someone he clung to with a pitiful hope—that they really were different from other high fey Saffron knew.

"Now…" Cylvan added, swaying slightly. He kept one arm wrapped around Saffron, as if by habit, and touched the book on Saffron's lap. "See what you can do with the spells in this book. Impress me."

Saffron cracked a smile. Then he laughed, unable to help it.

Opening Baba's grimoire, he flipped through the first few pages of instruction, so even the memory-stripped beantighe in him would know the steps to make. He had no rowan berries to actually perform anything impressive, but he would still go through the motions, even if just for Cylvan's appreciation.

Grabbing his candle, Saffron found the page of teacup circles in his sketchbook, hoping Cylvan assumed those had been put there before the window of what memories Saffron had lost. Luckily, Cylvan was probably drunk enough to fall for anything.

Choosing one, Saffron was unable to halt the little bubbles of excitement as he worked. Using the quill, he carved a circle around the circumference of the wax stick, followed by the feda marks according to the magic circle he chose. Not unlike the candles in the Kyteler crypt.

Strength.

He knew it wouldn't work without rowan berries, without offering deliverance, even though he'd seen something similar in the Kyteler ruins—but as far as he was concerned, it had the same power as the altar to his friends next to the window. It was the thought, the intention.

Lighting the wick, Saffron smiled at the little flame. Then he finally glanced at Cylvan again, who had claimed a seat on the edge of the bed during Saffron's process. The prince watched him with curious eyes, a tiny smile on his perfect mouth.

Saffron extended the candle in offering. Cylvan raised his eyebrows, then cautiously took it—and his eyes rolled back in his head, collapsing onto the bed and clutching his chest with a haggard gasp and a groan. Saffron lurched to his feet in a panic, but then Cylvan laughed, shaking his head and sitting back up again with a satisfied sigh. Saffron punched him in the shoulder, and Cylvan laughed again, before making a show of appreciating the linework in the candle.

"What is it for?" He asked. "Immortal life? A love spell, maybe? You admittedly look very pretty in the low light. It might already be working."

Saffron flushed, but was still mad about the trick. He grabbed a blank sheet of paper and stubbornly wrote: *Impotence*. Cylvan put a hand to his mouth with a gasp, and it was dramatic enough to summon a smile and an eyeroll from Saffron. He showed the actual spell on the page of teacup circles, and Cylvan considered it for a moment, before smiling.

"Thank you, beantighe," he said thoughtfully. "I'm... already feeling better than I have in weeks."

The words were rich with sentiments left silent—but Cylvan spoke them behind his eyes. Saffron could see each thought clearly, and they were the words he wished to express out loud, too.

I'm happy to be with you again. I'm happy you're here. I'm happy I get to laugh with you.

I still miss you terribly.

They might have gazed at one enough all night, had a drop of wax not melted and singed Cylvan's finger, making him cry out and declare Saffron a wicked thing bent on causing the prince undue harm. Saffron laughed, reaching for the candle, only for Cylvan to hiss and hold it away. He extended his burnt finger, instead—and Saffron rolled his eyes once more, then pressed a healing kiss to the side of it.

23

———

THE ECHO

Sunbeam was right about arid markings not translating into Alvish, which was both exciting and perpetually frustrating. But, at least, with the help of Cylvan's notes rescued from Beantighe Village, Saffron was able to transcribe the markings from around Danann House into more recognizable characters, despite still having no clue what they meant. He thought Cylvan might have a better idea, but the prince, who had claimed Saffron's bed while Saffron sat on the floor, just groggily looked at the page for a long time before sighing and flopping drunkenly back against the pillow. He mumbled a lazy excuse about *"the beantighe trying to force the prince to learn taboo magic,"* and Saffron wished he could laugh at the irony.

"Maybe the next time I go to Connacht... I'll be able to get something more helpful," he mumbled last, before snuggling into Saffron's pillow and inhaling a deep, exaggerated breath. "Good... like flowers. Saffron flowers... pretty Saffron flowers... pretty... taboo... arid flowers..."

Saffron giggled, reaching an arm to tuck the blanket over Cylvan, last. Little did the prince know, Saffron was eager for his next chance to sleep on that pillow, too. It would smell like pine and gardenia ravens.

After reaching the limit of what he could do with the hatch-marks, Saffron spent an hour familiarizing himself with every grimoire spell with wide, curious eyes. It was impossible to see and memorize every one, since not all of them were organized clearly, or they used words Saffron didn't understand, or even seemed to be protected by some sort of invisibility charm—but amongst those he did comprehend, he had to bite back disappointment that none were immediately applicable to what he needed.

There was no obvious mention of arid trials; no spell for charming royal fern engagement rings; no mention of manipulating true names except random spells to extend their reach, or something—which, apparently, was how patron rings worked. Saffron wished he could shake Cylvan back to the land of the living to show him, but an unthreaded beantighe wouldn't know why that was significant.

When Saffron filled himself to the brim with grimoire spells, he flipped through his sketchbook with a fluttering heart, thrilled to have it back within reach again. Upon finding the page where he once sketched his prince next to the nymph lake, Saffron gazed over his shoulder to where that same prince was limp on his bed, buried deep beneath thick sleep only beantighe moonshine could provide. His head was tilted to the side, one hand resting on his stomach while the other clung to the empty bottle of alcohol containing a single drunk pixie snoring inside. The other two curled up in his hair and under the collar of his shirt, using it like a blanket, though Cylvan's hand swatted sleepily at the creatures whenever they moved. His chest rose and fell evenly, dark eyelashes twitching, and Saffron hoped he was having nice dreams. He even snored a little bit, cheeks still flushed with inebriation, lips hanging open slightly. Saffron let his eyes linger as long as they wanted, refusing to ever take even such simple sights for granted again.

Inspired, he plucked one of the pristine pieces of charcoal from the box Cylvan once gifted him, settling cross-legged on the floor with the sketchbook propped against the side of the bed. It had been a few weeks since he'd drawn anything from reference, but Saffron allowed himself to be out of practice, willing to draw and re-draw Cylvan as many times as he needed until it was perfect. Just like he was. His prince, his raven.

Smiling to himself, Saffron wrote a label in the page margin just like he did with every other strange, wild creature he crossed in the Agate Wood.

> <u>*Night Prince.*</u> *(sídhe fey, wild). Spotted in yarrow fields and Danann House dormitories.*
>
> *Tall. Brod-shouldered. Long black hair. Horns (dragons?). More beautiful than leanan ~~shees~~ sidhes and daemons.*
>
> *Scary at first. Kind once he warms up to you. A thick skin that must be broken. Resoursefull. Top of his class. Smart and he knows it.*
>
> *Nipple-jewelrey. Well endowed. A soft mouth. Lovely to kiss.*
>
> *Plays the violin. Messy and cluttered. But still perfect.*

Perfect, Saffron's lips formed the word delicately, letting the tip of his charcoal trail off on the final stroke, looping around where he'd caught the impression of his perfect Night Prince resting peacefully, comfortably, in his own bed. Saffron promised it would always be the safest place for Cylvan to close his eyes.

HOLLOW SCRUBBED DISHES IN THE SINK WHEN SAFFRON descended the following morning, meeting each other's eyes and trading a silent greeting. His expression that morning wasn't so harsh or confused, and in fact even looked a little excited, like he was eager for everyone else to get out of the house. Saffron wondered exactly how friendly he and Cylvan had gotten while drinking together the night previous, unable to resist smirking at the mental image.

But Saffron's good mood fizzled the moment he found Taran standing outside where Kaelar should have been. Smoking a stick of floral tobacco in the air thick with rain, he glanced over as Saffron emerged—and Saffron realized, Taran wasn't even the biggest surprise of the morning. Opposite him, Daurae Asche poked their head out, and Saffron knew by their cloak and boots they would be joining the hunt. He couldn't help but frown in confusion, though didn't let it linger on his expression.

The ground was slick with mud from the previous night's rain, further sloshed as more fell from the sky in scattered rhythms. Saffron's boots sank into the grass and flourishing undergrowth with every step, already shivering by the time they reached the overgrown road and oppressive wall of mist. Kaelar must have told Taran about finding the gate to the ruins, which was why Taran joined that morning. Saffron should have left the fucker in the luggage trunk.

"You brought your bracelet, Asche?" Taran asked as Asche climbed from their shared saddle, saying it in a way that made Saffron wonder if it was intentional for him to overhear. His eyes followed the movements, pausing on a grey-brown woven circlet around Asche's wrist. Asche lifted it in turn, smiling at Taran in confirmation.

"Good. Make sure you stick close to the beantighe once you get into the fog, you wouldn't want to get lost."

"Wait," Asche's excited expression dropped. "You're not coming with us?"

"I'm going to search the outer area, here." Taran smiled handsomely. "I can trust you to keep an eye on the beantighe, right? And to definitely find a way inside?"

Asche's crestfallen demeanor snapped back into determination, smiling and nodding. Taran smiled and nodded back, before meeting Saffron's eyes, where the expression shifted into something else. Consideration, perhaps even skepticism. But Saffron was still stuck on the thought of the daurae entering the mist with him, instead of Taran himself, which was the last thing he expected. He then had to wonder what Taran told Asche they were looking for, as surely the daurae wouldn't be so eager to contribute to a fairy fruit hunt with the intention of drugging and manipulating their brother.

But by the way Asche smiled at Taran, Saffron had a nause-ating thought. Perhaps it didn't matter what Taran wanted—Asche looked like they would be willing to do anything he asked at all. Something about the way the daurae mimicked Taran's expression, even some of his movements, made Saffron's skin crawl. As if there was something more than simple admiration, and Taran had no intention of acknowledging it.

Saffron scoffed silently, but motioned for Asche to follow. He barely made it two steps before he was grabbed and yanked back by the wrist.

"Don't forget, beantighe," Taran breathed a low threat. "Back by sundown."

Saffron snatched his arm away, glancing at Asche and resisting the urge to scowl a second time. Turning into the mist, the two high fey exchanged final goodbyes, and Taran was left behind.

As much as Saffron would rather waste the day pretending like he couldn't find an entrance through the fence-line, he was too eager that morning to search the ruins for anything on knotted red threads, arid trials, Gaeilge, or whatever else might be useful to him, even if he couldn't enter the crypt with the daurae in tow. Not to mention—he was far more fearful of crossing paths with the beannighe while wandering around the outside with Asche. The last thing he wanted was for the old woman to take a chunk out of the Daurae of Alfidel.

Pretending to innocently search like anyone else, Saffron lead them on an indirect path to the gnarled tree and loose fencepost. As they walked directly within reach of the fence, Saffron couldn't help but glance over his shoulder, finding Asche completely unfazed by the iron. Perhaps it was something to do with the bracelet they wore.

He made a big deal out of *accidentally* bumping his hand

against the loose bar, and then *accidentally* knocking it away enough to climb through. Asche might not have even noticed if Saffron's efforts were clumsier, immediately shrieking with delight and shoving Saffron out of the way so they could crawl through, first. Saffron just picked himself back up out of the mud, slicking hair from his eyes and following behind in annoyance. Perhaps he could have waited for the beannighe to find them, after all—

As if summoned, something grabbed his arm right as he took the first step through. He whipped around to find the red-veiled crone's face staring at him with wide eyes.

"The queen's opulent silver—did that high fey place them on you?" She asked, tapping a chipped nail against one of his cuffs. "Why haven't you named them yet?"

"Named them?" Saffron asked in confusion, but the beannighe was already stretching backward to strip a branch from the nearest rowan tree.

"Yes, dear—a *name,*" she insisted, pushing the branch into his chest. "Just like you name anything else, so you alone can control it."

"A—" Saffron meant to reiterate his confusion, but the words caught in his throat when, for the first time, he recognized the ragged clothes the beannighe wore. A tattered button-down top. A fraying maroon skirt muddied and desaturated with age, cinched around her thick waist. And, somehow still pinned to her neck—a Morrígan Academy brooch.

"Beannighe," he said, mouth dry. "Were you... part of the Kyteler School, here?"

The beannighe frowned, aged face wrinkling deeper in annoyance. "What?" She snapped. "Aren't we all? Why ask something so obvious?"

Saffron smiled awkwardly, glad when her expression relaxed a moment later. Still, she didn't release her grip on him.

"I'm still waiting for you to come deliver for me," she scoffed. "I'm losing my patience, you know."

"I-I will as soon as I can," Saffron promised, despite still not understanding exactly what she needed. "Erm—will you still show me what you meant? About giving a name to my cuffs."

"Ah, of course." The beannighe sighed, wiping her hands on her skirt before reclaiming the rowan branch for herself. "I will show you, so you do not end up in any more trouble."

She pressed the broken end of the branch to the polished surface of his cuff.

"Give me a name, then. One no one else would be able to guess."

"Oh," Saffron considered it, combing through his memory for the first thing to come to mind. "Um... what about... Icarus?"

She nodded, holding the twig to the silver before drawing a vertical line and tapping feda hatchmarks into it. It left no mark directly on the cuff, but Saffron saw how markings appeared down the length of the branch, instead.

"Go on, try to compel it," she said, finishing her lines and handing him the stick. Saffron examined the markings on the rowan twig a moment longer, before extending his arm.

"Um... *Icarus, unclasp.*"

Nothing happened, so Saffron tried again, rephrasing the command and how he said the name. Again and again, the silver cuff remained right where it was until the beannighe finally sighed and put her hands up for Saffron to stop.

"Is there something already associated with your cuffs? Another branch? A ring?"

"Oh—there's a ring, yes..."

"That explains it. Bring the ring next time, and we can charm it, then. Give me the twig back for now," she said, taking it for herself and snapping it in half.

"Is this... something I could do myself?" Saffron asked. "Do I really only need a rowan branch? And the ring?"

The beannighe eyed him for a long moment, before shaking her head. "You're hardly more than a spring witch, aren't you? Here I thought you'd already made an oath. Perhaps I should not have been so hopeful. No, child, you must be rowan blooded to charm anything containing even a lick of opulence, like patron rings or giving true names."

"T-true names?" Saffron asked in surprise, but the woman was already shuffling him away. On cue, Asche called out from the fog as if it was really the first time they noticed Saffron wasn't following.

"Bring me the silver ring next time, and I'll show you once again. Now get going, I have too much work to do."

"But—"

Did she really mean—*true names were charmed with arid magic?*

"Um, just... one more thing, if that's alright!" Saffron couldn't resist as she lumbered away. "Those strings in the trees— what are they?"

The beannighe sighed once more, adjusting her red veil as a breeze caught it. "They are the final memories of those who pass in these woods. They provide some perennial deliverance for the barrier around the school—the same one that allows you to speak despite wearing opulent silver, by the way. It would be far too much for me, alone. Another reason I was hoping you to come and help..."

She grumbled the last part, before scowling as Asche called out again. "Go on, one of those spirits inside clearly wants to speak with you."

She waved her hand, but Saffron only saw the trees, the threads. *Memory threads.* He'd always assumed that phrase was merely a metaphor—but could unwoven memories actually be made tangible? To be manipulated by hand? Locked away and hidden?

Then, those knots beneath Taran's bed...?

His mouth went dry as a thousand ideas, thoughts, conspiracies exploded in the back of his mind—but Asche's feet were stomping through the weeds behind him, approaching fast.

"Beantighe!" They rang out, and Saffron took once last glance toward where the beannighe vanished, before sighing and step-

ping through the fence and reuniting with the daurae. He followed Asche's lead back into the trees, thoughts swelling so bright and thick he barely perceived anything happening ahead of them.

Why would Taran mac Delbaith hide memory threads in a box under his bed?

Were they his? Or someone else's?

If he really was ashen like Sunbeam said, was he the one to remove them? Or did someone else pull them?

Saffron frowned as they passed beneath a red rowan tree on the opposite side, recalling something else the beannighe said.

What did it mean to be rowan blooded, and how did it relate to arid magic and true names?

And—

Could Saffron do it himself, in order to protect Cylvan's name like he once promised?

THE CHAPEL

The last thing Saffron was going to do was walk the daurae directly to the library where all the fruits were hiding, so he continued the act of someone who had never been through the fence, before. He gasped and feigned shock as they approached the shadowy buildings on the other side of the trees, and Asche grew more and more excited every time Saffron pretended to be surprised.

More than once they exclaimed their thrill over how pleased Taran would be, which nearly shut down all of Saffron's patience in an instant. Was it possible to keep Asche as far away as possible from Taran until Ostara? He suddenly didn't want the daurae anywhere near the fey lord, worried there was something else going on that might make him ill. Puppy love? Misplaced adoration?

Wanting any distraction he could find, he led the daurae into every abandoned structure they passed, mostly just trying to burn time while also keeping his eye out for anything useful. The one time he nearly bumped into Sunbeam around a corner, he slapped a hand over her mouth and motioned for her to be quiet, grimacing when Asche called out to him from out of view. Her eyes went wide, but Saffron just hissed for her to stay out of sight, to which she nodded and snuck off again.

The sound of screeching metal caught Saffron's attention while appreciating carved stonework around the roof tiles of one sagging structure, jumping when Asche called out for him to come and see. But upon finding them, Saffron instinctively grabbed and wrenched them back again at the sight.

Bones lay strewn across a long floor dirtied with rubble from the crumbling ceiling overhead, many crushed into dust, others lying exactly where they first fell. A sight that filled Saffron with horror—but seemed to only excite the daurae, who wriggled against his grip and whined to be let go.

At the far end of the nave, what remained of pews lined like coffins on both sides, facing what Saffron only vaguely under-stood to be an altar and chantry. Growing up, Luvon had never been particularly religious except in making offerings to old gods at the turn of each season, but Saffron had joined him at commu-nion with fey friends who worshipped deities Saffron had never heard of. More than once, those deities were carried over from human traditions, which Luvon hinted at on their return home—but Saffron always knew no high fey would ever admit it.

The room where they stood reminded him of those memo-ries, though it didn't reflect any single one in particular. Asche remained overwhelmed with curiosity, finally tugging themself free and racing into the building. Saffron nearly called out for them to be careful, barely biting it back when reminded of his tongue-less state.

"Ohhh, Cylvan would be so jealous," Asche mused, voice echoing off the high ceiling. "Most Proserpina chapels have been burned or turned into Dagdan Monasteries ... but this one is so well-preserved. I wonder if there are any rare books left behind? If I take him one, maybe he won't be so mad about the shoes I ruined..."

Saffron gulped, staring at the interior again with a second perspective. The altar at the front was coated with thick dust; an array of golden candles cluttered the far wall, brittle with age; a tapestry dangled from the back wall, embroidered with a golden sun motif on a warm yellow background. Straining his neck upward, he even lost himself for a moment in the broken rose window high overhead, whose remaining colored panes of glass cast vivid rainbows across the bones and debris on the floor.

Proserpina's chapel. But—why would there be something like that on a human campus? Unless it was placed there on purpose, before the school was destroyed? A church dedicated to the Night Queen who hated the same students who walked the campus, who would eventually be the one to demand the school shut down entirely, whose king would hunt them down to kill or push through the veil. When the chapel was first dedicated to her, did the students know what would come?

Swallowing back his hesitation, Saffron gave in and followed the daurae farther inside. He picked through cracked bottles under the altar, popped open the almery lock and sniffed the oils and incense stored inside, then followed Asche through one of the back doors into what looked like a dressing room or sacristy. His curiosity piqued highest when Asche wrenched open a door heavier than both of them combined, revealing a dark room lined with books all the way up to the ceiling. Saffron nearly bodily shoved the daurae out of the way.

Searching out one of the candles on the wall, Saffron quickly lit it and occupied the entire little room with wide eyes and wandering hands. It forced the daurae to find something else to keep their attention, turning with a huff and a flip of their cloak.

Saffron had to wonder why none of those books had been carried into the protective belly of the underground with the others, left to the wiles of time and however it saw fit to treat them, instead. To Saffron's gratitude, it appeared the dark, locked room had done well to preserve a good handful of titles, however, resting without the scars of chewed pages and mold growing from the humid air.

Grabbing any and all he could find that were still intact and legible, Saffron made a circle on the floor around himself and flipped through with the light of his candle. Every now and again Asche would stop by, as if hoping Saffron had moved on so they could claim his place, only to huff and storm off again. Outside, the rain picked up, thunder rolling in the distance and making it difficult to know exactly what time it was. But Saffron just kept reading. He couldn't stop himself.

Most of it was nonsensical, or written in languages he didn't know, or simply replied on high-level words that went straight over his head. When he finally found something he could understand—he almost wished he hadn't. It made his heart race, fingers trailing down the handwritten title: *Proserpina's Silver*.

Written in the form of a personal diary, Saffron struggled to parse out most of the words within the flowery script, but gathered enough to understand. His heart pounded in his ears the whole time, though he pretended it was just more thunder in the distance.

The only documented form of complex, tangible opulence; more nuanced than simple opulent touch-charms.

Curious, he reached down the collar of his shirt for the amethyst pendant, squeezing it, then smiling to himself when it warmed in return. Did it count as a 'touch-charm'? Perhaps that explained how it still worked within the ruins, while his silver pieces didn't? Ah, the beannighe mentioned something about her barrier while they discussed naming his cuffs, and Saffron realized, that barrier must have specifically suppressed opulence. No wonder he never saw any pixies or sprites or anything else of wild fey within the iron fence.

Used for behavioral encouragement in both humans and high fey. See: Proserpina's Ten Hindrances of Human Perpetuity, ("")'s Three Tenets of Taming Insubordination, ("")'s Means of

Subduing Ironick Capabilities in Detained Iron and Rowan Witches, etc.

Sometimes used for recreational purposes. See: Proserpina's Sixteen Indulgences of Carnality, Tools For Empowered Sidhe Opulence and Magic Efficacy, etc.

Reportedly used to ease the effects of Ashen Periods on high fey affected by closed veil tears. Also used in hunts by prominent witch hunter families.

Means of fabrication held secret by mac Dela Sidhe family.

The mention of Ashen Periods would have gripped Saffron's attention in a vice, had the following line not swept in and clutched him harder.

"Mac Dela..." he whispered, before muttering out loud: "That's King Clymeus' family name, isn't it?"

Something scratched on the floor next to him, making him jump, thinking it a mouse coming to find their parchment lunch. But then one of the books suddenly shifted, and Saffron yelped, jumping backward and kicking it in surprise. It skittered under the shelf, but continued to scrape against the floor, and Saffron had to gulp and look, else the curiosity eat him alive.

Unlike all the others, the book in question wasn't nearly as well-preserved—the number of pages gripped by the spine were twice as many as they should have been, bending it over itself and on the verge of curling outward like toenails left to grow too long. As if it had been submerged in a well for all those centuries tucked away, only removed and instantly dried the second he cracked open the door.

Biting back the hesitation, he scooped the book back into view, relieved when it didn't bite him. Carefully forcing the pages apart, he watched in reignited interest, and then understanding, as new pages grew from the inner spine, like leaves from a tree. A book constantly filling itself with new information, like invisible hands scribbling notes on each new page. The scratching sound was a new sheet coming to maturity, and Saffron watched with his mouth hanging open as words appeared in black ink right in front of him, filling in lined columns labeled at the top.

KING AILIR'S DAY | SPRING | AOLORA BARRACH (SÍDHE) | (DE BHALDRAITHE (SÍDHE)) | BORN.

KING AILIR'S DAY | SPRING | THUVA BARRACH (SÍDHE) | (DE BHALDRAITHE (SÍDHE)) | BORN.

KING AILIR'S DAY | SPRING | MURVA MAC DELBAITH (SÍDHE) | (MAC DELA (SÍDHE)) | DECEASED.

KING AILIR'S DAY | SPRING | MICCHON Ó CÀIDH (SÍDHE) | (Ó CATHBAD (SÍDHE)) | BORN...

He nearly left it as merely an intriguing form of magical family history—until his stomach lurched, and his eyes flashed back to one of the names.

Murva mac Delbaith (mac Dela).

Why would those names...?

Searching the labeled columns along the top edge—Saffron learned quickly.

RULING COURT | SEASON | NEW ALVISH NAME | (OLD ALVISH FAMILY NAME) | STATUS.

New Alvish name—*mac Delbaith.* Old Alvish family name—

"Mac Dela," he rasped.

Taran mac Delbaith, who provided the silver needle to Elluin after Arrow's death, the one used to carve cruel accusations into Saffron back. Taran, who supplied Proserpina's silver choker, silver cuffs, and taught every other person the proper way to use them. Silver devices only fabricated by the mac Dela family...

Someone must have kicked Saffron in the back. The door must have slammed shut on his chest. Suddenly he couldn't read the words, feeling like he'd gone mad in that tiny little room. He tried to deny it, tried to find any reason why it couldn't be true—but the words were right there in front of him, even labeling them as a Sídhe family, just like Cylvan once said Taran belonged to.

But then, that meant... Taran mac Delbaith was a descendant of Clymeus mac Dela, the wolf king, the one said to have driven Queen Proserpina to closing the veil; to hunting, displacing, or killing humans, even demonstrated by the very chapel he sat inside of, surrounded by bones of dead arid students—

Saffron attempted to slam the book shut, but the overwhelmed spine split and pages exploded in every direction. Scrambling backward, he kicked them away, tumbling out of the room and against the opposite wall. He stared as the words on every sheet faded into nonexistence, erased the moment they were no longer bound together. But—Saffron had seen it.

Cylvan knew, didn't he? All of Alfidel knew, didn't they?

Why would they be so eager for someone from Clymeus' family to return to power, after everything he did? And Cylvan, as a direct descendant of Proserpina—even if they weren't directly related, even if he and Taran had so many cousins and relatives between them that there was no crossover at all—

Was it really because everyone believed the mac Delbaiths to be ashen, like Sunbeam said? As if high fey who couldn't perform magic wouldn't be any risk...? Did they think—Taran's connection to the old king could help him guide Cylvan toward peace, because he understood intimately what Clymeus once did...?

Why hadn't Cylvan ever mentioned it? Surely he knew, surely he knew what it might mean for Taran, for the mac Dela—mac Delbaith family to rise back into power?

How could Cylvan have once looked Saffron in the eye and

declared he didn't know who the wolf could possibly be, when Taran clearly mimicked the same Sídhe power as the old king? When he was literally a descendent of the old king? How could even Cylvan believe Taran was ashen, to declare to Saffron he didn't know what the wolf was, when there was an animal just like Clymeus hunting beantighes on Morrígan's campus, just like during Proserpina's Night Court...?

"Why...?" Saffron croaked, running fingers back through his hair as it all tangled in his head like spider threads. Sinking to the floor, he hyperventilated into his crossed arms. He pulled his knees in close, suddenly feeling like he was crumbling into pieces. He was going to be sick. He was going to be *sick*.

All he could think, was—if the people of Alfidel were still welcoming of Taran back into power, it meant—to them, the treatment of humans during Proserpina's Night was nothing to lose sleep over. As if no one feared what Clymeus did—but feared something Proserpina might have done if she hadn't been busy with the humans and the veil. If she hadn't been so intent on wreaking havoc on humans, specifically, the same as the human lover who spurned her and planted the first seed of resentment. As if there was something else Cylvan could bring that could be worse, that only someone who knew how to control a Night Ruler could prevent. Did high fey think Clymeus a hero? For turning Proserpina's ire toward humans, instead of on themselves?

Even if Cylvan wasn't the wicked Night King they all anticipated—would it even matter? Or would humans still become victims all over again, as fears festered and rumors spread?

What else could there possibly be to take?

Folding his arms tightly, Saffron pressed his face into the crooks of them—and screamed. It muffled the sound, though anything that might have escaped would have been buffered by the pounding rain outside. As if the sky felt what he did, mimicking the same torment stirring hot and wild and frantic in his chest. He wished to disappear beneath it, to vanish entirely in the rain, so that he might not have to leave again and face reality outside the safety of the iron fence—

Perhaps he begged a little too loudly, because the rain heard him. It heard him, and it obeyed—burying the roof of the chapel beneath pelting water, forcing it to groan beneath its own weight, then buckling down on top of him.

25

THE RAIN

Puddles the size of ponds blanketed the ruined campus as rain continued to pour. Saffron didn't know how he made it back outside—only that the world spun, and he wasn't entirely stitched within his body. Perhaps that was intentional, because the moment he attempted to return to it, the pain of his leg shattered into pieces made itself known, and Saffron shrieked in agony.

He was carried by Sunbeam. Up ahead, Asche scurried through the rain, helping to lead the path. Beneath the dizzying pain, Saffron heard them speaking to one another, back and forth, as if Asche hadn't been surprised to see Sunbeam at all. As if they knew each other. Saffron must have hit his head, too. He must have been dreaming.

With every step, the puddles weighed Saffron down, attempting to claim him, to suck him into the mounds as punishment for ever crossing the path of the old school. But as badly as he wished to accept his drowning fate for any chance to ease the horrific pain in his leg, Sunbeam wouldn't allow it. She supported Saffron with all the strength of her back and shoulders, dragging him between crumbling stone skeletons as the daurae fought back panicked gasps and attempts at using their magic. Again and again they tried to blast fire from their hands—but every time, there was only a puttering silence followed by a whimper of confusion.

It was nearly impossible to see through the rain and the encroaching darkness. At least—that's what Saffron told himself. It wasn't his vision going blurry from the pain. It wasn't the vomit he fought to bite back swelling higher and higher until it ate him alive from the inside out. Fuck. *Fuck*.

But as if unsealing the time-locked tomb of Proserpina's chapel infuriated the spirits trapped within the gates, Saffron suddenly witnessed shimmering glows everywhere. Milky white and opalescent like Luvon's eyes, floating between buildings, past shattered windows, between sagging walls, as if drawn by the white moonflowers blooming across moss and leaves and vines clinging to stone. He saw bones in every shadow, emerging from mud eroded by the torrential rain, turning their heads to look at him. He saw them. All of them.

"Fuck..." he begged as Sunbeam encouraged him to keep his eyes open, to breathe, they were almost there. But Saffron was steadily losing his will to continue, wishing either for his shattered leg to slough off entirely, or for the spirits to rip his soul from his body so he no longer had to feel it at all.

A single glowing spirit suddenly emerged from between two buildings, floating without feet on the path. Sunbeam continued as if she didn't see it—but Saffron did, and his body jolted. It knocked him out of Sunbeam's arms, hitting the ground with a shriek of pain before finally vomiting pink-tinged bile into the mud. Sunbeam scrambled for him, but Saffron just lifted his head and searched the dim edge of the path, desperate to see their face again.

"Arrow?" He begged hoarsely. Sunbeam heaved him back upright, forcing him to continue as Saffron fought against her, straining his neck to search for his friend. Opalescent. Transparent. Arrow's spirit, roaming the ruins despite never knowing them when they were a safe, welcoming place. Why did they have to be trapped there only once it became a prison?

. . .

HE DIDN'T KNOW HOW LONG HE WAS DRAGGED, exactly. All Saffron knew was, by the time they reached the iron fence, he was both shivering and drenched in hot sweat. His entire body throbbed. He was sure his broken leg had ripped away entirely. But that didn't alarm him—it was what he asked for, after all.

But one thought managed to surge to the front of the cacophony as they passed through the iron, and Saffron threw his hand out to grip the front of Sunbeam's shirt.

"Wait," he rasped. "Taran. Don't let Taran—see you."

"Don't worry about that right now—"

"*No*," Saffron insisted through clenched teeth, tightening his grip on Sunbeam's clothes. He knew, if Taran saw Sunbeam within the mist, it would only raise his suspicions. It would weaken any trust he had in Saffron. It would complicate the tentative peace they had. It might put Hollow in danger back at Danann House. Saffron wasn't going to risk it. He would drag himself on his stomach all the way back to campus before he let Taran lay even one eye on Sunbeam.

He grappled for the nearest branch he could reach, successfully yanking himself from Sunbeam's grasp. Barely managing to remain upright, it still twisted his leg, and he buckled over to puke what remained of the stomach acid in his gut. He met Sunbeam's eyes again as she glared at him, but Saffron would continue to be stubborn until she listened.

"What's going on?" Asche hurried back, not having noticed their companions falling behind. Sunbeam threw them a look, before pinching the bridge of her nose in frustration.

"I shouldn't go any farther," she said, and Saffron managed a relieved breath. "Can you help him, Asche?"

"I'll... I'll carry him," Asche finally squeaked. "It's my fault he's hurt, anyway... I took him into that building..."

Saffron grimaced, but put out a hand for Asche, who hurried

over. They pulled Saffron's arm over their shoulder, and Saffron tested their strength, letting out a miserable laugh when they nearly buckled beneath his weight. But he could hop on his good leg well enough. He just needed someone to help him balance. It didn't matter, so long as Taran never saw anything.

Thank you, he mouthed to Sunbeam as they passed, not wanting Asche to overhear him speaking.

"Asche, don't you dare let your fey lord friend ignore this," Sunbeam hissed at the daurae, next, clearly feigning naïveté when it came to Lord Taran. In response, Asche stiffened up like a royal guard. The fact they didn't argue was further proof they knew one another, somehow—but Saffron's mind spun too fast to hold on to the thought.

"Of course not!" They promised, pulling Saffron forward another few hopping steps. "I'll make sure he gets help. I swear. I —I won't tell anyone I saw you here, either, I promise... even when I go back to Avren, I won't tell anyone..."

"Good," she muttered, before throwing Saffron another annoyed look. Saffron just smiled, before leaning more on Asche and focusing on the terrain ahead.

Maybe it was the continued sapping of his cognizance, but Saffron swore the shadows in the mist had multiplied. Bulky, slender, slow-moving, rapid shadows that passed by on every side of them. More ghosts. More ghosts infuriated with the opening of the queen's religious tomb. Saffron would be back to apologize. He would be back to re-seal the prison as it was meant to be left. He only hoped they would understand.

Emerging from the treeline onto the overgrown road, Taran was already there waiting for them, as if he could smell the blood. As if he could sense the churning of the ghosts in the woods and knew something had happened. The look on his face when he spotted them and realized it was only Saffron who was hurt was bittersweet—because it meant Taran was capable of empathy when it came to the daurae, but he might also refuse to help Saffron, no matter what Asche said or did. Who was Saffron for

Taran to protect, anyway? What did Saffron actually do that he couldn't turn around and force on Hollow or another beantighe, instead?

"What happened?" Taran demanded, grabbing Asche and pulling Saffron away. Saffron hit the grass with a miserable grunt, attempting to push himself onto his back but sinking too quickly into the spongey earth. "Are you hurt, Asche?"

"We—we found a way into the ruins, but a building collapsed," Asche said quickly, attempting assertiveness despite their trembling voice. "The beantighe got trapped, and then I couldn't use my magic—"

"Come on," Taran interrupted, grabbing Asche's arm and towing them toward the horse. "You're freezing. Let's get you home."

"Wait!" Asche demanded. "We're not going to leave him!"

"You are my priority—"

"No!" Asche insisted, yanking themself from Taran's grip. "The beantighe needs help! We're not leaving him out here!"

"He's just a fucking beantighe, Asche, there are plenty more—!"

"I'll tell Cylvan!" Asche cried. "About all of this! I'll tell him everything! I'll tell him you've been sending the beantighe into the woods to look for the wolf!"

Laughter erupted from somewhere nearby—and then Saffron realized it was his own. *Sending the beantighe into the woods to look for the wolf*—was that really what Taran told them? To find the animal stalking campus? Oh, god—everyone in Alfidel really did believe Taran mac Delbaith was fucking ashen. Perhaps he was. Perhaps Saffron really had just imagined it all along, like Sunbeam once said.

"I'm taking you home," Taran insisted. "I'll come back for the beantighe, alright? If we all go together, it'll take twice as long and you'll catch your death."

"But he—!"

"He'll be fine. I'll come back for him, Asche, alright? You

don't have to tell Cylvan anything. There's no reason to make him worry. I'll drop you off then come back for the beantighe, alright? Now *get on the fucking horse.*"

Saffron wouldn't forget how Asche stood up for him, even long after they disappeared and the blanket of nighttime draped the Agate Wood. Even if Saffron died in the mud, alone in the rain, leg bent backwards. Even if he became just another ghost wandering in the mist.

Closing his eyes, Saffron sank deeper into the earth, allowing it to swallow him if it so wished. Allowing it to drag him into the mounds if it so wished. But there was one thing he needed to do, first. One intention to set.

Extending a shaky hand, Saffron recalled the Arid-Ogham, feda markings he'd spent the night prior memorizing. He drew a circle in the mud. Starting at the bottom, he carefully carved each line around the edge, whispering each letter into the earth in tandem.

S-I-L-B-H-A-N. The Old Alvish spelling that would be recorded in high fey history of any and all languages anywhere Cylvan was immortalized. A word that wasn't Alvish or Gaeilge or human or fey. Just a name. A spell of its own, as Saffron knew Cylvan would always come whenever he called it. And while the enchantment would be washed away in the rain before Saffron took another breath, he begged the earth to remember it.

Taran mac Delbaith would not become king. Cylvan would not be forced into submission by the same people, the same family who rent the Kyteler School of Arid Magic from its roots.

Cylvan would protect it. Cylvan would reinstate it, one day, and should he make it through the night, Saffron would help him. Saffron would make sure of it—and carving the prince's name into the forest floor was a promise that there was at least one person rising into power who could help. Someone who was different. The lingering spirits only needed to wait, and the Night Prince would come.

He always came when Saffron needed him.

Closing his eyes, Saffron pulled his hand back into his chest and let out a shuddering breath. He wondered if Asche and Taran had made it back to the house, yet. He wondered if Hollow had been allowed to go home. He wondered if Sunbeam and the bean-nighe were somewhere warm and dry. He wondered if Cylvan, or anyone else—would even notice he was gone, like Kaelar once said.

His three pixie companions found him in the darkness, right on the edge of the mist that otherwise banned them. Saffron appreciated their colorful lights. They scuttled around in the mud, waving their hands out to demand his attention, or perhaps in an effort to keep him awake, until Dewdrop zipped off into the sky. The remaining two put on a show with leaves for hats and twigs for swords, squeaking and squealing whenever Saffron's eyes slowly closed, as if insulted he would even think of going to sleep during their performance. A part of him wished they would flitter off like the first one did, wished he could just close his eyes and sleep and wait for the sun to rise.

Thump, thump, thump. The sound of feet hitting the road came over the rain, and Saffron cracked open his blurry eyes to search for Taran's horse. He was surprised Taran had come back at all, but sank back into the mud when he realized he may have only imagined it. Taran wasn't coming back. Taran had no reason to come back. Saffron was nothing, Saffron was only a disposable beantighe—

Feet rushed to meet him, and Saffron forced himself to look. It was too dark, the rain was too heavy to see anything clearly, but he made out the silhouette of something racing toward him. Coming within reach, it dropped to its knees, wrapping arms around Saffron's shoulders and immediately pulling him into the warmth of their cloak.

Oh.

"Cylvan," Saffron mumbled without thinking, smiling weakly. Cylvan stiffened. A frantic hand combed wet hair from Saffron's face, out of his eyes.

"Saffron," Cylvan responded. "What happened, Saffron? Are you hurt?"

Saffron grimaced, motioning feebly to his twisted leg. Cylvan's hand traveled down to touch it, jerking back again when Saffron cried out. Apologizing, he pulled Saffron closer to the warmth in his cloak, and Saffron let out a long breath of relief. From deeper within the covering, Dewdrop appeared with concerned squeaks and hands that pinched at Saffron's eyelashes, and Saffron mouthed a silent *thank you*.

"I'm going to take you home," Cylvan promised, before cursing under his breath. "For some reason I can't use my magic here, so we'll have to walk a little bit. But I'll carry you. It's going to hurt, but you just have to bear with me, alright?"

Saffron lingered within the comforting cloud too long, only returning to the surface when Cylvan patted his face. As if the moment he draped within Cylvan's arms, his defenses fell entirely, and he knew it would be safe to sleep. Saffron managed to nod despite the heaviness dragging down his eyes, and Cylvan whispered something before sliding an arm under Saffron's back, then his legs.

The instant Saffron's leg hung off the broken bone, his hand clawed at Cylvan's chest and a scream tore out of him. Cylvan apologized profusely, only pausing for a moment before moving again. It summoned another shriek of agony, but Saffron tried to bite it back, gripping anything he could knot his hands around.

Clinging to Cylvan's whispered comforts and encouragements, Saffron disappeared into the prince's body with his eyes squeezed closed and his breath held against the excruciating fire in his leg—and the only thing to pull him back again was the smell of wet fur. Rot. Blood.

Cylvan's movements stopped. Saffron strained to open his eyes, squinting through the downpour to find a black wolf heaving with breath and blocking their path. Beneath him, Cylvan's arms locked, and then trembled.

"That's..." he breathed, heart pounding next to Saffron's ear.

"The... the wolf. It's... it's real..."

Taran must have come back for Saffron in that form for a reason. Perhaps to make good time, perhaps to carry him more easily—or perhaps to finally show Saffron the same fate as Arrow, Cloth, Berry, like he intended from the beginning. But his own arrogance ended in the very last thing he wanted, which was Cylvan finally laying eyes on him. Proof that he existed at all, not just a lie made up to drive him mad.

It told Saffron one more thing, too—that they'd left the reach of the iron fence and the barrier that sucked opulence from the air. He opened his mouth, attempting to say something—and the squeezing of his collar was proof. The beginning of a thought formed, before dwindling.

Saffron just tugged on Cylvan's cloak. It took two more attempts before Cylvan finally broke his locked gaze with the beast to glance down at Saffron. Saffron raised his hand—and pointed to the sky.

Cylvan knew what that meant. His jaw clenched, and he glanced back at the wolf for another moment, before stepping back and taking off into the clouds. Holding Saffron against his chest, they left the beast on the road, and Saffron's dwindling thought sparked to life again with the chill of the sky.

That book in the chapel said Proserpina's Silver was sometimes used to remedy ashen states.

Perhaps everyone believed Taran and his family to be ashen—because they actually were. Perhaps they merely utilized their own silver to fake it.

Which meant there was a reason Taran couldn't enter the ruins. Perhaps why he realized even the mist wasn't safe. Because it denied the opulence in Proserpina's Silver, too.

Saffron erupted into laughter. Cylvan whispered his name in concern, but Saffron couldn't help it. He just laughed and laughed and laughed, until the collar tightened and he could no longer breathe, until the world went quiet and he sank into the pain setting his body alight.

26

THE THISTLE

The wolf was no longer just a beantighe myth. It was no longer only something students gossiped about while eating lunch, declaring they saw it stalking the woods outside the fete, creeping through the darkness at the whims of a rowan spirit.

Prince Cylvan had finally seen it for himself, in flesh and blood, and he clung to Saffron differently in every moment after.

Magnin used potions and poultices and other fey magic Saffron couldn't comprehend in an attempt to heal the broken bones, and Saffron's head was in Cylvan's lap the entire time. In his bed in the attic, Cylvan sat cross-legged at the head of it, caressing Saffron's face, brushing fingers through his hair, whispering dreamy little prompts between Saffron's miserable gasps and sobs. With every touch, pain jolted up the entire length of his spine, into his neck, his teeth, until he clenched his jaw so hard he felt something pop. It was only Cylvan's thumb brushing the corner of his mouth, then pressing between Saffron's teeth that finally forced him to relax before anything actually cracked in half. Cylvan's finger settled inside his mouth to ensure it wouldn't happen again.

Eventually, the burning heat and agony under Saffron's skin, in his bones, boiled his thoughts enough that he slumped into groping unconsciousness, and Cylvan could only whisper Saffron's name in an attempt to summon him back. But Saffron didn't have anything left, and allowed himself to be taken.

Despite the ease of sunsingers through the window, Saffron woke with a gasping jolt, eyes wide as he stared at the ceiling overhead. It took a moment for his memories to return—though some definitely had to be remnants of a dreams mixing with reality.

Groaning, he pressed a hand against his forehead as it pounded. His entire fucking being down to his stitched-up soul throbbed and ached—but nothing emanated with a white-hot pain like the bones in his left leg. Straining to look, he was reminded why upon lifting the blanket and spotting black bandages wrapped tightly from his hip all the way to his ankle, pulled tight enough that he could barely flex his foot, only a small gap over the knee to provide the slightest amount of bend.

"Oh, good." A voice came, making Saffron jump. He spotted Eias sitting at the writing desk with a blown-out candle and piles of books, scribbling something on parchment for a homework assignment. In front of them, a small ceramic tea set steaming from the pot. They wore casual clothes, looking exhausted with legs crossed. "I was wondering if you'd ever wake up."

Saffron instinctively opened his mouth to ask where everyone was, but the choker gave warning like it always did. He'd gotten so used to speaking freely in the mist that for his instinct to be an out-loud response was almost embarrassing. He clamped it shut again, forcing himself to sit up with a gasp and a grunt. Eias just watched, brushing their nose with the end of the quill until Saffron was done moving around.

"Your bones are technically in one piece again, but brittle like old bread," they explained, finally closing their book. "Magnin wants you to use a crutch while you continue healing, and you have to keep most of your weight off it for the next few days."

What about Cylvan? Taran? Asche? Saffron had to fight the urge to mouth the names or demand a pen and paper to write it down. Instead, he just grimaced, risking a light touch against the bandage over his thigh. It hurt just as badly as he remembered in the beginning, but more contained. It didn't resonate through his whole body, locked in his upper leg by the magic and the bandages. Saffron almost wanted to ask how Magnin finally figured out what to do, recalling the way he attempted at least a thousand different tonics and other methods, but bit back that urge, too.

"Oh, here," Eias went on. They poured something into a ceramic cup from the teapot in front of them, and Saffron hesitantly extended his hands to accept it.

"This will help with the pain. Erm—the prince also said you've been having nightmares lately, so drink it all the way. It should help you feel better."

Saffron narrowed his eyes. Hooking a finger through the loop, he stopped short before sipping at it. It smelled of roses and ivy, the surface shiny with flavor oils. But at the very bottom, he spotted the head of something that made his stomach flip in surprise.

Perhaps Eias never expected him to recognize it—but any beantighe would know weaverthistle. A spiney plant that bloomed crimson in the heat of summer, then again in the dead of winter. It was a common brew in Beantighe Village, because it helped to dull painful memories. Turning them into blurry, muddy shapes and colors, reducing them to visions seen through murky ponds. Saffron knew exactly how it would taste, exactly how it would feel in his mind, having had plenty of memories he wished to blur away during his time working at Morrígan.

It wasn't even the sight of it that made him so uneasy—by that point, he'd built up such a tolerance that one single cup would do nothing except file down the sharpest edges of the events the night before. No, it was the fact Eias had any of the crimson thistle at all. Not only had it, but apparently knew how to use it. Saffron always thought it was an old beantighe folk remedy, not unlike Baba's teacup circles in a way. A magical, medicinal plant that was almost impossible to find, and dangerous to keep around as discovery by Elluin or anyone else would result in consequences. For Eias to so blatantly offer it...

The prince said you've been having nightmares lately...

Saffron smirked. More likely, Taran asked Eias to brew it in an attempt to wipe Saffron's memory of the night before, period.

Saffron sipped as if none of those thoughts existed. Eias didn't say anything else, only nodded slightly when Saffron met their eyes and offered a timid, naïve-beantighe smile.

"The rest of us are going to Connacht for a few days, so you'll be left to rest and recover. Magnin will want to see you before we go, though, so get dressed and meet us downstairs in an hour. I'll go let him know you're up. Ah, your crutch is there, against the wall. Practice with it a little, first."

Connacht.

Eias left without another word, not knowing the frenzy they'd planted in Saffron's mind. Hadn't Cylvan said something about finding books in Connacht, when he came to Saffron's room drunk? While scouring Baba Yaga's grimoire, he certainly said something about finding useful texts there...

Gazing down at the tea in silence, Saffron frowned. He buried two fingers into the hot drink, fishing the thistle out and smashing it beneath his foot. Pixies immediately swooped down to investigate the vivid red thing like a ruby on the floor, before dancing around it like a fallen enemy and stealing the longest barbs to throw at one another.

Saffron had to join them in Connacht. He had to find the books he needed. Books about not just aridity, like Cylvan thought—but about arid trials. Proserpina's Night Court and her treatment of arid witches. Books about being rowan blooded, arid magic and true names, opulent silver...

Memory threads.

Once the barbs were stripped, the pixies doled out the wet crimson petals bundled inside. Wrapping them into scarves, into head bows, into ribbons to decorate their wings. Saffron just thought about how their color perfectly resembled the red threads in the trees. The red threads he'd found under Taran's bed, currently stored in the floorboards of the neighboring attic room with his other contraband.

He vaguely recalled spells in Baba Yaga's grimoire about memory threads. About witnessing them, preserving them. When he first flipped through the pages, he didn't understand what they meant, not knowing *memory threads* were actually tangible strings—but since speaking with the beannighe, he had a better idea.

Glad to find he'd been washed clean of the previous night's sweat and blood while unconscious, Saffron wriggled his way into pants and his black blouse, mouthing curses the entire time his leg complained and ached. Grabbing the crutch last, he double-checked his sketchbook, grimoire, and arid notes were still stashed the neighboring room's floorboards alongside what he then understood to be memory threads. Just in case anyone came snooping around while he was gone.

Slipping from his room, Saffron hurried down the corridor and through the wainscoting. Emerging again in the second floor hallway, he brushed himself off, made himself presentable, and adjusted his opal patron ring to ensure it was fully visible. Then— he knocked on Kaelar's door, and made sure to look as disappointed and pathetic as humanly possible that he hadn't been invited on the trip with everyone else. Kaelar took the bait in an instant.

27

THE TRAIN

In addition to his excitement to bring Saffron along and show him off, Kaelar was a little too eager to introduce a new piece of cruelty once Saffron joined him in the front vestibule. A long, delicate chain, one end dangling heavy with a silver sun motif like thorns around a coin, the other hanging with a crescent-moon piece of silver half the size of his palm.

"It's called a veil weight," Kaelar told him, clipping the heavy sun-shaped medallion under his veil, then threading the chain over the center of Saffron's head to nudge the half-moon into his mouth. Saffron recognized the sun shape on the opposite end right away, recalling the tapestry that hung in Proserpina's chapel in the ruins. "'Supposed to keep you from speaking, which isn't really a concern in our case, but—I just wanted to try it out. It's an heirloom of your new patron-family."

Of course it is, Saffron complained internally, a flush of whatever dignity he had remaining escaping as he clamped teeth down on the silver half-token. The remaining weight of the chained sun dangled over the crown of his head, peeking out from the back bottom edge of the chiffon for all to see. He understood the device's additional cruelty as soon as the weight pulled on his jaw, making it ache within moments—but if he allowed the half-moon piece to slip, the heavy sun opposite would rip his veil off. He suddenly didn't want to know what the secondary branching chain was for, assuming some sort of third contraption was meant to be included if the wearer allowed their veil to fall.

Danann House's other residents arrived in the front corridor one by one as the sun rose, and they each demonstrated only the briefest surprise at Saffron joining them. Maybe once they spotted Kaelar fawning over his beantighe-pet, they unanimously realized it was inevitable.

Eias' thick, dark waves were pulled back into a short, braided ponytail over their ears. Magnin knelt and adjusted the embroidered hem of Eias' skirt as it wrinkled, his own long, silvery-white hair draping over one shoulder, pinned out of his eyes with clips that matched the simple mauve tunic hanging off his frame. Something about the way he complimented Eias' skirt while adjusting it made Eias blush a little bit, though they expertly kept the expression otherwise off their face.

Kaelar wore a suede vertical-slit vest over a white linen shirt, sleeves pushed up to his elbows to show off gauntlets that matched the leather loop of his belt and made him look like more of a jackass than normal. Taran arrived in the front corridor, next, surprising Saffron when he approached and asked how he was feeling, if he was in a lot of pain, if he needed anything. All empty offers of compassion, so Saffron just silently shook his head, unsure whether to be apprehensive or embarrassed when Taran then proceeded to adjust the bottom edge of his veil, not unlike Magnin did with Eias' skirt. But then Kaelar implied Saffron would be joining them in Connacht, and Taran stiffened, before eyeing Saffron intensely. Saffron just smiled.

Perhaps also understanding the inevitability, and perhaps not wanting to make a scene, Taran leaned in close to simply whisper: *"Behave yourself."*

Saffron met his eyes with a flat expression. He didn't know whether to play innocent or something else, but Taran wouldn't have cared either way. Not when Cylvan and Asche came descending down the stairs, and Taran's attention pulled away in an instant.

Saffron disappeared into the effortless grace of Cylvan's silhouette, forgetting about every other person in an instant. He wore a single-shoulder cape decorated with golden embroidery, a fitted black doublet with a high collar underneath, and high-waisted pants shaping his waist and thighs. On his hip, a clearly-decorative, gold-pommeled sword dangled from a loop on his belt, poking out from the back of his cape as he rested a gloved hand on the grip. His long hair draped loose over his shoulders and down his back in the way Saffron liked best, though something about it was more regal than Saffron had seen him in some time. It made Saffron's heart race faster than a hummingbird flapped its wings, only intensifying when Cylvan turned his way and smiled in greeting.

"How are you feeling, beantighe?" He asked, tone remaining casual. "Lucky I spotted you the other night, hm? Perhaps I should explore these woods more often."

A weak excuse, but Saffron wasn't going to argue. Even Taran laughed lightly, as if wishing to change the subject as soon as possible, having no interest in pushing the truth as he didn't want to accidentally make himself suspicious, either. Something about that was deliciously satisfying.

Saffron nodded, bowing slightly in gratitude. Cylvan nodded in return, while Asche just looked at him like they had a frog trapped in their mouth. Apparently even they knew better than to blurt anything in present company, whether it be Cylvan, Taran, or the others who had no business overhearing whatever they meant to say.

"Is—is your leg all better, now?" The daurae managed to string alternative words together. Saffron smiled awkwardly and nodded, not expecting how Taran placed a hand on his shoulder.

"Magnin did all he could, but we will be getting something more appropriate soon," he said coolly. "Until then, you'll have to keep an eye on the beantighe until he's used to walking on his own, especially since it'll be crowded with the street festival."

"The beantighe is joining us in Connacht?" Cylvan asked sharply, and Saffron gave him a look.

"I imagine Kaelar wants to show off his newest possession... but considering what you told me you saw last night, Cylvan, perhaps it isn't safe to leave him here all by himself, anyway," Taran answered gracefully.

Still, Cylvan's defensive posture didn't change. Saffron wondered when and how Cylvan brought the wolf up to Taran at all, and what exactly the conversation entailed. Including the lies Taran told while Saffron wasn't there to hear them.

CLOUDS SWALLOWED THE BRIEF MORNING SUN BY THE time they prepared to leave, low thunder ringing overhead and swirling the garden greenery with incoming wind. It was only then Saffron realized he'd lost his cloak in the ruins and had nothing else to protect him from the rain, grimacing and stepping away from the circle of conversation.

Limping to the coat closet, he was just beginning to accept having to sit in the rain and freeze to death, surprised when a weight suddenly draped over him. Grabbing it before it slipped to the floor, his fingers recognized the luxurious wool exterior and fur lining, but most of all—the perfume on the inside.

"Are you feeling alright?" Cylvan reiterated, but that time it was offered under his breath with a hundred additional layers of unspoken sentiments. When they met eyes for just a moment, Saffron smiled and nodded, pulling the offered cloak farther over his shoulders. Cylvan nodded, too. He grabbed a different covering for himself, but first, his eyes lingered on Saffron's mouth as if anticipating a word or two to escape from it—or perhaps he could see the thin chain emerging from between Saffron's lips. Either way, he said nothing else, returning to the door to leave with the others.

Outside, Saffron was lifted into Kaelar's saddle, not bothering to fight for a specific placement that time. He just pulled up the hood and snuggled down into the fabric as deep as he could, unable resist smiling to himself in pure bliss.

Crossing Morrígan's barrier veil, Saffron flexed his stiff leg as it already ached, not looking forward to the two-hour journey all the way to Connacht on Kaelar's horse. He tried to busy himself with the foggy scenery on either side of them until the others eventually caught up to Kaelar's lead and passed by. It was easier then to steal glances at Cylvan's stately silhouette on the back of his horse, and he even occasionally met Saffron's eyes. Cylvan always smiled when he did, before frowning at Kaelar in turn, and Saffron had to bite back every amused giggle.

Letting his mind wander, the conversations melted into background noise, even Kaelar's occasional promptings existing as nothing more than blurred sounds. But when the group broke off from the main road against what Saffron knew of the journey, he perked up again in uncertainty. Upon laying eyes on a new structure within the trees, accompanied by a long walkway of stone jutting out from the entryway, he realized perhaps they wouldn't be traveling by horse, after all.

Iarnród Station. A train station. Saffron had heard of them, giant snakelike carriages that belched steam and could draw a dozen passenger cars at a time. He'd never seen one for himself, never even heard them rumble by, though Luvon once described them as alerting their arrival with the sound of a beansidhe shriek.

The station outside of Morrígan's protective barrier must have been fairly new, as Saffron had never heard mention of it before arriving on the back of Kaelar's horse. He nearly passed out from shock as it wailed on the tracks, then wondered if it was shrouded in a similar silencing-spell as Cylvan's suite. Otherwise, it would certainly screech for everyone on campus to hear.

A crowd of onlookers gathered around the boarding platform, though very few actually stood in line to purchase tickets. Saffron recognized many of them to be students from Morrígan, dressed in their uniforms and gawking even so early in the morning, while a handful of others tilted straw hats while leaning against their carts as if just passing through and pausing to witness the most recent invention. Saffron wondered why they would ever choose to continue by horsecart or by foot with such a powerful alternative—until he approached the ticketing gate on Kaelar's heels, and saw the cost of boarding for himself. 200 gold chaplets, the same amount sent to Luvon for a month of Saffron's work. Just for a trip to Connacht?

With tickets purchased, the travel party grouped together on the platform until it was their time to board, and Saffron's leg quickly ached beneath his weight. Shifting back and forth on his feet, when he noticed Cylvan watching, he tried to force himself to relax again—but then the prince sidled over as casually as he could, claiming a place next to Saffron close enough that Saffron could lean against him and take some of the weight off. He audibly sighed at the relief, making Cylvan chuckle.

Eventually motioned to enter the individual cars at the end of the line, Eias, Magnin, and Asche boarded into one, while Taran and Kaelar stepped through the neighboring door. Saffron was left waiting as Kaelar took his goddamned sweet time, rocking more and more on his heels as the pain in his leg was beginning to split his spine in two—only to be swept into the wrong door by a clawed hand, tucked into a seat next to Asche before he even knew what was happening. Cylvan then clicked the sliding door shut, ignoring when Kaelar was suddenly there knocking on the window and complaining. Eventually, he had no choice but to give in and find his seat elsewhere, though Saffron wished his ego would have left him stranded on the platform.

The passenger car was lush with velvet seating, adorned with romantic tapestries of fey frolicking in meadows on the walls, a complimentary tray of wine and cheese and other desserts rattling in the corner with every movement. Saffron self-consciously pulled his crutch in close, making himself small in the corner of his seat as Cylvan nudged Asche out of the way and claimed the cushion between them. Clearly not meant to comfortably fit three bodies, it meant the line of Cylvan's hip down to his knee sat flushed with Saffron's, and Saffron was once again grateful for his veil to hide the blood in his cheeks.

Once the train lurched forward, though, all embarrassment raced out of him. It was replaced by pure elation as the platform slinked away, allowing rolling hills, farmland, forestscapes thicker than even those in the Agate Wood to stretch out to the horizon. Saffron couldn't help pressing his face into the glass as landscapes blurred by, wanting to see everything as it came and passed. That was, until Cylvan leaned in slightly and teased him.

"Careful, beantighe. You'll give yourself whiplash."

Saffron blushed, attempting to settle back into his seat again, though was quickly drawn right back out the window for a second time. All the while, Cylvan's hand remained on Saffron's leg, even squeezing slightly every time Saffron jumped when something particularly interesting flew past in the blink of an eye.

"Are you able to put any weight on it?" Magnin suddenly asked, but Saffron didn't respond, not considering how he might have been the recipient—but then Cylvan squeezed his leg again, and Saffron snapped around with a scowl, only then finding everyone's attention trained on him. Startling, he clambered for his crutch as it almost toppled.

Shaking his head, he smiled awkwardly, then shrugged, only more embarrassed when Cylvan whispered something and attempted to lift his veil out of the way. Saffron quickly diverted his hand again, not wanting anyone to see the veil weight in his mouth. The self-consciousness only grew as Magnin suddenly left his seat to crouch on a knee in front of him, pawing at the tight bandages and making Saffron flinch.

"There was a lot of bruising around the fracture, which may hurt more than the repaired bone does. I wasn't able to do much for the crushed muscle, sorry. You'll just have to heal that on your own."

"Crushed muscle?" Cylvan asked flatly, and the temperature

in the train car dipped. Cylvan examined his nails as if pretending to be disinterested, as if it was only gossip, but everyone else knew. He did it on purpose. "You know, I'm still so curious what the beantighe was doing out in the woods at all. Do any of you have any idea?"

"Oh..." Magnin cleared his throat as casually as possible. "D-Daurae Asche, you were with the beantighe for one of your class audits, weren't you...?"

Asche stared at Magnin like a deer facing a bear, frozen while gripping a handful of candies halfway out of the bowl in the corner.

"Um..." They wheezed, before glancing at Saffron, as if Saffron could offer any sort of plausible excuse. Saffron just watched the panic flicker behind their eyes "Well... yeah. Professor Adelard... mentioned there were some... um, oh, some *rare mushrooms* in the Agate Wood that would be good for charms... so I asked the beantighe to go with me... but we got separated... and then he was attacked by that wolf... right, beantighe?"

"Hm," Cylvan muttered with an unappeased smile. "Thank goodness that beast didn't spot *you*, Asche, or else it might have had a good meal. How would I ever explain to father his golden child was chomped up by Morrígan's wolf?"

Asche frowned. They went back to the candy bowl without an answer.

Saffron, meanwhile, extended a hand while pretending to regain his balance as the train took a curve. In reality, he squeezed Cylvan's knee to get his attention. To hint there would be a chance to discuss it later—but Cylvan's eyes remained directly on Magnin, as if he knew Magnin had a secret. Terrifyingly, Cylvan also smiled politely the entire time, and Saffron didn't envy anyone on the receiving end of a look so threatening.

Magnin cleared his throat again, choked by invisible hands. He then dropped Saffron's foot without warning, and Saffron grunted. Slowly bending his leg back, he draped it with the cloak, but left Cylvan's hand in place on his opposite thigh.

"Another question, Magnin." Cylvan crossed his legs and rested an elbow on his knee. The icy smile never faded. "Taran mentioned the beantighe would be getting something *more appropriate* for his leg, soon... as his healer, do you know what he meant by that? Perhaps an offering of silver?"

He said the last words intentionally, not knowing Saffron knew exactly what he was referring to. Proserpina's Silver, only forged by the mac Dela family. Then—Cylvan did know who Taran descended from. Magnin must, too, as he went a little pale, buying some time by pouring a glass of wine and gulping it down.

"A-as it is, L-Lord Taran has been... teaching me some things about Proserpina's Silver, actually. I believe it can be beneficial for the beantighe in this scenario, yes. But only for the means of healing, your highness. Of course."

"Of course," Cylvan's voice came low and firm, but his dark lips curled into another bitter smile. Saffron suddenly didn't want to know what would happen when Cylvan discovered the silver choker and cuffs he wore hidden beneath his collar and sleeves every day. Ah, no, that wasn't true—Saffron would have loved to know. Perhaps it was even something to look forward to.

Magnin seemed to be having the same thoughts, eyes hovering over the base of Saffron's neck before flickering back as Cylvan spoke again.

"You know—not even I know how the silver works. They keep it so tightly under wraps. I'm curious—did you forge that silver cuff that trapped me in Danann House a few weeks ago?"

Magnin went white as a sheet.

"Um—n-no, your highness! I didn't even know... there was such a thing, or that you..."

"Taran must have a number of pieces on hand, then," Cylvan interrupted. Saffron spotted a tendon flexing in his neck, as if doing everything in his power to remain coy and aloof and terrifying. Like a snake arching back to strike, but not before swaying with curiosity. "Will Taran provide the raw silver for you to forge? Is he fetching it for the beantighe on this trip? Ah—perhaps he will get the ingredients while with his family for the funeral. God rest Lady Murva's bones. May her pyre collapse, or whatever. That's what Winter Court funerals do, isn't it?"

He glanced at Saffron that time, and Saffron jumped. He nodded without thinking—then frowned when he realized that meant the mac Delbaith branch of the mac Dela family came from the Winter Court like he did. He was unexpectedly annoyed at the thought.

"Is this really a good choice of conversation?" Eias interjected with a forced laugh. "Especially considering... present company."

"Hm? Oh, you mean the daurae?" Cylvan swung his head exaggeratedly toward Asche, who was busy sorting their candy treasures by wrapper color and shine. "Asche knows as well as the rest of us what we're talking about."

"Know what?" Asche asked, but Cylvan waved them off. Asche scoffed.

"Um... Lord Taran will provide the raw silver, yes, your highness." Magnin's voice cracked, as if knowing Cylvan wouldn't be so easily distracted from his earlier question, wanting to answer sooner rather than later. "This will be my first attempted forging of opulent silver, as well. I am confident in my abilities, however."

"I assume it will be a form of healing silver?" Cylvan coaxed more information, that time placing his hand directly on Saffron's injured thigh and making Saffron flinch. "Will you shape it to the beantighe's leg, yourself?"

"Erm—y-yes, your highness, I assume I will. I already have sketches drafted for my idea, if you are curious enough to know..."

"No need," Cylvan's hand cupped over Saffron's mid-thigh shifted, stroking it slightly. Saffron pretended not to notice, though it was like pretending not to notice a leanan sídhe crawling between his knees. "I only look forward to seeing the final product. It's quite significant for you, you know; the mac Delbaiths are so very protective of their family secrets. I hope your parents are proud."

"Well—it's all in preparation for you and your future court, your highness," Magnin flashed a handsome, though uncertain smile. "Just like Eias is practicing their thread—"

Eias slammed an elbow into Magnin's stomach, and Magnin buckled over his legs with a wheeze. Eias cursed under their breath, before smiling awkwardly back at Cylvan again. Despite their attempt to stop him, though, Saffron heard that interrupted word and made the connection right away. It was obvious when also considering their weaverthistle brew that morning. Eias was a threadweaver in training—and Saffron had to wonder if they were also the one who pulled the memory threads hidden under Taran's bed.

"Where should we shop first when we arrive in Connacht?" The fey gentle changed the subject with zero grace. Cylvan was coy enough to play along, though wore a mischievous smile the entire time. Quickly, Magnin jumped back in to discuss the entertainment for their trip, and then Asche joined in, talking about clothing boutiques, needing new school supplies, stopping by a cobbler, perhaps a bookstore... and the whole time, Saffron bit back a smile of his own.

All the talk of opulent silver reminded him of his realization while held in Cylvan's arms outside the ruins, facing down the wolf in the rain. If Taran truly relied on Proserpina's opulent silver to transform into the wolf—Saffron merely needed to take it away from him. Whether it be a ring, an earring, a bracelet.

He could simply... take it away. If he took or controlled whatever silver thing Taran used, Saffron could control Taran. Own him.

To own a Sídhe lord, to own their opulence, to own their entire magical capability... and then to use it to summon a gruesome wolf on command, just like Elluin wanted...

Saffron glanced at Cylvan, who glanced back. He smiled. Saffron smiled in return.

Perhaps some things could be so simple. Especially with Ostara on the horizon, Saffron hoped that to be the case.

28

THE SHOPS

It wasn't technically Saffron's first time in Connacht, though he'd previously only stopped in for a day at a time while Luvon was visiting.

Apparently named after a human town that once sat mirrored on the opposite side of the veil, most buildings were constructed from wood and glass, naturally feeling *cozier* than Morrígan's dark stone exteriors and metal spires. Perhaps it was also partially due to the way Connacht smelled constantly of bread and pastries, seemed to always flourish with random festivals and celebrations, and boasted a population as diverse as the wild things that lived in the woods.

As a bustling trade-port on the Connacht River, the town saw more people coming and going in one day than Saffron might see in his entire life—and he could have spent that same amount of time just sitting and watching those who passed through. With their unique clothing, the fabrics they wrapped themselves in, the varying hairstyles and makeup, even down to the jewelry they wore and how they jingled when they walked. All of it intermixed with a myriad of languages and physical characteristics far different from the relatively homogenous beauty and grace of the students who walked Morrígan's campus every day. Horns, wings, tails dotted more people than Saffron saw anywhere else, and even Cylvan's and Asche's obsidian horns didn't stand out in the crowd.

Alternatively, it was normally Saffron who could blend into crowds effortlessly. When visiting with Luvon, he was never made to wear his white Morrígan uniform and veil, though even if he had, it would have hardly raised any eyebrows or turned any heads. But that morning, stepping off the train onto the busy platform, wearing all black down to his veil, silver sun motif dangling down the center of his spine—heads turned. People looked. They gave him a wide berth, and he knew it wasn't because he needed a little more room to limp with his crutch. They turned their noses up, then whispered to one another, then hissed things in every language Saffron did and didn't know. He just kept his eyes low, kept in close to the others, tried not to notice. Tried not to think about how, with every bitter look, strangers' eyes would oftentimes flicker to Saffron's injured leg, his crutch, then to Cylvan at the head of the group, as if looking to see if the prince held the opposite end of a leash.

Hardly more than an hour passed before the Danann House party of fey had scattered entirely. Taran left the group early to re-board the train for the next town, but not before offering Cylvan a kiss on the cheek in goodbye. Cylvan even wrinkled his nose the second Taran turned his back.

Eias and Magnin eventually went their own way without a word of goodbye, though they'd been in their own world since arriving, seeming to forget they'd come with friends in the first place. Even Kaelar had left in the opposite direction, distracted by something or someone, not giving Saffron a second glance, that Saffron really thought he was losing his mind. Was it because Saffron inserted himself into the trip last second, he was so easy to forget? Admittedly, it happened in the brief moment Saffron stood in a shop with Eias and Magnin, right before they parted— so perhaps Kaelar assumed Saffron was being chaperoned by them?

All he knew was—as much as he wanted, he wasn't supposed to be left alone with Cylvan. If Taran found out, he would be furious. And the longer Saffron went without guidance, the higher his anxiety spiked—but Cylvan was always there, pressing a hand into the small of Saffron's back and encouraging him forward.

With every gentle touch, with every sense of Cylvan's perfume or the sight of his reassuring smile, Saffron's anxiety ebbed a little more. A little more. Saffron even slowly numbed to the turning heads and staring eyes, always seeking Cylvan out whenever anything made him self-conscious.

It was only when Saffron's attention snagged on a placard pinned to a board that he realized part of the potential reason so many people stared as he passed:

REPORT ALL IRON WITCHES
TO AUTHORITIES;

REPORT ALL SUSPECTED
USE OF IRON MAGIC.

Saffron knew from context what *iron witches* and *iron magic* referred to, immediately jolting backward and nearly knocking a group of strangers to the ground. He might have even bolted in the opposite direction, had the crowd on the street not been so thick, had Cylvan not suddenly curled an arm around his back.

Still, Saffron couldn't pull his eyes from the sign even as Cylvan comforted him. Branching off the O's of "iron witches" and "iron magic," he swore he recognized additional markings, searching his memory before realizing they were similar to some he'd seen in the Kyteler crypt. But the edges of the letters were so aged, the wood was so cracked and weathered, he decided he must have only been imagining it.

"The signs don't mean anything," Cylvan reassured in a low voice, coaxing Saffron to continue down the street. "It's social suicide to accuse someone else's beantighe of practicing taboo magic, worse than whatever reward they would receive. No one is going to bother us—especially when they see who is with you."

He said it so easily, so calmly, and Saffron nervously glanced up to meet his eyes. He immediately knew what Cylvan meant by *'when they see who is with you,'* as if no one would dare accuse the coming Night Prince of harboring an iron witch, at least so blatantly, especially not while Cylvan looked so intimidating. Wiping it from his mind, Saffron leaned in slightly to Cylvan's body as the prince maintained an arm over his shoulder, always meeting Saffron's pace as he balanced on his crutch.

One more thought itched at Saffron, though—and that was how, when Elluin first made her accusation of him in Danann House, Kaelar hardly bat an eye. How true could it really be that accusing someone's beantighe of iron magic was *social suicide*, when Kaelar was seemingly eager to sell Saffron out...?

Biting his lip, Saffron adjusted his veil, then checked the line of his buttoned sleeves, wishing to at least look as presentable as possible while people stared. Cylvan noticed, even helping to re-tuck Saffron's blouse into the back of his waistband. Saffron immediately flushed at the feeling of the prince's warm hand.

"We make a nice matching pair, don't you think?" He leaned in close again, clearly referring to how they both moved like dark shadows donning all black down the street. Saffron couldn't help but chuckle, taking the chance to adjust the buttons on Cylvan's sleeve cuff, too. Cylvan smiled like a hungry wolf, locking eyes over Saffron's shoulder with any pedestrians who dared let their gaze linger too long.

It was while he kept close that Saffron noticed a pattern of anyone passing by the Night Prince—once out of eyesight, they would let out a sigh, as if holding their breath, then pinch fingers together and draw an arch from shoulder to shoulder over their heads. The third time Saffron saw it, they stood at a pastry stand while Asche ordered something to eat, and the worker in the back made the same motion after turning their back. Saffron tugged on Cylvan's cape, and Cylvan leaned down to listen. Saffron made the motion in question, and Cylvan's smile turned sarcastic.

"They're cleansing themselves of my creeping Night," he whispered, and Saffron frowned. Cylvan mimicked the motion, explaining: "It's an old gesture of beseeching a Day Court. People also use it to cleanse themselves of bad luck, or if they think they've been cursed."

Saffron's frown sank further. He pinched his eyebrows before stubbornly making the same motion, but backward, sweeping it down over his chest from shoulder to shoulder. Cylvan laughed, shaking his head before gently taking Saffron's hand. He formed Saffron's fingers into a crescent, like a waxing moon from the tips of his fingers around the curve of his thumb.

"Now you can make the arch, if you really wish to beseech my calamity," Cylvan prompted. Saffron did—but wasn't expecting the melancholy smile that crossed the prince's face at the sight. Cylvan must not have expected it, either, because he quickly cleared his throat before turning to Asche and snapping at them to hurry up. Saffron just watched him, before gently clasping their hands beneath his cloak again. He would beseech Cylvan's Night Court every single day, if it comforted him to know there was at least one person who cared for him more than they feared his curse.

SAFFRON TRAILED BEHIND THE PRINCE AND THE DAURAE for the rest of the morning, occasionally slipping into silent ghost-liness, but regularly brought back to the land of the living every time Cylvan glanced over his shoulder to ensure Saffron still followed. Sometimes, he pointed out something pretty dangling from a shop window. He offered to buy Saffron a new jacket. Tucked a sugar-iced pastry into Saffron's hands and distracted him when someone turned their nose up or made the Day Court gesture again. Saffron sneered at one passerby when he noticed, and Cylvan snorted, before pulling a face, too—and they burst out laughing as the blood drained from the stranger's face.

But when Saffron was refused entry at the third shop in a row, Cylvan finally snapped. Pulling Saffron through the door anyway and into the back, he grabbed the veil and tugged it off. Saffron let out a small sound of surprise, nearly losing his teeth on the chain. Grappling for the chiffon on instinct, Cylvan was already wadding it up into a ball and tucking it into Saffron's hand.

"Taran's at a funeral in the next town; he won't be back for a few days, so you don't have to wear this until then. By royal decree. Danu bless. Amen."

Saffron flushed, but nodded, not expecting the intensity of Cylvan's tone—or the expression that came with it. Keeping Saffron's eyes with his, staring at him for a moment longer than would have been casual. When Cylvan's hand suddenly lifted to touch Saffron's face, then push his mussed hair back into place, Saffron held his breath.

"I prefer to see your face, anyway..." Cylvan mumbled, before pulling his hand back with what sounded like a tiny curse under his breath.

Cylvan was suddenly grabbed and yanked toward the boutique's fine clothes by Asche demanding attention. Cylvan stumbled after them, and Saffron took his first breath, hobbling his own way to a bench where he could sit and rest his leg—as well as his pounding heart.

Without the veil making him self-conscious, Saffron was able to enjoy the sight of Cylvan and his sibling rifling through clothes, changing into different jackets and skirts and blouses, pinched and prodded by the designer who offered all sorts of suggestions to adjust the fit. Every time Cylvan lifted his eyes to Saffron and asked what he thought, Saffron stiffened, opening his mouth and nearly speaking on instinct. Not that it mattered that he couldn't —his answer would have been exactly the same, every time.

You look beautiful, Cylvan.

Everything fits you perfectly.
You're always so handsome.

It made Saffron blush constantly, unable to keep away the bite-sized fantasies that formed whenever Cylvan pulled on another ensemble and looked more stunning than ever. With his broad shoulders and chest, narrow waist and hips, long legs that Saffron knew were stronger than they looked... even just watching his hands work over buttons and loops, Saffron was mesmerized by the tendons, the way the sharp points of his nails moved with perfect accuracy every time. His favorite moments were when Cylvan was in the middle of trying on something new, and Saffron was tasked with guarding his half-cloak and rapier, unable to resist breathing in the smell of him whenever no one was looking.

Was that what it would have been like to be Cylvan's... what? Saffron would never expect to be Cylvan's singular choice for a lover, especially since it was common for high fey, especially courtiers, to have a myriad of partners on the side. Even Luvon and his wife, Catrín, had wide circles of intimate friends they would go on long "trips" with.

But—despite being only a human, despite how he would live for only a fraction of Cylvan's natural life, despite being naïve with not a lot to offer, except maybe a few taboo arid spells for entertainment, Saffron didn't need anything more than to be Cylvan's simple peace. Someone he could rely on whenever needing warm affection or companionship or stress-relief. If it meant Saffron could enjoy the little things like following Cylvan between shops, complimenting his outfits, then later helping him back out of them again between groping hands and hot mouths... Saffron could be happy with a simple life like that.

At least—to fantasize about such a simple, joyful life made him happy. Maybe in another world, Saffron could have something so peaceful.

But in that where he walked, that simplicity was not possible. Not for him. Never for him, when there was too much else he'd seen, too many secrets he'd learned, too many risks he knew he would have to take because there were too many people he cared about protecting.

Saffron might never know what it was like to live a simple, peaceful, wonderful life with someone he cared for—but perhaps, if he did everything he could, he could ensure that opportunity for someone else like him in the future.

That person—might even be the same handsome Night Prince in front of him.

29

THE SYMBOL

Once he noticed it, Saffron couldn't stop seeing it. That symbol from the iron witch warning placard, that circular mark with the pointing arrow. The one he recognized from the books in the Kyteler crypt that were indicative of arid magic.

On signs, on lantern posts, sometimes carved into doors or engraved into cobblestones. Always small enough to blend with the texture of the background, easy to miss unless someone was specifically looking. And Saffron was.

When he spotted it on the hanging sign of a bookstore—Saffron's instincts claimed him in an instant, grabbing Cylvan's hand and pulling him back to point and silently beg. It took only that one moment of Saffron's captured interest for Cylvan to lose track of wherever they'd been heading, steering Saffron straight through the doors in an instant. Saffron bit back a laugh.

It was, perhaps, the only time and place Saffron could lose interest in Cylvan entirely.

The bookshop on the other side of the doors was even larger than the Grand Library on campus. With a fireplace burning in the middle of the main atrium, the air smelled of warm cedar and coffee from the counter on the far wall, chairs and couches spotted with patrons lost between pages while more people milled between the shelves on the first, second, and third floors. *Three floors of books.*

It must have been clear on Saffron's face, because Cylvan leaned in close from behind, handing him a piece of folded parchment.

"Don't look so excited, and try to avoid drawing attention to yourself," he said in a low voice, before adding at a normal volume: "Gather these books for me, will you, beantighe?"

Saffron nodded right away, unfolding the paper—before pausing, and looking at Cylvan again with his eyebrows raised.

Anything you like.

Really? He mouthed, and Cylvan smiled mischievously.

"I mean it," he said. "Anything at all."

Saffron could have kissed him. He almost did—but managed to channel that enthralled energy into Cylvan's hand, grabbing and squeezing it hard enough that the prince barked and laughed. Cylvan nudged Saffron forward to get started, patting his ass in encouragement and making Saffron yelp and he hurried down the stairs.

Mythology and Folklore; Classic Literature; History of Alvish Courts; Opulentology (Applied and Theory); Saffron could have spent hours, weeks, years just *looking*, let alone actually grabbing books to pull down and read. Less than an hour into his search, he already had one of the push-carts full to the brim with anything at all that caught his interest, whether by title, subject, or even just the way the cover looked. There were even entire sections dedicated to fine art and drawing, and he scoured every single volume for any and all references he could get his hands on. He even picked up a sketchbook the size of his palm, unable to resist the gold-leaf filigree around the edges.

Yet, in the back of his mind, there was a constant reminder of the specific things he needed, but couldn't seem to find. Arid magic, Aridology, Gaeilge language reference, Ogham-Arid reference... no matter where he looked, in the Opulence sections, Language sections, History sections, he continuously came up blank.

Finally, he located a far corner labeled *Linguistics and Anthropology*, searching the shelves with a finger touching every single spine so he wouldn't miss anything on accident. When one did catch his eye, he stretched on his toes as tall as he could go, extending his arm overhead but still coming in just shy of grabbing it. He almost lost his balance, but upon grabbing the edge of the shelf, he paused. His fingers draped over something carved into the edge of the wood, sensing the texture not unlike when he found the carving beneath his bed in the attic.

Engraved in the fibers, small and faded enough that it could go as easily missed as all the others in the city, a familiar circle-and-arrow shape greeted him. Its placement at the end of the row reminded him of the signs on the shelves in the Kyteler crypt, and he curiously stepped to the next line down the way. He bit back an excited smile at the sight of another symbol. That time, however, the direction of the arrow was tilted, slightly. As if indicating direction.

Keeping out of the way of fey patrons, Saffron carefully followed every symbol that preceded the first, more than once losing his way as some were so worn down they barely existed. The trail ran cold as he reached the far corner of the third floor, all the way in the back with walls stacked high with what looked like spillover inventory. There, he was met with only a mirror as tall as he was.

He frowned at the reflection gazing back at him, barely recognizing them, never before having any desire to know what every inch of himself looked like—but then his curiosity prickled, suddenly suspicious that there was some sort of charm on the glass. The unfamiliarity with his own reflection stemmed from how it appeared to smooth his skin, brighten his eyes and cheeks, dull the appearance of his scars. He nearly turned away in annoyance, before spotting the decorative gilding around every edge of the frame. He crouched to appreciate the artistic touch, even though it meant he remained within the reflected stranger's line of sight the entire time.

A variety of soft greens, blues, and gold adorned the glass in shapes of ferns, flowers, vines, berries, and long grasses, encircling every side as if the viewer gazed into a reflecting pool. It charmed him instantly, smiling to himself—before spotting the arid circle-and-arrow marking in the bottom corner. Nestled within a bundle of gold-painted rowan berries, his heart flipped in a sense of validation. That time, the symbol pointed straight up, as if indicating there used to be a passageway straight ahead of him. He tried not to be too disappointed, realizing he might have been following a long-dead trail left by ghosts as old as the Kyteler students still haunting the ruins.

He almost touched the symbol in reverence, but resisted. The last thing he wanted was for anyone who might be watching to notice and wonder what had the black-clad beantighe so curious in the furthest reaches of the bookstore. Clearly, the markings were only meant to be seen by the people meant to see them—and Saffron wasn't sure he was one of those chosen few. Despite being human, despite seeking information about aridity, there was still a part of him that felt like an imposter at the idea of declaring himself an arid witch or user or practitioner or any of those labels.

He regarded the decorative edges of the mirror one more time, before finally rising to his feet. At the last second, he touched the mirror in curiosity, pulling away again when it was warm beneath his fingers. His thoughts wandered, and a sudden idea struck him.

In the Kyteler crypt, they'd asked him to answer a question only a human would know the answer to. His response of "*Cerberus*," referring to a human Greek myth, was enough to open the door to the stairs. He'd thought it'd been the spirits to open the door for him—but he suddenly wondered if that wasn't the case. What if his answer satisfied some sort of vocal enchant-ment? Sunbeam mentioned spoken magic systems, didn't she? And the beannighe spoke so insistently about naming objects to control them, even going so far as to claim true fey names were just arid magic...

Perhaps they were the same concept? Perhaps something similar applied to the door into the crypt? Perhaps—something like that was common across all sorts of secret arid places?

The trail of the marks ended at that mirror, which might have been enough to halt his search, except that something about the verdant designs around the edges reminded him a little too much of another human myth he'd spent nights pouring over. *Echo and Narcissus.*

The problem was—even if Saffron was right, and the mirror would respond to a spoken command, he didn't know the ques-tion. Even if he did, he couldn't speak it out loud.

He thought back to the myth, gazing at himself in the reflec-tion. He knew his eyes weren't *that* green, his face wasn't *that* pretty, his teeth weren't *that* brilliant—but perhaps the glass wasn't meant for someone like him, despite the arid symbol in the bottom corner. For all he knew, the mirror had been charmed long before or after it was marked, and was never meant to be anything more than a unique toy for high fey bookstore patrons to *ooh* and *ahh* over when they passed by. He could even imagine Asche responding the same way, before searching every inch to learn every magic ingredient that went into the charm.

The irony made Saffron smirk. Did passing fey find their visages so lovely and perfect and beautiful that they stood there appreciating themselves like Narcissus in the human myth?

His heart thrummed. Another thought tested him, though he knew it likely stemmed from the same desperate urge that searched for connections where they might not exist.

Why would human spells use fey language?

Why would the voices in the crypt ask a question any fey could answer?

What was the opposite of how a high fey would respond to a charmed mirror like that?

Saffron felt foolish, but decided to try just one thing to ease his curious urges. It was easier to swallow the appearance of foolishness knowing he was far away from any potentially searching eyes, at least.

He pictured a pretty fey cooing over their reflection in the mirror—and did the opposite by closing his eyes. The opposite of a fey's reaction would be to not see himself at all, right? To block his vision. To be un-tempted by the face that gazed back at him. But upon extending his hand, he still only found solid glass blocking his path.

Sighing, he opened his eyes again in disappointment—only to find a fellow moon-eared human smirking over his shoulder. Saffron jumped, whirling around to meet her.

"You've got the right idea," she encouraged, and Saffron's cheeks flushed hot in embarrassment.

He put his hands up in defense, smiling awkwardly to insist he wasn't trying anything strange—only to raise them higher in surprise when the stranger suddenly rushed him. Saffron instinctively stumbled away—only to trip backward, tumbling through the mirror and landing on the other side.

30

THE DEALER

Saffron's head clunked against a wood floor, groaning and rubbing the back of his skull in annoyance. But upon cracking open his eyes, he realized immediately, he was no longer in the same section of the library. Scrambling upright, feet nearly tangling in his crutch, he faced a classic painting of Narcissus hanging on the wall in front of him—then screamed when someone suddenly poked their head through with an excited grin.

"Welcome," they said, phasing through the rest of the way. "I was wondering if you'd figure it out. I'm impressed, especially since I haven't seen you around Connacht before. And..."

She glanced up and down Saffron's outfit.

"... Well, considering what you're wearing... perhaps I shouldn't be all that surprised. Let me guess, you've been caught practicing once before, already?"

"Not exactly," Saffron mouthed—before realizing the words escaped no differently than when speaking in the mist. He squeaked in surprise, hand flying to his mouth. "Oh, god, I can speak here too!"

"Those are some nasty pieces of silver you've got there," the stranger went on in consideration, stepping in to touch one of his cuffs. "You need help getting them off? I can give them a name for you, if you want."

"They..." Saffron laughed awkwardly at the sudden closeness. "They're paired with a ring, already, I think..."

"Ah," she sighed, taking her hand back. "Sorry to hear that. Then is there anything else I can help you with, sweetie?"

Saffron took a tiny step back. He glanced around where he'd fallen through, slightly comforted when the interior of the room matched that of the library on the other side of the passageway that had since become a painting. Even taking a step toward the window and stretching to look, he recognized the Connacht street on the other side. He really had just fallen through some secret portal in the mirror.

The room where they stood was circular, with a corridor branching off into a neighboring space of the same size. Both were lined with bookshelves stacked high with spines of every color, language, age, and Saffron nearly vanished into scouring them instantly. He only stopped upon seeing the line of what looked like red paint around the edge of the floor, interspersed with randomly-spaced black candles flickering with crimson flames.

"What... is this place?" He finally asked, glancing back to the portrait entrance, then to the woman. She wasn't as muscular or tall as Sunbeam, but carried an equally intimidating air of 'prepared to break Saffron's arm if he asked the wrong questions or gave her the impression he wasn't someone who could be trusted.' He decided it would be best to keep his companionship with the literal Prince of Alfidel under wraps.

"You're looking for arid tomes, aren't you? That's why you followed the iron symbols around on the third floor," she asked, and Saffron nodded after a moment of hesitation. He realized then, she wore the embroidered blouse and apron of a bookstore employee.

Saffron raised his eyebrows, then bounced slightly on his toes as the woman raised her eyebrows, too, then nodded her head toward the books at her back. "Well, whaddya need?"

His heart thumped hard enough that his mouth dropped open.

"These—! These are—!"

"Yeah," she laughed, crossing her arms and leaning back against the shelf. "And I'm your local dealer. Is there anything specific you're looking for?"

That question wasn't nearly specific enough.

Saffron wanted everything. All of it. Every single book on those shelves. Cylvan promised to buy anything he wanted, right? How could he organize the transportation of every arid book in that hidden library, without anyone finding out?

No, no—he shouldn't take all of them just for himself. Where would he even keep them?

"Um... ah..." He stammered, still too overwhelmed to form a coherent thought. "What about... Gaeilge? Gaeilge dictionaries? Alvish to Gaeilge...?"

"Oh, sure." The woman nodded like it was nothing. "For what level? I have basic, beginner, intermediate, advanced, and oath-taken."

Saffron stared at her in silence. She laughed as if he wasn't the first completely ignorant fool to literally stumble into her secret corner of illegal books.

"Do you have anything that's just..." he wheezed. "General use?"

"Ha—sure. Wait here, the barrier's only in this part."

"The barrier?" Saffron asked, skimming the floor encircled by candles again as the woman left through the corridor into the neighboring room. She called out from where she scoured the shelves:

"You're in an anti-opulence circle, it's the reason you can speak despite the silver."

"Right..." Saffron said, unable to resist a tiny smile of familiarity. "I've actually seen something like this, before. How does it work?"

"Just like any other arid-ogham circle," she answered. "The candles are standing in for feda marks."

"How?" Saffron asked again, crouching on the balls of his feet to observe the nearest one. Despite flickering with life and dripping over the edges, he couldn't tell if the black wax actually melted. "Is it, um... oh, what did Henmother Salma call it? Delivering... thunder?"

"*Asunder?*" The woman clarified with a friendly smile, returning to the front room with a thick book in her hand. It was the size of Saffron's palm, leatherbound with shiny red-sprayed pages. "Not exactly—this circle is delivered perennially through the flames. Erm—that means *always,* unless disturbed. Deliverance is just a transfer of energy, and fire is a form elemental energy, right? Actually, here. Take this, too. I can tell by your face, you need it."

She grabbed one of a multitude of thin, hand-bound books piled on the shelf, handing it to him.

Intro to Aridity: A Beginner's Guide to Magical Terms, Crafting, Spells, and Concepts for Spring Witches.

"Oh..." Saffron said breathlessly. He trailed fingers down the cover page. "What's a *spring witch?*"

"A rookie," she smirked, and he pouted. He couldn't argue, though.

"Then an *iron witch* is technically...?"

"Someone formally trained in aridity."

"Hm," he huffed through his nose, flipping quickly through the pages. A handful of terms he skimmed were familiar from Baba Yaga's grimoire, and his heart skipped excitedly. "How can I buy these? Surely I don't take them to the front counter...?"

"Oh, *Christ,* don't do that," she snorted.

"Actually... my name is Saffron."

"... Right. Sorry. I'm Pimbry," she chuckled, putting out a hand to shake. Saffron just stared at it, suddenly confused. Were they making a deal...? When he didn't respond, she pulled it back.

"It's nice to meet you, Saffron. Do you only have a beantighe name? Do you need help picking another one?"

Saffron raised his eyebrows, then shook his head. "No. I like my name."

"It's very pretty," Pimbry agreed with a nod, before touching the books in his hands. "Consider these gifts, little witch. The only cost is that you protect them, continue learning all you can, and teach any other humans who come along after you. Agreed?"

"O-oh!" Saffron inhaled sharply. "Um, thank you, of course!"

Pimbry nodded with another smile.

"Good," she said, before grabbing a white stick candle from the sconce on the wall. Adjusting the books to lay flat in Saffron's hands, she poured melted wax into the top corners of both, before stamping them with an iron seal donning feda marks.

The amethyst pendant down Saffron's blouse suddenly burned hot, making him jump. Scrambling for it, he grabbed it right as Pimbry tilted her head in curiosity.

"I should probably get going," Saffron said, realizing Cylvan must be looking for him. He offered Pimbry a bow of gratitude, promising to pay forward the cost of the books like she asked. She thanked him, wishing him luck and walking him back through the portrait to the main shop—but they barely crossed through before a horned fey swept around the end of the shelves, eyes wide and frenzied.

"Saffron!" He practically shouted, grabbing Saffron's arm to pull him away—but Pimbry stepped in suddenly, breaking Cylvan's grasp without hesitation. Cylvan turned on her with fury, half a second from ripping her apart had Saffron not rushed between them and stole Cylvan's attention back. He waved his hands to assure the prince it wasn't anything to worry about, trying to show Cylvan the books to prove it—only then realizing the wax seal had glamoured them to pass as tourist pamphlets.

Saffron turned to Pimbry again, bowing one last time in gratitude, and Cylvan noticed. His emotions tempered in an instant, though he still grabbed Saffron's arm and held it tightly. He and

Pimbry locked eyes, and the woman nearly spoke to ask if there was anything he needed—

"There are witchhunters patrolling the walkway right outside," Cylvan told her in a low voice, and Pimbry's expression flickered in surprise, then darkened. "More are gathering. There are others glamoured inside the store. Get every human you know and leave."

"I'm afraid I don't know what you mean, your highness," she answered flatly. Cylvan wrinkled his nose, practically sneering in impatience, clearly so agitated his cool and calm demeanor had sloughed away entirely.

"Then so be it. But I warned you."

Pimbry stared at him. Saffron did, too—but Cylvan wasn't going to wait for another reply. He squeezed Saffron's arm again, offering Pimbry one last nod of finality, before pulling Saffron away. Saffron glanced over his shoulder to where they'd left the human woman who'd helped him—but she was gone in an instant.

THE SCORN

They barely made it to the bottom of the stairs when the shop's front doors slammed open, a flurry of armed guards rushing inside. Cylvan immediately grabbed Saffron around the waist and pulled him back, but the guards swarmed the bookstore without giving them a second glance. Shoving the other assistants away, they spread out between the shelves, barking commands at employees and patrons, alike. It was no time at all before there was a crash from an upper floor—and Saffron's breaths turned icy at the sight of Pimbry forcibly dragged down the stairs between two sets of commanding arms.

Every lingering high fey erupted into conspiratorial gasps, staring as Pimbry was forced out the front door. The witnesses raced after them to see what would happen on the street right outside.

Saffron lunged to follow, too, but Cylvan grabbed his crutch and stopped him. Saffron twisted and wrenched free without argument, shoving through the pursuing crowd and emerging into overcast light and the start of rain outside.

He barely knew her. They'd barely exchanged more than a few words of shared understanding and camaraderie. She asked if he needed help. She asked what he was looking for—then offered it to him for free. Eagerly. Encouraging him to continue arid work in the shadows of the high fey who wished to eradicate it from Alfidel. She was—proof that Saffron wasn't alone. Baba Yaga wasn't alone. There were other humans trying to reclaim their magic, too. They were only out of sight.

In Pimbry's face as she was dragged away—Saffron saw the spirits of the Kyteler School. He heard rushing feet on the stairs to and from the crypt, arms heavy-laden with the same books protected behind the charmed mirror on the third floor. Desperate attempts to keep their magic, their culture, their heritage safe and alive so it wouldn't go extinct like the high fey in power wanted.

Saffron smelled the smoke of buildings burning. He heard the screams—

No, those weren't the cries of students in his head. They were the people on the street.

Burn her.

Try her.

Iron witch.

Rowan witch.

Burn, burn, burn.

If high fey chanted those words in King Ailir's Day Court—Saffron couldn't imagine what calls reverberated through the sky in Proserpina's Night.

Elluin's threat burrowed deeper into the marrow of his bones.

You'll undergo the five trials of aridity used by Queen Proserpina.

Prove you can perform arid magic at will…

Or I will force your henmother to perform them.

Everyone will be investigated and tried with conspiracy.

Burn them. Try them.

Iron witch. Rowan witch.

Burn, burn, burn—

Saffron shoved his way through the crowd, to the front of the line.

Pimbry was pushed to her knees in the road. The excited, jeering crowd quickly formed a circle around her as guards stood at the ready, though gave a wide berth. She said nothing, just stubbornly blew a piece of dark brown hair from her eyes.

"Pimbry Scott," the head of the guard announced, reading from a long scroll in his hands. In the dim light, Saffron noticed innumerable other names written down it, some marked off and at least a dozen more unaccounted for underneath. A horrifying thought struck him—was Baba Yaga's name somewhere on a list like that because of Elluin's accusation? Was Saffron's?

A hand suddenly grappled the back of Saffron's shirt, before hooking around his elbow and roughly yanking him back. Saffron stumbled, before locking his good leg and meeting eyes with Cylvan. The prince's expression was contorted in a mix of anger and panic, attempting again to pull Saffron away, but Saffron grit his teeth and shook his head. Cylvan's expression abandoned any gentleness that remained, grip tightening enough that Saffron's arm bruised beneath it. Around them, bystanders recognized the Night Prince, throwing looks before whispering to one another, attempting to give him as much room as they did the human on the road. Cylvan noticed—but not because they'd noticed *him*. Because their eyes always turned to Saffron, next.

"It's time to leave, beantighe," Cylvan growled through clenched teeth. "You do everything I say, remember? *Without question.*"

Saffron knew why Cylvan spoke that way, especially with so many listening ears around them—but the words were cold and harsh, his expression furious enough that Saffron's heart raced with an ounce of fear. Still—he shook his head. He silently pleaded for Cylvan to *wait*, just wanting to see if there was anything he could do—but Cylvan still pulled. He continued to dominate Saffron's balance, and might have grabbed Saffron off his feet entirely if the crowd wasn't so thick around them.

Twisting his arm, Saffron managed to break Cylvan's grasp again, though only momentarily. Cylvan's hand returned to his elbow in less than a second, but Saffron was already turning back to the scene unfolding. The crowd roared again and drowned out any more words Cylvan attempted.

The guard with the list continued speaking, and the crowd fell silent at the words *iron trials*. Elluin's words rang in Saffron's head.

Cylvan's grip twisted harder, snarling Saffron's name under his breath, but Saffron barely heard it. He barely saw what was happening in front of him at all—he just saw Baba Yaga on her knees where Pimbry Scott sat. He saw the students of the Kyteler School. He saw—himself, one day, inevitably, where he would have to kneel in front of Elluin, too.

One of the guards wearing a vaguely familiar, triangular silver brooch stepped forward, uncorking a glass bottle of opalescent liquid. He forced Pimbry's mouth open to drink it, and Pimbry never looked away. She never flinched. Just gulped it back before jerking free from the man's hand.

The crowd went silent. Even Saffron's heart stopped, watching, waiting, as if he knew what would come.

"Saffron, please—" Cylvan's voice swept close, sounding desperate. *"Don't watch this."*

But Saffron couldn't look away. Not while the woman's eyes traveled around the edge of the circle, as if searching for something. Saffron followed her gaze as it paused, and he saw other human bookstore attendants clustered in a shadowed alleyway at the back of the crowd. They stared at her, too, stone-faced and empty.

She smiled and nodded at them—then erupted into orange flames.

A shriek tore from her mouth, splitting the rainy air and cascading across the dark clouds overhead. The crowd surged backward, almost knocking Saffron to the ground. Cylvan's arms caught and encircled him instantly.

Protected against the rushing feet and shoving elbows of onlookers, Saffron only saw the orange flames, so unnaturally bright. He felt the heat of them on his face. Heard how they devoured every one of the woman's screams of agony like burning leaves. Cylvan's hand attempted to cover Saffron's eyes—but Saffron shoved it back down, only to desperately cling to Cylvan's wrist as every inch of him trembled in fear.

Pimbry Scott's skin bubbled. Blistered. Burned away, as if devoured from the inside out. But even as she screamed, as she collapsed to her side, as her body desiccated into a pile of ash, Saffron never took his eyes away.

His breaths hitched as Pimbry's cries trailed off into a moan—and then silence. Saffron held his breath until he couldn't, inhaling sharp enough that it was a cry in itself.

Cylvan finally had enough. He pressed his hand over Saffron's eyes, and Saffron flared with bright emotions, attempting to scream, choker cutting him short as he thrashed and attempted to pull free again. But Cylvan was stronger. He was always stronger.

"Your highness," a voice came from behind, and Saffron fell still again in an instant. Cylvan turned slowly, and Saffron followed, glancing over his shoulder to find the man with the familiar silver brooch smiling at them. "I did not realize we had such a prominent witness to this horrible affair. I do hope you know Connacht is not rife with iron witchcraft."

Cylvan didn't answer for a long time. When he did, Saffron didn't recognize his voice. It belonged to a stranger—to someone who knew exactly how to speak when on display.

"I am impressed with your swift actions, general."

"Thank you, your highness. Ah—would you and the daurae like to assist in cleansing the shop? It would be an honor for our city."

Cylvan paused again. His hands around Saffron's body held him tightly, as if remaining completely still would allow him to go unnoticed. Saffron's heart just pounded in his ears, staring through fuzzy vision as Pimbry's body smoldered in the middle of the road. Would no one come to take her?

"Asche," Cylvan's cold voice called out. "Come here."

He released Saffron, and Saffron sank to his knees. He stared at what remained of Pimbry Scott, before the sound of new flames caught his attention. Looking over his shoulder again, he watched in silence as Daurae Asche shakily used their fire to light a torch in Cylvan's hand. Cylvan took it—and threw it through the front window of the bookstore. With a gust of wind from his hands, the fire inside swelled, kissing every page within reach. An entire shop destroyed—because of one hint of arid magic.

Even just having them drawn in your book...

If anyone found you with them, they would execute you on the spot...

And investigate every single person you've ever spoken to.

It was no different from Cylvan's warning in his suite. Anything, everything, any person who even brushed up against arid magic—was destroyed upon discovery.

Did high fey really fear human magic that much—or did they merely despise it?

Saffron felt nothing except the warmth on his back. The bookstore succumbed to the fire with ease, every text inside devoured by Asche's flames sweltering beneath Cylvan's ecouraging wind. In the back of Saffron's waistband remained the only two books to survive—books that would have earned him a body of charred flesh just like the person burned alive on the street in front of him.

Even if he found a way to protect Cylvan. Protect Baba Yaga. Protect his friends. It didn't matter—because the only way to do so—was through the magic that would get them killed for simply knowing him, anyway.

He would inevitably die by the only thing that could save him.

Saffron suddenly comprehended exactly how, the way Cylvan originally tricked him into learning arid magic, from the very beginning—was so heartless.

32

THE REMAINS

Kaelar thought Saffron had been with Eias and Magnin.

Eias and Magnin looked at him like he was an idiot.

Cylvan claimed Taran asked Asche to keep an eye on the beantighe, and Asche nodded like it was a fib they'd already practiced. Saffron just stood in silence while everyone discussed whose burden it should have been to watch him.

He wasn't allowed to enter the restaurant they choose for dinner, so he stood by the door. When asked to wait somewhere else by the owner, he stood a little farther away. When too many people bumped into him on purpose, spit on him, cursed him after gossip spread about the arid witches in the bookshop, Saffron found a quiet place around the corner to wait, instead. He wasn't sure how long he did, staring blankly at his feet while his ears rang, far away from the rest of the world.

Eventually, Kaelar stumbled drunk around the corner looking for him, trapping him against the wall and planting a wet kiss on his cheek. Saffron barely felt it. He might not have felt anything at all, though Eias still tore around the corner and dragged Kaelar away.

Returning to the inn, the fey retired to their rooms amongst drunken conversation and laughter, while Saffron hovered in the main sitting area. Cylvan approached with a drunken flush in his cheeks just like the others, touching Saffron's shoulder and asking if he wanted anything for dinner. Saffron shrugged away from him on instinct, not quite sure why. He shook his head with an empty smile, motioning for Cylvan to go to bed. Cylvan hesitated, but nodded, looking like he wished to say something else—but instead averted his eyes, and left.

Saffron didn't light a candle against the lessening sunlight. He sat on the buttonback couch by himself, staring down at the smoke-rich Gaeilge book on his lap. He barely managed to hook a finger under the cover—before emotion flooded him, and he had to press a hand to his mouth to keep the gasps at bay.

The sun fully set and Saffron vanished into the darkness. Tears streamed silently from his eyes, hardly moving except to breathe. He replayed the events over and over again. Not to search for a way he could have stopped them, or to reiterate how close he'd come to his own death, or anything else—except to simply force himself to relive every moment for the sake of penance to the woman who had died right in front of him. To recall all the arid books lost because of him. It felt selfish not to force himself to witness the mistake again and again and again and again. Selfish. Impertinent. Arrogant.

Hours passed, and he was suddenly met with sniffling. Shuffling feet. The buzz of a presence that approached him.

Lifting his head, Saffron found Asche facing him in the darkness. Their face was puffy and wet from crying, and Saffron assumed it was from another nightmare. Uncurling his locked limbs, he intended to search the kitchenette for tea to brew, but Asche slumped down on the couch, first, and took Saffron's hand.

"C-c-can I ask you something?" They stammered between weak sobs. "You will l-laugh, but I have to know."

Saffron nodded. He pushed past the ringing in his ears, having grown used to it in the silence. Asche's voice was loud in comparison, though Saffron knew they were only whispering.

"I-I had no choice, didn't I?" Their face contorted more before hunching forward and crying into their hands. "I had no choice but to burn everything, right? No one believes I did that—because I wanted to, right?"

Saffron turned the question over more than once, wondering at first if Asche was as drunk as the rest of them. But then he recalled the first conversation between them and Cylvan, the night Saffron brewed lavender tea. About Asche's nightmares, burning down King Tross' design room, needing to practice their Sídhe ability more, calling it *unpredictable*, being too afraid to talk about it...

The image of Pimbry Scott's skin blistering, splitting, burning away surged into Saffron's memory. The peeling tear of screams as the flames devoured her.

Saffron didn't actually know whether or not Asche could have refused. Saffron didn't know anything about that moment from Asche's perspective, or even from Cylvan's, or the pressure felt by the both of them to be perfect royal children punishing humans performing taboo magic. With everyone watching. With rumors already spreading.

Cylvan was supposed to be different—but Saffron was suddenly unsure of that, too. Cylvan, who descended from Proserpina. Who never even once mentioned Taran's lineage as reason to refuse the marriage. Who barked at Asche to contribute flames, who used his wind to embolden them to devour everything inside.

Who—tried so hard to pull Saffron away. To cover his eyes so he wouldn't see. Who even told Pimbry Scott about the oncoming threat, giving her just enough time to get all of the other humans out of the shop...

Asche's whole body shook. Their muscles clenched, clinging to Saffron's arm as if desperate for an answer. Saffron knew nothing—but even so, he wouldn't deny someone so young, so broken, a safe place to rest their head.

He put his hand on Asche's clinging to him, then nudged one of their horns. Asche lifted their puffy, swollen eyes, and Saffron managed to smile calmly.

I believe you, he mouthed as clearly as he could. Then he brushed some hair from Asche's eyes, summoning the daurae's head to his lap. Asche collapsed without hesitation, face scrunching up as they sobbed further, tears soaking Saffron's blouse while they cried until nothing was left. Saffron brushed their hair as they did, closing his eyes, holding his breath.

For just a moment, Saffron wondered if a younger Cylvan ever had anyone to hear his sobs. To hold him, to offer reassurances of his inherent goodness, too. Was that why Asche cried as if they had blood on their hands? Because they saw what happened to their brother, and they were terrified of a simple mistake being used against them by someone like Taran mac Delbaith, while everyone else in the world thought them to be bloodthirsty and wild and cursed to bring calamity and misfortune?

Saffron clenched his teeth. He focused on comforting the daurae whose weeping slowly petered out, giving way to hiccupping breaths and whispers of apology. Saffron just kept brushing their blonde hair until, eventually, their breaths settled into the predictable rhythm of sleep.

Saffron closed his eyes, holding the daurae protectively as a myriad of understanding rained down over him.

Maybe Cylvan really was different, like Saffron hoped.

Cylvan was also afraid.

Cylvan was trapped in a desperate, but futile performance for Alfidel of who they thought he should be—and the person Saffron knew in secret, in private, was actually who he wished to be.

Perhaps Asche was different, too—but they'd learned what was right and what was wrong by watching how people treated their brother.

Perhaps Asche feared their own magic, their fire, so much that they even refused to practice at home—because they were terrified to one day be as ostracized as their brother for an act they were forced to perform.

33

THE PARTY

Perched on the cushioned sill of the inn window, Saffron held his hand through the pane. Loose raindrops speckled his knuckles, his dry nailbeds, the heavy opal ring on his finger. The day prior had passed in a blur, spotted with vague memories of waiting outside while the others ate breakfast, shopping with Kaelar while Cylvan and Asche hung close by, eating lunch on the river, preparing for a fete that coming night. He'd spent the entire day avoiding eyes, avoiding drawing any attention to himself at all, though constantly smelled burning flesh on the air.

Every hidden arid symbol around the city, including on the first declaration where Saffron noticed it, had been scratched off overnight. In one devouring flame, in one destroyed bookstore, underground iron magic was successfully purged from Connacht. Saffron had made Connacht unsafe for arid humans—and he had never felt so numb.

With Taran still away at his family funeral, Kaelar made sure to strip Saffron out of his black clothes of disgrace for something a little more fitting, something a little more revealing, talking the whole time about how excited he was to show off his first official beantighe-pet. Saffron never resisted, never protested, ears ringing as he pushed every thought away instead.

A pale blue, sheer wrap-blouse pulled open in the front to expose the length of his neck, the intersection of his collarbones, and a wide line of skin; a soft corset belt that gathered spilling fabric at his waist; high-waisted taupe pants that clung tighter than he knew possible, laced down the front between his hips; boots with an inch of heel that clacked with every step; hair coiffed out of his face. Saffron didn't look like a beantighe. In some ways, he even looked like any other high fey, except a little uglier, a little shorter, and with ears that never fully grew into points.

Upon catching his reflection in the mirror on the way out, he couldn't decide if he liked it, or hated it so much he nearly tore his skin off. Especially with the silver choker on full display like any other piece of jewelry, like something pretty meant to be shown off. He couldn't look for too long, else he might actually be sick.

Not used to showing off so much skin, Saffron felt every eye that looked as he and Kaelar joined the others near the front entrance of the inn. Asche, clearly trying to pretend like the day and night prior never happened, squealed and complimented him. Then Eias approached to fix the way his shirt bundled aesthetically over the corset belt, mumbling about how surprised they were that Saffron could clean up at all. Saffron just kept his eyes low. He didn't need to be reminded of how shocked they could all be when he was dressed in expensive clothes, made to look "presentable" by fey standards. Like a little cat put in a bow.

Eias and Magnin weren't ones for indulgent parties, and Cylvan outright refused to allow Asche anywhere near a party where there would be copious amounts of drugs and drinking, so the three of them went their own way once the group emerged back onto the road. Saffron watched them go, then glanced back at Cylvan, whose eyes hovered over Saffron's collar. It was the first time he'd seen it so outright—but he said nothing, turning away and motioning that they should get going. Saffron and Kaelar followed behind him.

The prince's outfit was simple that night, though no less regal than usual. He wore a rich, dark blue tunic cinched at the waist with a thick belt, a smiling crescent moon like the profile of a person as the buckle. The tunic fabric was thick, especially along the bottom seam where embroidery and beading swirled along the hem, hanging long enough that it could have passed as a short dress. Still, Cylvan wore shiny hosen underneath, legs sinking into knee-high boots laced all the way down the front and with heels only slightly higher than Saffron's. Following him down the walkway, Saffron spotted the wide keyhole in the back of the tunic, last, flushing slightly at the visible smoothness of Cylvan's skin underneath.

Heads turned for a different reason that time, and Saffron pretended it was simply because Cylvan was the most beautiful thing beneath the moon—not because of the bookstore fire. Not because of the gossip. Cylvan was simply impossible to ignore.

It admittedly made Saffron more self-conscious to be dressed in such a revealing top after trying so hard to blend in, scowling down at the bare skin of his chest as they walked. Kaelar kept a hand on his lower back the whole time, which didn't help his nerves. Saffron just watched the way Cylvan's legs moved. The rhythmic sound of his heels against the cobblestones. The way his long loose hair swayed back and forth with every step.

Arriving at their destination, the smell of incense struck Saffron before the full sight of the interior did. Blinking a few times as they passed through a curtain to the other side, fire bowls and torches illuminated a great room filled with bodies standing, reclining, chatting, laughing. A cerulean pool sank into the floor just inside the entrance, swimming with fish of every color. Where the pool ended, thick rugs decorated the stone floors, and open spaces overflowed with pillows, tables, blankets, bottles of wine, and trays of fruit, with additional spreads of food on opposite sides of the room. Anywhere uncovered by rugs sprawled with tiled mosaics, and Saffron might have lost himself in them had Kaelar not nudged him farther inside.

Enormous floral bunches mixed with the incense burning in thick clouds, swirling from golden animal heads on chains between white stone columns. The cacophony of scents made Saffron drowsy, aromas seducing everyone who entered the room into a state of relaxation. Saffron didn't know if he appreciated it or not; at least it wafted away just as quickly as it burned, swept up through the open ceiling where the night sky boasted a few pinpricks of stars between clouds.

Saffron barely took another step as Kaelar's hand encouraged, but Cylvan appeared suddenly and offered an opaque, pink-tinged drink in a champagne glass. The prince held his own in a different color, and Saffron swore he recognized the edges of an apple notch floating on top. He nearly lunged to take it away, but Cylvan met his eyes and offered a subtle shake of his head. Saffron gulped.

"So the beantighe doesn't get sick later and ruin the fun," Cylvan interjected Saffron's thoughts with an unreadable smile. Kaelar seemed equally surprised at the offer, but then jostled Saffron with a laugh and tipped the glass between his lips. Saffron had no choice to swallow, or else drown. Saffron silently begged Cylvan knew was he was doing. He silently begged—

Cylvan was different.

The prince was pulled in another direction not much later, a dozen voices and pairs of hands coaxing him toward a cluster of pillows in the back corner. Saffron wasn't prepared for the swarming jealousy unleashed in his chest like wasps, tinged with additional bitterness as he knew those same people were the ones gesturing Day Court arches over their heads when Cylvan wasn't looking. To suck up to his face, but curse him behind his back—if Saffron wasn't immediately pulled in the opposite direction, he might have shoved his way through the crowd to go wherever Cylvan did. To smack any ugly, arrogant fey face that so dared as sneer with his crutch.

That was, until Kaelar grabbed Saffron's crutch and tossed it away with the cloaks on the wall. Saffron was reduced to hopping on one leg while clinging to Kaelar, which was clearly Kaelar's intention, but Saffron still did everything he could not to make contact more than he had to. Whenever he did, he made sure to pull on the back of Kaelar's shirt for balance, choking him at the collar. To grab a handful of fabric and take a fistful of hair with it. At one point, he even knocked Kaelar toward the fish pond, where the fey lord dunked a whole foot before shoving Saffron away with a barking insult.

Saffron wanted to hold Kaelar's head under the pool until he fucking drowned. He wanted to beat Kaelar's face into the mosaic floor, and the temptation grew stronger every time Kaelar groped Saffron's ass, pulled him close to nibble at his ear, slid a hand under the collar of his shirt, introduced him as his *prettiest silken-beantighe* who *pleasured him for hours every single night*. Embarrassment swirled with rage and fear still seeping from Saffron's bones after the events the day prior, creating a noxious mixture— and Saffron was going to snap.

It was only a matter of time before Kaelar tried something more forcefully, and that moment came two hours into the party. Three of Kaelar's friends, then Kaelar himself, suddenly got to their feet mid-conversation, and Saffron knew what to expect before they ever hooked arms under his shoulders and dragged him away.

Thrashing, Saffron was pulled out of sight. They threw him down onto the stone steps of a back stairwell, and Saffron attempted to flee, only to be shoved down again with a twist of his leg. A commanding hand then gripped Saffron's chin, forcing his mouth open while pinning him against the stone steps, edges cutting into his spine.

Saffron fought to shove them away, but Kaelar made a command of *"restraint,"* and the silver cuffs snapped. Attempting to bludgeon with them, his arms were just shoved over his head, and a chocolate-dipped pink strawberry was buried between his teeth. Before he could spit it out, matching pink wine spilled into his mouth, and hands pinned his jaw shut. His whole body shook as he finally swallowed, gasping for breath—only for another fairy fruit to be shoved inside. Then another, and another, as the stairwell rang with laughter.

Saffron felt the alcohol before the dusted fruits, which was both unexpected, and equally frightening. He'd managed to avoid fairy wine up until that point, but like the matching fruits, he knew the effects would kick in hard and fast. He would be drunk, stumbling, simpering in another few minutes.

But when the draping cloud of fairy inebriation took longer and longer to come, even the fey seemed perplexed. Shoving more fruits into Saffron's mouth, pinning him down, fighting off his hands, their attempts at force-feeding him only grew more insistent, until one of them sat back in annoyance.

"Your beantighe sucks, Kaelar," they muttered, pummeling Saffron with a loosed apple and making his nose bleed. "What the fuck fun is it if they can't even get drunk?"

"What's wrong with you?" Kaelar demanded, grabbing one side of Saffron's shirt. Saffron spit a mouthful of fruit into Kaelar's face, blouse and chest soaked with pink wine and strawberry juice. Kaelar shoved him back against the steps, getting to his feet and brushing himself off.

"Whatever," he muttered, before his eyes lingered on Saffron's opal patron ring. Ice filled Saffron veins when Kaelar smiled in a different way, taking Saffron's bound hands and kissing the gaudy stone. "Perhaps this is a better time to test my patronage, hm?"

34

THE SÍDHE LORD

Reclaiming a seat next to Saffron, Saffron yanked his hand away, but Kaelar roughly grabbed his face and leaned close.

"Kiss me on the cheek."

Saffron's mind went blank. He pressed obedient lips to Kaelar's scruffy face, and Kaelar's friends laughed.

Another compelling command came, and then another. Saffron's consciousness went silent. Restrained vomit burned in the back of his throat as the game passed in a blur, kissing, laughing, teasing, doing whatever Kaelar said without any way to resist.

"Do you know what would be funny?" One of the others asked as Saffron licked wine from Kaelar's fingers. "We should find out exactly how seelie our favorite prince is."

"Oh," Kaelar grinned, and Saffron's blood curdled.

If Saffron did anything too intimate with Cylvan, especially after the events of the day prior, Taran would kill them both. Kaelar had to know that—but Kaelar was too drunk to consider the consequences. It was clear in the way he swayed slightly, grasping Saffron's cuffs and pulling him in to whisper.

"Go find Prince Cylvan and sit on his lap. Then..." Kaelar smirked. *"Kiss him."*

No—

Saffron stared at him, mouth hanging open—but magic took ownership of his body. He attempted to fight the urge driving him to stand, wincing as it strained the fragile bone in his leg.

His breaths came fast, realizing he couldn't stop himself. Limping down the narrow corridor, he used the wall as support. The whole way, he buried nails into any crack he could find, but his body just kept moving. No, no, *no—*

Behind him, Kaelar and his friends cackled in pursuit. Wanting to see for themselves. Wishing to know exactly *how seelie the prince was—*

It took only a moment of searching the pillows and bodies before Saffron spotted Cylvan across the room. Seated within a circle of pretty fey with a glass of wine in his hand. Perhaps it was the alcohol in Saffron's own system, or the enchantment digging teeth into his blood, but Cylvan looked—*ethereal.* He looked so enchanting, sitting there amongst the pink curtains and perfumes and spilling flowers and every other pretty face.

Saffron stumbled straight for him. Cylvan looked up just as Saffron entered the circle of fey, who all scoffed at his audacity. Cylvan's eyes flickered to Saffron's wrists still locked over his stomach, about to ask if everything was alright—but Saffron spread his legs over the prince's lap. Surprised, Cylvan's hand moved to Saffron's sore thigh, as if knowing how badly it hurt. He managed a single word to ask what Saffron was doing—but Saffron took his face, pressing their mouths together before another syllable could escape.

The surrounding fey gasped and giggled. Cylvan let out a sharp sound, dropping his glass and burying fingers into Saffron's waist. Saffron just tangled his lips over Cylvan's on a command that wasn't his own, matching the familiar shape of Cylvan's response with ease. Tasting wine and fruit, he slid his tongue between Cylvan's lips, pushing deeper, kissing the prince as if he were walking ambrosia.

In any other circumstance, the taste would elate him—but it

was everything Saffron could do to fight back tears. That exact moment, one he'd looked forward to earning honestly, one he'd prohibited himself from fantasizing about too much, risk tumbling into lonely nothingness—had been taken with a few words from Kaelar's mouth.

It was an eternity before the enchantment faded. Saffron finally pulled away just enough to separate their lips—but didn't dare move farther as tears crested and spilled over his eyes. He clung to Cylvan's tunic with shaking hands still restrained, not knowing what to do next. The humiliation was petrifying, turning him to stone as everyone in the audience laughed and howled with mockery.

"Seelie Prince Cylvan, why don't you keep kissing it?"

"It looks like it wants more, your highness."

"Go on, show us what else it'll do for you."

Saffron wept quietly, hunching more, wishing to disappear—when a gentle hand brushed his cheek. A warm mouth kissed a line of tears away. His pinched eyes cracked open, barely lifting to meet Cylvan's gaze in the low light, only for Kaelar's voice to emerge from the crowd again.

"Go on, beantighe—slide your hands down Prince Cylvan's chest. Kiss him on the neck."

Another miserable sob broke from Saffron's mouth, pressing his face into Cylvan's shoulder before kissing the soft skin below his ear. His hands pressed flat against Cylvan's body, where a heart pounded impossibly hard beneath the touch. Every other muscle was stiff, hard as rock, and Cylvan had stopped moving entirely. Perhaps humiliated just as Saffron was.

Cylvan stared straight ahead as everyone else laughed, a crowd gathering while offering suggestions for Kaelar to make, next. When a glass of wine suddenly dumped over Saffron's head, drenching him—all he heard were gasps and cries of shock, then more laughter. His blouse, soaked, had gone transparent, putting every carved word on his back on display.

"Selfishness, impertinence...!" Someone exclaimed, and Saffron

jolted when fingers touched the letters. Cylvan's arm hooked around him in an instant, lunging far enough to shove whoever it was away with a snarl.

Saffron just clung to Cylvan's tunic, until another compelling word from Kaelar forced him to return his mouth to the side of Cylvan's neck. Cylvan's fingers dug deeper into Saffron's waist.

"What are you doing, Kaelar?" Cylvan finally asked, breath hitching when Saffron's mouth found the skin below his jaw.

"Don't you like it?" Kaelar laughed. "I thought our seelie prince would overheat at the thought of a simpering beantighe touching him all over. Or would you prefer some privacy?"

Cylvan's heart pounded harder, skin burning hot beneath every place Saffron touched. Finally, he grabbed Saffron's hands, shoving them away. Saffron slumped against his shoulder, terrified to meet his eyes. Wishing he could apologize. Biting back bile.

"Is this how you demonstrate authority as a patron-fey?" Cylvan went on, voice inflamed with rising anger. "By embarrassing your beantighe like this?"

"Figured I might as well do all that I can now," Kaelar answered. "Before some human breaks your heart like Proserpina, and you bring the Night Court we've been promised."

More whispers, and Saffron realized—he was bearing witness to the start of a new rumor. A new malicious lie to be passed between the crowd surrounding them, where it would spread to the people on the street, then across all of Alfidel until there was no way to stop it.

Seelie Prince Cylvan, who didn't play along in harassing a beantighe. A seelie Night Prince, due to step into Queen Proserpina's place, whose own Night Court stemmed from a human lover who rejected her. Who learned the woes of seelieness, of showing mercy and kindness to humans. Thank god for unseelie King Clymeus by her side, who showed her the root of her grief, who directed her anguish toward the humans who hurt her, instead of the fey she ruled over—thank god for King Taran mac Dela—*mac Delbaith*, who would do the same when seelie Prince

Cylvan inevitably brought darkness because he'd softened his heart to humans just like his great-grandmother...

Burn, burn, burn. Saffron bit down hard on his tongue, fighting back the emotions swelling in his throat.

Alfidel didn't care that Cylvan wasn't anything like Proserpina. They didn't care that his Night Court hadn't even been formally predicted, yet. It was just like Cylvan once told him as they laid in bed in the Aon-adharcach suite, while wearing the same controlling silver cuff Saffron did.

Everyone already believes I am destined for a Night Court. Even as a child, filing down his horns, forcing himself to smile, silently pleading for people to give him a chance to be a Day King, too, but—

It didn't matter what Saffron did. It might not even matter if Taran became Cylvan's Harmonious King or not. It didn't matter, because—courtiers believed a Night Court was imminent. The courtiers of Alfidel would manifest a Night Court of their own. And when it came, humans would be the sacrifices made to appease it. Like offering gifts to an ancient god controlling the darkness. Just like the first time.

Perhaps that was why they ever reserved some humans as beantighes on their side—so if a Night ever resurfaced, they would have the fodder to quell it back. Again and again and—

Saffron's hands clenched into fists. He pressed his face harder into the side of Cylvan's neck. The fury in his body bubbled, overflowing until he burned just like Pimbry Scott. Surrounded by fey who cheered and laughed and chanted. One more sacrifice to the unseelie god of darkness that would soon come. Humans who would force the Night, and then save them from it.

Burn, burn, burn.

Shoving away from Cylvan, Saffron broke his cuffs apart. He grabbed Kaelar by the front of the shirt—and slammed a fist into his nose. Hard enough that the bone crunched, shattering into pieces like new teeth.

Kaelar shrieked, falling to the floor and taking Saffron with him. Shouts erupted from every direction, but Saffron just reeled back and punched Kaelar again. More hot tears filled his eyes as he landed a third pulverizing hit. He wrenched back for a fourth, but Kaelar jerked sideways at the last moment, and Saffron's fist crashed into the mosaic floor. Splitting pain bolted up his arm, screaming—and a dozen hands tore him off of his victim.

Shoved facedown, Saffron thrashed and spit. A hand grabbed him by the hair and slammed his head against the tile, making the world spin. Something pressed into the back of his neck, pinning him as Kaelar sat back up, blood drenching the bottom half of his face, nose fully askew.

"You absolute—*fucker!*" He cried, blood flying from his mouth. "I'll have you begging! Turn him over—!"

But the atmosphere suddenly thinned into paper, cutting Kaelar off.

Not just him—the entire party plummeted into silence.

Sharp, guttering breaths bounced through the crowd like skipping stones on a lake. Hands lifted to throats, glancing at one another with wide, confused eyes.

The closest fire pot snuffed, and heads turned in surprise. Down the way, the next went dark. Then the next, and the next, dragging the room into darkness.

The fey lady pinning Saffron pulled away, and Saffron scrambled backward, eyes wide as he watched her clutch her throat and gasp. Another body fell to their knees close by, and another followed. All of them, like a dark ocean wave crashing against the beach, a ripple of bodies groaning and choking and sinking to their knees. Saffron clung to the remaining air in his own lungs, just trying to escape the creeping suffocation of everyone else, searching for a way out—until his eyes landed on the shadow of one other person unaffected.

A horned leanan sídhe. Tall and unmoving, standing over Kaelar who coughed at their feet, clinging to the bottom of their tunic in desperation. The shadow's eyes glowed like pricks of indigo starlight, observing the pitiful form of a fey lord begging for breath on his knees.

The shadow pulled away from the clutching hand, bending a knee and shoving Kaelar against the mosaic tile. They whipped the rapier from Kaelar's belt, slamming a heeled boot into Kaelar's chest and whisking the point of the blade within an inch of the fey lord's straining windpipe.

"That beantighe is the only one who has earned protection from my Night Court," Cylvan whispered. "And creatures like you would be wise to cower beneath what I am willing to bring in order to protect him."

Cylvan, draped in choking darkness, was unrecognizable. A daemon cloaked in shadow as if made for him. An ancient god of the deepest night—who would demand blood in exchange for allowing the sun to ever return.

Saffron's most innate human instincts writhed, begging him to run far, far away—but then Cylvan's indigo eyes turned to him, and Saffron couldn't pull away from such a commanding gaze.

Even when Cylvan released him again, Saffron didn't move. He watched every moment as the Night Prince raised his boot— and smashed it into Kaelar's already destroyed face. Hard enough that Kaelar's jaw snapped and dangled grotesquely from its hinge. Cylvan then buried the rapier through one of Kaelar's hands, lifting a foot to smash between his legs in tandem. Kaelar just cried, begging for mercy with whimpering groans.

Only when the fey lord went still, staring at the open sky overhead, did Cylvan toss the sword away. He then turned to Saffron sitting petrified on the floor.

The tap of heels on the mosaic tile were loud, echoing off the walls. Saffron pushed himself away as the shadow approached, then held his breath as if suddenly terrified to prove he still inhaled freely.

Cylvan crouched in front of him, and Saffron finally, without question, witnessed the face of his raven prince. Cylvan opened his mouth to say something, perhaps to assure Saffron it was going to be alright—but Saffron threw himself forward, grappling for Cylvan with a shuddering gasp. Cylvan's arms encircled him instantly, and he pressed his nose into the hair at the back of Saffron's neck.

"I'm going to take you away from here," he promised. Saffron bit back a quiet sound, squeezing his eyes closed and nodding.

Wrapped within Cylvan's protective grasp, air stolen from the lungs of surrounding bodies swirled around them. Saffron didn't dare breathe any more than he had to.

Cylvan held him close, and the floor sank away. Ascending into the night sky, the prince said nothing else, and Saffron never opened his eyes to look. But he heard it, like the mounds renting open for every deceased soul to cry out—those gasping moans of breath rushing back into lungs, reclaiming their lives nearly stolen.

35

THE QUIET

Rain prickled Saffron's skin when they reached the peak of Cylvan's arch. Still, he didn't pull away to look where they were going. He just clung with white knuckles, shivering as the fire in his bones no longer kept him warm. Cylvan never said anything, either, only cupping his hand against the back of Saffron's head to support him. Protect him. Cylvan was taking Saffron away, just like he promised.

When they returned to solid ground, instead of excited chatter, music, busy streets meeting his ears, Saffron heard only the rain. Croaking toads. Wind through wet branches. It was enough that he finally cracked open his eyes.

Even with blurry vision, Saffron recognized looming trees in every direction. Cylvan's shadow stretched long behind him by a warm glow at Saffron's back. Horses nickered from a tying post, others latched to wagons off to the side of the dirt road where they stood. The smell of rain intermingled with spiced meat and vegetables, and Saffron hesitantly straightened his stiff neck to glance over his shoulder. A rustic tavern greeted him, though he had to squint against the firelight emanating through the windows.

Cylvan's boots thunked as he stepped onto the building's

walkway, a bell chiming as they entered through a rattly front door. It was pleasantly warm inside, and Saffron couldn't bite back his little sigh of appreciation. Cylvan chuckled.

Hushed voices conversed around scattered tables in the main area, though none of the patrons even lifted their heads as the door clanged shut on Cylvan's heels. The smell of food was stronger once they left the embrace of the rain, wafting with broiled meats, potatoes, steamed vegetables, fruit pies, even rich chocolate and coffee. A far cry from the expensive shops Cylvan had spent the previous days patronizing, and Saffron suddenly wondered how they must look in a place so rustic.

"Do you want me to put you down?" Cylvan's voice brought Saffron back, and Saffron shook his head, tightening his arms around Cylvan's shoulders. Cylvan adjusted his arms and held Saffron steadily, subconsciously brushing the back of Saffron's hair before approaching the front desk.

"A room for the night," he requested, and Saffron lifted his head slightly again, meeting the eyes of the attendant. Cylvan then patted the side of Saffron's leg, whispering: "Will you pull the purse from my belt?"

Moving stiffly, Saffron shivered as if frost broke from his skin the second he unfolded. He groped the prince's lower back, his hip, his ass until finally finding the hard leather pouch in question. Snapping open the top flap, he pulled out the bag inside, offering it to Cylvan, but Cylvan just motioned with his chin to the counter. Saffron met the attendant's eyes again, but was too exhausted and chilled to be embarrassed. He just extended a hand to drop the bag of gold coins in front of them.

"What kind of room are you looking for, your highness?" They asked with an uncertain smile, further caught off guard upon undoing the bag string and seeing exactly how much money was stored inside.

"One that comes with the *utmost discretion*," Cylvan replied, and they stiffened, before nodding fervently.

"Oh, of course! Of course—come this way, I have just the

thing for you... It's not particularly lavish, I must admit, but the bed is soft, and—"

"Anything you have is fine," Cylvan reassured with a handsome smile, and the attendant hurried around the end of the counter.

Carried up two flights of stairs, Saffron kept his face pressed into the curve of Cylvan's shoulder, arms wrapped around the back of his neck. At the top, the attendant used a brass skeleton key to unlock the door and push it open, dropping a second key into Cylvan's hand. Cylvan stepped inside without another word, going straight for a soft place to drop the passenger clinging to him.

"I can bring a second cot right away for your beantighe-servant—" The attendant began, but Cylvan interrupted smoothly.

"No need," he answered, before crouching just enough to settle Saffron on the edge of the mattress. Saffron still didn't break his arms looped around Cylvan, already missing the warmth of being so close. Cylvan obeyed on his own, kneeling and flattening his wide hands over Saffron thighs. Without turning away, he spoke again to the attendant still in the doorway.

"Could we also get a meal and a change of clothes?"

"Of course, your highness."

The attendant offered Saffron a final, fleeting glance, before scurrying out and closing the door. Even once they were gone, Cylvan remained in front of Saffron, captured within his arms and doing nothing to escape. He just sat on his knees, hands gently cupping the outsides of Saffron's thighs, searching his face as if wishing Saffron would say something. Saffron couldn't even bring himself to meet Cylvan's eyes for longer than a few moments at a time.

"Did Kaelar feed you fairy fruits?" He finally spoke.

Saffron frowned. He averted his eyes slightly more, curling a piece of Cylvan's rainy hair around a finger. Cylvan waited patiently for an answer, and Saffron finally pressed his lips together, then nodded. Cylvan's eyes trailed down Saffron's neck, pausing on the silver collar, before regarding the stains on Saffron's blouse.

"I thought he might," he muttered. "Let me guess—the fruits didn't have any effect, which is why he resorted to compelling you?"

Saffron nodded again, strangely embarrassed. He finally pulled his arms away, resting his hands on his lap and unconsciously picking at the dried scabs on the backs of his knuckles. In the heat of the inn, his bruising hand tingled and swelled where it collided with the mosaic floor, but Saffron was glad when nothing appeared to be broken.

Cylvan curved a finger under Saffron's chin, encouraging him to turn. He did, meeting Cylvan's eyes.

"That's why I gave you that strawberry drink first thing," he said with a tiny nod. "It's actually meant to protect against allergic reactions, but... fey also use it to draw out their inebriation, so they can drink and eat more without getting sick... Seems it works on humans, too. You'll probably feel the effects of the fruits soon, though, once the tonic in your stomach washes away..."

That wasn't what Saffron was expecting, raising his eyebrows, before recalling how Cylvan drank something similar with an apple piece inside. That meant—Cylvan really had been keeping an eye out for him, even before...

Saffron was reminded of the way the party ended in darkness, echoing with the sounds of choking, gasping. He pinched his eyes closed, furrowing his brows before meeting Cylvan's eyes again.

He touched his throat, then pressed fingers to Cylvan's chest. Cylvan watched him quietly, before gently reclaiming Saffron's bruised hand and kissing his fingers.

"I'm sorry if I frightened you," he whispered, breath hot against Saffron's skin. "But I am not sorry for what I did."

His mouth remained on Saffron's fingers, but his eyes flickered open, gazing at Saffron intensely through dark lashes. Saffron's heart fluttered in intimidation.

"Every one of them, Kaelar especially... deserves to die choking on their own vomit for how they taunted and touched you."

Saffron's heart drummed faster, but his skin flushed with ice. He cupped Cylvan's cheek, and Cylvan melted into it, closing his eyes and pressing into the curve of Saffron's hand. As if it was the first time he'd ever felt anything warm.

Saffron's thumb brushed the mole under Cylvan's eye, before his fingers trailed in a line to Cylvan's mouth. His lipstick was faded, smeared somewhat from Saffron's own lips moving against it. He bit his tongue, then let out a tight breath.

I'm sorry, he mouthed weakly. Cylvan's expression twisted in a sudden fury, eyes bright as he straightened up on his knees. Taking Saffron's hand, he clung to it.

"Don't apologize to me," he said firmly. "You had no choice. I will not forgive you for something you did not do on your own. It's Kaelar who should be apologizing to me—apologizing to *you*, for what he did. If I had not enjoyed the look on his face while he suffocated so much, I might have forced him to do so right there on his knees. And then ripped out his tongue to offer you as a gift."

Saffron's mouth hung open slightly as the words dangled between them—and then he surprised himself when he smiled, and then gave a hoarse little laugh. It caught Cylvan off guard, too, and his expression softened. As if the sound wore away any remaining thorns under his skin. His hand slid over Saffron's bandaged thigh again.

"Are you in a lot of pain?" He asked. Saffron shook his head no. In reality, the ache in his leg blossomed as brightly and painfully as his crushed hand, but he didn't want Cylvan to know that. He didn't need Cylvan to worry any more than he already had.

Still, as if he could sense it, Cylvan's hand trailed up and down Saffron's leg. Saffron disappeared into the sensation, until Cylvan touched his chin again to pull his eyes back.

"There's a tub in the next room," he said. "Do you want to take a warm bath until dinner comes?"

Saffron smiled wearily, realizing that was the nicest thing he could possibly be offered. Nodding, he put his hands out to push himself to his feet, but Cylvan coaxed them around the back of his neck before gently swinging Saffron into his arms.

36

———

THE CAKE

Drawing hot water in the near-dark, Saffron held a single candle in a hooked brass cup as Cylvan bent over the faucet. The pipes creaked and rattled before belching water into the basin, and the prince straightened up again, wiping his brow with an uncertain smile.

"At least the water runs clear," he chuckled. "You know... the bath in my suite back home is far nicer. If this one doesn't satisfy you... you're welcome to use it whenever you like, instead."

Saffron smiled, knowing Cylvan was thinking of the first time Saffron actually had used his bath. He wished he could mention it, too, wished he could tell Cylvan how that was the first time he ever decided to fully trust him—but he would have to hold that sentiment just a little while longer.

Cylvan clearly wanted to ask what Saffron was thinking, but instead just bit his lip again, then examined the complimentary bath oils and poured a few in. Mint, sage, roses bloomed in the form of suds across the surface of the rising bath-tide, and Saffron peeked with the light hooked on his finger.

Cylvan gently swept the candle away, setting it on a table next to the wide basin. His nimble fingers found Saffron's waist-corset, undoing the laces cinched around his middle. He avoided

Saffron's eyes, though Saffron swore there was a slight flush on the prince's cheeks.

"Despite the miserable time..." Cylvan mumbled, pausing to gaze at the silver collar around Saffron's throat. Saffron almost pulled away self-consciously, but Cylvan's attention flickered back down to his hands again. They found the internal buttons of Saffron's blouse, opening them one by one. "You looked... very nice tonight, beantighe. I would be lying if I said..."

He trailed off. Saffron waited impatiently, wanting nothing more than to know what Cylvan was thinking—

"... I'm surprised you clean up so well."

Saffron smirked, then rolled his eyes. It clearly wasn't what Cylvan originally intended to say, but he swallowed his disappointment and pretended not to notice. Cylvan smiled sarcastically as well, though it faded as the silence returned and his hands pinched open the few remaining buttons.

Saffron's blouse fell to the floor, and Saffron held his breath as Cylvan didn't move right away. He could feel Cylvan's eyes on him—but didn't dare lift his gaze to meet them, not even when a light touch suddenly trailed up his back. Saffron closed his eyes, holding his breath, knowing his scars were visible, reflected in the mirror over the sink. Surely, those were what Cylvan's gentle finger trailed over.

"They were so cruel to you," Cylvan whispered, but it sounded more like an admittance to himself than words offered for Saffron. "Without hesitating, they were... so cruel to you, who only... who couldn't..."

Saffron finally put his hand out, tugging on the bottom of Cylvan's tunic. It snapped Cylvan out of it, and his touch quickly left Saffron's back.

"Erm... sorry," he muttered, putting his hand to his forehead like he couldn't believe what he'd just done. "I'll... ah, I'll leave you to warm up. Perhaps dinner has been brought, already. Take as long as you like."

He left faster than Saffron could stop him, and the sudden

silence of being left alone was sharper than Saffron expected. Especially upon catching a glimpse of his scars in the mirror, Saffron's heart sank embarrassment. Scars that hadn't healed with the help of Magnin's tonics and magic like his broken wrist and the bite marks around his shoulder. No—the words on his back scarred beneath beantighe herbal lotions and tea leaves, skin barely stitching together while Saffron was forced to continue working day by day, until his body nearly succumbed to the stress of it all.

Those letters he would carry forever—*IMPERTINENCE, SELFISHNESS, AR...*—were gnarled like tree bark. Visible from a distance. Discolored and unsightly. He'd been able to ignore them through strategic avoidance until that point, never looking in the mirror, always using a brush to scrub his back in the bath, even wearing one of Cylvan's shirts when they had sex the first time—

But there, in the dark bathroom, they were more visible than ever. He just heard the chanting mockery of the party guests once he was drenched in wine, fabric clinging to every carved mark, read aloud for everyone to hear.

His hands shook. He grabbed the blouse back off the floor, quickly pushing his arms back through the sleeves and fastening enough of the buttons that it wouldn't fall away. He left the pants on, too, realizing he didn't want to see the bandages around his broken leg, either. Would there be ugly scars there, too? Scars, marks, imperfections he never before ever thought twice about—until mocked by an entire room of perfect people who had never known what it was like to have calloused hands?

Saffron sat in the bath, fully clothed, until the hot water turned to ice. He emotionally prepared for the moment he returned to the main part of the room and, after seeing and touching Saffron's unsettling scars up close, Cylvan would be long gone.

At least the reassurance of being alone meant, by the end of washing up, Saffron was able to pull the wet clothes off to dry himself. He avoided the eyes of the mirror the entire time.

But upon leaving the bathroom, Saffron came face-to-face

with Cylvan sitting at the foot of the bed. He was mid-bite of something in his hand, a table weighed down with food and pulled up to the edge of the mattress in front of him.

"Sorry," he said, mouth full. "I'm starving."

Too surprised to think, Saffron smiled—then laughed. Cylvan motioned for him to come closer, patting a folded piece of clothing on the bed next to him. It was a clean nightshirt from the front desk, and Saffron approached timidly, thanked him, then took it and stepped aside to pull it on over his wet hair.

Cylvan was... still there. Cylvan smiled at him like nothing had happened, like nothing had bothered him at all...

The nightshirt only dangled to his knees, and a part of Saffron wondered if Cylvan did it on purpose. Still, he hesitantly claimed a place on the mattress as Cylvan scooted over to make room. The prince still wore his dark blue tunic and leggings, though had kicked the shoes off and unbuckled the belt cinching the fabric around his waist. He smelled like rain and perfume, and Saffron almost forgot what he was doing upon sidling in close. He tried not to sink entirely into Cylvan's side, but it was difficult as the mattress bowed between them.

On the table, the spread of the meal was both traditional and lavish. Beef roast, sweet potatoes with glaze, breaded croquettes, butter and garlic asparagus with mushrooms, chestnut stuffing, wine, and, finally, strawberry and cream cakes that made Saffron's mouth water.

"Go on," Cylvan encouraged, and Saffron didn't hesitate. It was the first full meal he'd been able to enjoy since coming back to life from his attic grave, and he wasn't going to be shy about it. He even bypassed a plate at first, forking asparagus and potatoes into his mouth, biting a croquette in half, sitting on his knees to lean across the table for the wine at the opposite end. Cylvan, meanwhile, just sat back and watched with a satisfied smile.

"Good," he said, squeezing one of Saffron's ankles. "You've looked a little withered lately, beantighe. Does it taste good?"

Saffron blushed, but nodded, knowing there were crumbs on

his face. Cylvan bit back another smile, eyes lingering on Saffron's mouth before motioning for him to continue. Saffron did. When Cylvan joined him, it was to take Saffron's face and feed him bites of the roast, carrots, croquettes dipped in gravy.

Every time Saffron tried to pull away, Cylvan just squeezed his cheeks tighter until Saffron burst out laughing and submitted. Cylvan seemed to get a thrill out of deciding what he ate and in which order, commenting the entire time on how he'd looked pale, lately; he'd looked a little sick, malnourished; how Cylvan knew Saffron never had a chance to enjoy the meals he made for the rest of the house. Saffron didn't argue, didn't see any reason to fight back, enjoying every bite as much as he enjoyed every playful touch from Cylvan's hand. Eventually, Saffron did the same, offering a bite of sweet potatoes to Cylvan on the end of the fork, only to petrify at the sensual way Cylvan curled his perfect lips over the offering.

As they ate, Cylvan asked how Saffron was feeling, if there was anything else he needed, if he could feel the effects of the fruits kicking in, yet. Saffron just shook his head, a part of him hoping he'd bypass any fairy fruit inebriation at all. He wasn't sure what would happen if reduced to something floaty and simpering, especially while Cylvan looked... *like that*. Sitting so close. Smelling so nice. Smiling at him so handsomely. Saffron had to resist sliding a little closer.

"I think we'll stay here another day or two," Cylvan went on, helping himself to a sip of wine. "Until the excitement dies down in Connacht. Would you like that?"

Saffron smiled, but tugged on Cylvan's sleeve as if to reiterate, *"you'll stay with me?"*

Cylvan smiled, offering the edge of the glass between Saffron's lips and coaxing him to have a drink, too.

"Yes," he promised. "Though I will have to return to Connacht briefly in the morning to establish our alibis. Maybe get some of our things from the inn. Check on Asche. Put on an apologetic performance for Kaelar, wherever he ended up..."

Saffron frowned. He pulled stubbornly on Cylvan's sleeve again, thoughts buzzing with the start of drunkenness. He hoped it was only from the wine—but then Cylvan smirked, shaking his head and offering Saffron another drink. It was the most beautiful thing Saffron had ever seen, and heat swirled in his extremities. Oh, no.

"It's my duty as the prince to keep the peace," Cylvan muttered, offering Saffron another bite of something to eat. Saffron accepted it, before reclining against Cylvan's shoulder without realizing what he was doing. "I must always act the bigger person. Even if I nearly slaughtered an entire room, heh. I promise it's only for show and nothing else. Perhaps I'll bring you his tongue, after all, like I promised earlier."

Unsatisfied, Saffron's grasp around Cylvan's sleeve tightened.

Oh—he was definitely sinking into fairy drunkenness. How could Cylvan look so breathtaking just in the light of the fireplace?

"What are you smiling about?" Cylvan asked as Saffron was indeed captivated by him, cheeks flushed while resting a chin on Cylvan's shoulder. He opened his mouth to answer, before closing it again in disappointment. He squeezed Cylvan's cheeks until his lips puckered, giggling.

Handsome, he implied, gazing at Cylvan's mouth in appreciation. Cylvan said nothing, though smiled through Saffron's demanding hand.

"You're definitely getting drunk," he murmured, voice garbled by his squeezed cheeks. Saffron giggled again, shaking his head. Cylvan hooked a finger under Saffron's chin, searching his eyes. "I can see it. Fairy drunkenness puts a pink glimmer in the eyes of its victim, and yours are lighting up like fireworks."

Saffron just kept smiling. He released Cylvan's cheeks, only to wrap his arms around Cylvan's waist, instead. He let out a long sigh, pressing his nose into the chest of Cylvan's tunic and breathing him in deeply. Cylvan's hand found his shoulder... then his back... his waist, where it hesitated... before creeping slightly lower to Saffron's exposed thigh, his nightshirt having lifted slightly as he wiggled around.

"You're flushed," Cylvan commented, but his voice was thoughtful that time. "Do you feel alright?"

Saffron nodded, though his eyes closed as he disappeared into the feeling of Cylvan in his arms. The scent of him in his nose. The sound of his heart, beginning to race beneath Saffron's ear. Everything about him was—intoxicating, even more than any fairy fruits ever would have been. How had Saffron ever resisted? He wasn't sure how much longer he could, especially while his body tickled with warmth, while he couldn't stop smiling every time Cylvan even breathed. Ah—he never realized how large of an emptiness was left behind when forced to pretend Cylvan didn't exist. And while they weren't wholly back in place with one another again—Saffron just wanted to revel in the reminder of how perfectly he fit into Cylvan's shape.

It was impossible to even consider pulling away as Cylvan's hand continued to stroke the outside of Saffron's thigh, occasionally hooking his finger and thumb over the narrow part above his knee, as if trying to determine exactly how much weight Saffron had lost in the previous few weeks. Soon, he coaxed a bite of strawberry cake into Saffron's mouth, and Saffron accepted it gladly.

"Is it still your favorite?" Cylvan asked under his breath, and Saffron sighed before nodding. Cylvan offered another bite, and Saffron sat up to take it. He exaggerated his movements, meeting Cylvan's eyes and licking the end of the fork with a teasing smile. Cylvan mumbled *"stop that,"* but still scooped another bite to offer. Saffron wanted to make Cylvan blush.

Taking Cylvan's hand offering the cake, Saffron met his gaze again, elongating the movements of sliding the bite off the fork with his tongue, then licking his lips. Cylvan flushed slightly, before averting his eyes.

Saffron giggled. He stretched over the table, dragging a finger through the cream frosting of one of the additional pieces of cake.

Licking it off sensually, he found Cylvan's eyes again, laughing when Cylvan only stared at him, stone-faced. But a tendon popped in his neck, beneath where he gulped down something hard.

Saffron nearly teased him again—but his hand slipped under his weight, collapsing to the table and smashing the cake beneath him.

He burst out laughing, never knowing it was possible to become so drunk, so fast. The fruits devoured at the party came for him like a sudden rainstorm, soaking him through until he was nothing but petrichor and floating mist and gasping mirth.

On his back on the table, Saffron sighed between the amusement, wiping cream from his neck and sucking it off his fingers. He coyly offered one of the strawberries on his shirt to Cylvan, grinning in surprise when Cylvan leaned forward to take it. His mouth was hot around Saffron's fingers, and Saffron giggled.

"You're acting like a messy high fey," Cylvan scolded gently, propping one hand on the table in the curve of Saffron's waist and hovering over him. "What am I supposed to do with you now?"

Saffron smiled firtily, hooking messy fingers over the collar of his nightshirt and tugging it down to offer a peek of his chest. He liked how Cylvan's eyes followed, like a raven eyeing something colorful in the grass. It made wanting heat glow between his legs, and he had to squeeze his thighs together to hide it.

Extending a hand, next, Saffron drew a line of white cream down Cylvan's cheek. Cylvan's mouth found his finger, and Saffron's breath hitched as it disappeared between two soft lips, all the way to the knuckle. A warm tongue teased it, before amethyst eyes opened again to find Saffron through dark lashes. Saffron's skin boiled.

"I always knew you weren't as demure and innocent as you pretend..." Cylvan accused with a smirk, and Saffron giggled more. Cylvan caressed Saffron's finger with his mouth again, taking in a second and a third, before pulling away with a sigh.

"But—as tempting a dessert as you are, I am not going to ravish a drunk beantighe."

A withering complaint left Saffron's mouth, collapsing back to the table in disappointment. Cylvan laughed, then scooped a hand beneath Saffron's head, pinning it to the side and sweeping over him. A hot tongue glided up the length of Saffron's neck, licking away the cream and strawberry filling on his skin. Saffron shuddered, gasping and moaning softly in surprise, taking handfuls of Cylvan's tunic in an attempt to remain in his body.

"What am I going to do with you?" Cylvan repeated, before biting at Saffron's ear. One of Saffron's arms wrapped around the back of Cylvan's neck to keep him where he was, terrified in his drunkenness that the moment the prince pulled away, his heart would break into pieces. Saffron—wanted it. He wanted more. He wanted the heat between his legs to meet the warmth of Cylvan's body, else he burn away like an old wick.

Cylvan's opposite hand found Saffron's hip, as if he couldn't resist, either. His mouth returned to Saffron's neck and jaw, tasting every spot trailed with strawberry cake. When Saffron couldn't take it anymore, he turned his head—and caught Cylvan's mouth in a desperate kiss.

It engulfed him in an instant. That feeling, that ambrosia he'd spent so long wishing to taste again. He had it on his mouth again—and suddenly the world was full of light and warmth and nothing terrible at all. He was taken back to the edge of the nymph lake, where he and Cylvan kissed the first time—back when everything was perfect. When there was only the open sky, the green grass, the wildflowers, and his raven prince.

"*Mmh—!*" Saffron inhaled as Cylvan's hands buried into him. He was flattened against the table in an instant, crushed beneath Cylvan's mouth demanding more after a single taste. It drew the breath from Saffron's lungs, and he locked his arms behind Cylvan's head as their mouths fought for dominance, gasping between scraping teeth and twisting tongues. Cylvan shoved Saffron harder against the table, fully commanding every inch of him as wineglasses and plates crashed to the floor.

"Damnit!" Cylvan hissed suddenly, pulling away. Fingers replaced his mouth on Saffron's, burrowing between Saffron's lips and almost making him choke. Saffron's back arched with a sharp breath, clutching Cylvan's tunic with shaking hands as Cylvan tugged the collar of Saffron's nightshirt down, kissing his neck again, then his collarbones.

"Pl—" Saffron attempted, before the choker cut him off. His vision spun upon opening his eyes again, hazy with heat and desire and intoxication. Cylvan's fingers buried deeper into his mouth, making him whimper as sharp nails tickled the back of his throat. Spit dripped from the corner of his lips, flushing as Cylvan pressed between his legs.

"I want to hear you ask for it, Saffron," Cylvan growled. Saffron only moaned, breaths hiccuping as he sucked on Cylvan's fingers filling his mouth.

But then the fingers suddenly pressed harder, gagging him— and two more hooked under the silver choker, ripping it away with force.

37

THE TONGUE

Saffron's hands flew to his throat as hot blood bubbled from where the silver prongs tore free—but upon gasping, the hint of pressure was gone.

Before he could panic further, Cylvan's mouth found the front of his neck and licked the fresh blood away.

"I know you have a tongue," he accused in a low voice, and the fingers in Saffron's mouth pressed deeper, making his breath catch. "I've known since the beginning, Saffron—but I won't hold back anymore. I want to hear—every sound withheld from me."

Saffron shuddered. Cylvan finally pulled his fingers free, a line of spit trailing behind as Saffron could only crack open his watering eyes to look at him. He wanted to ask *how*—but knew he hadn't done anything to try and hide it, either. As if a part of him hoped to one day hear Cylvan say those words, to hear him make that demand. To clear him of consequences if Taran ever found out. *Prince Cylvan insisted. He found out the truth, himself.*

"Cy—" he rasped, taking Cylvan's hand and pulling it to his chest. He pushed it under the collar of his shirt. "Cylvan—please, touch me more."

Cylvan inhaled as if he'd been hit in the stomach. His hand

obeyed Saffron's request, cupping the upper curve of his chest before rubbing his thumb against the nipple beneath his palm. Saffron shivered, gripping Cylvan's tunic again before pulling him down into another breathy, desperate kiss. The movement was sloppy, melting beneath the first wanted sensual touch he'd felt in weeks—and it being at the hand of Cylvan made it all the more consuming.

"Say my name again," Cylvan breathed between their mouths.

"P-Prince Cylvan," Saffron answered instantly, hitching as Cylvan's opposite hand stimulated the heat between his legs, covered only by the thin hem of the nightshirt. He arched his head backward with an open-mouthed gasp, only for Cylvan to help himself again to the pinpricks of blood bubbling in the wake of the silver collar. His tongue swirled over the wounds, before trailing down again to find Saffron's chest and lick all the places that made Saffron shiver and gasp. Saffron's hands tore at Cylvan's tunic in return, and Cylvan pulled away just enough to shirk it off over his head.

"I want you," Saffron begged. "Please—I want you, I'm not drunk, I'm not—Even before, all I wanted—was you, Cylvan—Your highness—ah—"

"Even before?" Cylvan asked coyly, and Saffron could only feverishly nod. He rolled his hips against Cylvan's hand still fondling between his legs, growing more and more desperate. His own hands groped Cylvan's body, wishing to refamiliarize himself with every dip of the muscles in his stomach, the firm expanse of his chest, the strength of his shoulders.

When his fingers stumbled over the jewelry in Cylvan's nipples, the sound Cylvan made in response nearly drove Saffron mad. His hands found the waistband of Cylvan's leggings, finally, attempting to open them—but Cylvan's hand snapped out, grabbing both of Saffron's wrists at once. The prince pulled away, furrowing his brows with a deep exhale through his nose. He met Saffron's eyes, half-lidded and conflicted.

"I... We... shouldn't," he whispered, voice tight. *"Fuck*—I shouldn't. You're... you're not in your right mind. This isn't... this isn't how I meant..."

He trailed off. His grip around Saffron's wrists tightened until Saffron winced, proving how hard he fought to hold himself back. Saffron wanted to beg, to *plead*—but he thought of Cylvan's similarly conflicted demeanor at the party, how he stiffened beneath Saffron's mouth and hands. Even though the circumstances were leagues apart, the last thing Saffron wanted was to coerce Cylvan into anything he wasn't pleading for, himself.

"Don't get me wrong," Cylvan added, as if reading Saffron's mind. He braced a hand on the table, leaning close again with his jaw clenched tight. "There is nothing I want more right now—than to throw you on that bed, and have my way until sunrise. But—not like this. Not until I know for sure... you want it, too."

"I—!" Saffron nearly exclaimed, but bit it back. He pressed his lips together, gazing down to where Cylvan still gripped his wrists, then nodded weakly. "Can we... is it alright if we... at least... keep kissing?"

Cylvan's expression softened, and he pulled Saffron in for exactly what he asked. That time, though, it was gentle. A more unbearable rush of emotion washed through him, leaving him heavy.

"If you still want it in the morning, I won't hold back," Cylvan continued, and Saffron couldn't help but laugh breathlessly. "I'll devour every inch of you, all for myself. You won't be able to stop me."

Saffron kissed him again.

"Do you promise?" He asked, and Cylvan released his own breathy chuckle.

"I have never been more sure of anything."

Saffron kissed him again.

"Will that be before or after you go back into Connacht?"

"Oh—*fuck*," Cylvan groaned, collapsing and crushing Saffron back into the table. Saffron burst out laughing, pinning Cylvan against his chest, even wrapping his legs around Cylvan's waist to keep him there. Cylvan's hot voice rumbled against his skin when he answered. "Perhaps I will have to keep you awake long enough that you sleep the day away, so I can go do my chores."

"There are many ways to keep me up all night," Saffron encouraged, and Cylvan pinched and twisted Saffron's nipples in agreement. Saffron shrieked, and Cylvan laughed harder than Saffron had heard in a long time.

"You're right," he finally agreed, lifting his head and resting his chin on Saffron's chest in order to look at him. "There are plenty of ways to keep a wicked beantighe awake into the early morning hours—but perhaps not how he wants. You're going to answer every question I have for you."

Saffron's mirth plummeted into ice—and so did his expression, apparently, making Cylvan grin darkly and pinch his cheeks.

"The more satisfied I am with your answers, the more times I will let you come tomorrow morning."

"That's—" Saffron wheezed, but Cylvan was already plucking him from the messy table. Saffron wiggled, tightening his arms and legs around Cylvan's body like a vine on a tree, heart pounding as he was carried back into the bathroom. Cylvan helped wiped him down and rinse his shirt of food and cake, but didn't begin his interrogation right away. He had no chance, as their mouths hardly left one another after reuniting again.

"Why did Taran lie about your tongue?"

Saffron had a new piece of cake from the tavern kitchens, more fruits with cheese and bread cluttering the tray between where he and Cylvan sat on the bed in the dark. The additional food in his stomach helped to ease the horny drunkenness that previously controlled him, though he was still bitter about being left in the cold.

Saffron took his time answering by indulging in a bite of dessert, then gazing introspectively out the tall windows over the head of the mattress, windy trees whipping around on the other side. He absentmindedly rubbed a hand up and down the bandages of his extended leg, massaging the sore muscle underneath. When he took too long to answer, Cylvan knew he was procrastinating, throwing a blueberry at him.

"I don't know," was his sloppy answer. Cylvan continued immediately.

"Why were you wearing Proserpina's choker?"

Saffron nearly answered *"I don't know"* again, but knew if he avoided answering every question, Cylvan would only become more demanding.

"... He said... I was being punished for something I did." Saffron chose his words carefully. He still wasn't sure exactly how much he wanted to reveal, but also juggled with how badly he wanted to spill the entire truth. He tried to walk the path between both, for as long as it existed. "Something I don't remember, that was taken in my memories. Erm, something about... that wolf, I think. Maybe the one we saw on the road, the other day...?"

His eyes flickered to Cylvan for the briefest of seconds, but Cylvan was scowling at a piece of bread on the platter in front of him. Saffron shifted where he sat.

"Was that the same wolf you mentioned in my room the other night? The one Elluin blames you for..."

"I'm certain," Cylvan muttered, finally grabbing the bread lying victim beneath his harsh gaze. He wadded it up around a piece of white cheese and claimed an animalistic bite. Saffron took what remained from Cylvan's hand in a coy show of defiance, and Cylvan smirked like he wanted to tear Saffron wide open. A part of Saffron still hoped he would.

"We must have been... close," he feigned after taking a bite of his own, gazing down at the morsel of cheese and bread that remained. "Especially if... I got wrapped up in whatever Elluin had out for you... right?"

"Close'..." Cylvan considered. He helped himself to a plump strawberry, before offering the second half to Saffron, as if expecting him to steal that, too. Saffron smirked, claiming it with

his mouth, never breaking eye contact. Cylvan smiled wistfully to himself. "I think... we were *becoming* close, yes. We actually only had a little bit time together before..."

He trailed off. Saffron chose another strawberry, biting off half and offering the rest to Cylvan, just like Cylvan had him. Cylvan accepted it with the same flirty movement of his lips.

"Before I had my memories taken," Saffron answered for him. "You can say so, your highness. I won't be upset. I've... come to terms with it, already."

The lies came easier than Saffron thought they would, though his voice still cracked with those final words. He finished the mouthful of bread and cheese in his hand.

"You know, the reason we..." Cylvan cleared his throat. The words started almost reminiscently, but cracked like Saffron's voice had. Saffron pretended not to notice, helping himself to more fruit and cheese while Cylvan took as much time as he needed. "The only reason you began studying arid magic was because of me."

"I remember you saying something like that in the kitchen," Saffron smiled, ignoring the initial pinch of dread as he first thought back to Pimbry Scott and the bookstore. "But what business does a high fey prince have learning arid magic?"

"Well... you were going to charm this ring of mine, and ended up following the trail of arid magic to get there. We... made a geis over it."

"A geis?" Saffron grinned, knowing even an unthreaded version of himself would be amused by the realization. "Like Derdriu and Naoise?"

"That's right," Cylvan chuckled, before it trailed off again. "But the whole time, you had no idea... that I was leading you toward it, intentionally. I was... manipulating you into learning, so that if something happened and we were found out, it wouldn't ever get tied back to me. Because I was terrified of..."

Cylvan's mouth dangled open, as if the words clustered at the back of his throat, too frightened to emerge.

"I was terrified of... this," he finally said. "Of *this*, of exactly what happened, where you had your memories taken. I was worried some oracle would unweave your threads and learn what I'd been trying to do through them. I suppose... it was a self-fulfilling prophecy of my own hubris."

"I like that word," Saffron whispered. "Is that the thing that makes you so charming?"

Cylvan smiled wearily. "Some people say it's what makes me so... disagreeable."

Saffron giggled. Cylvan did, too. A tiny exchange of a shared memory, without ever expressing as much out loud. Saffron spread more cheese over a piece of bread before piling it high with every apple slice Cylvan couldn't eat.

"It doesn't seem like any oracles learned your secrets from my threads," Saffron promised, trying to keep the tone casual and lighthearted. He crunched into his pile of apple-cheese-bread, slurping up a deluge of juices that spilled from the corners of his mouth.

"Wow, stunning," Cylvan mumbled. "Remember earlier when I said you cleaned up nicely? I take it back."

"Hm. We'll see if you still feel that way in the morning," Saffron muttered, licking juice off his thumb and giving Cylvan a knowing look. "I've been told I'm hard to resist with other things dripping down my chin."

"Al—*right*," Cylvan wheezed, hunching over and putting a hand up in defense. Saffron smiled, licking his lips before taking another bite and promptly dropping three apple slices that disappeared into the blanket. He searched for them between his legs before precariously balancing them back on the cheese. Taking another risky mouthful, he raised his eyebrows at the sight of Cylvan smiling so fondly at him.

"What?" He mumbled, mouth full. "I never claimed *everything* I did to be irresistible."

"Nothing," Cylvan said thoughtfully, shaking his head. "I suppose I am only... relieved to see you as yourself, despite everything that's happened. It's easy for me to spiral, thinking every part of you I liked best was taken when you were unthreaded... but then I remember... it's only a few weeks that were taken, wasn't it? And while that's still not something I *enjoy* thinking about, ah... What I mean to say, is... I'm relieved to find you're still exactly the person I came to care so much for, before."

Saffron stared at him with hot-blooded cheeks, eyes wide as his heart raced. He gulped.

"O-oh..." He managed, embarrassed.

"Perhaps..." Cylvan went on, using his thumb to wipe a line of juice from Saffron's lip, then coyly pressing it into Saffron's mouth to lick clean. "Even if you never recall our first memories together... that just means we will have to make new ones. Better ones. And now that I know exactly what you mean to me, I can ensure every memory thread going forward is one of joy."

Saffron smiled.

"Did I mean a lot to you?"

"Yes," Cylvan answered without hesitation. "And you still do, even if one of us is starting over as strangers. Perhaps it's for the best—I can be on my best behavior this time, and ensure you really fall for me."

"That's not very fair," Saffron teased. "Is there a way to get my old memories back? Just put them back in."

Cylvan smiled, closing his eyes and dangling his head backward.

"Yes," he answered again. "It wouldn't be easy, but... it's possible to place memory threads back where they belong. So long as the oracles in Avren preserved yours, we can have them returned as if they were never taken."

Preserved. Saffron thought about Taran's red strings, taking another bite of his bread and apples.

"Really?" He insisted with another full mouth.

"Yes. But perhaps only the happy ones."

"If you're returning my memories, I wish to get all of them. Even the bad ones, please."

"What for?"

Cylvan's tone remained teasing, but Saffron's chest squeezed in sincerty. He gazed down at his bread, taking another slow, considerate bite.

"Because... bad memories make the good ones more special," he whispered. "And... even if they're bad, if they're with you, I want to have them back. I don't want you to... carry the burden of bad things all by yourself. I'll help you."

An unthreaded beantighe wouldn't be so sincere—but Saffron couldn't help it, like a choking plea for Cylvan to understand without saying it outright. A planted seed, so that one day, when all the truth came out, Cylvan would know for certain that Saffron never left him at all.

"Well," Cylvan laughed weakly after a long moment of silence. "Danu has been cruel to me, and therefore to you, lately, so I wouldn't speak so soon."

Saffron scoffed. "Do not blame Danu. I have spent one whole week in Danann House, and I already know exactly who it is treating you cruelly."

"Oh?" Cylvan smirked, and Saffron realized perhaps he'd said too much again. He stuffed his mouth with another crumbling bite of the food in his hand.

"Daurae Asche, obviously."

Cylvan barked a laugh, throwing his head back again before shaking his head.

"Gods—you have that right. That little twat. Being away from them tonight is actually quite the relief. I haven't had a peaceful night's sleep since they got here."

"Because they have nightmares?" Saffron asked.

"No—because this is the first time they've had a captured audience to listen to their ramblings for so long. I love them to death, but if I have to hear them explain magic charms one more time..."

Saffron laughed. "I quite liked their charm lecture. I thought it was very interesting."

"Of course you would—you're the most wild-fey obsessed person I know. And since a majority of charms stem from wild fey and forest magic, Danu help us, I'm sure you could entertain one another for years on end."

"I think Asche is charming," Saffron defended further, loving the way Cylvan's nose wrinkled in what might have been a pinch of jealousy. "Especially when they try to be demanding, then wilt beneath a single look."

"They don't have much practice being as icy and pushy as I am."

"You are neither icy nor pushy," Saffron reassured him, biting a black cherry from its stem before popping the pit back to the tray.

"No?"

"No. You are peppery and withholding. Hm, like Baba Yaga's cat."

"A *cat!*" Cylvan scoffed. "If I am a cat, then what are you?"

"... Perhaps I am also a cat," Saffron laughed. "I suppose Baba's cat also hunts wild things and likes to sleep in the sun like I do."

Cylvan smiled like Saffron was his most favorite thing in the world. He extended a hand, brushing the back of it down Saffron's face.

"Then I will always provide a sunny place for you to sleep, so you can rest from any bad memories you hold on to."

Saffron smiled. He couldn't resist tucking his face into Cylvan's hand, closing his eyes and memorizing how it felt to be caressed so gently.

38

THE PROMISE

Saffron slept beneath the earth. Beneath the mounds, where others lost to the grips of the underworld lay. He sank into velvet sheets of warm soil, smooth as silk beneath his hands, only ever emerging enough from the darkness to exhale a contented sigh and turn. To pull the blankets closer, to nestle deeper into Cylvan's sweet scent and settle as close as he could without ever opening his eyes. He'd never smelled anything more luxurious than warm fabrics tinged with a certain night lord's perfume. If that was what it meant to die, Saffron had to wonder why Persephone in myth ever thought to return to the surface at all. He would take her place without question.

"Saffron," Cylvan's voice eventually coaxed him from the furthest reaches. "I'll be back soon."

But Saffron turned, lifting his arms sleepily from beneath the blankets to wrap them around the back of Cylvan's neck. Pulling him down into a sleepy kiss, Saffron held him for a long time, drowsily moving their mouths together. There was no timid beantighe act that time, too exhausted from everything that had come before it, too worn down until only his base wants existed like bone through a wound. Saffron, the real Saffron—didn't want to wait any longer.

"You promised," he mumbled. Cylvan chuckled. He knelt back onto the bed, accepting Saffron's plea and kissing him more.

"I won't be long," Cylvan whispered. "I'll devour you when I get back."

No—Saffron had waited long enough. He'd been good and obedient long enough. He wanted to be selfish, for once. And the more he kissed Cylvan, the more the prince's resolved wavered in turn, as if he thought the exact same thing.

"Prince Cylvan," Saffron breathed, making his voice extra pitiful. "I just—want you to touch me. Don't make me wait anymore."

He could feel how Cylvan's eyelashes tangled into his own; how his mouth claimed every one of Saffron's breaths, how it almost claimed his words carried on them.

"How do you want to be touched?" Cylvan asked with a voice like silk, and Saffron finally opened his heavy eyes. He smiled playfully.

"Touch me... like it'll bring back all my memories of you."

Cylvan's nails burrowed into Saffron's hips, making Saffron inhale sharply—but it was quickly stolen again by a merciless mouth.

Saffron arched his back, hands finding Cylvan's chest and coaxing the nightshirt over his head. He threw it to the other side of the room so Cylvan couldn't try and leave again, searching for his mouth once more and groping his warm skin the moment they found one another. His fingers teased the bumps of the jewelry in Cylvan's nipples, summoning the most delicious inhale of breath Saffron had ever tasted.

Cylvan pulled the blankets away from Saffron's body, and Saffron shivered as chilly morning air spilled over his bare legs and through the thin fabric of his shirt. Through the windows at the head of the bed, rain pattered on the glass, sunsingers chirping in the woods right on the other side. It was—a perfectly serene way to wake up, only to dissolve into Cylvan's touch.

It wasn't like the night before, which had been carnal and

demanding—but there was still a level of ownership Cylvan took over every part of Saffron's existence where his hands gripped, his mouth dominated, his tongue tasted. Every inch, lingering in the places that summoned shaking gasps from Saffron's mouth, pulling away just as Saffron tingled and leaving him wanting for more, more, more—

"Show me your eyes," Cylvan cooed, and Saffron knew it was so the prince could search him for fairy inebriation. Despite feeling sober as ever, Saffron turned away in an instant, arching his back on his knees and hiding his face against the pillows. Cylvan muttered something, but Saffron just pressed his hips into Cylvan's body, rolling against him until sharp nails found his waist.

The bottom of his nightshirt was pushed up his spine, draping from the curve of his back—and a hot tongue found the base of his hips, before curling lower, circling his entrance and making Saffron whimper. He moaned and gasped into the pillow, moving his hips desperately, silently begging for more. Cylvan's hand found his bandaged thigh, caressing it, but Saffron barely felt the tightness of the muscle. He felt nothing but Cylvan's tongue.

Cylvan knew how to tease him, and Cylvan enjoyed every moment of teasing him—and nearly brought Saffron to climax with his mouth alone, opposite hand leaving Saffron's thigh to stroke between his legs until he was trembling and helpless.

Cylvan tore three of his sharp fingernails away using his teeth, then dripped floral oil taken from the bathroom the night before over his fingers. A line of spit dripped from his mouth to where his fingers teased, and Saffron shivered in pitiful want. A thumb found its way inside, then a finger, gently stroking in and out and teasing every inch as they went. It was only Cylvan's arm hooked under his hips, arching him upright, that kept Saffron from collapsing.

"Is this alright?" Cylvan asked affectionately, adding another finger and kissing the base of Saffron's spine. Saffron whimpered in pleasure, nodding with his eyes squeezed shut. His legs twitched, toes curling as the sensation flooded up his back, branching out over the rest of his body with every push of Cylvan's fingers.

"Is it enough?" Cylvan went on playfully, and Saffron groaned in complaint. "Tell me what you want, beantighe."

"I want—" Saffron choked as Cylvan pressed all the way to his knuckles, already losing his grasp on what words were. "I want—more, Cylvan—"

"Who?"

Saffron croaked a bitter laugh. He moved his hips against the rhythm of Cylvan's fingers.

"I want more, *your highness.*"

A hot breath of laughter escaped Cylvan's mouth, followed by his fingers removing themselves. Saffron sank into the pillows as he was relieved of the pressure, gazing feverishly over his shoulder as Cylvan undid the waistband of his pants, revealing his growing length and stroking oil up and down it. He met Saffron's eyes, and Saffron bit back a smile, moving his hips again in invitation.

"Who taught you to act like this?" Cylvan asked through a heated smile, grabbing Saffron's waist hard enough to restrain him. "You must not know—what it means to bend beneath me, beantighe."

"Then teach me," Saffron invited coyly. "I want to know what it means to submit to the Prince of Alfidel, *your highness.*"

"*Fuck,*" Cylvan grunted at the challenge, centering himself— then immediately burying flush with the backs of Saffron's thighs. Saffron buckled forward with a sharp gasp, legs and back spasming as Cylvan filled and nearly split him in half.

"Cyl—*Cylvan!*" He begged, breathless as his eyes watered. "Oh, god—P-Prince Cylvan—*mh!*"

Still gripping Saffron's waist, Cylvan pulled back and pressed inside again; slowly that time, then increasing as Saffron warmed to the size of him. It rendered Saffron speechless, just gripping the pillow, the sheets, mouth strained open wide for only gasps of sweetness to escape.

"Do you regret begging?" Cylvan asked, bending over Saffron to press deeper, summoning a small whimper of submission from Saffron's mouth.

"N-no, oh—god," Saffron managed, syllables hiccuping between thrusts, shoulders coiling in and out every time Cylvan's hips met the backs of his legs. "F-fuck, Cylvan—!"

"You insist on being so informal with me," Cylvan teased in a low breath, cupping a hand under Saffron's chin to curl his neck back and meet his eyes. "Would you like it—if I moaned your name like that, too?"

Saffron attempted to swallow, but it caught in the strain of his throat. He hazily met Cylvan's eyes, mouth contorting every time Cylvan slammed back into him. Again and again and again until his eyes watered and dripped. A weak smile found his lips.

"Yes," he rasped. "Please—please, your highness—"

Cylvan kissed him from above, before sliding a hand down the curve of Saffron's throat. His mouth then found the underside of Saffron's jaw, then the side of his neck, biting at the inner curve of his shoulder.

"You—are like nothing I've ever had, *Saffron,*" Cylvan breathed, hot against Saffron's back and making him tremble. "You are the most decadent thing I've ever tasted, *Saffron.*"

Saffron fell back into the pillows, shaking with bliss and stretching out his arms to grip the bars of the headboard. Cylvan coaxed the rest of him flat to the bed, pinning Saffron's legs together between his knees and allowing himself more weight to thrust inside.

Cylvan's hand flattened against Saffron's back, trailing his palm over every textured scar of the words carved in his skin. Saffron shivered, offering Cylvan a glance over his shoulder. But Cylvan didn't see him—he stared at the words, alone. That was the first time he'd seen them so close, in direct light, unlike in the dark bathroom the night before; it was the first time he touched them fully, with his entire hand. Saffron had hidden the scars from Cylvan the first time they tangled up in one another, but in that moment, Cylvan touched them as if it was one of his biggest regrets once he was told Saffron was gone.

"Beautiful," he whispered, and Saffron's heart squeezed. "You're... perfect, Saffron."

"Don't," Saffron whispered back, hiding his face against the pillow. But Cylvan's hand continued touching every inch, every letter.

"Do you know... you have a line of freckles down your spine?" He breathed, trailing a finger as he said it. "And a beauty mark here, at the top of your shoulder..."

He kissed the spot, and goosebumps flushed Saffron's skin.

"Everywhere I touch... is softer than the last," Cylvan continued, never slowing the pace of his hips. "Every part of you... is more perfect than the last."

Saffron just shook his head, but Cylvan's mouth, his thoughtful touch, carefully broke down the insecurity, the embarrassment at the thought of someone Saffron thought to be perfect seeing something so gruesome on his body. He realized—an unthreaded version of himself wouldn't know what Cylvan talked about, let alone how he'd gotten the scars at all, but Saffron didn't want to play that game. He didn't want to acknowledge it. Just like he didn't want to pretend he didn't know about Arrow and Berry and Cloth. He wasn't sure he could, if asked. He wasn't sure he could stomach lying about his friends who died.

I'm not perfect, he wanted to say, instead. *I'm covered in scars. My skin is uneven. My hair is a mess. My fingernails are chipped.* All the things Taran tried to fix in the first week of Saffron's stay in the attic. He'd learned, that day, every single imperfection every high fey saw when they looked at someone as pathetic and small as he was.

But Cylvan dé Tuatha dé Danann, the Prince of Alfidel, the embodiment of what it meant to be perfect—venerated every inch of him, as if... he meant it, that time he called Saffron a treasure. Something to be appreciated. Memorized. Every part of him, even the scars, the stretch marks, the things Saffron never thought were even something to be insecure about until some fey made a comment.

Cylvan pressed deeper inside, as if wishing to summon a sound from Saffron's mouth. It did, and Saffron moaned into the pillow, clutching it in his arms before biting down on the fabric. Cylvan hunched over his back, hooking fingers into Saffron's mouth and pulling him free.

"I want to hear all of it," he breathed, and Saffron whimpered, fists trembling as they clutched the cushion desperately. His eyes fluttered closed from the overwhelm, spit dripping between Cylvan's fingers as the prince's opposite hand gripped Saffron's hip for leverage. Plunging deeper, again and again, Saffron thought he might break into pieces. Gasping and crying out in pleasure, he prayed Cylvan's name between hiccuping breaths and want for more.

"I want—to see you," he begged next, turning pathetically to reach out an arm. Cylvan didn't hesitate, removing himself and taking Saffron's extended reach, pulling him into his chest before pressing him back into the pillows. Saffron wrapped his arms around the back of Cylvan's neck, opening his legs again as Cylvan pressed back inside, vanishing into shared gasps and pleas on one another's name. Saffron kissed him selfishly, closing his eyes and rolling his hips to meet Cylvan's movements, wanting him deeper, harder, more and more until they might never be separated again. Cylvan obeyed every silent command, all the while supporting Saffron's bandaged leg, ensuring there was never any weight applied enough to hurt it.

"You're so beautiful, Saffron," Cylvan repeated, kissing Saffron's cheek, then his sweat-flushed forehead, his hair. "Like nothing I've ever seen before."

Saffron shook his head again.

"Don't—tease me," he whimpered, but Cylvan responded with a long, reverential kiss that numbed all of Saffron's denials.

"You're beautiful," he reiterated, pressing their foreheads together. "And the only person—who can ever make such requests of me."

Saffron smiled weakly, and something about it made Cylvan thrust harder. Choking on his breath, Saffron's hands found Cylvan's shoulders, clinging to him, clawing lines into his skin.

"Don't go," Saffron asked, meaning more than simply back into Connacht. *Don't go, don't go, don't leave me again, I can't be without you again.* "You can't go—"

"Not yet," Cylvan promised, nipping at Saffron's neck. "Not when you feel so good."

"Do whatever you want to me," Saffron practically begged, pulling Cylvan closer. "If it means you'll stay."

"I'll do whatever I want to you—because I'm your prince," was Cylvan's answer, and Saffron bit back a laugh.

"You said—*mh!*—I could make requests of you…"

"I never said I would listen."

"You…!" Saffron bucked backward as Cylvan's hand stroked between his legs, crying out as ecstacsy flooded between his hips, waking every nerve in his body as it swelled like bottled champagne. Higher and higher as Cylvan coaxed it—until Saffron gasped and choked at his peak, releasing over Cylvan's stomach. Cylvan immediately hunched over to press their foreheads back together, kissing him, complimenting him, telling him how beautiful he was—all the while, his own movements growing more intense, losing their constant rhythm in demand for release. Saffron could only cling, legs wrapped around Cylvan's waist while he was dominated—before Cylvan grunted and spilled inside of him, in the most satisfying way.

Saffron collapsed to the pillows as the world spun, a flush of ice grazing his skin as his heart squeezed and slowed in the afterglow. Breathing heavy, Cylvan bent over to kiss him, pushing sweaty hair from his eyes to kiss his forehead, last.

"Beautiful," he whispered one last time like a promise, and

Saffron managed an exhausted smile despite unable to find the rest of his body.

"I'll come back for you," Cylvan's voice returned, floating overhead. Saffron pouted his lips, managing to open his eyes again. It made Cylvan laugh, kissing him one more time before coaxing himself in and out with a few final rolls of his hips. Saffron's face contorted in pleasure, summoning a satisfied sound from Cylvan in reply. "There is no way for me to possibly... be apart from someone so perfect, for any time at all."

"Do you promise?" Saffron asked, the exhaustion of crashing pleasure racing to meet him. Cylvan kissed him again.

"I promise," he said. "By the old rules of human and fey—I always come back for what belongs to me."

Saffron smiled, closing his eyes and sinking heavily into the pillows. Cylvan pulled away, trailing a line of kisses across Saffron's collarbones, then his damp hair.

"My treasure," he whispered in finality, and Saffron attempted to smile at the joy those words brought him—but he disappeared too quickly back to the mounds, summoned to that safe, dark place where he could sleep and wake again to the sound of Cylvan's voice. Deep enough that he never once worried about propping the door closed, or being caught off guard.

39

___

THE OFFER

Saffron slept deep enough to escape dreams. Deep enough that once his heart floated back to a place where it could beat again, summoning him from the darkness, he wasn't sure where he was. Who he was. Why he was. Only that he ached with saccarhine warmth emanating from his back, his stomach, between his legs.

He might have even remained in the earth, had something in the open air not caught his attention. *Knock, knock.*

Flickering back to life, Saffron's heavy eyes cracked open, squinting against the sun breaking through overcast clouds on the other side of the windows behind him. Lifting his head slightly, he blinked around the room as thoughts pieced themselves back together, only at the last moment realizing—he wasn't alone. There was a stranger in the room with him, door propped open behind them. Had he not been so heavy, Saffron might have screamed, clambered away, attacked with the first thing he could grab—but then he realized, he recognized them. It was the clerk from the inn's front desk.

Sitting up slowly, somewhere in the depths of his awareness he knew he was naked and littered with lovemarks and half-moon crescents in the shape of Cylvan's teeth, but for some reason, it didn't bother him. He just watched the clerk bring in what Saffron recognized as luggage bags without ever meeting Saffron's eyes, and then Saffron's attention moved to where the dinner table had been cleaned of old dishes and replaced with a breakfast spread filling the room with delicious scents. Cut fruits with powdered sugar; eggs, bacon, honey ham, glazed salmon beneath a glass lid; steaming coffee in a porcelain carafe; a bouquet of tulips and fresh lavender spilling out of a crystal vase in the middle.

On the opposite nightstand, an additional surprise waited for him, and Saffron plucked it up before sinking back into the pillows with a long exhale. Smiling to himself, he touched the front where his name was written in Cylvan's handwriting, opening the card and wiggling his feet in glee.

STAY WHERE YOU ARE. YOU ARE SAFE.
IF YOU WAKE BEFORE I RETURN, I DESERVE
  PUNISHMENT WITHOUT MERCY.

The inn attendant left the room not much later, though Saffron noticed how they glanced last second back to where he rested, disheleved, useless, exhausted in the bed. Saffron almost smiled at them in reassurance, but they turned away again too quickly—and made the sign of beseeching a Day Court as they went. As soon as the door closed behind them, Saffron frowned, making his own for a Night in response.

Keeping the note in one hand, he crawled on wobbly hands and knees to pick at the breakfast offerings on the table, eating directly from the platters. Spreading coils of salted salmon on crackers, sucking on chocolate strawberries, sipping at champagne and orange juice with more alcohol than anything else. He wondered how such a quaint tavern and inn managed to provide such an impressive display twice in a row, though he wouldn't be surprised if Cylvan had somehow arranged for it to all be delivered from Connacht nearby.

Knowing how far they were from the city center, recalling

how long they soared in the sky after leaving the party, was both a relief and another reason Saffron's insides twisted up in anxiety. Far enough that he might not be found; far enough that he wouldn't be able to make excuses if the others were looking for him.

You are safe. You are safe.

Slumping back into the fluffy pillows with another fat strawberry between his fingers, Saffron rubbed a palm up and down his bandaged thigh while sucking on the red fruit, smiling at the hand-painted flowers encircling a hanging lamp overhead. It was fitted with what Saffron recognized to be electric lights, something he'd overheard Eias talking about as they approached on the train. How had they described it? *A fast-growing trend in Avren, spreading across Alfidel. Illuminating rooms and streets without the need for candles or matches, like magic. Someone finally figured out how to get lightbulbs through the veil without the glass shattering...*

Oh, god—Saffron was thinking about the *lights.* He was thinking about the interior decor, when his whole body throbbed so deliciously. Grinning and kicking his feet like a fool in love, he allowed himself to follow the memories back to every moment. Every second. Every touch, and taste, and smell, and—

He had to grab the card again, reading *"You are safe"* once more as adrenaline slammed for a second time. He drowned in the pure elation of exactly what he'd done, but also cowered at the thought of how he'd put himself and Cylvan in horrible danger by giving in to his selfish urges, how if Taran or Kaelar or anyone else found out exactly what happened, Saffron surely wouldn't live through the week—

You are safe. You are safe. You are...

"Safe," he whispered. He sank back into the pillows, tracing his fingers over the handwritten letters. Cylvan's words. Just for him. His name, a promise, a spell—just for him.

Perhaps... all was not lost. Cylvan knew Saffron could speak again—but Saffron hadn't told him much else. As far as Cylvan knew, Saffron's memory threads were still gone, he'd simply... fallen for the prince's undeniable charm and allure, all over again.

"Who wouldn't?" He mused, thinking about how handsome, perfect, irresistible Cylvan looked while they ate dinner the night before, how his muscles moved as he thrust in and out of Saffron that morning, the way he filled Saffron to the brim, the sound of his breaths and grunts of pleasure—and Saffron prickled with embarrassment, kicking his legs again and giggling. *Fuck.*

EVENTUALLY LIMPING TO THE BAGS DELIVERED BY THE desk attendant, Saffron was surprised at how *completely* they were packed. All of Cylvan's clothes, all of Saffron's clothes, including those Cylvan bought for him on the first day, as well as a few new pieces he didn't recognize. Even his arid books were in Cylvan's bag, and Saffron's amethyst pendant was tucked away safely alongisde them, where he grabbed it to drape over his head. Even his crutch was propped against the wall by the door, he noticed last.

Assuring himself Cylvan was just being thorough, Saffron grabbed the crutch and hopped back to the breakfast table, spreading another piece of toast with salmon and cheese before snagging the gossip digest tucked under one of the platters.

Flopping back to the bed on his stomach, he skimmed through the pages unfurled like feathers on the pillow, ankles crossed and swinging with the food balanced on the tips of his fingers. Beantighes weren't usually privy to daily, weekly, or monthly digests, except when a patron specifically mailed one to Beantighe Village for one reason or another. Depending on the publisher, they discussed politics, or gossip, or festivals, scandals, and none of that had ever interested someone like Saffron who would much rather repurpose the paper for his sketchbook.

But that morning, it only took until the second page for something to grab his attention and hook into it like a pair of talons.

MATRIARCH MURVA MAC DELBAITH, KNOWN FOR HER PHILANTHROPIC ENDEAVORS, RETURNS TO THE MOUNDS BY PYRE. FAMILY ORACLES STATE INHERENT MAGIC WAS 'HEAL- ING' UPON POSTHUMOUS WITNESS. FAMILY SAYS TAPESTRY WILL BE WOVEN TO RESEMBLE ANCESTRAL HOME IN THE WINTER COURT...

Saffron scoffed, hating to be reminded that the mac Delbaiths were also from the Winter Court. That must have also been the same funeral Taran attended while everyone else was in Connacht. Saffron hoped the burning pyre failed to collapse beneath the deceased's body, signifying the mounds wanting nothing to do with her. There wasn't a single part of him that believed the words *philanthropic endeavors,* either, despite not being completely sure what they even meant. Unless it was about cruelty, or war crimes, or the courtiers' overall distaste for her while alive.

One other thing did stand out to him, however—that mention of *inherent magic.* What did that mean, if the mac Delbaiths were ashen? How could an oracle figure it out in death, but not in life?

Burying another bite of toast in his mouth, Saffron rested his head on an outstretched arm while reading the headline over a second time and then skimming through the dry recounting of the woman's life. He only sat up again at the sound of a key in the door.

Stretching his neck, instincts urged him to leap to his feet and scramble out the window—but he forced himself to remain calm. Cylvan promised he was safe.

Still, he couldn't help but sigh in relief when it really was Cylvan who opened the door and stepped inside. Carrying a paper bag in one arm and a bouquet of flowers in the other, Cylvan kicked the door shut with his foot, before smiling as Saffron sat up on his elbows with a grin of his own.

Cylvan nearly said something in greeting, before his eyes trailed up Saffron's bare ass, back, shoulders, exposed on the bed. Swaying his legs, Saffron smiled flirtily from his naked place within the pillows, laughing when Cylvan immediately stuffed everything he carried onto the nearest chaise and pounced.

Cylvan stole the last bite of salmon on toast, and Saffron barely had a chance to squeak before the prince's mouth pinned against his, then turned him over.

"My little strawberry cake," he breathed between their lips, tucking Saffron against the pillows and captivating every additional thought Saffron had.

"Were our bags delivered?" Cylvan went on, but hardly gave Saffron a chance to respond. He lifted a knee onto the bed, gliding his hands over Saffron's chest. Saffron shivered beneath the touch, gently hooking his fingers around Cylvan's wrists. Cylvan responded by rubbing his thumbs into Saffron's nipples, making Saffron gasp sharply as a mouth found a ticklish spot under his ear. He giggled, then laughed as Cylvan hiked himself farther onto the bed, pinning Saffron beneath straddling legs.

"I'm going to take you away from here, Saffron. Just like I promised," Cylvan went on against his skin. Saffron's eyes fluttered slightly in question.

"What do you mean?" He asked. Cylvan kissed him again, smiling excitedly, handsomely, then took Saffron's hands to kiss his knuckles and under his wrists where the silver cuffs sat.

"I've chartered a carriage for the Winter Court," he answered, and Saffron's eyes widened. "We'll leave tonight, after the sun goes down."

"You—" Saffron pushed Cylvan away in sudden alarm, just enough to stare at him. "You did what?"

Cylvan's smile grew, clearly getting the reaction he wanted—but it wasn't what Cylvan thought. No, Saffron's words weren't rooted in thrilled surprise; they filled Saffron with fiery, icy fear in an instant.

They couldn't leave. Saffron couldn't go to the Winter Court with Cylvan, as tempting as it was. They couldn't run away together, as badly as Saffron wished it was possible—not when Hollow's life was so vulnerable. Not when Elluin still detained Baba Yaga. Not when Saffron hadn't figured out a way to protect Cylvan and his name, yet. They couldn't just... run away. They couldn't just leave everything behind—

"We..." he croaked, holding Cylvan's face. "We—we can't, Cylvan. I'm sorry, but—we can't go. Not like this."

Cylvan's sunny demeanor clouded slightly. He furrowed his brows, smiling in confusion and brushing his thumb over Saffron's cheek.

"Why not?" He chuckled. "Don't tell me... you would prefer to go back to Danann House?"

"No!" Saffron sat up quickly, nearly headbutting Cylvan who sat back just in time. "Of course not, I mean, I only... it's just..."

He didn't know how to say it. How could he possibly explain without saying too much? With Cylvan's offer to whisk Saffron away... With preparations already made...

Saffron knew, if he suddenly offered too much of the truth, Cylvan would only further root himself into his plan. If Cylvan knew the extent of the threat on Saffron's wellbeing, both from Taran and Elluin, Cylvan might even force Saffron to go against his will. Might even compel him to run away. But if they left, if Saffron never returned home from Connacht...

Taran would take it out on Hollow.

Elluin would take it out on Baba Yaga. And then they would both take it out on Beantighe Village.

Saffron could only hold Cylvan's face, staring at him pleadingly.

"What about Taran...?" He croaked.

Cylvan scoffed. "What *about* Taran? I'll make sure he never finds us."

But his purple eyes grew dark, as if on the verge of saying something else, as if he could sense Saffron's true hesitation. As if he suddenly wished to do exactly what Saffron feared, to exert his will as the prince, or a Sídhe, or something else—but instead, he closed his eyes. He clenched his jaw, and Saffron felt how hard it tightened beneath his hands.

"Have I done something wrong?" He asked flatly, and Saffron straightened upright.

"No!" He insisted again, nudging Cylvan's face to look at him. When his eyes still refused to meet Saffron's, Saffron huffed and pulled him more forcefully. Cylvan continued to resist, and Saffron finally realized, Cylvan seemed almost embarrassed.

He exhaled a soft breath, then kissed Cylvan gently.

"You want to take me away somewhere safe," he reiterated thoughtfully. "*Thank you,* Cylvan. That's so kind of you to think of me that way. Truly."

Cylvan softened slightly beneath Saffron's hands.

"I want nothing more than to disappear to the Winter Court with you one day, too," Saffron continued in promise, kissing Cylvan's cheek. "You must look so beautiful in the snow and the mountain lights. We would drink Luvon's frost wines and eat warm nutmeg cakes with ice berries. And then we would read books by the fire, and fall asleep under fur blankets..."

"Yes," Cylvan answered under his breath. Saffron smiled, nuzzling into the curve of Cylvan's jaw.

"I wish to do that, too," he promised. "Just... not now."

"Why not?" Cylvan insisted. Emotions flared in his body again, Saffron feeling each and every one beneath his hands, how Cylvan's heart pounded. Like he was one weakened resolve from breaking open and flooding the room with wind. Not in anger, not in rage, but in—confusion. Saffron kept smiling gently.

"Because... I don't want to run away knowing we will have to live in secret. I know you would keep me safe... but I don't want you to *have to.* I want to live freely by your side, without ever having to worry about people like Lord Taran ever again."

He kissed Cylvan's forehead.

"You are so kind," he repeated. Cylvan's hands found the

crooks of Saffron's arms, trembling slightly. "It makes me so happy to know you wish to take care of me, Prince Cylvan."

"Then let me."

"I will."

"When?" Cylvan's gaze cut into him; if Saffron didn't know any better, it might have even frightened him. But despite how big and explosive Cylvan's emotions could be, Saffron had no reason to be afraid of him. Still, he returned a look of matching intensity. Cylvan didn't back down, a muscle twitching in his jaw as if sifting through every possible arguement he could counter with. Saffron spoke again, first.

"I will never deny anything you wish to do with me..." he started, pulling Cylvan down to hang over him on the bed. Extending his arms, they crossed behind the prince's head. "...when we no longer have to worry about Taran mac Delbaith."

"It's not that simple—"

"I thought you were a prince," Saffron whispered, and Cylvan's eyes narrowed, nostrils flaring in a rush of genuine anger. Saffron didn't mean it, feeling the first flicker of uncertainty pinch in his chest—but he just pulled Cylvan down to kiss him again. And then again. When Cylvan still didn't respond, Saffron shook him stubbornly.

"Say something, your highness. Or am I making you angry?"

"Yes."

"Do you still want to take me away?"

"Yes."

"Even when I make you angry?"

"*Yes.*"

Saffron cracked a weary smile.

"Do you understand... what I'm trying to say?"

Cylvan's jaw flexed again. He pressed his lips into a line, closing his eyes and knitting his brows, but nodded. Not in a way he agreed—but he at least understood. Saffron kissed him again, softly. He would keep kissing him, again and again, every time those overwhelming emotions flared up to the surface, like a reminder that they were still on the same side. There was no animosity in disagreement—at least, Saffron didn't want there to be. It made him wonder who taught Cylvan to believe such a thing, though a part of him already knew.

"Don't be angry with me, your highness," he teased in a pitiful, coquettish way. "Oh, Prince Cylvan, what can I do to make it up to you? I spoke out of turn~ it was so rude of me."

"It was."

"What can I do?" Saffron pressed his mouth to the base of Cylvan's throat, then trailed his tongue up the side of his neck. Cylvan's breath shuddered, catching hard when Saffron's hand moved down the center of his stomach, teasing the waistband of his pants. "Is this alright?"

"Y-yes," Cylvan said roughly, and Saffron smiled, sliding his hand into Cylvan's pants to play with him. The trembling breaths he summoned from the angry prince hovering over him was enough to warm every inch of Saffron's body, finding Cylvan's mouth and kissing it again.

"I want to disappear with you," Saffron repeated. "As soon as we can be together freely."

"I..."

"Until then—you have me here. Until tomorrow morning, when we have to go back, you have me all to yourself. Can we pretend until then?"

"I don't want to have to pretend!" Cylvan exclaimed. Saffron pulled his hands away immediately, and Cylvan's head drooped, shaking back and forth. "How much longer? How much longer —must I sit back and watch as you stand with nothing to protect you? Don't you understand what will happen to me if I lose you again, Saffron? I can't..."

His voice cracked. He shook his head again, and Saffron jumped when the smallest fleck of heat dripped to his neck. He took Cylvan's face again, staring as emotion welled in Cylvan's eyes. Cylvan avoided his gaze, but it didn't matter. Saffron saw everything that flickered across his expression.

"I can't... do it again," he admitted weakly. "I can't—lose you again. I can't lose *more* of you again, I can't..."

Saffron wiped Cylvan's tears away, sitting up to embrace him. Cylvan sank against him in return, and Saffron pet the back of Cylvan's hair in comfort.

"I'm sorry; I'm here," he promised with every ounce of honesty he could give. Saffron needed Cylvan to feel it, even if he couldn't speak it—though Saffron suddenly felt the crushing weight of his lies more than ever before. The weight of how badly he hurt the same person he held, who only ever wanted to protect Saffron, too.

But as badly as it hurt, as much as Saffron hated himself for knowingly hurting Cylvan further, when it would be so easy to open his mouth and explain everything—

Saffron was... terrified. He was *terrified* of witnessing this person he held in his arms break down into pieces, again. To crumble beneath his hands, realizing what Saffron had done to protect him. A terrifying Night Prince—who would never admit to needing help from anyone, but would cease to exist, otherwise.

Saffron was terrified of losing his friends. Of losing Hollow, who was being held over Saffron's head like an object at ransom. Of losing Baba Yaga, who had never been given a fair chance at a good life. None of them had.

But if Saffron just maintained his act a little bit longer, just a little bit longer... he might be able to offer everyone he ever cared about something that was more than simply living, day by day.

"I'm here, Cylvan," he begged his raven to understand. To hear the words he couldn't speak, yet. Just a little bit longer. "We only have to pretend for a little bit longer. I promise."

"How long?"

Saffron pressed a shaky kiss to Cylvan's hair. He didn't know how to answer. It was easier to sew his promise, to show his devotion through his hands, his mouth, his body, rather than speak anything into the universe that could be captured and twisted.

Saffron didn't know when they could stop pretending. He

didn't know when he could stop lying. He didn't know when, or if, he would ever be able to live peacefully with Cylvan at all.

That was why—he had to savor every single moment of peace he was given. Just like the first time.

He couldn't squander it, just like the first time.

Not when the alternative terrified him into near nonexistence.

40

THE LOVELIER CHOICE

Cylvan helped Saffron into a straw-padded wagon outside the inn, handing over his crutch before climbing up, himself.

Journeying back to the city, they sat close to one another as Saffron sketched using new pastel colors and a palm-sized sketchbook, surprise gifts from Cylvan's morning in Connacht. The passing trees, occasional peeks at some wild fey crunching through the undergrowth, another passenger's intricately stitched luggage, Saffron's hand moved like water over the page as Cylvan picked straw from his hair and complimented his work.

It was quiet. Peaceful. Perfect. And every time Saffron remembered it wouldn't last much longer, he nestled closer into Cylvan's side. Under his arm. Resisted the painfully strong urge to take the prince up on his offer to escape to the Winter Court, after all...

But Saffron had to think of Hollow. Baba Yaga. Everyone in Beantighe Village. There would be plenty more chances to run away together, to go wherever they wanted—but not until Saffron made sure the people he wanted to protect were safe, first. Saffron's books in Cylvan's bag, those given to him by Pimbry Scott, were his best chance at exactly that.

In Connacht proper, they met the others outside of the train station. Approaching as nothing more than beantighe and high fey, Saffron even kept a few paces behind as a sign of submission, though Cylvan made dirty hand movements behind his back the whole time. There were a multitude of reasons Saffron wanted to grab and drag the prince away somewhere private.

Kaelar stood a distance away as Eias handed Saffron his black veil. Saffron bowed in gratitude, relieved he hadn't lost it. Asche watched them the whole time, before harassing Cylvan for abandoning them with Eias and Magnin who were so *dull* for going to bed early; it summoned retaliation from Eias, who complained about Asche keeping them all up too late at the street festival. Saffron bit back more amusement, especially once the silver choker squeezed around his throat, slightly. An unwelcome reminder of its return.

Waiting on the train platform for their turn to board, Cylvan remained in a great mood, and Saffron had to bite back the pure bliss of just witnessing it. The prince teased Asche, complimented Eias' souvenirs, told Magnin his hair was looking particularly shiny that afternoon—and actively ignored Kaelar entirely. All three of them raised eyebrows like they knew something was different, and Saffron had to cover his laughter behind a badly-timed cough.

Boarding one after another, Saffron was settling in place when Magnin cleared his throat, then pulled a lacquered black box from their bag. It was half of Saffron's height, and caught Saffron's attention in an instant—which seemed to be Magnin's intention.

"Will you step into the next empty carriage with me, beantighe?" He asked. "I want to get these braces fitted on you as soon as we can."

Saffron glanced at Cylvan, who was distracted by something shiny Eias was showing off. Smiling to himself, Saffron nodded, getting back to his feet. It shouldn't take too long; Cylvan might not even notice he was missing.

Slipping through a hidden door in the wall, they stepped into a narrow passageway on the other side that ran down the length of the train car. Clearly meant for the passage of drink carts and other hospitality workers, Saffron didn't say anything, just followed Magnin to another door at the far end. They stepped inside right as the train rumbled beneath their feet with preparation to chug ahead.

Saffron claimed a seat on one of the cushions, and Magnin hooked the end of a long chain beneath the edge of the bandage at his ankle. Feeding it up the length of Saffron's pantleg and over his waistband, Magnin pulled it through, the hook slicing through the bandages like pulling a zipper. Saffron was grateful to not have to strip entirely, though the pain of losing the stability of the bandages made his jaw clench uncomfortably.

When the carriage jolted forward, Saffron grabbed Magnin for balance, surprised at how tightly the fey held himself—and then the outer door of the car suddenly slid open. Someone stepped inside within a moment of the train taking off, before closing it again without a word.

Saffron's lungs froze as Taran shook out his hair. He met Saffron's eyes, then casually smiled.

"Hello, beantighe," came his greeting—but something unreadable tugged at the corner of Taran's mouth as he said it. "Did you have a nice time in Connacht?"

Magnin pulled away from Saffron to offer Taran a bow, but Taran put his hand out.

"Don't let me get in the way," he said cooly, stripping off his cloak and settling onto the cushion opposite where Saffron sat. Saffron could only watch, heart drumming as loud as the tracks clanging beneath the train.

Hardly another moment later, the back door suddenly opened, too, and Kaelar stepped inside. Saffron's heart slammed harder.

"You look nervous," Taran said thoughtfully, resting his cheek against a bent finger. There was no more gentleness in his voice. His normally golden green eyes were dark, never pulling away except to blink slowly. Kaelar, meanwhile, remained in the back corner. Saffron realized with a thud of his instincts, he might have been blocking the exit on purpose. He eyed Saffron no differently than Taran did, with bruises around his nose despite a healer's best attempts at fixing what Cylvan broke with the heel of his boot.

Taran spoke again.

"Magnin, will you remove the beantighe's collar? There are some things we need to discuss before returning to Morrígan."

Magnin nodded. He reached around Saffron's neck and unclasped the silver. Saffron gulped as he did, swearing the air in the car whisked away the very moment he could inhale freely. He prayed it was because Cylvan had noticed him missing, wind rushing from his hands, already on his way to intervene...

But Cylvan never came. And Taran didn't say anything else, not for a long time. He just watched as Magnin used a small needle to pop holes within the seams of Saffron's pants, then undid the clasps on the lacquered box and lifted the lid. Saffron didn't know whether it was better to keep Taran's gaze or pretend like nothing was amiss, finally shifting his eyes toward the box Magnin knelt in front of. Inside, four silver plates were nestled into a shiny black interior, laid out in the shape of a leg.

"Explain what you're doing, Magnin," Taran's voice came again, and Saffron jumped. Magnin cleared his throat.

"With the opulent silver you provided, my lord... I was able to fashion these braces for the beantighe's leg. But first, I have to form them to his anatomy. His bandages have hardened enough to keep their shape, so I will be using them as a mold..."

"Ingenious," Taran flashed an impressed smile. "I knew I could count on you to be so creative, Magnin. Truly outstanding."

"Th-thank you, my lord," Magnin seemed genuinely complimented, but at the same time, as on edge as Saffron was. No—that was impossible. Saffron was about to plunge directly through the floor.

He focused on Magnin's hands, suddenly desperate to cling to anything that wasn't Taran's gaze. They rolled up the bottom of Saffron's pantleg as far as it would go, taking the bottom edge of the leathery bandages and gently coaxing them free. Like pulling a sheet of bark from a tree without tearing it, resulting in a single piece that could be shaped, just like Magnin intended. Saffron might have easily fallen into all the memories he had of harvesting sheets of bark to replace roof shingles on the cottages—

"Kaelar told me a very interesting story about the party you all attended."

Saffron's pounding blood stopped with a whimper of his heart. He moved his eyes slowly back to Taran, who just kept smiling.

"Apparently he and Prince Cylvan got into an argument, causing a whole scene. Is that true?"

Saffron gulped. His eyes flickered to Kaelar, who smiled slightly, then back to Taran.

Saffron nodded, knowing there was no point in lying or playing dumb.

"I gave you the ability to speak."

"... Y-yes, my lord," Saffron's voice cracked as the air grew thinner.

"Kaelar said it started because Cylvan was jealous of his behavior toward you. Is that true?"

Saffron glanced briefly to Kaelar again, who still said nothing.

"No, my lord." Was Saffron's answer.

"Go on, then."

Saffron swallowed again.

"L-Lord Kaelar—"

"That's no way to address your patron-master."

"... Master Kaelar... compelled me to k-kiss Prince Cylvan, in front of the rest of the party. And then to grope him. It was—it was humiliating for him, my lord, I'm sure—"

"For Kaelar?"

"No, for Prince Cylvan..."

Taran's smile twitched.

"And that is why the prince sucked the air from the room, assaulting all two-dozen people there? Because he was embarrassed to be kissed by a beantighe."

Saffron couldn't breathe, as if silver hands were still pinned around his throat. As if Taran's voice was made of the same choking magic.

He tried to be distracted by Magnin's movements, watching as he pressed the bandages into the curve of the silver. Watching how the silver, as if still warm, easily molded to take the shape. How, as it solidified, a shine spread over the surface—

"That's not the story Kaelar told me," Taran urged. Saffron closed his eyes. He picked at the skin of his nails in anxiety, but managed to glance back at Taran again.

"I don't know what Master Kaelar would have told you," Saffron said, trying to keep his voice calm. "He compelled me to assault Prince Cylvan, and Prince Cylvan retaliated."

"Prince Cylvan protected you."

Saffron pressed his lips together, knowing, more than ever, he had to be careful of the words he chose.

"I don't know if I would call it that, my lord—"

"*'Seelie Prince Cylvan allegedly stole the breath of an entire party in Connacht when kissed passionately by an attendee's beantighe...'*" Taran's response was rehearsed, and Saffron realized why as Taran removed a gossip pamphlet from the inner pocket of his jacket. "*'Partygoers say the prince then swept the pretty beantighe into the sky, and they were not seen in Connacht again the following morning or afternoon. Perhaps Prince Cylvan has a taste for humans just like his great-grandmother, Queen Proserpina, once did. Who's to say whether this beantighe who stole his heart will be the one to also break it, and induce the Night Court promised?'*"

Saffron could only listen. When he did answer, his voice shook, though he tried to cover it with a naïve smile.

"Isn't that—good for you, my lord?" He asked. "I thought you wanted Cylvan's reputation to get worse. How else are you supposed to be Alfidel's savior if there's no villain threatening it?"

He intended it to pose as genuine offer of peace, but the words formed into a sarcastic accusation faster than he could stop them. Taran just kept smiling, then swished the pamphlet between his fingers.

"They did actually mention me by name, here," he said. "But not as the coming savior. Just like every other gossip column of the past year, they poke fun at the clear lack of affection Cylvan holds for me. This one asks if, perhaps, the reason he is so 'flaccid in our bedroom' is because he actually prefers soft, pretty, innocent beantighe servants, instead. And then they have the nerve to claim it no surprise, as *'the beantighe seen stealing the prince's heart was described with emerald eyes, knowing hands, and hair like brown sugar. Far from the harsh beauty of Taran mac Delbaith.'* Ah—and here is my favorite part. *'Perhaps soft loveliness is what the icy prince actually needs to tame his cruelty, rather than the strong hand of a mac Delbaith...'* Isn't that interesting?"

Saffron's smile grew more desperate. He shook his head slightly.

"That's just gossip, my lord. It doesn't mean—"

"And now—" Taran interrupted. "I heard Prince Cylvan intended to return to the Winter Court... with one guest. There's no name for his intended partner on the itinerary, though. Do you happen to know anything about that?"

Saffron stared at him. His mouth dangled open, waiting for something clever and cunning and perfect to escape—but nothing did. There was nothing for him to say; Taran already knew everything.

Taran crushed the pamphlet in his hand, throwing it in Saffron's face. Saffron barely flinched, just clenched his fists harder over his knees.

"I—" He attempted.

"Magnin," Taran interjected. "I think you ought to check the beantighe for injuries, considering the perilous night. Unbutton his shirt and pull it open, will you?"

"That's not—!" Saffron exclaimed—but Taran leapt from his

seat, slamming Saffron back against the wall with a forearm pinned against his throat. Saffron choked, throwing his hands out in an attempt to shove him away, but Taran's opposite hand was already ripping his shirt through the buttons. They scattered like teeth across the floor, the pendant following suit with a sharp sound before clattering to a halt. Saffron's open shirt revealed a swathing tapestry of love marks and bruises and bites left by Cylvan's passionate mouth the night and day previous.

Taran jerked away, staring at them—before grabbing Saffron's open collar again, and slapping him. Again and again, until Saffron buckled backward with a cry and threw his hands up in defense. The onslaught only stopped when Magnin pulled Taran away, Saffron's face swelling and burning hot as blood dripped from his nose.

"I told you what would happen!" Taran roared, spit flying from his mouth as Magnin fought to hold him back. "I told you what would happen if you ever touched him again, *you useless bint!* I knew I couldn't trust a fucking human to keep its legs closed—I should have ripped your fucking memories out when I had the fucking chance!"

"There's nothing stopping you now!" Saffron snarled before realizing. *"Try me,* you ashen cunt!"

"I'LL KILL YOU!" Taran's hands found Saffron's shirt again. "And then I'll kill every beantighe roach living in that dump in the woods! Perhaps then I'll kill *Cylvan* to finally be *fucking done with it!* There is still one more royal sibling *eager* to marry me, and I will not hesitate—Gods know it'll be easier to stomach than *THIS DEGRADING SHIT!* And it'll be all because of *you,* beantighe—every single fucking *human,* your *fucking gods-damned prince,* will die a horrible death because *you* couldn't resist *spreading open for Cylvan's cock!"*

The train screeched as it approached a stop on the way. Taran's frenzied eyes flew to the carriage door as the platform rose into view outside, then came to a halt. The sliding *thunks* of a dozen carriage doors sounded off.

Saffron lunged for the exit, but Taran grabbed him, first. He slammed Saffron back to the seat, knocking the air from his lungs. Saffron thrashed his arms—but Taran smashed a fist into his jaw, knocking Saffron's reality loose. His body sagged, thoughts curdling and swarming.

"*Fuck!*" Taran seethed, raking fingers back through his hair. "Kaelar, come on. *Now!*"

"*Restraint,*" Kaelar commanded, and Saffron's wrists clacked together. He bent over to pick up the amethyst pendant from the floor, all while additional enchantments came. "*Be still. Be silent.*"

Saffron slumped. Numb, motionless, disconnected as if his spirit had been locked out.

"Oh... it's warm," Kaelar chuckled, fondling the pendant before draping it over his neck and appreciating the color. "How pretty."

Dragged from the seat, Saffron was folded up in the back corner, away from view of the carriage door. Kaelar took Saffron's place on the cushion, next—and with a nauseating turn of Saffron's stomach, the fey lord glamoured himself, from head to feet, to resemble Saffron perfectly. All the way down to his messy brown-sugar hair. His emerald eyes. The scar on his cheek. His mouth, his hands. Cylvan's lovelier choice.

"Whenever you're ready, your highness," he said, thick with sarcasm, perfectly sounding in Saffron's own voice. Taran cursed him, planting a knee between Kaelar's legs—and pressing their mouths together.

Saffron could barely stomach to watch, witnessing himself wrapped in a passionate embrace beneath Taran mac Delbaith's hands and mouth, moaning and whimpering in all the most horrifying ways—

Saffron didn't think the nightmare could worsen— but then the carriage door slammed open, and Cylvan stood on the other side.

Kaelar gasped innocently, hiding behind Taran who snapped at Cylvan to leave. Cylvan inhaled sharply to say something—but then stopped short. He stared a moment longer, as if memorizing every detail of the sight in front of him. Saffron under Taran. His mouth kiss-bruised, shirt pulled open to reveal his bare chest. Flushed and breathless. Taran's knee pressed between his legs—

Cylvan took a step back. He put a hand to his mouth, furrowing his brows—then turned, and took off into the sky.

"No!" Saffron cried through clenched teeth, tearing against Kaelar's enchantment like a hardened shell. *"No—! Cylvan!"*

But Cylvan was already gone. And as soon as he was, Taran stepped back, wiping his mouth before spitting on the floor.

"How was I?" Kaelar asked, still wearing Saffron's face and fluttering his eyelashes, licking his lips, opening his legs. Taran just smacked him on the shoulder and told him to shirk the glamour before he was sick.

Saffron just strained his neck toward the window, asking, begging why—*why* Cylvan would ever think Saffron would—

Why wouldn't he say anything, do anything—

But then Eias appeared in the open doorway. They peeked inside, meeting Taran's eyes and bowing their head slightly.

"Perfect timing," Taran complimented, and Saffron thrashed again beneath the weight of the enchantment pinning him. He tumbled to his side on the floor, and Eias glanced at him for only a second, before averting their eyes again. They glanced at Magnin, instead. Saffron glanced at Magnin, too, but—he wouldn't meet Saffron's eyes, either.

Saffron had to wonder—if it had been planned all along.

Queen Proserpina, who sought comfort in Wolf King Clymeus following the betrayal of Adone, her human lover...

Seelie Prince Cylvan, the coming Night King, heart broken by a human, just like his great-grandmother—who only a descendant of Clymeus could comfort and control...

"What did you tell him, Eias!" Saffron pleaded, voice cracking. Eias still wouldn't look at him. Behind them, the train horn announced its departure from the station. Saffron threw his body in every direction, fighting to rip through what remained of the

numbness in his bones, desperate to fling himself from the train car, to call out for Cylvan in the open sky—

But Taran stepped to where Saffron lay, grabbing Saffron's open shirt and dragging him to the middle of the floor. He took Saffron's chin and forced their eyes to meet.

"Take as long as you want to bring me my fruits," he started, but Saffron spit in his face. Taran sighed, wiping it away in annoyance. "You'll want to listen to me, beantighe. You'll regret it, otherwise."

Saffron's fighting stopped. Frustrated tears filled his eyes.

"Take as long as you want to bring me my fruits," Taran repeated in a low, cruelly sensual voice, "but every evening I don't have them until Ostara... I kill whatever beantighe is assigned to work in Danann House that day. Starting with Hollow. Tomorrow."

"You can't—!" Saffron jolted, but Taran just smiled, shoving him back down. He grabbed his cloak and threw it over one shoulder.

"Is there room in your car with the daurae, Eias? We better hurry," he said, and Eias stepped out of the way as Taran exited. "Magnin, get the beantighe's leg all fixed up. We want to make sure he's got the best chance to do what I ask, after all. It's only fair. Kaelar will help if there's any more trouble."

Kaelar said something. Magnin said something. Taran said something else. Eias said something last. The carriage door slid shut. Latched. The train blared again, and the ground shifted. Saffron's reality closed in.

What did you say to him, Eias?

What could you possibly say—for Cylvan to ever think...?

Saffron stared at the ceiling. Choking on his own breath, even without the collar to squeeze him.

Falling from a great height, the wings on his back were nothing but melted wax and scattered feathers.

He never should have flown so close, no matter how warm and decadent Cylvan's light had been.

41

THE FINAL WORDS

Saffron's cuffs were restrained once more when they arrived outside Morrígan. The collar was returned to his neck. He was pulled onto Taran's lap on the back of his horse for the journey, arms dangling around the back of Taran's neck. Chest to chest. Sensing the fey lord's hot breath on his skin the entire time.

Something inside of Taran had snapped, and Saffron wasn't the only one who saw it.

The moment they arrived at Danann House, Saffron shoved away. He hit the dirt with a thud, then pushed himself to his feet and raced through the door. It was almost effortless with the silver braces compressing his leg, opulent silver infiltrating his bones with healing magic—but by the time Saffron made it to the top of the servant's stairs, it still ached. It throbbed like it'd snapped all over again.

He just had to get Taran's memory threads. Baba's grimoire. His new arid books. *Anything.*

There had to be *something* in *any of them* Saffron could use. He had no other choice. He had nothing else—

Before rushing into the room where he hid his things, though, he realized his own bedroom door hung ajar.

Inside, a windstorm had blasted through. Books were scattered across the floor, ink spilled over the top of the desk and dripping off the side. The window had been thrown open from the outside, latch torn away from the wood. The good luck charm for his friends was knocked to the floor, scattered across the chaos. He thought for a moment it had been Taran to rip through his things while they were away—but then saw exactly what was on the desk, half-smothered in ink. His heart stopped, and brought the world to a halt with it.

The Alvish-Gaeilge book, given to him by Pimbry Scott, was spread open over a piece of brown paper. One covered in feda markings diligently scribbled down from everywhere in the house.

Alongside each mark, a nightmare unfolded in the form of Cylvan's handwriting.

NO BURN.
NO HEX.
SHARP CUT.
NO POISON.
SEALED AIR.
NO ATTACHMENT.
FRESH SCENT.
NO LEAKS.
ONLY INTENDEES.
OUT OF SIGHT...

Cylvan's translations grew more frantic as they went. More and more, until the nib of the quill tore through the page, slicing an arch across the wood underneath and hurling the inkpot against the wall. Kitchen spells; housekeeping spells... they weren't actually Saffron's final words.

Saffron had known that all along; god, he'd even forgotten about them entirely amidst everything else happening—but they were the first place Cylvan went. The first thing he sought out after whatever Eias told him, after what he saw on the train. The last words of the person he lost.

And Saffron, without ever realizing how badly a heart could hurt, had let him believe it.

Silent tears dripped from his eyes. He just stared at the words, at the familiar handwriting, at the ink plipping with every drop to the floorboards. Below his feet, something bumped.

Cylvan was in his room. Cylvan was right downstairs. If Saffron could only explain, if he just told Cylvan everything, including that he never lost his memories, was never lost at all, not a single part of him—

Saffron needed something to prove himself honest, especially after what Cylvan thought he saw on the train, especially not knowing what Eias had told him. Saffron threw himself out the door again, into the neighboring room where he ripped up the loose floorboard and yanked out his leather bag containing his sketchbook, Baba's grimoire, Taran's threads, and—the Greek myths. The ones Cylvan started annotating for him, the ones Saffron continued. If Cylvan didn't believe Saffron when he said he'd never lost his memories—the book would prove it. A lying, threadless beantighe would never know all the things he wrote inside.

He removed Cylvan's ring from the spine where it broke through the pages of Icarus, and pushed it onto his finger.

Rushing from the room, Saffron knew exactly where to go to push through the third floor wainscoting, but he still almost lost his way. The panic, the adrenaline, the fear—all of it, blown out by the repeating image of Kaelar glamouring himself to Saffron's visage; how it felt to watch him caress and kiss Taran so sensually; Cylvan meeting who he thought was Saffron's eyes through the train door. How Saffron couldn't move the entire time. How neither Eias nor Magnin would meet his eyes, after. Taran's final threat—

Saffron shoved through the wall panel, only to crash into someone rushing up the stairs on the other side. Daurae Asche hit the floor with a grunt, before scrambling to gather the random crystals and notebook they'd dropped. Saffron barely had the patience to help them back to their feet before hurrying by—but his wrist was grabbed last second, pulling him back.

"Wait!" Asche croaked. Saffron tried to pull away again, staring straight at the Aon-adharcach door, ears ringing—"I said *wait,* beantighe! Cylvan isn't going to listen to you, you're just going to make it worse!"

Saffron turned on Asche with fury, and Asche stumbled backward in surprise. They threw their hands up, but didn't back away. That was when Saffron noticed the hands-and-dagger ring on their finger—as well as his amethyst pendant around their neck.

"Listen to me!" Asche exclaimed, shaking their head. "I know what happened—I know everything that is happening, as well as what Taran told you, alright? And I—I want to help. I even—I even told him I want to have a party at the house tonight, but just so you and I can leave without anyone noticing... He thinks he can trust me, but..."

They trailed off, and Saffron saw a flicker of rage cross Asche's own expression. They swallowed whatever they meant to say, instead insisting:

"Please, Saffron, let me help you. But for now—we have to leave Cylvan alone."

"No—!" Saffron managed the short word just before the collar went tight. Asche pressed their lips together, but nodded empathetically.

"Cylvan won't listen to anyone right now," they whispered. "Please, trust me. I know him. What he thinks he saw—there will be no explaining in a way he'll listen. At least not right now. Please. The best we can do is let him be, just for a little bit. And while we're gone, we'll find a way to help him. Right?"

Their eyes flickered to the book in Saffron's hand, held upright like a weapon.

"Is that for him? Look, I brought some things, too," Asche

held out two red, hexagonal crystals in one hand, and a black leather notebook in the other. "Why don't we leave them together? I'll take them into his room and leave them on his bed, alright? Then he'll see them after he calms down..."

Saffron pulled the book into his chest, opening his mouth to protest—

"*Please,*" Asche insisted gently. They put their hand out for the book, and timidly offered the pendant in exchange. "Let me. If you go in there, yourself... I worry he might say or do something he regrets. He's not thinking clearly. He really thinks you..."

Asche trailed off. Saffron could guess, though he had to halt the immediate stream of thoughts, lest his legs give out beneath him. The betrayal Cylvan must have felt, from the one person he thought he could trust to always care for him...

Squeezing his eyes closed, a few restrained tears dripped out— but Saffron slowly extended the book to Asche, and traded it for the pendant they offered. Asche took it with a reassuring smile, and held it like something precious. In exchange, they pulled the silver ring off their finger and tucked it onto one of Saffron's. Then, they reached around his head and undid the choker. It tumbled into Saffron's cupped hands, next to his pendant.

"You'll be able to leave the house with that ring. Why don't you go grab a horse, Saffron? I'll come meet you right away."

They said Saffron's name with so much kindness. More tears filled Saffron's eyes, but he wiped them away and nodded. Asche nodded, too, and their silent agreement was made.

Still, despite the promise, Saffron hesitated on the opposite side of the wainscoting. He squeezed the pendant hard. He braced for the moment Asche opened the door to the Aon-adharcach suite, breaking the silent barrier—

"*—He's gone—I never had him back—Taran has taken everything from me, everything—*"

Saffron clamped hands over his mouth, fighting back agony that surged like blood up his throat.

42

THE MEMORIES

The cool air was a balm on Saffron's overheating thoughts that wouldn't stop racing.

He must have been somehow close to death, because he swore he witnessed more wandering spirits than normal as he and the daurae made their way through the dark Agate Wood on the back of the horse. Perhaps the spirits were just curious about the red threads in Saffron's bag. The arid grimoire right next to them. The prince's family ring on Saffron's finger, clutched tightly in his opposite hand so he wouldn't squeeze the amethyst pendant, instead.

He didn't have Pimbry Scott's arid books.

He didn't have Taran's supposed piece of opulent silver used to turn into the wolf.

He didn't even have time to cry out while crushed beneath the new, demanding weight of having to figure it all out in only one night, else he lose everything. Everything.

All Saffron had was one last hope of learning something, anything at all about Taran mac Delbaith through the knotted threads.

"Did you know?" He mumbled, slumped with his forehead

pressed into Asche's shoulder. "That he's ashen. And Clymeus' heir."

"... Most courtiers know," Asche answered like it was any other light gossip. A chat over brunch. Perhaps they knew anything else would make Saffron bolt off the horse and race back to Danann House.

"I didn't."

"Well—it's not a *secret*, but people don't talk about it," they continued, each word trailed by hesitation before the next. "The mac Delas are a Sídhe family—and a well-respected one. The mac Delbaiths are a branch of them, but no less part of the larger tree."

Saffron scoffed, and Asche shook their head.

"I know what you're thinking, since they come from Clymeus... but they've always been charitable. And friendly. And philanthropic. And... never showed bitterness for losing their magic, at least in public. I don't think they're all bad... For the most part, they're well-loved amongst courtiers, really... Which is why this is all such a shock..."

Asche sniffed, and Saffron suddenly felt bad for asking. But not bad enough to stay silent.

"How did they lose it in the first place? Their opulence."

"... Verity Holt took it away from Clymeus from Proserpina fell, and cursed his entire family tree. Every branch of them, including Taran's."

Saffron cracked his eyes open. He watched colorful wisps bounce between the trees a few yards away, wishing to lure the visitors to a different fate. His mind floated on the pain and the exhaustion, swearing he suddenly knew how it felt to chip into pieces beneath the pressure.

Verity Holt, along with her twin brother Virtue, were the humans who overthrew Proserpina. They were the ones to put an end to her Night Court, bringing her son, Elanyl, into power instead. Elanyl ruled an Evening Court—one with more sunlight than his mother's, but still rife with unease. Fragile. One that could slip back into darkness again, if he wasn't careful. Elanyl only ruled for a decade before dying a silly death, leaving his only son, Ailir, to ascend to the throne as a toddler. Elanyl, the foolish king, who Alfidel lauded even more than the human twins who did the hard part. Perhaps Saffron shouldn't have been so surprised.

"When they become kings... could Cylvan... give Taran's family their magic back?" Saffron's chest hurt when he asked.

Asche stiffened beneath him, as if they'd never considered that, either.

"Oh..." They breathed, and it was answer enough. Saffron just closed his eyes. He didn't want to think about it. He didn't want to think about how there were so many reasons for Taran's claw for power, so many reasons he justified using Cylvan for his own wants. And how Alfidel was going to give everything to him, without any fight at all. With open hearts and arms. All for protection against a Night Court that might never come.

"Do you want to know a secret?" He asked softly. Asche nodded. "Taran... never took my memories. I've been pretending this whole time."

Asche didn't respond for a long time, then nodded, as if they'd already figured that out, too. Still, they asked: "Why?"

Saffron grimaced. "He knows I have influence over Cylvan— but not like you think. I never drugged him... I never tricked him... I only..."

He trailed off. He watched the wisps in the trees again.

"I think... I love him," he whispered, unsure if the words were meant for Asche or the incoporeal spirits. "At least... I know I will, if we are ever given more than just a few weeks to get to know each. It's like I already know I'm supposed to fall in love with him..."

Asche was quiet. Up ahead, the horse finally reached the abandoned road, pausing before the wall of mist.

"I see the way he looks at you," Asche said, like a promise. "I used to think he loved Taran... I used to think *I* loved Taran... but maybe I just... didn't know any better. The way my brother looks at you, though... the way he touches you... the way he talks about you all the time, even when you aren't there... I think he's meant to love you, too, Saffron."

Saffron closed his eyes. New tears flooded, and he smashed his face into the back of Asche's shirt as he cried. He didn't know what Cylvan heard on the train.

He didn't know what Cylvan was thinking. Saffron had turned his back on his raven, again—leaving him all alone in Danann House when he needed comfort, *again*, but—

"I'm going to do everything I can to save him," he wept, "so one day, maybe I can hear him say that for myself."

SAFFRON'S SILVER LEG BRACE FELL VICTIM TO THE beannighe's barrier. The magic silver had, at least, been potent enough to heal some of his injury in its limited time, allowing him enough strength to walk—but every step was agony.

Stumbling through the darkness, they followed sprawling moonflowers up the walking path toward the empty library. The entire time, Saffron was nearly convinced he'd slipped through the veil between life and death and wandered the plains of asphodel rather than the abandoned school. If it wasn't for Asche supporting his weight and encouraging him to continue, he might not have made it to the ruins at all, let alone the limbo fields.

Perhaps it didn't matter where Saffron walked, so long as his spell worked. He had everything he needed. He didn't have to wait. Didn't have to prepare. He could only pray there was something valuable in Taran's threads.

Asche screamed at the sight of wild fruits in the library; Saffron just bent his knees, plucking the nearest pink strawberry and taking a bite. It quelled the anxiety in his soul in an instant, and he sighed like a thirsty man finally getting a drink of water.

"I thought you didn't know where they were!" Asche demanded, proving they really did know everything that was going on. They swatted the fruit from Saffron's hand. "Why would you lie about them, even while Taran—!"

"Taran isn't getting his hands on anything," Saffron grunted, helping himself to a handful more. "I found them on my first day here—and I still never told him. And I never will. Never."

Asche whispered something pitiful, before apologizing and gathering Saffron back into their arms. Following Saffron's directions, they climbed the stairs to the empty second floor where Sunbeam had nearly finished her work on the veil circle.

Choosing one of the shelved corridors with the fewest fruits, Saffron clumsily tugged Baba Yaga's grimoire from his bag, asking Asche to open it to the page he'd already marked. As they did, Saffron pulled out the other ingredients already gathered, working with squinted eyes as his head throbbed and made his vision flicker in and out.

Weaverthistle picked from the edge of the ruins, where he wondered if the memory threads in the trees fertilized them like seeds; a bowl of water; a thick fairy apple; a rope to loop around his wrist.

Asche read the instructions out loud, and Saffron worked in silence. Mashing the red weaverthistle flowers and shells, he dunked them in the bowl of water, using his hand to make sure they combined entirely. Next, he soaked the first of Taran's four memory threads in the mixture, watching the water turn cloudy in response. Dipping the fairy apple into the swirling bowl last, he paused to let his body relax before taking as large of a bite as he could, juices spilling from the corners of his mouth.

Grabbing the bowl, he plucked the knotted thread out and threw it to the floor. Gazing down his bookshelf corridor, he double-checked the loop of rope around his wrist and made sure the daurae clung securely to the opposite end. Asche looked a little faint, but Saffron smiled at them in encouragement.

Finally, Saffron took a deep breath—and threw the water toward the ceiling.

Prepared to be immediately soaked, the water, instead, lingered overhead—then bubbled, pulsating and whipping into a thick cloud.

Stretching wide until it ricocheted against both sides of the shelving, the fog then stretched downward to the floor. It never once lost thickness, no matter how far it reached. Wider and taller, the dark thunderhead draped and spread over Saffron's feet, where a chill nibbled his boots.

Gulping back nerves as his body tingled with fairy drunkenness, Saffron tugged on the anchoring rope one more time—then followed the final instruction, and stepped inside.

Saffron emerged in the dark, chilly night air. Straightening up, he searched in every direction, but quickly realized—no matter which way he turned, his perspective stayed the same.

Gazing straight ahead, the surroundings passed as if traversing Morrigan's campus despite never moving his feet. The path was a familiar one, even in darkness so penetrating it had to be at least midnight. He was making his way from Danann House, down the stretch of Quartz Creek separating campus from the edge of the Agate Wood.

Following the path, he came to a stop at the base of Agate Bridge. His instinct was to continue forward, briefly thinking he could race across and into the woods, all the way back to Beantighe Village—but his body still didn't respond. It just stood there, waiting, eyes locked on the dark trees on the other side.

When something suddenly emerged from the shadows, Saffron jumped. He recognized the person who appeared—he'd seen her face many times in passing—and just once, up close. Cloth.

Stark realization sliced through the cloudy memory making it hard to think straight. The memory thread he'd chosen to swim through—was the night Taran killed Cloth.

Ahead of him, Cloth approached, looking pale and frightened.

"Well?" Taran's perfect, polite lilt left Saffron's mouth.

"I'm—I'm sorry, my lord, I couldn't find them in time. If you could spare me another day or two, maybe..."

Cloth's voice shook, but her posture was perfectly straight. Never once did she look away, meeting Taran's gaze directly. A part of Saffron was proud to know she approached the fey lord with so much confidence—but another part of him wished she would look somewhere else. Anywhere else, knowing he would have to keep her eyes the entire time. Knowing exactly what would come next, no matter how badly he wished to stop it.

It came as quickly as he feared. Without warning, without offering another word to her request, Taran took a step back. Every bone inside of him sweltered with white-hot heat, as if smelting metal to claim the shape of claws, legs, haunches of an animal as large as a horse. And then—Taran chased her down. Off the bridge. Under it, where she tangled up in mud on the bank. She begged for mercy only once, before Taran's teeth clamped down and silenced her.

SAFFRON HIT THE LIBRARY FLOOR WITH A GASP, staring at the opaque mist that swirled where he'd fallen through. It slowly disintegrated once he left, like water vapor returning to the air. Soon, nothing was left except a blanket of dew kissing every inch of the shelves.

Asche rushed to meet him, dropping to their knees and checking if he was really still alive. Saffron just stared between the shelves toward the window, realizing the sky was beginning to lighten.

"How long was I in there?" He asked hoarsely.

"A few hours," Asche said, and Saffron shuddered. He didn't allow himself to linger on how that was possible, knowing it only meant he had less time than he thought. Especially with so many threads left to search.

Grabbing the next one, he repeated the process.

THE SMELL OF MORNING FORESTRY FILLED HIS NOSE. Then came the sound of sunsingers, a babbling creek, and—footsteps, crunch, crunch, crunch, crunch, beneath him. Ahead, someone else tromped through the thickets. He paused.

From a grove of trees, a wanderer suddenly emerged, nose buried behind a tattered piece of parchment. Distracted enough that they didn't notice Taran in the shadows. Instinctively, Saffron attempted to call out just like with Cloth, his voice didn't register. Even if it had, the greeting would have lodged like a stone in the back of his throat.

Lifting their head from the parchment—the wanderer was Berry.

Saffron's vision shifted, lowering into the shadows as his friend turned to search the direction where he stood.

"Sunny?" Berry called, before frowning and gazing back to the map again. Saffron tried to call out again, terrified of what he was about to witness—but it was too late. His perspective shifted, lunging and burying teeth into Berry's flesh.

Saffron fought to shield himself, tried to close his eyes so he wouldn't have to watch, but it didn't matter. In Taran's memory, he'd been nothing but hyper-focused. Moving with pinpoint accuracy, with every intention to kill without blinking. And Saffron— was forced to watch, feel, and taste every moment. Every mouthful of his friend's blood that spilled between the jowls of the wolf he'd crossed paths with before even knowing what was happening.

In the last moment, Taran examined Saffron's map left in the grass—eyes lingering in the unexplored corner Saffron since learned to be where the ruins sprawled.

. . .

SOMETHING TUGGED ON SAFFRON'S WRIST, STRETCHING taut, and he reflexively grabbed back. Crashing to the floor, vomit raced up his throat, and then screams, pressing the horrified sound into the blanket of leaves and fruits. Curling up tight, he knotted fingers in his hair as he couldn't even cry, couldn't even think, could only scream and scream until he finally evicted every last coppery taste of blood from his mouth.

But even as every part of him begged for mercy, begged for even a moment to recover, he couldn't. There were two strings left, and the sun was even higher in the sky. He couldn't wait. He couldn't waste it.

"If Sunbeam comes soon, don't let her interrupt, alright?" He croaked, gathering the ingredients again.

"Are you alright?" Asche insisted, placing a hand on Saffron's shoulder. Saffron didn't answer, he just worked faster.

His first slam of hesitation came in a moment of pause, which he knew would be his downfall. That single moment that allowed the horrible thought scratching at the back of his mind to speak up.

Cloth. Berry. There was only one other beantighe Taran killed on campus—that Saffron knew of. One more beantighe, but two more threads.

He had to. Saffron had to. He couldn't turn his back on Arrow, on anyone else, ever again. He had to know why Taran had his memories of killing the beantighes plucked, why he kept them, why he hid them. There had to be a good reason, even if it was a horrific thing to taste and know. There had to be something. There had to be *anything*. Alfidel wouldn't care about dead beantighes. There had to be *something else* Saffron hadn't figured out yet.

Closing his eyes, clenching his teeth, Saffron's hands shook around the bowl. It made the water ripple, breaking the crystalline surface. A cold hand suddenly pressed against his, and he opened his eyes to tell Asche to stand back—only to find no one there. No one that he could see, though he could still feel their touch. As if drawn by a familiar memory, even if it wasn't theirs—and their vicious emotions flooded him.

It wasn't grief—it was anger. Resentment. Hatred.

Squeezing his eyes closed, Saffron swallowed the lump in his throat.

"I'm here to help, Arrow," he whispered. "Sorry it took so long."

Show me what Taran did to you.

43

THE FIRST

"I know where to find them, but I can't reach them. Give me another day. My friend will help me."

Arrow stood tall, not unlike Cloth in her last moments, too. Saffron felt annoyance swirl in the body that wasn't his.

"What do you mean, can't reach them?" Taran growled from the mouth Saffron borrowed. Arrow straightened up in response, squaring their broad shoulders. The Imbolc fete at Danann House cast a bright light on the other side of the trees, illuminating them from behind, making them appear even wider than Saffron remembered. It was no wonder Taran felt so threatened.

"I mean, I literally can't get past the iron gate into the ruins. It's too big, it must be negating your fancy ring that unlocks everything," Arrow raised a hand, sarcastically wiggling their fingers to show a silver band around one of them.

"I don't fucking think so," Taran insisted in a low voice. "Iron has no effect on that silver, so I suggest you stop lying to me, beantighe. Before I run out of patience."

"I'm not lying, damnit!"

"What makes your friend so special?" Taran went on, crossing arms over his chest. "I told you I needed the fruits tonight. Why *would I wait until you get a whole squad of useless humans together?"*

"He knows the woods and everything in them better than anyone. He could figure out how to get in," Arrow replied, and had Saffron been in his right mind, in his right body, he might have felt the full extent of pain those words caused. Because Saffron knew— Arrow was talking about him. *Even after Saffron told them off only moments prior, Arrow still believed Saffron would help them, later. And—he would have. Saffron would have, if only—*

"That ring will get you in, damnit!" Taran snapped, taking a step forward, only to lean back again when Arrow responded with a similar motion.

"YOUR RING DOESN'T FUCKING WORK!"

"Well, then—why don't you tell me the name of your friend, and I'll ask him for help myself?" Taran's words were thick with resentment, and Saffron felt the exasperated smile on his face as he said them. But Arrow didn't back down, didn't even loosen their shoulders.

"Go fuck yourself. You're not going anywhere near him without me."

Taran put his hand out.

"Return my ring."

With no hesitation, Arrow popped the ring off their finger—but then paused before handing it over.

"This is one of those bone rings, isn't it? Made from Sidhe remains," they asked, and Taran went stiff. "I grew up in Avren. In one of the queen's abandoned monasteries, actually. Mac Dela gravediggers were always coming around disturbing old family plots for things to munch on..."

"Be silent, foundling," Taran hissed, thrusting out his hand for the ring. Even Saffron felt how it lacked any compelling enchantment; Arrow must have noticed, too. They watched Taran with a new shimmer of question.

"Is that why you can't enter the ruins, yourself? You use some sort of secret ash magic, too? Let me guess—it doesn't work when you

approach the gates, either. I'm telling you, my lord, the iron gate is too—"

"It has NOTHING TO DO WITH IRON!" Taran snarled. His extended hand twisted backward unnaturally, as if fighting the wolf that thrashed beneath his skin. "Return my ring, beantighe!"

"Then what?" Arrow asked. "Because if it's not the gate, and your magic ring can't even open it—then it's something else. Something no beantighe is going to be able to figure out. But if you tell me what it is keeping you from entering the ruins, yourself, I can be of more help—"

The raging fire erupted too hot in Taran's body, tearing through his skin. Hot and wild and excruciating, every inch went up in flames as flesh and muscle and sinew made way for the beast hiding underneath.

Saffron watched as Taran torn his friend open; he felt every single moment, as if the wounds were his own.

THE ROPE WRENCHED SAFFRON BACKWARD, OUT OF THE memory cloud. Collapsing, he pressed his face into the floorboards, entire body shaking and soaked with sweat. He grappled at his skin to make sure he hadn't actually split open from the inside out. He couldn't think, couldn't speak—only saw Arrow's face. Heard their voice.

Bone ring. Gravediggers. Ash magic. Doesn't work on the gate. Nothing to do with the iron.

"F-fuck," Saffron rasped. He stared at his leg, where his only pieces of Proserpina's Silver remained. Flattening his hand against the top brace, his heart pounded as scattered understanding clicked together.

Taran leaving Connacht right away to attend a family funeral, where a Winter Court pyre burned the deceased's body—*Murva mac Delbaith, inherent magic determined to be 'healing' upon posthumous witness—*

"It's... bone ash," he croaked, squeezing the plate on his leg.

"Its opulence... comes from dead Sídhe fey... dead mac Dela bones... That's how it has opulence; it must be... according to their inherent magic..." His ears rang. "Then Taran, Taran must be..."

Saffron's heart stopped.

The reason the beannighe claimed Wolf King Clymeus stalked the Agate Wood—

Taran—ashen, resembling Clymeus mac Dela's wolf—

He turned to vomit again, but his stomach was empty. Everything inside of him was empty, there was nothing left to purge. He was forced to feel every single scraping thorn of understanding.

The reason the beannighe sensed Clymeus in the woods, the reason Taran was able to change into a wolf despite being ashen—was because he used the bone ash of the dead wolf king to mimic his Sídhe ability.

With shaking hands, Saffron clutched the last remaining thread. Why go to such lengths to hide it? Wouldn't Alfidel be thrilled? Wouldn't they find a reason to celebrate it?

What else—could Taran mac Delbaith be so frightened of, that he had it pulled from his own memory?

"Saffron?" Asche asked nervously, and Saffron met their eyes. The daurae looked terrified, staring at him as if Saffron suddenly wasn't making sense. Saffron wished he could explain. He wished he could tell Asche everything was going to be fine, that he'd figured it all out—but there was still one more thread before they had to return to Danann House.

"One more," Saffron reiterated. He gathered the ingredients for one final excursion. Sweat dripped down the back of his neck, hands trembling, mind racing as he tried to guess what he might find. In the cacophony, one reassuring thought returned louder than ever. Something he already knew.

If I can learn where he keeps it, I can take it. I can make Taran vulnerable. He will not hurt anyone else.

I will control him.

I will save Baba Yaga. Hollow. Cylvan. Everyone I love.

Saffron buried his hand down his shirt, clinging to the amethyst pendant—and that time, it warmed against his palm. His determination surged.

Cylvan was waiting for him. Saffron could tell Cylvan everything.

He threw the water, drenching himself in what he hoped would be his salvation—and Taran's undoing.

44

THE HEIR

"This is going too far, Anysta!" Taran's voice ricocheted off the coffered ceiling, chased by the banging door in his wake. On the other side, Anysta had her face between the trembling legs of a low-fey girl, who jumped and whimpered when Taran suddenly burst into the room. He hardly perceive her. Taran only saw his sister, who barely lifted her eyes from stroking the girl's length to smile at him.

"What now, dearest brother?" She cooed, and the girl beneath her shuddered, biting down on fingers to stay silent. Anysta pushed her skirts out of the way, coyly tugging the fingers from the girl's lips and demanding to hear every sound.

"This is going too far," Taran repeated with added vitriol. He waved the letter in his hand, only a single line written across the front. But Anysta still didn't care, going back down on the girl who writhed and moaned and clung to Anysta's Dagdan priestess garb.

"I must admit, I don't understand what the problem is," she eventually said, but still didn't meet Taran's eyes. "We all have to do our part."

"I've done mine!" He shouted, throwing the letter at her. "What I've done—giving my bones for his, is it not enough? Will it ever be enough?"

"As the one who will reap the benefits of being king, brother, isn't it only fair that you carry the heaviest burden?"

"They'll execute me for this."

"Only if they find out."

"They perform thread searches on anyone they want, Anysta, with no warning at all—!"

"So then remove it," she smirked, sliding fingers into the girl and making her moan. Anysta lifted her head slightly, appreciating the way her partner gasped and arched her neck backward.

"They'll find a gap," Taran insisted through clenched teeth, heart pounding in a mix of fury and fear.

"Have the ladies not taught you how to weave filler-threads, yet?"

"Filler—? If this doesn't get me executed, Anysta, filler threads—!"

"I'll take that as a no."

Fury sweltered into rage, ripping through Taran's body, melting the bones helping him remain upright. Storming forward, he came within a foot of the chaise where Anysta pleasured the girl—only to stumble back again when his sister suddenly lunged upward, pointing a knife at him. Caging her partner protectively against the cushions, Anysta's golden eyes were sharp like the dagger in her hand. Taran took a step back, but his anger didn't subside. He could only heave with hot breaths.

"Oh, baby," Anysta finally smiled again, circling the tip of the knife in Taran's direction. "Don't tell me... there's even more to be disappointed about with you? You remember how upset mother was when you didn't take Clymeus' ability to compel, don't you? What is it this time? Gasp—don't tell me, mother's favorite can't even manipulate threads? You? The chosen one?"

"Stop it," Taran hissed. Anysta smiled more, kissing the edge of the blade before teasing the girl with it, who giggled and blushed.

"I suppose there's still time to take the bones back out of you," she went on, using the knife to snip the laces of the girl's corset up to her

chest, kissing sensually at her nipples. "Perhaps you were simply never cut out to be the wolf king's heir. Would you rather take my place as a priestess? Proserpina's tapestry might appreciate your company, since you resemble Clymeus so much—"

"Anysta!"

Anysta slumped. She buried her face into the tan skin of the girl's stomach, before sitting forward to smile at her.

"Do me a favor," she cooed, and the girl sat up slightly in question. "Cover your ears for me, darling. Just for a moment."

The girl glanced at Taran, before doing as she was told. Anysta kissed up her stomach one more time, before throwing her brother an exasperated look. Placing her hands over the girl's as well, for good measure, her eyes went icy in a second.

"There's no point in dragging it out, Taran. Just do what mother asked, then go back to the party, fuck your stupid prince senseless like you do every other night, and let the rest unfold as it must."

Taran's face went hot. He thought he might be sick. He didn't want to do that, any of that, not to Cylvan—

"Everyone... already thinks he's bringing a Night Court," he said, though it lacked the same aggression as before. "This isn't necessary."

But Anysta wasn't listening. Anysta wouldn't listen, that much was obvious from the resentment in her eyes. She always looked at him like that, ever since she was forced into priesshood while her baby brother received the wolf king's final remains.

There was simply nothing Taran could do.

He left the room, moans and gasps trailing behind him. Pulling the door closed into his back, he grit his teeth, clenching the note into hardly more than withered fibers.

Breathing in deep through his nose, he grounded himself in the moment. He pushed away his disdain, his annoyance, his frustration, his fear.

The air was rich with sea spray. Avren always smelled like that, but within the halls of Mairwen Academy right on the coast, the scent was stronger than ever. He could even faintly hear the crashing waves on the other side of the windows, and was reminded of the long morning he spent on the jagged coastline, riding horseback with Cylvan while reminiscing on their childhoods together. It was the first genuine moment he'd been able to share with his old friend in years—and less than a few hours later, the request to ruin it all came. To clinch his place in Cylvan's life. To ensure it.

Alfidel's savior, to tame the bloodthirsty Night Prince. Just like Clymeus and Proserpina.

Letting out a long breath, Taran forced the thoughts away, and pushed off from the door.

He'd chosen his family. He would choose nothing else. Not even Cylvan, his oldest friend, to whom he'd told only lies since first disappearing when they were children. Perhaps, one day, when the grip around Taran's throat loosened as he stepped into kinghood, he would be able to tell Cylvan the truth. Perhaps there would be a time where even the Tuatha dé Danann would provide him more protection than the mac Delas ever could.

But that wouldn't come for centuries—and only if Taran was by Cylvan's side.

The ballroom glistened with sparkling chandeliers, shimmering gowns, embroidered jackets, moving feet. The air was lively with string music as bodies swirled and danced, feet tapping rhythmically on the wood. It wasn't hard to find Cylvan amongst them, laughing with a group of friends by the buffet of food on the far wall. Taran went straight for him.

Taking Cylvan's hand, Taran kissed it. Despite everything else roiling in his gut, as always, Cylvan's natural beauty made Taran's heart flutter when their eyes met and Cylvan smiled at him. He looked so handsome, like nothing had ever, or ever would, bother him at all. Taran knew the truth, Taran knew there was an endless myriad of things tearing Cylvan apart in secret, things Cylvan had confessed only a few nights prior while alone in the dark—but Taran wouldn't allow himself to follow that memory. If he did, he might not be able to do what had been asked of him.

Maybe, one day, he would be able to tell Cylvan everything.

Kissing the back of Cylvan's hand again, Taran's tongue flicked against his warm skin, tasting perfume.

"Are you coming to bed soon?" He asked, then shook his head as Cylvan offered a sip of the champagne in his hand.

"Soon enough. I have to stop by the library, first."

Taran's stomach turned, but he kept his expression calm. "Meeting with that beantighe again? People are going to start calling you a seelie prince."

Cylvan rolled his eyes, taking another drink. Even that sarcastic movement was flawless, somehow.

"Don't be jealous, Taran. Glass is only a friend. She has a rare text to give me, that's all—a first edition of Old Alven Mythology, isn't that exciting?"

"...Just don't drink too much," was all Taran could think to say, realizing only afterward the way it was an unintentional seed to be planted. "You always overdo it and end up getting in trouble."

"Don't worry about me."

Taran left a kiss on Cylvan's cheek, then excused himself.

Leaving the party, he stepped into the corridor.

Down the long, dark hallway, he came to a halt in front of a mantle mirror surrounded by flowers, framing him like a royal portrait.

He regarded his face. His tan skin, wavy brown hair, gold-green eyes. Features that resembled King Clymeus, as Anysta said. Staring into them for a long time, he finally pulled away before the hesitation could grow any stronger. He turned his eyes to his hands, flexing his fingers and exhaling through his nose.

His skin prickled with warmth, then a sparkling kiss of magic emerged from the deepest reaches of his bones. Magic that wasn't his to own, but his to use. It was hardly more than a flutter compared to the roiling heat that came when taking the form of the beast.

Taran's fingertips paled, and the color washed down his palms.

His fingernails grew, dark and pointed. He lifted his eyes back to the mirror, only for a moment—and a face that didn't belong to him gazed back with amethyst eyes.

"I told you to watch how much you drank," he muttered with Cylvan's voice. "Now look what you've done, Cylvan, throwing a beantighe to the waves..."

45

THE WOLF KING

Saffron slammed to the floor, kicking his feet and shoving as fast as he could away from the lingering cloud. He crashed into a pair of legs, the owner of them snapping his name and scrambling to gather him by his shirt.

"Taran—!" He cried, grappling Sunbeam's clothes. She was drenched in a vivid sunset orange, nearly blinding him. "He—! Nimue, it was him—!"

"Saffron!" Sunbeam took him by the shoulders, attempting to both shake and settle him. "What the hell are you doing here? What is *Asche* doing here? Oh, god—what the fuck kind of magic—!"

"I have to—!" Saffron lurched away, but the floor shifted. He nearly collapsed, pressing hands to his head and begging the world to go still. He felt it—that burning, melting, tingling in his bones. In his bones, his own bones—

The silver—was in Taran's bones.

He wanted to scream. He wanted to scream until the whole world tore itself apart. There was nothing for Saffron to take, nothing he could steal, nothing he could put in Cylvan's hands to say, *"Look! Look what I've found! He can't hurt you anymore..!"*

Saffron learned the truth about Taran, his silver, his magic, the reason he couldn't enter the ruins and beseeched then killed beantighes instead—but Saffron's chance at doing anything about it never existed. Not unless Saffron ripped every bone out of Taran mac Delbaith's body—

The sun was setting. Saffron had to get back to the house. Taran was going to kill Hollow if he didn't get back in time, unless—

Plummeting to his knees, Saffron ripped frantically through the fairy plants, shredding fruits and leaves and vines to shove into his bag. Sunbeam grabbed him, pulling him away, demanding to know what was going on as Asche just cried and begged Saffron to *stop!*

"What am I supposed to do!" Saffron shrieked, fighting against Sunbeam before losing his footing and hitting the ground again. "What the fuck am I supposed to do now! His bones—!! It's in his fucking *bones, godDAMNIT!!"*

"What are you talking about, Saffron!"

But Saffron was already back on his feet, racing for the door. His leg screamed between the silver plates, barely able to keep him upright. All he knew was—Hollow was going to die if he didn't get back to the house. Everyone he loved would die if he didn't give Taran the goddamn fruits—!

Claws tore down Saffron's arm the second he burst through the doors, throwing him to the walkway. Scrambling to right himself again, Saffron turned onto his back—and met bright yellow eyes, a wrinkled snout, teeth bared as the wolf paced only a few yards away.

Sunbeam and Asche rushed behind him, and Sunbeam grabbed the daurae the second she laid eyes on the beast.

"How is he..." she asked, but Taran kept his eyes locked on Saffron in the dirt.

"The barrier didn't last as soon as I destroyed that woman's circle," Taran heaved between breaths. His voice was grating, crackling with every word, biting back mad hysteria. As if something happened at Danann House to snap him further than he'd already gone. Saffron was suddenly terrified for Cylvan.

"Without the circle, without the threads, there is no more barrier," Taran continued. "... Which means I can hunt on my own. Which means I don't need you—I don't need Cylvan—I don't need—"

"Taran?" Asche begged alongside Sunbeam, but Saffron didn't dare turn to look. Taran's yellow eyes saw them, though, bulging and taking a slight step back while bowing his head in uncertainty. But it was too late—Asche had seen him. One by one, the people he thought he could use as bartering chips flaked away as they realized who he was, what he was willing to do to get what he wanted.

"It's him, Asche," Saffron found the courage to say, and Taran's eyes snapped back to him. "He wants wild fairy fruits—to drug Cylvan into proposing."

Taran snarled, pawing at the dirt and swinging his giant head back and forth, as if to disagree—but if he spoke again, he would only dig his grave deeper. As if Asche hadn't already heard him, as if they hadn't already realized.

"The fruits?" Asche demanded, shoving out of Sunbeam's arms. "That's why you want wild fruits—to force my brother into marriage? *That's* what this is all about? I know everything you said in the train car, Taran, but this is—!"

Taran's ears flattened against his head. He took another uncertain step back.

"That's right!" Asche shrieked. "I know what you said about using me if Saffron didn't get what you wanted! About killing my brother! I thought—!"

Asche ground their teeth together. They lunged, but Saffron jumped in their way, first. Nails tore into Saffron's arm, brandishing him with every ounce of Asche's rage.

"I thought you loved him!" They cried. "Me, too! My whole family! I thought—! I thought you were different, you always promised you were different! But you fucking mac Delbaiths—all you want is to get your fucking opulence back, don't you! You don't give a shit about anyone else! You don't even care about being king, do you! You just want to use Cylvan to get your gods-damned magic back—! No wonder Cylvan won't fucking propose to you! And *NEITHER WILL I!*"

Taran's nose wrinkled deeper, snapping his teeth. Saffron attempted to pull Asche back one more time—but the daurae broke through his arms.

They thrust out their hands. unleashing a torrent of golden flames. Hitting the earth, they spilled like ocean waves, biting into plants and overgrowth before shifting bright orange and all-consuming. Silhouetted by their light, Saffron saw how Asche's slight frame heaved with furious breath, long blonde hair wafting out behind them as the fire grew higher and more enraged.

"Fuck you!" They screamed. *"Fuck you! Fuck you!* You'll never lay a hand on my family—*ever again!*"

They turned sharply, citrine eyes piercing straight past Saffron and Sunbeam toward the library. Throwing up their hands again, they drenched the front entrance with devouring fire that glowed pink with berries fueling the flames.

"No!" Sunbeam begged, throwing her hands up—but it was too late. Hungry flames tasted the walls, chewing through anything palatable within reach of hot tongues. Her veil circle would be left to fend for itself—just like the fruits. Just like the crypt below.

Taran saw the color. He heard the hissing and popping of ripe fruits boiling in their skins. He must have smelled the hot sugar on the air—and realized what was right on the other side, on the verge of extinction beneath Asche's flaming hands.

He lunged, but Saffron slammed his shoulder into the beast's ribs before teeth could sink into the daurae's shoulder. They both hit the ground, and Saffron barely rammed his heel into Taran's foaming mouth before it could gut him.

"Take Asche away!" Saffron cried, and Sunbeam wasted no time heaving the daurae over one shoulder. Asche screamed, kicking and flailing their hands, threatening to burn her to a crisp just as well, but she took off in the opposite direction before any threats could be realized.

Saffron locked his arms around Taran's neck, choked by fur and flesh as the wolf thrashed against him, tearing at his clothes and skin with claws, slamming him against the road with every movement of his head. Gritting his teeth, Saffron waited until he knew for certain Sunbeam would have a head start, finally snapping away and scrambling backward.

Taran twisted back to his feet. Gathering his bearings, he only stared at the growing flames of the library, prickling and sparkling with loosed fairy pollen. The heat grew as Asche's rage was insatiable, shifting Taran's fur, blowing Saffron's hair around his face with hot fingers and embers. Saffron hoped the spirits protected their books just like the first time. He hoped they weren't frightened.

"No more of this, Taran," Saffron said, wiping blood from his mouth. "Those were the only fruits in all of the Agate Wood. I know it—and they're gone."

Taran's head swayed toward Saffron, mouth hanging open slightly. Loose embers and falling ash swirled around his mouth between every huffing breath. But the beast's golden eyes weren't filled with the rage Saffron expected—they were bright, piercing, and a guttural sound emerged from the back of his throat. Saffron clenched his fists, stomach turning over when he realized, the sound was laughter.

"No," Taran groaned, shaking his head again. "No, no, *no*, I'm not close to being done. There's still one more thing I can use, *beantighe.*"

Saffron's instincts screamed at him to *move*, and he took a step back, but Taran followed. One step back, one step closer.

"I know... there's a reason Cylvan is so infatuated with you." The words dragged along the ground as Taran descended. "I know... you're controlling him, somehow. Why else would he have been so brokenhearted—and then so angry? I've never seen him so angry before, beantighe, it really was quite a sight... and the whole time, he just asked me over and over and *over and over* where you were, what I'd done with you... I know you have something he wants... you have something to offer. Cylvan dé Tuatha dé Danann does not bend over... and play someone's pet... unless there's a reward on the other end. So tell me what you've promised him, and I won't spill your entrails across the road."

"You..." Saffron still couldn't believe it. "You really think I have something a *prince* could want?"

Taran scoffed, kicking up more ash from the dirt. Saffron shook his head. He flattened a hand against his chest, fingers closing around the front of his shirt and feeling the pendant still hot underneath.

"Does that drive you *mad*, Taran, knowing Prince Cylvan gladly *bent over* for whatever I had to offer, after your family came up with an entire plot to make you his only friend?"

"You think yourself smart, like you have this all figured out," Taran snorted. Over his shoulder, something red emerged from behind a crumbling structure, and Saffron's heart pounded. "But even an ashen Sídhe lord—has more pull in this world than a *worthless beantighe*. It doesn't matter what you do now, because Cylvan is *mine*, no matter how much you cry and bitch. You've taken advantage of my mercy long enough—and I've run out of patience."

Saffron nodded, but his eyes were locked on the crimson veil approaching. He met the beannighe's eyes—and she smiled at him. He couldn't help but smile back, a rush of pure thrill devouring him like the flames did the library.

Her wolf king. The beannighe would finally get her wolf king.

"You're right," he agreed. "I am definitely worthless—but I know the thing you've been hiding."

Taran bared his teeth in agitation.

Saffron's mouth twitched into another smile. He flexed his legs to run. "I know those bones don't belong to you, Taran—and I know whose they really are. And..."

He could hardly keep the splitting grin of anticipation off his face.

"I know someone who has been looking everywhere for you, *wolf king*."

The beannighe tore through the smoke, crashing against Taran's back and burying teeth into flesh. Skin and muscle flayed beneath her demand, a fountain of blood spewing between her lips and drenching her in even brighter red. Taran threw his head back with a roar, snarling and twisting his neck, burying his own teeth into the beannighe's leg to tear her off—but Saffron didn't see what happened, next. He was already running.

46

THE NAME

Danann House was alight with the fete Asche requested as a cover, overflowing with students come to eat, drink, fuck—and, in Saffron's case, to burst from the trees, screaming Cylvan's name. He held back gasping pain as his leg bent beneath the effort, feet slamming into the earth, torn by roots and stones, moon on his back—and the entire time, clawed feet tore after him. Snarling, grunting, heaving with the breaths of an animal that wouldn't hesitate to kill him, that time.

Saffron emerged in the dark apple orchard behind the house. It took him a frantic moment to reorient, ignoring the group of half-dressed fey pleasuring one another amongst the rows of trees. Saffron turned toward the glow in the darkness. The house. Cylvan. Cylvan was in there. If Saffron could just—

The fey screamed, and Saffron turned just in time to witness the monstrous shadow rip through the branches. Taking off down the row, Saffron barely dodged between two trees as Taran nearly buried silver teeth into his back. Weaving in and out, Saffron just searched for the lights of the house every time he lost his bearings.

Throwing himself over the back garden fence, he hit the grass on the opposite side and kicked away from the darkness. A hunched silhouette rumbled on the other side. Right on the edge of the light, burrowed within the blackness. Taran didn't want to be seen as the wolf—and by the gaping wound still gushing blood on the back of his neck, he must have known better than to change back, too. Fey Taran would bleed out in an instant.

"Cylvan—" Saffron managed to wheeze, coming back to his body and grappling for his hands and knees. Pushing himself upright, he raced for the house.

Up the terrace stairs, he shoved through the back door. It smacked one of the party guests on the other side, who grabbed Saffron's sleeve and wrenched him back in retaliation. Saffron just ripped himself away, pushing deeper into the crowd.

"Cylvan!" He shouted over the voices, but his prince was nowhere to be found. Not in the kitchen, the dining room, the parlor, the study—Saffron's raven was nowhere at all.

Racing up the stairs, Saffron thought of the Aon-adharcach suite, but it was just as empty. He shoved through the wainscoting, praying Cylvan would be in the attic, even crying out in relief upon bursting through the door—but it wasn't Cylvan waiting in front of the open window on the other side.

Kaelar grabbed him just before he turned. Gripping Saffron's hair, he twisted and shoved Saffron facedown on the desk, pressing against him from behind and cooing for him to *relax, it's all going to be alright*. His mouth then found the side of Saffron's neck, biting down, leaving a mark over where Cylvan had tasted the night before.

"I knew you'd be back; I knew you'd come right to me," he grunted as Saffron shoved against him. "I enjoyed gutting your friend Hollow, you know. He screamed and cried and pissed himself, all while calling out your name, too. I told him you weren't coming. You never cared about him, anyway. You only care—about your prince's cock, right?"

Saffron twisted out of Kaelar's grasp, pulling his arm to fight back—but Kaelar shoved him out the open window, and he fell.

Three stories rushed by—and he hit the grass with a heavy *thud*.

SAFFRON LOST EVERY SENSE THE MOMENT HE COLLIDED with the earth—but they crept back slowly, one by one.

Hands grabbed him, dragging him deeper into the darkness.

He smelled fresh soil, verdant leaves, rotten fur.

He heard Eias' voice whispering something, and then crunching feet before Kaelar joined them.

He tasted salty dirt as a garden towel was shoved into his mouth.

Jolting, an arm hooked around his throat from behind, pinning him back into Kaelar's body. Saffron attempted to twist free, but Kaelar's opposite arm wrapped around his waist. Cooing into his ear, Kaelar whispered once more for him to *relax*, just like in the attic. Just like the very first time, nearly three weeks earlier.

"Eias," Taran growled from somewhere nearby, and Saffron wildly searched the darkness. They were surrounded in every direction by thick foliage, with a garden trellis blocking most of the sounds of the party. Saffron finally spotted Taran over Eias' shoulder, who sat stiffly in front of him, holding themself small. As if they had reason to be just as frightened as Saffron was. "See what Cylvan likes so much about this beantighe."

"And if they can't find anything up here," Kaelar breathed, combing fingers through Saffron's hair before biting the curve of his ear. "I'll take a look other places."

Spit dripped from Saffron's muffled mouth as he screamed and fought against Kaelar's arms, throwing his head back and forth, arching his back, bending his knees up and slamming a heel into Eias' stomach. Kaelar compelled him to *be still*, and his muscles collapsed until motionless.

"Go on," Taran grumbled, huffing through his snout against the back of Eias' head. Eias jumped, but their eyes remained locked on Saffron, wide and—*apologetic*. As if the request actually surprised them, as if they didn't know exactly who they fucking worked with willingly—

Whether or not they were surprised, Eias still lifted their hand. They inhaled a small breath. Kaelar curved his hand under Saffron's chin to hold him still.

Eias pressed a finger to Saffron's forehead, then closed their eyes—and Saffron's insides crumpled into ice, blood solidifying into thick slush as the world sucked away beneath the gardens. He heard himself whimper as gravity vanished, plummeting into it. Like falling asleep, like tumbling into a vivid dream waiting for him right on the other side.

Memories flooded from every direction, scattered pieces breaking and forming—or was that Saffron's own body, forced through pinholes dug by Eias' hand, pricked by their finger through every scene woven by memory threads? Tapestries meant to only be seen, not touched, not perused, never meant to carry the weight of anyone more than just Saffron who created them.

Eias' search followed no rhyme or reason at first, sifting through mental images like trinkets for sale in a shop. Sifting, sorting, pausing occasionally. Saffron mentally begged them to pull back, to release him, to not dig any deeper—but there was no reaction from the searching hand, poking holes through each hazy scene, forcing Saffron to follow as if dragged on a leash.

Meeting Asche outside the Aon-adharcach suite. Cylvan's agony on the other side.

Witnessing Kaelar wearing his own face and straddling Taran's lap. Taking his amethyst pendant.

Disappearing between sheets in Connacht; the silver choker being torn away.

Kissing Cylvan while straddling his lap; being force-fed fairy fruits at the party.

Their search traveled backward, following breadcrumbs one after another, and Saffron felt every moment. Relived every sensation, every experience, though they were all muffled beneath a cloud of someone else's perception.

Sometimes he saw the memory as himself within it; sometimes, he was thrust into an omnipotent perspective, as if Eias had been there watching the whole time. It was humiliating, violating, for someone to sift through Saffron's most intimate moments—and it would prove he and Cylvan had been absconding the entire time. There had been hardly a moment at all where Saffron kept himself away from Prince Cylvan's gravity.

The train.

The pain of his leg crushed beneath debris.

The chapel.

Cylvan visiting him drunk, bringing his books.

The crypt.

Sunbeam. The beannighe.

His deal with Taran. Silence, restraint, disgrace.

Donning the red veil; claiming himself a rowan spirit.

Realizing Cylvan's intentions, leaving his rings on the Aonadharcach bookshelf.

Their first night draped in one another's warmth.

The nymphs.

Floating to the ceiling to caress Derdriu's face.

Heart racing whenever he met Cylvan's eyes. How it felt to be embraced by him.

His growing fever. Being thrown in the lake.

The wallpaper.

Arrow.

The geis.

Imbolc. Brìghde's walk around Beantighe Village.

A yarrow field.

Saffron slammed backward, breaking through Kaelar's enchantment like a fist through glass. His hands lashed out to grapple Eias' arm, staring without seeing, burying his nails into skin, desperate to rip himself free—

"N—o!" He gagged against the towel, more spit dripping from his mouth. Hot tears flooded his eyes. A flicker of the real world came into focus—before Eias dragged him back. Echoing outside of it, Kaelar whispered more encouragements. *You're doing so well.*

No—

No, no, no—*no, no, no, no, no, please—!*

"It's more than just a ring. Come on. Let me brag a little bit."

Cylvan's confident smile, crooked and arrogant. His eyes burrowing into Saffron, burning themselves into Saffron's existence.

"Eias—what are you doing!"

Magnin's voice erupted at the edge of the yarrow field—no, Magnin wasn't there, his voice came from the gardens outside Danann House, Saffron wasn't in the yarrow field, he could run away before Eias found anything else—

Taran snarled, lunging and snapping his teeth at Magnin in threat. Saffron surged back to the surface just in time to watch Magnin stumble backward—before shouting Eias' name again.

"What are you doing!" He demanded again, voice cracking. "This is going too far, Taran! Don't make them do this! Eias, you don't have to—!"

"Eias was mine, first, Magnin—and if they stop before I get what I want, I'll have every thread ripped from you, just like I should have done with this beantighe from the start."

"Go, Magnin—" Eias' begged weakly. *"Please*—just go."

Their hand trembled against Saffron's forehead. A shaking gasp escaped their mouth—and then they pushed back into Saffron's mind, like a knife pressing between his ribs.

A sharp gasp tore from Saffron's throat—then a scream. A plea, reeling backward and slamming against Kaelar's chest again, who just tightened his grip against Saffron's windpipe and made it impossible to breathe. Saffron screamed more, expelling the towel from his mouth and throwing his head back in an attempt to detach from Eias' hand. When he couldn't, more terrified tears spilled from his eyes—and he shrieked Cylvan's name. Again and again, he screamed for Cylvan, only for Kaelar's hand to wring tighter around his throat and cut him off.

"I wonder if you're someone I could trust to help me, too?" Cylvan's coy words emerged from the tapestry.

"You want me to compel you?"

"That's right."

Saffron fought harder to shove Eias away; Kaeler pulled his head farther back, until Saffron's neck strained over his shoulder. Kaelar whispered more crude encouragements into Saffron's ear, promising it would all be over soon—

"What's your name?"

No—

"My name is... um... Dewdrop."

No, god—don't—

"It's nice to meet you, Dewdrop—"

Please—

"My name is..."

"Cylvan—" he rasped beneath Kaelar's hand. But he couldn't stop it, he couldn't stop the memory from unfolding, pulled from him like threading his heart through his mouth.

"... Sybil."

"No, *no*—"

"When you enchant me, start... with my name... so the ring knows... who you're influencing... alright...?"

The images warped. Slowing to a crawl, Cylvan's voice stretched like long strings of sap from a broken branch.

Eias' finger finally pulled away. Saffron slumped back into Kaelar's body, disappearing into the starry sky overhead, like a puppet with snapped strings.

"He..." Eias' voice was right there—but far away. Saffron was lost to it. *No more. Don't take anymore.* Saffron had nothing left at all to give.

"He—!" Eias attempted again, voice shrill, followed by a gasp. "He knows P-Prince Cylvan's—! His true name—!"

Saffron plummeted from the heavens, crash landing back into his body. The puppet strings surged. He reeled back—then slammed his forehead into Eias', tearing through Kaelar's grasp in one motion.

Eias tumbled backward, unconscious, forehead split open as Saffron twisted and smashed his fist into Kaelar's mouth. It earned him just enough time to shove away, losing his balance but scrambling toward the terrace stairs. Taran snarled behind him. Saffron heard him prepare to lunge—

Saffron slammed into a body on the stairs. He nearly tumbled backward, but arms caught him around the waist. Instinctively, Saffron threw his hands out to fight back—

"*Púca.*"

He froze—and slowly met Cylvan's eyes. Bright, like amethyst coins. Staring at him, wide and uncertain. Over his shoulder, Magnin stood in the doorway, breathing heavily with his jaw clenched in anger, having fetched the prince, himself.

"Cy—!" Saffron gasped when he heard movement from the garden. He threw his head to look, but Cylvan grabbed and pulled him back. Saffron attempted to push away, to shove free of Cylvan's arms in a panic. "Cylvan—you have to go, please—! Please, you have to go far away from here!"

"Do you remember me, púca?"

Saffron stared into Cylvan's eyes pleadingly, seeing his shared desperation. It was the same expression he wore the morning before in Connacht, begging, *"How much longer do we have to pretend?"*

Saffron—didn't want to lie anymore. He would never lie to Cylvan again, just so Cylvan's perfect features never twisted into such agony even one more time.

Saffron took Cylvan's face—and kissed him. Like he always meant to. As a person butterflied open to reveal every knot and thorn and tangle of weeds suffocating him from the inside out. Saffron kissed him like the first time; like the last time. Like someone returning suddenly from a place no one could follow. With every plea for forgiveness tracing their breaths.

"I never forgot you," he sobbed, barely pulling apart. "I could never forget you, Cylvan. I'm so sorry—"

The ground tore away. Saffron threw his hands out, clinging to Cylvan against the rushing wind sucking air from his lungs.

At the top of the arch, Cylvan pulled Saffron close, shuddering with breath before kissing him again. Saffron's hands tangled in Cylvan's hair, trying to pull him closer, apologizing endlessly between their moving mouths. Saffron just kept kissing him, desperate for his warmth, his forgiveness—

"Saffron," Cylvan finally breathed, amethyst eyes splitting Saffron open further, to purge the weeds from his chest once and for all.

"Close your eyes and sleep."

47

THE RESURRECTION

Saffron didn't dream. He didn't move. Did he even breathe?

Pulled beneath the mounds and wrapped in moss. Mouth, ears, nose, filled with thick, dark soil so that nothing at all could stir him. Until the darkness kissed his forehead and summoned him with gentleness.

"Come back to me, púca."

Cylvan. Saffron sought the root of the voice, searching the darkness, purging the comforting, heavy soil from his lungs and his mouth in order to find him. The only voice he would abandon serenity for. That voice promised fruits more decadent than serenity.

Morning light filtered through Saffron's lashes, eyes cracking open and closing again as they stung and stuck together. His body shifted, fingers twitching against one another where his hands were tucked safely into his chest, pressed into another body that was warm and perfectly shaped to fit his.

Something touched his hair, then his face. Another whisper of his name, and Saffron fought to open his eyes again.

On the other side—bright purple irises came into focus. Alabaster skin framed by long dark hair. A scratchy linen tunic gaping open at the collar and revealing Cylvan's bare neck and chest, the silver chain of his pendant shining in the light. Draped over them, a familiar moth-eaten blanket softened by years and years of use.

Saffron was in Fern Room. He recognized the old wallpaper, the feel of the mattress beneath him, the smell of the pillow he shared with Hollow. His heart fluttered in a thick relief he wasn't expecting, wishing he could sink deeper into that place where memories of Danann House didn't exist at all.

"Cylvan," he rasped with a tiny smile, closing his eyes and collapsing back against the pillow. He was answered with Cylvan's mouth against his. Breathing in through his nose, Saffron stretched his neck to respond, relishing in how he tasted. It had to be a dream—a lovely dream. A perfect thing. He wished to stay there, forever, even if it meant never waking up again at all.

"What have you done, púca?"

Saffron cracked open his eyes again, just enough to witness the perfect person in front of him. He trailed fingers down the side of Cylvan's face, appreciating the shape of his jaw, his chin, his nose, his lips... Cylvan looked so much like he was meant to live in the sun.

"I just... wanted to keep you safe," he breathed. "I'm sorry. I couldn't do it, I couldn't... I'm just... just a..."

Cylvan's mouth found his again. Saffron kissed him as disappointment coiled in his stomach, then body-sinking melancholy as the reality of his failure was strong enough even to penetrate such sweetness. He didn't want to wake up. He didn't want to go back to that place, that attic, where hands were rough and words were harsh and there was nothing he could do but accept the fate he was given. He could no longer fight. He had nothing left. He was not meant for the divinve mercy of other heroes in high fey myths.

"I'm sorry," the words choked out, followed by tears swelling in Saffron's eyes and bubbling over his lashes. They soaked his cheeks in an instant. "I'm sorry, I'm sorry, I'm so sorry, I'm so useless, I haven't done a single thing right—"

"Asche told me what you did."

Saffron sniffed. He pulled away, wiping his eyes and looking at Cylvan in question. His prince's smile was so gentle, so affectionate, it brought more silent tears to spill over.

"You've been searching the woods for fairy fruits."

Saffron's breath caught on a sob he tried to swallow back. He nodded, then shook his head, whispering more apologies as Cylvan tucked hair from his eyes.

"Taran never took your memories, because... you agreed to find the fruits he wanted to drug me. You found them on the very first day, but still never told him."

Saffron nodded miserably again.

"It took... searching your memory threads for Taran to get what he wanted."

Saffron broke down again, crying into Cylvan's chest as he was reminded. He could never wake up. He couldn't ever face Cylvan, knowing what he'd done, how he'd ruined everything because he wasn't smart enough, strong enough. Worthless—useless—impertinent—selfish—arrogant—

"I love you too, Saffron."

"Don't," he begged. "You can't, you can't say that..."

"Why not?" Cylvan asked softly, kissing the backs of Saffron's knuckles. "Isn't it what you wanted to hear?"

Saffron refused to meet Cylvan's eyes. It was too cruel, to know he would wake up again to a place those words didn't exist.

"I don't deserve it," he wept. "Not after what I've done to you."

"You deserve it."

"But you're—not real," Saffron insisted. "You're not real..."

Cylvan chuckled. He curved a finger under Saffron's chin, offering him a kiss, then a dozen others over the tears on his cheeks.

"I'm as real as you are."

Saffron attempted to argue again, but Cylvan stole the words with his lips. Again and again, every time Saffron attempted to declare him a dream, Cylvan kissed it away.

"I'm real," he promised. "And so are you. *And so are you,* gods —thank the gods, you're real, I never lost you..."

Saffron wiped his eyes again. His heart puttered with a gush of anxiety, and he held Cylvan's eyes, before turning his head. He took another moment to glance around the room, which should have been formed to his memory, as only a dream—but it was different from what he remembered.

Letty's shared bed was surrounded with books and stacks of paper, scrawled with practice sentences as if she was learning how to read alongside Hollow. Tacked to the walls, notes about magical plants, dried grasses, long strands of seaweed knotted not unlike Taran's memory threads.

Saffron sniffed again in confusion, wiping his eyes, then his nose. He recalled what Kaelar said, right before throwing him out the attic window—but Saffron saw hints of Hollow everywhere, and it urged his panic back down. Hair ties woven from reeds. A long branch tucked in the corner with recently-flayed wood as he carved a new practice sword. Even the pillow and blankets beneath them clung to Hollow's natural scent, something that would have faded away if he'd really died when Kaelar said.

Saffron turned quickly back to Cylvan, who remained on his side, head resting in his hand on a bent arm. He smiled as if watching the realization bloom behind Saffron's eyes was particularly satisfying. Saffron wiped his nose again with a frown, planting his hand on Cylvan's stomach and making him wheeze.

"You're real," he said in a crackly voice. "I'm not... I'm not dreaming."

"No," Cylvan finally sat up, intertwining his fingers with those flattened on his stomach. "This isn't a dream. This is real— and I love you."

Saffron flushed, but he couldn't turn away. His lips parted slightly in uncertainty—and Cylvan sat forward to kiss them.

Saffron kissed him back, pulling his face closer before releasing a shaking breath.

"I love you," he replied in a whisper. "I'm sorry for lying to you, but—"

Cylvan kissed him again, like he wished to drag out the peace just a little bit longer. Saffron embraced the thought, taking that moment to cup Cylvan's face with a relieved smile. There wasn't a single crack on him.

"What did Eias say to you?" Saffron finally found the courage to ask. "What you saw on the train—it wasn't real, I would never—"

"I..." Cylvan's voice hitched. He furrowed his brows before taking Saffron's hand and kissing it. "I... I know, Saffron, I'm sorry. I'm so sorry, I should have known it was a trick, but in the moment I really thought..."

He couldn't bring himself to say any more, shaking his head. Leaning over Saffron, Cylvan reached an arm under the bed to pull out Saffron's leather bag. Digging around inside, he removed a black leather notebook that Saffron recognized as the one Asche had outside the Aon-adharcach suite.

"Asche... had tracking charms on both Eias and Magnin. They placed them apparently after they were acting strange while together in Connacht."

Saffron held his breath that time, taking the notebook that Cylvan offered. Flipping through it, he was intrigued by the writing inside, sloppy and ink-splattered, crammed onto the pages as if written with one's eyes closed.

"Their charm is able to take words spoken out loud and transcribe them onto these pages, here... it's not perfect, as you can see, and doesn't punctuate anywhere, but... you get the idea."

Cylvan flipped to the page in question, and Saffron's stomach sank as he began reading. There were no names or delineation between who said what, but he was able to guess.

*it is nice to know taran and the beantighe are getting along so
well dont you think*

what makes you say that

*they are always having tea with one another and i swear ive seen
the beantighe go into tarans room more nights than not which i
must admit makes me a little bit jealous as its unusual for taran
to invite people into his room that he doesnt trust*
  *i sometimes wonder what they talk about and it makes me
want to be careful with my words you know just in case the
beantighe is sharing all of our secrets behind our backs*
  *sometimes i swear im put in a position to admit something by
the beantighe and i wonder if it is only so that they can share it
with taran afterward ha ha ha*

do you really think taran and the beantighe are that close

*i suppose i dont have to guess im pretty sure i have even overheard
them enjoying one another most nights which is so shocking since
taran has never shown interest in humans before now but the
beantighe must be something truly special no wonder he is so
protective of it when it comes to kaelar because he wishes to keep it
all to himself to keep his bed warm and learn all our secrets...*

Saffron slammed the book shut. He almost buckled over the
edge of the bed to puke, but Cylvan swept the notebook from his
hands, first, tossing it away as if he didn't want to see it any longer,
either.

"I'm sorry," Saffron didn't know what else to say, shaking his
head before kissing Cylvan again. "None of it is true, Cylvan,
please believe me—"

"I do," he insisted. "I never fully believed it, Saffron, but just
hearing the words... and then seeing what I thought was happening... my thoughts went mad thinking—thinking Taran was the

reason you really insisted on returning to Morrígan. Why you refused to go to the Winter Court with me. It was—foolish of me, I know it was foolish, I should have asked you directly, but—I suppose I... couldn't handle the thought that I really had nothing. That I'd made a fool of myself fawning over you, when you actually favored Taran all along. That Taran had truly taken everything from me, even you, when you didn't even know it..." He pulled Saffron into his chest, arms locking around Saffron's back. "But... I never lost you."

"You never lost me," Saffron reassured, wrapping his arms around Cylvan in return. "I never left you, just like I once promised..."

"Oh, gods..." Cylvan whispered. "Say it again."

"You never lost me."

"Say it again."

"You never lost me!"

"What else?"

Saffron giggled. "I never left you."

"And?"

"And..." he trailed off, before smiling again. He kissed Cylvan's forehead. "I love you, Prince Cylvan dé Tuatha dé—*ah!*"

Cylvan buried a hungry mouth into Saffron's shoulder, and Saffron squealed, kicking his legs as he was on the verge of being devoured. But no matter how he tried to fight back, Cylvan's grasp was stronger, and Saffron couldn't bite back the laughter.

"There's so much more I want to say," Cylvan growled. "Not to mention so much more—I wish to do to you, but..."

Voices came from the other side of the door.

"There isn't time."

"There isn't time?" Saffron questioned, just as the Fern Room door slammed open. Saffron snapped up, then burst into more tears as Hollow stood on the other side. Untangling from the blankets and knocking Cylvan away, Saffron threw himself into his friend, wailing against his shoulder in relief. It lasted just until

Letty tore around the corner, bodyslamming Saffron and Hollow onto the bed with rebuking shrieks.

Next came Sunbeam and Asche, but most surprising of all after them—was a two-legged Nimue wearing Letty's pinafore, and nothing underneath. Around her neck, a chain of seaweed woven with a dry reed.

Everyone Saffron cared about—was perfectly safe.

It wasn't often Fern Room was so full of bodies. Asche eventually snapped, ramming the creaky window open to let in the breeze, but that only allowed a hoard of pixies to rush inside and assault every inch of Saffron in demands for treats and attention. It almost made him cry again, never having realized exactly how much he missed all of them. The three who joined him in Danann House were with the cluster, and Dewdrop, who favored Cylvan most, went straight to work nesting in the prince's black hair.

According to the others, Saffron had been in and out of sleep for two days. Learning everything that happened while tucked in Fern Room made his insides squirm.

Taran had not come searching for Cylvan in Beantighe Village, yet.

Baba Yaga was still being held by Elluin, but she was safe. Letty, Hollow, and Fleece had been checking on her every day in secret since Cylvan and Hollow first visited her drunk.

Letty explained that in Saffron's time away, she'd been learning how to read with Hollow, while also working with Silk and henmother Hector to learn more about not only medicinal plants, but magical ones. She and Silk even helped to heal what remained of Saffron's leg, as well as any other cuts and scrapes they found while he slept beneath Cylvan's command. Professor Adelard had been dragged into the conversation at some point, as well, and Saffron couldn't help the pinch of jealousy when he thought about all the things he'd missed.

On the second day, a raven found Cylvan in Beantighe Village. He and Hollow hiked out into the woods before opening the letter it carried, just in case there was a tracking charm inside. Instead of a tracking charm, they found an apology signed by Eias and Magnin, written in opal ink. According to Cylvan, lies written in opal ink turned brown in the sun—so the fact Eias' words were still shimmery meant they were honest. Saffron read the note at least a hundred times while the others talked, every single time finding something else to tangle his thoughts.

Your highness: I will never be able to fully express my grief for what I've done. I know I have put you in great danger. I swear, while I saw your true name in Saffron's memory threads, I did not declare it to Taran. But—there is a gap in my memory. I think he may have taken it from me, but I do not know how. He should not even be able.

Saffron: I do not deserve your forgiveness, and I will not ask for it—but please believe me when I say, I never once wished to search your memories. I know that must be hard to believe after what I did, but I never expected Taran to ever ask for such a brutal thing. The person who commanded me that night is not the one I grew up with. I will not make excuses for him, but he is no longer someone I wish to be by the side of. I will be leaving with Magnin as soon as it is safe for us to do so. I will no longer be at Taran's call.

If there is anything you need from me, I will do it with the utmost discretion. It is the very least I can offer for the pain I have caused.

—Gentle Eias Lam.

It was easy for Saffron to have his doubts, but Eias had apparently kept their back and forth with Cylvan well enough a secret that Taran never came looking. Magnin even knew exactly where Cylvan was, according to the prince, since he'd been there the night of the fete when Cylvan read Asche's charmed notes, realized what had happened, and was preparing to whisk Saffron away to Beantighe Village the moment he returned to the house.

It had been Sunbeam who brought Saffron's sketchbook and Baba Yaga's grimoire from the library ruins, meanwhile, where she even reassured Saffron the veil circle had survived the flames. When he asked if she would be passing through, soon, however— she went quiet.

"Chandry never responded to my message," she said, but added nothing else. Saffron knew better than to ask.

Later spreading Saffron's map of Morrigan and the Agate Wood on the floor of the crowded bedroom, Letty, Nimue, Asche, Hollow, Sunbeam, Cylvan, and Saffron gathered around as Sunbeam pointed to all the places she'd found changes to Morrigan's campus barrier, by Cylvan's request.

"Taran is trying to keep Cylvan from escaping," Saffron whispered the obvious, but Sunbeam shook her head.

"I don't think it's attuned to Cylvan... it's attuned to humans. I think Taran knows Cylvan wouldn't leave without *you*, Saffron. They're trying to trap *you* inside."

"Cylvan should just go on his own, then," Hollow interjected. "Saffron can stay here. We can hide him."

"That's not safe for you," Saffron argued. "Taran wants Cylvan—but Elluin wants me. If she thinks I'm hiding here... she threatened to flatten Beantighe Village to find me once before, I don't think she'll hesitate to do it again. It would be better for me to go to Avren, so she'll leave you all alone."

"Why does she want *you?*" Letty frowned. Saffron shifted where he sat.

"I'm... the reason Baba Yaga was arrested, and is still being held. Because Elluin wants me to prove that I can do arid magic. Otherwise, she'll..." He shook his head. "She'll formally accuse Baba, and then... accuse everyone in Beantighe Village of conspiring with her. Everyone will be executed, unless I do what she wants."

"*What?*" Cylvan hissed, claws digging into Saffron's thigh where his hand sat. Saffron took it in his own, but didn't meet Cylvan's eyes. He was too embarrassed.

"But..." Letty started, before shaking her head. "She already knows Baba Yaga can do magic. She knows *all* the henmothers can do magic. Hector told me they all studied magic together... the henmothers, I mean. Elluin was even a student at Morrígan at the same time, and she became headmistress around the same time humans were turned into beantighes. Why would she only want *you?*"

"Because... I'm the one who embarrassed her when I wore the red veil," Saffron sighed. "And she's still hung up on figuring out who is controlling the wolf, which makes her look bad as headmistress... and if she has proof I can perform arid magic, she'll have every right to investigate every person close to me, including all of you, as well as..."

He glanced at Cylvan, who had a muscle twitching in his cheek. A muscle of restraint, as if there was something he wished to say. Saffron shook his head.

"She'll investigate Cylvan, too. I think she genuinely still believes he's the one behind the wolf; Taran hasn't actually told her everything, like she thinks..."

"Does Taran know what she's done?" Cylvan asked flatly, and Saffron shook his head.

"I don't know. When she came to Danann House to accuse me, she acted like she didn't know anything about my memories being taken, so I assume not. But Kaelar was with her, so... perhaps he is the one playing both sides."

"Of course Kaelar would get involved with performing arid trials," Cylvan spat, squeezing Saffron's hand hard enough that Saffron flinched. "His family is a bunch of disgraced arid witchhunters—if he was able to catch one on his own, he might get his honor back, or whatever."

"I'm a little surprised *more* people aren't accusing his-nightness of other crimes," Nimue mumbled. "Seeing as he has a history, and all."

Saffron's breath caught. He didn't mean to stare at her, but Nimue frowned, then narrowed her eyes in threat, as if to challenge him to say something in Cylvan's defense. But—Saffron knew something they didn't. Something that made his stomach turn when he thought about it.

"No..." Saffron started, and Nimue smirked before opening her mouth to immediately argue—but Saffron shook his head more insistently. "I mean—yes, people think Cylvan was the one to kill you Nimue, but..."

"... But?" She asked impatiently. If words could roll their eyes, hers would have. Saffron bit his lip.

"I... found memory threads under Taran's bed. I learned a spell so I could witness them. I thought, if I searched them, I could find something to use against him... but instead, I just saw how he killed our friends... and how..."

He glanced at Cylvan, who watched him with concern. Saffron's mouth went dry. He wasn't sure how to say it.

"You were supposed to meet Glass in the library the night she died," he whispered, and Cylvan stiffened. Nimue's nostrils flared in annoyance, as if any mention of that night incensed her in an instant—but Saffron shook his head again, silently begging her to listen. "It wasn't him, Nimue. It wasn't Cylvan who killed you."

"How *dare* you, Saffron!" Nimue snarled, jolting like she wanted to grab him, but Letty held her back. Saffron watched her miserably.

"I'm sorry—I'm sorry to tell you like this, but I saw it in Taran's memory. He glamoured himself to look like the prince, then went to find you on purpose. I think... I think someone else asked him to do it, like his mother, or someone, but... it was all on purpose, to make Cylvan look like a murderer. Like someone who needed to be *tamed*. And... it worked."

Nimue's expression twisted in fury, shoulders rising and falling with heavy, hard breaths, but she didn't say anything. She didn't try to argue, or even to declare Saffron a liar. Even Cylvan remained silent, just staring at him. But then, slowly, he looked at Asche, whose own expression was of disbelief.

"Asche," Cylvan said weakly. "Do you remember... what you told me, a few days after Glass died?"

All eyes turned to the daurae, but their eyes were locked on Cylvan. They'd gone pale, mouth hanging open.

"I asked who had a key to your bedroom... because I heard you come home late. But then when they accused you of killing her, I knew it couldn't have been you, because you would have been on the beach..."

Cylvan shook his head. "Then..." he whispered. "I really did go home right after the party... I didn't get too drunk... I didn't... I didn't..."

He finally met Nimue's eyes. The air grew heavy.

"He really killed you," Cylvan croaked. Nimue ground her teeth together, but still didn't say anything. "Taran really killed you, my friend... to make me look bloodthirsty. To force me into hiding, to force me by his side, promising he could help improve my reputation..."

"But you still wouldn't propose, so he started asking beantighes for wild fairy fruits," Saffron gently added. He wanted the others to hear it, too. "When beantighes couldn't bring them, he killed them."

"Taran is the wolf," Asche confirmed, and Saffron saw how they met Sunbeam's eyes. Her jaw flexed. "I saw it, myself. He doesn't just control it—he *is* it."

"That's impossible," Sunbeam whispered, but kept Asche's gaze. She said it less as a confrontation, and more an expression of confusion.

"Everyone thinks he and his family are ashen," Saffron agreed, and Sunbeam looked back at him. "And they are—but they use Proserpina's Silver to fake it. Taran is no different. He's using King Clymeus' opulent bone ashes to change into the wolf, which is why—"

"The wolf king," Sunbeam raised her eyebrows. "The bean-nighe kept saying..."

"I've never seen Taran use opulent silver before," Cylvan added in shared disbelief. It seemed reflexive, as if he'd been trained to defend Taran on such accusations.

"... Because it's in his bones, Cylvan," Saffron whispered, squeezing his hand. "It's not something he *wears* like my choker or the cuffs. That's how he can physically change into the wolf, and glamour himself... things to do with his own body. But he can't compel. I didn't think he could manipulate memory threads, either, like Eias said in their letter, but... I know he can't do anything requiring opulence directed at other people."

Cylvan stared at him for a long time—then rose to his feet, as if it was all too much. He paced the room, intertwining fingers behind his neck, searching for whatever crushed his back.

"... *Damnit,*" his voice cracked, dragging his hands down his face. "*Damnit, godsdamnit... oh, gods...*"

"I'm going to kill him," Nimue's words were harsh—but spoken out loud, she was breathless, like she'd been kicked in the chest. "I'll kill him, I'll kill that fucking bastard for using me—for making me think—and for hurting you..."

Her expression twisted more, before leaping to her feet and rushing from the room. Cylvan went after her, and Letty hurried to follow, leaving the rest of them in silence.

48

THE SIMPLICITY

Over the rest of the afternoon and into the evening, they compiled a list of potential ways to escape Morrígan Academy. Saffron hated that such a list was the first time Cylvan witnessed his improved handwriting.

> *Other ways out of campus not charmed; through the*
thicker parts of the woods. Over the mountains.
> *Cylvan can fly us out.*
> *Leave the night of Beantighe Ostara (tomorrow), maybe*
able to pass with the rest of the crowd coming and going.

The moment they arrived in Avren, Cylvan would bid for Baba Yaga's release and Elluin's dismissal, first and foremost. Then he would discuss Taran with the kings.

According to him, if they could prove Taran had King Clymeus' bone ash in his own body, it would be enough of a scandal to leave a black mark on the mac Dela-mac Delbaith family. Apparently, desecration of a corpse, on top of preserving parts of the body, especially after performing funerary rites, *especially* after a full living tapestry had been taken and woven for the tapestry hall in Avren—was a crime almost as grievous as glamouring oneself to resemble a member of the royal family. In order to commit a murder and slander their name, no less.

Saffron hadn't failed entirely, after all. Taran's threads had contained exactly what he needed, after all. He hadn't wasted his time, after all. He and Cylvan hadn't suffered for nothing.

Taran, Taran's entire family, would be ruined by what Saffron learned. And even though he no longer had Taran's specific memory threads, the fact he witnessed them, himself, created threads of their own that could be used as proof.

It was no wonder Taran had them stripped from his own mind, and then hidden under his bed. He never should have underestimated the house-beantighe he designated for chores.

But Saffron had learned never to accept any truth that was *too simple*. He would never allow himself to fall victim to anything that was *too simple* ever again. If they were going to move forward with something *simple*, he was going to ensure there was an additional protection in place, just in case. He wouldn't lose his chance to protect Cylvan because he got too arrogant, again.

FOLLOWING A MAP SKETCHED ALONGSIDE SAFFRON's chosen spell in Baba Yaga's grimoire, he and Cylvan found a break in the ruins' fenceline and crossed through hand-in-hand. Cylvan wore Asche's woven bracelet for the iron sickness, though still complained as they passed through. Once they were clear of the gate, Saffron asked him to do some magic and test the barrier, and Cylvan summoned a small gale to nearly blast Saffron's shirt over his head. It made Saffron laugh, shoving Cylvan into the grass before taking off running through the trees while chased by a wild fey lord.

All the way to the north of the ruins, they wandered overgrown paths between the trees, coming upon crumbling structures no longer resembling anything on Morrígan's main campus. Exploring each shell of a stone building with curiosity, they wondered out loud what each could have been; they made up stories of the human students who might have attended there, after Saffron told Cylvan about everything he'd seen in the crypt; they called out to one another every time there was a weird bug, or a salamander, or a toad; they whistled whenever the birds did, and tried to see who could get a response; Saffron showed Cylvan safe mushrooms and wild mint to chew on.

Cylvan went on long monologues about language, linguistics, ancient magic, the relationship between magic and religion, how they all interconnected—and Saffron wanted to bottle up every word, realizing he was hearing the root of what drove Cylvan to annotating books, to researching taboo magic in the first place. He was especially captivated by Cylvan's stories of his occasional trips into the human world to learn about the theologies and religions trending on that side, unable to stop laughing every time he talked about someone spotting his fey form and accusing him of being something called a *demon* from *hell* and attempting to *exorcize* him.

They talked about Gaeilge being the language of not only Baba's teacup circles, but the feda markings around Danann House, and how the human language shared similar linguistic roots with Alvish. The way Cylvan's eyes lit up with every excited contribution Saffron made, made Saffron's heart race. Every time Saffron taught Cylvan something he didn't already know, and he looked at Saffron with glowing curiosity and pride, Saffron nearly melted. Had Cylvan ever been able to discuss that obsession of his so freely with someone else?

It was all so simple. Saffron wished they could continue doing it forever. Just two ghosts. Living... freely.

It was almost over. It was almost over—and then he and Cylvan could spend the rest of their days enjoying one another's company with nothing biting at their heels. Just like they promised one another in Connacht, to live without worrying about someone coming to find them. To live freely, happily, wandering the woods in search of ancient ruins while chasing salamanders and whistling at birds.

Beantighe Ostara would begin once the sun set. Humans would celebrate the spring equinox for themselves, and fey would prepare for the season's turn the following night.

Saffron and Cylvan and Asche would escape amidst the celebrations. They would arrive in Avren amongst more. Hidden beneath the moon, Saffron would enter the next wheel of the season hand in hand with Cylvan, and, hopefully, never have to let it go again.

49

THE RITUAL

Finally stumbling across a small clearing at the end of a footpath, Saffron's breath caught as he gazed across the ceremony space they'd been searching for. Calling out for Cylvan to come, the prince landed next to him with a gust of wind, grinning and grabbing Saffron in excitement. A circular henge of seven flat stones stood twice as tall as Cylvan did, blanketed in lush green moss that matched the thick carpet of grass in the center, speckled with little white flowers like flecks of snow against a verdant meadow.

Removing the book from his bag, Saffron refamiliarized himself with the steps of the spell as they approached the standing stones. Cylvan brushed his hand along the front of the nearest one, talking out loud about how stone circles were thought to be some of the first intentional passages through the veil before the spells became more nuanced. It made Saffron pause, smiling at his Night Prince appreciating the ancient structure, until Cylvan threw him a sarcastic look.

"What's so funny?"

"Nothing, it's just... when I was a kid, before I knew more than I wanted about high fey... I used to fantasize about meeting an ancient king of the forest while I was out in the woods."

"I must be a dream come true for you, then."

Saffron laughed, interrupted when Cylvan scooped him up into a kiss, then asked what the first step was. Saffron searched the page as Cylvan carried him into the circle on one arm.

"This certainly seems like a lovely place to have my true name stolen," Cylvan went on, digging the toe of his boot into the grass.

Saffron sighed, flipping the page again in a final attempt to memorize every detail of Baba's old handwriting. *Bridging a true name (rowan witch)*. A spell that, according to the description, would allow Saffron to take the benefits of Cylvan's true name, and at the same time, be the only other person who could use it against him. Like a living patron ring, according to Baba's spell.

One step even described '*cupping his hand over his partner's chest, then pressing it into his own*', and Saffron realized it was just like when the beannighe attacked that fey lord in the woods outside the revel, or Kaelar after that, and read their true names out loud. Saffron was sure she had no reason to take them for herself, which was why she never completed the motion—but Saffron, himself, wouldn't let the name he inevitably grasped in his hand go.

"There are three ways to initiate the peak of the spell," Saffron read aloud, still perched in the crook of Cylvan's arm and using his horns as a bookrest. "It depends on our preferred method of emotional climax—sexual, physical, or metaphysical."

"That is definitely the most creative way you've asked me to fuck you."

Saffron laughed again, suddenly thrown over Cylvan's shoulder. With his free hand, Cylvan tugged the book from Saffron's grasp and tossed it from the circle, followed by his bag, then his shoes, as Saffron just wiggled and kicked his legs.

Flung down into the green carpet and white flowers, Saffron shook with more laughter as Cylvan claimed his hands and kissed the backs of his knuckles.

"I'm the fairy king of this forest," he said in a low, sensual voice, pinning Saffron's wrists together and pressing them into the grass over his head. "And I've been searching for an arid witch to claim my name for themselves. Are you the one?"

Saffron smiled, then giggled as a hand slipped under his shirt, tickling his stomach.

"I've been searching for a fairy king to claim. I can do whatever you ask of me, if you grant all my wishes from this point on."

"What do you wish of me?" Cylvan asked, pushing up Saffron's shirt to kiss a line up his stomach, and Saffron's amusement melted into small gasps.

"I wish..." He gulped, arching his back and resting his head backward. "I wish... to never be apart from you, ever again."

"Don't wish that," Cylvan argued, tongue finding one of Saffron's nipples and making Saffron shiver. "I will give you that freely."

"It's all I want—Cylvan."

Cylvan's hands pressed into the inner curve of Saffron's waist, pulling his hips up to tilt against the tops of his thighs. It curled Saffron's back, opening his legs for Cylvan to nestle between, and Saffron had to fight to catch his breath.

"Then I will grant it," he promised. "Once you own my name, we will only ever be apart if you command it."

"I'll make you mine," Saffron breathed. "My king of the forest, Day or Night."

"Then do so," Cylvan kissed him again, and Saffron pulled him into it before pushing out to turn Cylvan onto his back and straddle his stomach. It left Cylvan breathless, face flushed as dark hair fanned out behind him. Blades of rich grass and white flowers poked through each strand like strokes of black paint, and Saffron wished to memorize that living painting to keep just for himself, forever.

Flattening his hands against Cylvan's chest, he smiled again in promise.

"I'm going to make you only mine."

Closing his eyes, he recalled the steps of the spell. Every detail he'd memorized, to the point he could recite every word if he needed to.

Breathing in the heavy, humid smell of plantlife in the overgrown circle, he sought comfort in its familiarity. The comfort of a place hidden in the trees, where they wouldn't be found except by the wild fey and wisps and spirits and even older forest gods that already resided there. Ancient creatures who might know the magic Saffron used, who would keep their distance as to not interrupt.

"Will you undress me, your highness?"

Cylvan's hands moved without additional provocation, and Saffron's matched. Undoing the string at the base of Cylvan's neck, Saffron pulled it over Cylvan's head. Cylvan's hands undid the buttons of Saffron's shirt. Unlacing pants, stripping away hosen, braies, it was nearly impossible for Saffron to resist placing his mouth over every inch of his fey king the moment they sat naked together within the looming stones. Cylvan clearly shared the sentiment, collapsing into the grass with a grunt of restraint as his fingers buried into the skin of Saffron's hips.

Stretching long over Cylvan's head, Saffron reached for his bag that contained handfuls of red rowan berries still attached to a branch. Cylvan couldn't resist kissing the center of Saffron's chest as he hovered, making Saffron giggle and scold him.

Plucking a cluster of berries, Saffron smiled down at his prince who watched in curiosity. Saffron couldn't resist, leaning forward to kiss him one last time.

"Don't kiss me again," he breathed upon pulling away. "Unless you want your tongue to burn."

"I would do more for worse," Cylvan promised, making Saffron smirk, before palming the berries into his mouth. As he chewed, he used the end of the stick to carve a circle around where the prince lay, adding the hatchmarks last. According to the grimoire, it didn't have to be a physical mark; intention alone would be enough.

"A ring of invocation," he explained as he went, repeating Baba's notes. "To summon the magic to us."

He drew a second circle inside the first.

"A ring of evocation to clash against the first, forming a natural exchange within and without, ourselves in the center."

A third circle behind the crown of Cylvan's head, overlapping the first two.

"An intangible chaplet at the crown of opulence, partially within and partially without."

Weaving the thin rowan branch into a circlet of his own, Saffron settled it into his hair.

"A tangible chaplet at the crown of aridity, partially within and partially without."

Cylvan's hands puckered Saffron's skin where they clung, and Saffron nearly lost his focus, chuckling a little bit and pressing his impatient fairy king back into the grass. Leaving his hand there, he settled it flat over the center of Cylvan's chest where he'd seen the beannighe steal true names from high fey who got too close. That place Cylvan's own lived, the name Saffron would take for himself to protect against people like Taran. It wasn't exactly by the terms of their geis—but it would be enough.

But then Saffron hesitated as the weight of the demand squeezed his lungs. What if he failed? What if he couldn't perform it correctly, and was letting his own ego get in the way of thinking clearly? Were they just wasting time playing games?

What if he got his hopes up again—only to be proven wrong?

"Go on then, my arid witch," Cylvan urged as if he could sense Saffron's hesitation, but it didn't ease Saffron's nerves. Cylvan noticed, expression softening as he reached a hand to cup Saffron's cheek. "What is it, púca?"

"What if I can't do it?" He asked weakly. "What if I do it wrong—and it doesn't work? What if Taran comes—"

Cylvan pulled him down into a kiss, and Saffron trembled against him. Pulling back slightly, he closed his eyes, shaking his head, but Cylvan just adjusted the rowan crown in his hair.

"I trust you," he promised. "Even if it doesn't work this time, you have not failed. Everything you do is astounding. We will simply try another spell, again and again, until we figure it out. No one, especially not me, can expect you to have learned and mastered an entire taboo magic system all on your own..."

Saffron grimaced. He pressed his hands to Cylvan's chest again.

"Will you still feel that way if I truly mess it up? What if I turn you into a toad?"

"Every arid witch needs a familiar," Cylvan reassured. Saffron smirked, then shook his head.

"Alright—don't kiss me again until I say so."

"Ribbit."

Closing his eyes, Saffron slid hands up Cylvan's torso, searching for the taste of rowan iron in his mouth and body again. Beneath him, the prince dramatically writhed and gasped, begging to be cursed, hands finding Saffron's waist.

Gazing down at the handsome fey prince pinned beneath him, Saffron smiled to himself. Licking what remained of the berries from his fingers, he met Cylvan's eyes as his tongue flicked over the ends, and Cylvan's muscle tightened. Nails buried deeper into Saffron's waist.

Even if it didn't work... Saffron wouldn't be a failure.

They would keep searching for answers, together. Always together.

"Tell me... if it hurts," Saffron breathed. Stretching over Cylvan's head, he pressed his hand flat into the grass at the peak of Cylvan's crown, the southernmost mark. Closing his eyes, he held his breath—and recalled what Baba Yaga told him in Cottage Wicklow's kitchen, that morning he tried to save Berry.

Summon the wounds into yourself. You will not split open—but if you do it correctly, you will feel it.

He was not there to heal Cylvan's wounds, but rather—to absorb the power of his name. A name given by arid magic, placed there by arid hands, just like his. He didn't yet know how it worked, or when it was given, or by whom—but Saffron would take it into himself, and Cylvan would reclaim it back. Back and forth, until the name became Saffron's, until the magic that placed it became Cylvan's, until the name of *Sybil* would only respond to Saffron's voice, to Cylvan's. A shared vulnerability—a shared protection. A shared name.

Not unlike when he passed the injuries between himself and Berry, Saffron felt a shift. Something warm and tingling, like sparkling wine left in the sun. Sweet and comforting, a sensation that was more familiar than he expected—but perhaps he should have known it would be a welcome feeling, after spending so much time familiarizing himself with every part of Cylvan he could. To then experience his opulence, to blend their magics into one another for the sake of protecting one another—that was merely another intimacy to memorize.

"Oh—*mm*, Saffron," Cylvan sighed like he could feel it, too, and Saffron smiled through the haze.

But when an unexpected stab of ice struck him in the chest, Saffron buckled forward with a surprised cry. Cylvan gasped his name, but Saffron didn't move, pressing his hand flat against his chest as a line of sweat dripped from his hairline. It felt like—his heart was going to stop, clutched between two hands that squeezed and twisted, setting his ribs, his sternum, on fire.

Straining, he turned his eyes down to search Cylvan's chest, but—there was nothing. Even Cylvan didn't appear to feel it, eyes wide in concern. Saffron just clenched his teeth, shaking his head, not wanting him to worry.

Ice soon gave way to heat, which gave way to numbness—and when the horrific grip on his heart and muscles retreated enough that he could inhale a breath. Saffron pulled both of his hands away with a shaking gasp, staring down at Cylvan's chest. It was like nothing had happened at all—but then Cylvan's fingers flashed upward to trace down the center of Saffron's, and Saffron's eyes followed, seeing faint remnants of a mark that hadn't been there previously. Lines that wove in and out of one another, not unlike the knots that kept Taran's memory threads intact. Was that—Cylvan's true name, imprinted in Saffron's skin?

Saffron smiled, then giggled—then he burst into hysterical laughter, only shrieking with more glee when Cylvan threw his arms out and locked their bodies together. Twisting, Cylvan threw Saffron on his back against the grass.

Interrupting his gleeful howls of mirth, Cylvan kissed him hard, rough, demanding, making Saffron gasp.

"You—are like no one I've ever met before," the prince said like a prayer. "Saffron—my witch—let me worship you."

Saffron smiled through his gasping breaths, meeting Cylvan's mouth again and writhing beneath him.

"We have to share an emotional climax—to fix the bond." He barely got the words out before Cylvan smiled darkly, sliding a hand between Saffron's legs and stroking in a way that summoned a sharp sound.

"Gladly," he agreed in a low voice. "I will ensure this bond is immortalized, even in death."

Wrapping his arms around Cylvan's neck, Saffron rolled the prince onto his back again. Trailing his mouth from Cylvan's jaw down his neck, his chest, his stomach, he found the base of Cylvan's length. Saffron closed his eyes and smiled as Cylvan breathed lewd encouragements, calling him things like *forbidden beantighe-witch* and knotting fingers in Saffron's hair as his hips rolled in desire.

Saffron pulled away just enough to wet two of his fingers, before his mouth and tongue found the tip of Cylvan's length again and teased as much as he could. Extending his hand between his own thighs, his wet fingers curled and pressed inside, and he moaned against Cylvan's hardness at the back of his throat.

"Fuck, Saffron—!" Cylvan gasped as Saffron's head moved, tongue curling around the end and cracking open his eyes to appreciate the look of overwhelm on Cylvan's handsome face.

Saffron wanted to see him break, wanted to revel in knowing he had a new, entire control over his fey prince, the king of the forest, who was always so stoic.

Cylvan twisted fingers in Saffron's hair, before pulling roughly to meet Cylvan's mouth again. Moving on his knees, Saffron straddled Cylvan's hips, easing over him with a wince and an inhale of breath. Leaning forward, he collapsed against Cylvan's shoulder while fighting to catch his breath, rogue hands sliding up either side of his ass as Cylvan's erection eased itself inside.

"You don't have to rush." Cylvan's sincerity crept through the play, pressing a gentle kiss to the side of Saffron's neck. "Does it hurt?"

"I just... want you," Saffron shuddered.

"Every piece of me belongs to you," Cylvan promised, kissing Saffron again—and thrusting himself inside. Saffron gasped sharply, throwing his head back. "And you—belong to me. Every word, every sound. All of your magic, your cunning—is owed to your king."

Saffron laughed hazily, placing his hands on Cylvan's shoulders and smiling while moving his hips. Pressing Cylvan deeper inside, he rolled his back, flexing his legs and taking him in and out in all the ways that made Cylvan gasp and curse in pleasure. Hands gripped Saffron's thighs, his hips, his waist, as if struggling to find any place to anchor himself against the overwhelming way Saffron rode him.

"And what of yours belongs to me?" Saffron asked, smiling again as Cylvan's lips parted, eyes closed as he lost the ability to speak. Saffron's hands found Cylvan's chest, teasing his jewelry, kissing the center of his throat. "You once offered me your kingdom—but I don't care about power, or land, or anything someone else can take from me."

"You can have—anything," Cylvan breathed, expression brightening as he struggled to breathe. "Anything you want—is yours, Saffron."

"You know what I want," Saffron laughed softly, kissing under Cylvan's jaw. "Just you, only you. Every part of you. Your name, your voice—your body, your hands... your devotion."

"*F-fuck,* yes," Cylvan choked, and Saffron grinned—before he was suddenly grabbed by the crook of the arm and turned onto his back. Cylvan nearly bent him in half, gripping Saffron's wrists in one hand and pinning them over his head.

Slamming himself to the hilt with deep, merciless thrusts, Saffron gagged on every breath. He grappled weakly at Cylvan's shoulders with each twist of his insides, nails dragging down skin and leaving marks behind.

"Promise me," Cylvan leaned close, pushing himself as deep as he could go and making Saffron's toes curl. He edged in and out with rolling hips, and Saffron swore at him in whimpering breaths. "You'll never—make a deal with any other fey, ever again. Only me."

"Cyl—" Saffron begged, tightness flushing in a pool in his stomach, between his legs, the rhythmic in and out of Cylvan's hips pushing him closer and closer to the edge of breaking. Cylvan sensed it—and his hand found Saffron's length, stroking it knowingly.

"Promise me, Saffron," Cylvan demanded. "You'll never go where I can't find you. Ever again."

"I—!" Saffron writhed in pleasure, unable to find his mouth, clutching at Cylvan's arms in a beg for mercy. "Cylvan, I'm—!"

"Not until you say it, beantighe," came Cylvan's response, a smile coating the words. His hand between Saffron's legs stroked and teased more, almost making Saffron scream as the growing pressure between his hips crested and broke against his insides—

"I p-promise, Cylvan!" He pleaded, a mix of desperate laughter breaking out of him. "I won't—I won't leave you, again, please—!"

Cylvan pulled Saffron in as he tightened with climax, spilling over Cylvan's chest and stomach. Trembling with overwhelmed gasps, Saffron's entire body sparkled, heart dancing like human feet on Beltane. He sank back to the grass as Cylvan kissed him, then kissed under his chin, his neck, his chest, before pulling Saffron's legs together over one shoulder, and thrusting inside again.

Saffron's world spun, lapping in and out of reality as saccharine exhaustion made his body throb and tremble, feeling it swirl again between his legs as Cylvan buried inside. The prince's movements grew more demanding, pressing deep enough, with enough force, that Saffron thought he was going to split apart. Moaning, Cylvan bent Saffron's legs forward to give himself more leverage —before burying himself with a final gasp, and filling Saffron with spreading heat. Hunched over Saffron's bent body, with Saffron's legs still draped together over one shoulder, Cylvan breathed heavily as stray drops of sweat hit Saffron's stomach.

When Cylvan carefully removed himself, Saffron complained between biting his lip, but Cylvan hardly shifted away any farther. He kept Saffron's legs over his shoulder, kissing the curve of his knee, stroking fingers up and down the outside of his thigh. He only moved again when Saffron extended his hands, pulling Cylvan back down over him, just—wanting to be within reach. Begging for more. Begging to be filled again. No single touch was enough. Nothing else commanded every part of him like his fey prince who could grasp pieces of his soul and keep them warm, even in the loneliest of winters.

THEY REMAINED IN THE GRASS UNTIL THE SUN BEGAN to set, drifting in and out of awareness on the breeze, relishing the sensation of one another, kissing and fucking until Saffron could hardly remember his name. Making up for time lost. Making up for emotions repressed. As if the memories of Danann House would unfurl and fall away the more they traded ecstasy.

Lying on their backs in exhaustion, Saffron trailed fingers down Cylvan's chest, the muscles of his stomach, his strong shoulders; Cylvan kissed Saffron's collarbones, the tiny scars left on his windpipe, his wrists, his leg, anywhere Proserpina's Silver had tasted him. He found and memorized every spotted scar where the prongs pierced, kissing each one with reverence.

Could that really be what Saffron could look forward to by Cylvan's side? Now that they'd protected him and his name, now that he could refuse Taran and his plan by telling the kings what Saffron had learned about Nimue? The wolf king's ashes?

"I love you," Saffron whispered, tucking a stray hair from Cylvan's eyes. Cylvan claimed his hand, kissing his palm.

"I love you," he breathed into it. "Saffron, my arid witch."

"My fairy king," Saffron giggled, resting across Cylvan's chest, listening to his heart, drawing a finger down from the center of his collarbones where his true name hid underneath. "My raven."

"My treasure."

Saffron grinned. He kissed Cylvan one more time. Another geis sealed on their lips; the first of another infinity that would surely come.

GAZING UP AT THE CLOUDS PAINTED PINK AND ORANGE with the setting sun, a creeping chill soon came to tickle Saffron's skin and make him shiver. But even after pulling their clothes back on, they still didn't leave the circle, instead exploring more of Baba Yaga's grimoire as if searching for any reason to remain within the quiet peace of the henge. Or, perhaps—because the thought of leaving, of using Beantighe Ostara as a cover to escape through the woods, risking discovery, risking putting the entire village in danger, was overwhelming. Cylvan might have even been able to sense it on Saffron's voice, the way it trembled slightly whenever conversation brushed up against the topic—but he never once mentioned it being time to head back. As if he wished to stay right there, too.

But there were other powers less willing to wait. Less willing to search, where they might have found that peaceful circle where

Saffron could vanish like a wild forest spirit in the arms of his ancient fey king.

Other powers knew exactly how to draw Saffron to them, rather than wait any longer. And Saffron knew exactly the trap that had been set, when he spotted pluming smoke rising over the trees from the direction of Beantighe Village.

50

THE FIRE

Saffron abandoned everything in his bag, taking off into the trees like a bolting deer. Cylvan called out after him, but Saffron barely heard it, barely remembered there being anyone else at all—until hands suddenly hooked under his arms, and they launched into the sky.

Grappling for balance, Saffron only had a second to gather himself as the wind whipped above. Finally witnessing the extent of the blinding inferno within the trees, he screamed, nearly tearing from Cylvan's arms.

Racing shadows fled through the fence into the trees, Saffron was relieved to see—but the feeling didn't last the moment he spotted a handful of figures standing in a half-circle in the festival clearing. Kneeling within them—Saffron recognized silver hair.

"B—" His throat closed on the smoke. *"Baba Yaga!* Cylvan, we have to—!"

"No, Saffron, wait!" Cylvan commanded as Saffron attempted to pull him into a nosedive, but was interrupted by a blackbird suddenly flashing past, talon slicing through Saffron's cheek and making him jolt backward with a cry.

Half a dozen more pierced from the darkness like arrows, beaks and talons tearing into Saffron's arms, Cylvan's hair.

Cylvan instinctively pulled Saffron's face into his chest, hunching around him as he cursed and attempted to swat the birds away.

"Púca, hold your breath!"

Saffron did—and the air vanished, only a thin layer remaining for Cylvan to tread. With nothing to brace their feathers, the blackbirds tumbled until catching themselves again. They didn't attack a second time, scattering back into the trees.

Air crashed back around them like a muted thunderclap, Saffron inhaling sharply and recognizing a faint glow in Cylvan's eyes. Saffron grabbed his face, wishing to pull him out of it—but a loud snap resounded from below, followed by the whistle of something approaching fast.

It collided with Cylvan's shoulder, and he reeled backward with a snarl. Saffron nearly slipped from his arms, barely caught before freefalling—but it didn't matter, as Cylvan's balance was thrown askew. They rolled backward, plummeting to the forest outside the village gate.

Saffron hit and tumbled to a halt over the road. Lifting his head, Cylvan crashed to the undergrowth behind him, rolling over with a grunt and a curse. Saffron frantically crawled to where he was, helping him up—and blood stained his hand the moment he touched Cylvan's arm.

"Cylvan!" He choked, but Cylvan threw his strained gaze over Saffron's shoulder as four horses emerged from the inner flames of the village gate. Saffron attempted to lunge to his feet, wanting to put himself between them and the prince—but Cylvan grabbed his hand first, wrenching him back down.

"Saffron, look at me. Look at me!" He commanded, and Saffron did. His heart pounded behind his vision, making it undulate. He just saw the dark spot seeping through the shoulder of Cylvan's shirt, where the end of a broken arrow still protruded.

"Go into the woods. Run as fast as you can. Go back to the ruins and wait until—"

"No!" Saffron cried, but Cylvan grabbed him before he could fight further.

"It won't be for long," Cylvan promised, taking Saffron's face with urgency. "Those guards are from Avren. Taran might have called them—but they'll take me back to the capital, just like we planned. Just like we planned, remember? They'll do all the work for us. I can speak to the kings about everything, and then I'll come back for—"

"Sybil."

Cylvan went still. Saffron froze, eyes locked on Cylvan's face—but Cylvan's eyes stared over his shoulder, again. Saffron didn't have to ask. He already knew. A shriek of fear rippled through his being.

He turned his head, just slightly, just enough to look.

Taran stood on the road, illuminated by the sweltering flames of the village. Behind him, three guards waited in a line, one of them gripping Daurae Asche's arms as they screamed Saffron's name—and begged for his forgiveness.

"Take that beantighe by the throat."

Saffron had no chance to gasp before Cylvan's hand lashed out, slamming Saffron to the ground with a choking grip on his windpipe. No—no, no, *no,* the spell hadn't worked—

"Bring him here, darling."

Cylvan's tense expression didn't change, fingers flexing against Saffron's neck before lifting him back up again. He hardly flinched as Saffron clawed at him and thrashed for release.

Dragged through the bushes, Cylvan pulled Saffron onto the road, shoving him to his knees in front of Taran whose face was wild with bloodthirsty thrill.

"I was wondering where you two had gone off to." He smiled. "I was so worried, I had no choice but to call the royal guard. What a relief to find you mostly unharmed, your highness. We'll get your shoulder looked at on our way to Avren."

"He's not going anywhere with you!" Saffron snarled, but Cylvan's arm hooked under his chin and wrenched him backward, cutting off his words. Saffron jerked against Cylvan's grasp as Taran approached, kneeling in front of him. He squeezed Saffron's face.

"You were a useless pain in my ass, right up until the end," he cooed, before patting Saffron's cheek in gratitude. "As much as I want to take you with us to face judgment for taboo magic... I promised the headmistress she would have the honor, whether you pass or fail your final trials. She's waiting for you right on the other side of the fence, beantighe, so don't linger too long. Perhaps we'll see you again in a few days... where you can congratulate us on our engagement. It's all thanks to you, after all."

Saffron spit in his face, and Taran's fist slammed into his mouth. It knocked him free of Cylvan's grasp, landing face-down in the dirt but rolling over again as quickly as he could—just to watch Taran take Cylvan's hand, and pull him into a kiss.

"Say you wish to marry me, Sybil," Taran commanded sensually. *"Say you'll make me your Harmonious King."*

"I wish to marry you, Taran," Cylvan said, taking Taran's hands and kissing the backs of them. "I'll make you my Harmonious King."

"No!" Saffron begged, leaping to his feet—but Kaelar's voice emerged from the burning village, compelling him back to his knees.

Hitting the ground hard, Saffron hunched forward to catch his fall. He turned to find Kaelar approaching with a smug grin and arms crossed over his chest.

"It's time for you to perform the rest of your trials, beantighe. The old woman will suffocate on the smoke, soon, otherwise."

His eyes lifted to Taran and Cylvan, and Saffron followed, heart sinking at how Cylvan's hand curved around Taran's waist, gazing at him. His face was—empty. Blank. Trapped in his own body. Saffron wanted to scream, wanted to leap and rip Taran away, to tear him open, tear his throat out with teeth—but Kaelar grabbed him by the hair, shoving him into a bow, instead.

"Congratulate the prince and his fiancé, beantighe. Don't be rude."

"Thank you, Lord Caoimháin." Taran smirked. "We'll be expecting you at the engagement celebration tomorrow night."

Saffron spilled onto his side, slamming his foot into Kaelar's stomach, thrashing and spitting and demanding to be let go—but even screaming Cylvan's name, begging him to do something, anything—was useless. Cylvan might not even be able to hear him. Cylvan might not even remember what happened once morning came. Saffron stood no match against the power of a true name.

Perhaps he should have accepted that sooner.

His scalp burned as Kaelar dragged him toward the flames. Through the front gate.

Saffron wrenched back and attempted to free himself once more. His thoughts were as inflamed as every beantighe cottage burning around him, suffocating slowly as the fire scorched the breatheable air. Saffron scrambled to recall Kaelar's true name, to compel him, even just to find and grab something to break his arm, anything—anything that would set him free, so that he might chase after Taran, who had his final hooks in Cylvan, the person Saffron swore to protect, to stay with—

"Your henmother almost got away, you know," Kaelar grunted as Saffron nearly pulled loose, finally hooking an arm around Saffron's throat like Cylvan had held him. It made Saffron choke, clawing fingernails into Kaelar's arm as he was carried deeper into the inferno. "She didn't get very far in to the trees before we dragged her back, though—perhaps she's simply too old to go on. What do you think? Would it be more merciful to put her out of her misery, Saffron?"

Saffron landed a kick to Kaelar's groin, released for just a moment long enough to hit the dirt and push off again—but Kaelar tackled him a second later, slamming Saffron's face into the road and making his head spin.

"Taran is going to purge any human beantighe with connections to arid magic, you know," he growled, grabbing Saffron again and forcing him back to his feet. "Which means, even if you —prove yourself arid, and save your stupid village in front of Elluin—it doesn't matter. Every single one of them—is marked for execution, anyway."

His words bucked and broke as Saffron threw his fists, his feet, his head, knees only going weak at that final threat. He knew that already, he knew Taran rising to power was going to be catastrophic for all humans, not just beantighes, not just arid witches—but hearing it said so blatantly, Saffron wanted to scream.

Dragged toward the ceremonial field, Saffron's eyes burned against the heat and smoke in the air, searching the clearing for his henmother. Sure enough, in the center of the stone spiral meant to be where they partook in Ostara supper together—Saffron saw the hunched shape of Baba Yaga on her knees. Standing over her, Elluin grinned at the sight of Saffron stumbling in their direction.

Shoved to his knees in the grass, Saffron immediately turned to his henmother—but saw only red. A red veil, trailing on the scorched breeze behind her. He could have sworn he'd seen her silver hair from the sky...

But then the face hidden by crimson turned to meet Saffron's eyes in return, and his stopped heart slammed hard enough to crack his ribs.

Your henmother almost got away, you know. She didn't get very far in to the trees before we dragged her back...

Something rushed up the back of Saffron's throat—and before he could stop it, a shrill explosion of laughter erupted out of him. He howled, practically screaming with the hilarity of it, shoved into the grass by Kaelar who barked at him to *shut the fuck up*. Saffron just laughed more.

Next to him—the beannighe bubbled with amusement of her own.

51

THE HEADMISTRESS

"Today, we witness the performance of arid trials at my interrogation," Elluin announced over the snapping flames and crashing debris of Beantighe Village—and Saffron's restrained hysterics.

Sweat dripped from Saffron's face and made the fabric of his shirt cling to his back, speckling him in dust and ash as he still couldn't fully keep his composure. Any time he chuckled, the old woman next to him did, too.

"We will begin with a search for iron marks on the beantighe," Elluin went on, clearly annoyed as her prey weren't cowering at her feet and begging for forgiveness. It was only when she removed a black leather box from the inside of her jacket that Saffron's mirth muzzled itself, the reflection of flames on a silver needle and quill turning his heart to ice. "Master Kaelar, if you would please strip your beantighe so that I may begin the examination."

Kaelar's hand found the back of Saffron's collar—

"Keep your hands off him, Broderic," the beannighe snapped, and Kaelar pulled away in an instant. Elluin flared her nostrils, opening her mouth to screech at her—but Saffron just shook his head and untied the string keeping his top cinched. Removing the

extra fabric tucked into his waistband, he pulled it off over his head on his own volition. Elluin seemed even more annoyed by that. Behind him, Kaelar grumbled something in shared disappointment.

"As you wish, headmistress," he said as he finished. "If you tell me what you are looking for, I can direct you right to it. The love marks left by Prince Cylvan may mask what you're hoping to find."

"Disgusting," Elluin spat, but clearly something about the words, or perhaps Saffron's obedience, made her uncertain. She glanced to the beannighe, who she thought to be Baba Yaga, and cleared her throat. "You undress as well, Nora."

"That will not be necessary, headmistress," the beannighe responded more articulately than Saffron expected. "You know very well what I am capable of. These theatrics exist only as fodder for you high fey to pleasure yourselves while imagining, later."

"You—!" Elluin gasped, and Saffron burst out laughing again. "You will obey me, Nora Everhart! *Undress so that I may examine you for the mark of an oath!*"

The compelling intention was strong enough that even Saffron's muscles twitched—but the beannighe didn't move. She just smiled through her red veil at Elluin, whose flyaways caught and floated in the heat of the fire encircling them.

"I said, *undress yourself!*" Elluin compelled once more—

"Your words do not work on me, silver-blooded bitch," the beannighe finally answered, voice like stones scraping a blade. "I am not enchantable by such malleable fey magic. Try to compel me one more time, Elluin mac Darbhy, and I will show you exactly why you are better off without that tongue in your mouth to start with."

Elluin stared at her—and so did Saffron.

"How..." Elluin straightened up. She puffed up her chest. She wanted to fight back—but the words caught in her mouth. "Who are you?"

The beannighe grinned. Finally, she pulled the veil away, and

Elluin's eyes bulged. Stumbling backward, the thrust a finger in accusation—but no words fell from her gaping mouth. The beannighe just kept smiling, before turning to Saffron and offering the red veil to him.

"I believe this belongs to you, rowan spirit."

He reached for it—but Elluin lunged, attempting to rip it away from them both. Before her fingers touched the fabric, the beannighe leapt off the ground—and sank teeth into Elluin's neck.

Saffron tumbled backward as Elluin screeched and flailed and clawed at the woman pinning her in the grass. The beannighe didn't bother to scoop the headmistress' true name away, seemingly satisfied just with tearing a mouthful of flesh from bone with her teeth.

When she pulled away again, she met Saffron's eyes, the bottom half of her face drenched in wet crimson. Beneath her, Elluin writhed and moaned, clutching her gaping wound before searching—and her eyes landed on Saffron. To his disbelief, she extended a hand toward him.

"Help me, beantighe," she croaked, what remained of her vocal chords plucking like lute strings. "This mad woman—controls the wolf, beantighe, she must. Help me—and you can go free."

Something in Saffron's chest squeezed, choking him—only to erupt as more laughter. He nearly shrieked at her to *just fucking die, already!*, but the red veil was suddenly pulled from his hands, twisting and slamming back against his windpipe. His wrist caught in the hook, which was the only reason Kaelar's forceful movements didn't decapitate him entirely.

"Y—you're coming with me, beantighe," he said, voice shrill with obvious fear. "I'm your patron master, you belong to me. I'll forgive you of your sins, I'll take care of you—just don't let that woman touch me. You'll live in comfort—I'll even share you with the prince, just—"

"Get—off of me!" Saffron hissed, attempting to jerk himself free. Kaelar tightened the loop around his neck.

"You speak boldly for an ó Caoimháin witchhunter," the beannighe spoke to Kaelar, next, and Saffron choked as Kaelar instinctively cinched his grip again. The beannighe just tilted her head in observation, before nodding to herself. "Oh, yes, I see the resemblance. Your true name, even—it's from your great-grandfather Broderman, isn't it? That old cunt. I was the one who cinched him up outside the Kyteler gates, you know."

"Yes, and how did that work out for you!" Kaelar snarled. "It brought Clymeus straight to your door, you old bitch!"

"The wolf king was coming for us, anyway," she said, before smiling with bloody teeth. "At least my students had the thrill of gutting a witchhunter-general beforehand. Do you want to know how I killed him? Would you like a demonstration, Saffron?"

Saffron strained against the veil, how it pressed into his neck and twisted his wrist. He managed to nod. Kaelar wrenched him back again, opening his mouth to argue—but the beannighe just bent over to pick up the silver quill on the ground. Then—something shimmered from the grass next to Elluin, and Saffron bit back a cry of alarm as the headmistress' silver needle lifted, then sliced through the air.

It was thin enough to not make a sound—but the loop around Saffron's throat loosened, and Kaelar sank backward.

From the center of his forehead, the end of the silver rod emerged.

Saffron screamed, scrambling backward. Kaelar slumped fully onto his back, staring into the fire-rich red sky with unblinking eyes that glazed over without a drop of blood. That was—until the needle shuddered, sliding out with a slippery sound and stained red.

Saffron turned back to the beannighe, whose eyes lingered on the needle as it exhumed itself from the fey lord's skull, then hovered like a wisp awaiting another command. Saffron didn't have to ask to know she was the one to control it—but she must have sensed his confusion, because her eyes flickered to him.

"This is why you must give *names* to opulent silver; controlling tokens like rings and quills aren't enough," she grinned, fluttering the quill between her fingers. Saffron's heart danced in tandem. She'd once told him the same thing about his cuffs, and even tried to help him do so for himself.

"You're controlling it?" He asked weakly. The needle floated to him in reply, but he didn't flinch away, even as it buzzed like pixie wings and hovered in circles around him. Unlike when Elluin carved the words into his back, the needle didn't mimic the movements of the quill. It seemed to act on its own, just by the beannighe holding its feathery companion. "How?"

"No differently than how high fey can compel humans," she said. "Opulence overpowers aridity; but aridity overpowers opulence. Silver overpowers iron; iron overpowers silver. Sídhe compels rowan; rowan compels Sídhe. The fey have spent these last centuries declaring themselves more powerful, more pure, the only kind of magic that needs to exist—but they are simply one side of a veil that requires both for balance. They made themselves vulnerable when they failed to kill every rowan witch like Proserpina wanted."

"Rowan witch?" Saffron's voice cracked, getting slowly to his feet. The needle continued to follow his movements, as if it recognized him from the first time they met. "Is that something different from a-an iron witch? Is that why my ritual with Cylvan didn't work?"

"If you attempted a rowan-blooded spell without a veil oath, you did nothing except put on a performance for the trees, child. Don't you remember what I said as we tried to name your silver cuffs?"

"Ah..."

You must be rowan blooded to charm anything containing even a lick of opulence...

Saffron thought he was going to be sick—but then a hot rush of realization crashed into him.

If Taran's bones were made of opulent silver, no different than Saffron's cuffs—perhaps he didn't have to physically take them to control them.

Perhaps—Saffron merely had to give them a name.

A name was to control them, and to control Taran mac Delbaith. To control the wolf.

Saffron only had to become rowan blooded, first.

"Tell me," he said. "Tell me what I have to do. I'll do it, if it means I can protect him. Tell me how I can become rowan blooded."

The beannighe's smile curled into something more curious, more sinister. Behind her, Elluin groaned and gurgled on her own blood, barely clinging to breath. The beannighe disregarded her entirely, despite the headmistress' blood still caked on her chin and cheeks.

"This is what you will become when your bridge-partner on the other side dies," the beannighe said, motioning to her mouth. "A wild thing like me. Bodies weren't meant to contain this much magic without someone to help carry the burden. And you, little witch—I would not even consider you iron. You are only a spring berry."

"Tell me," Saffron insisted, clenching his fist around the red veil and pulling it into his chest. "I don't care—just let me try. Let me help Cylvan, so that I can help everyone. Everyone whose home burns around us, and everyone whose home burned beneath the last Night Court."

The old crone's eyes sparkled. She looked almost thrilled to deny him again, as if loving every moment he insisted—but from the treeline, a voice came.

"Headmistress," Baba Yaga emerged, and both Saffron and the beannighe turned to find her. At the henmother's back, shadowed behind trees illuminated by the flames of the burning village, Saffron recognized those he wasn't able to protect. "Show him. No one has made an oath with the veil in centuries—perhaps it will extend him mercy."

"Nora," the beannighe grinned. "You were always too tenacious for your own good. I see nothing has changed."

Baba Yaga's expression was intense, made more biting in the shadows of their crumbling homes.

"If there is anyone who can help us now, it is Saffron and Prince Cylvan. Let him try."

The beannighe turned back to Saffron, meeting his eyes. Saffron squared his shoulders. He would do anything to save his prince, his friends, the magic he was owed. No longer would he accept any fate that forced him to choose one over the other—he would force his own that gave him everything he wanted.

He would be the human in myth who forced their own fate despite the will of the gods.

He would be the divine mercy that tore Cylvan from the fate Taran forced him to accept.

He would be the sun Taran mac Delbaith flew too close to.

Blooming smoke turned the moon red. Saffron couldn't help staring as she hung overhead, guiding them. Into the darkness, flames grew ever-distant at his back as they trekked between the trees, past shadowy wild things that watched as a rowan-blooded witch clambered through undergrowth younger than she was.

From the shadows, Saffron heard voices. Hands reached from the darkness to touch him, to trail over his arms and cup his hands, as if extending Imbolc wishes as he passed. He would be back to grant them. He would be back to offer peace and safety. He would no longer wait and beg for Brìghde to hear him—he would force her to obey.

If it meant Saffron could save Cylvan, he would do it.

If it meant he could keep Taran mac Delbaith out of power, he would do it.

If it meant protecting the people he cared for most, no matter the cost—Saffron would do it. No matter what it took, he would give it for the promise of protecting everyone who ever protected him. Even if it eventually turned him mad like the bloody crone, the beannighe, the one who protected the school beneath a circle of memory-threaded deliverance, for centuries. Even if the initial beg of the veil killed him—Saffron would try. He would force his fate. He would no longer bend to the fey who expected his life to be one of always accepting the lot he was given.

Approaching the ruins beneath a crimson moon, the overgrown entrance gave way to a single touch from the beannighe's hand. It bent inward upon creaking hinges, ripping vines between the bars.

"Baba Yaga called you *headmistress,*" he whispered as they entered the trees on the other side. The thick mist was gone, the pure silence was gone, inundating them with the sound of opulence sinking into every once-cleansed pore of the soil, the trees, the air. "What is your name, beannighe?"

"Names are power," she muttered in reply. From the trees, a host of pixies suddenly emerged, swirling around her silver hair before searching Saffron and kissing anywhere blood dried on his skin. "I cast mine off long ago."

Saffron understood that sentiment. It was the power of a name that drove everyone to madness around him, after all.

"I will really be able to help the person I love?" He asked. The words were like thorns trailing up the back of his throat. "If I become rowan blooded, I can protect the people I care about?"

"You will be able to do anything you like, without any high fey interference at all," she smirked back at him, eyes flashing in the low red light of the moon. "Why else do you think the queen tried to kill every single one of us? We were the only ones she truly couldn't anticipate."

Grief, determination, resentment gripped Saffron's heart. Reaching down into his shirt, he pulled out the amethyst pendant and squeezed it. When the icy surface never warmed in response, his heart twisted in a fury.

Unlike Queen Proserpina, there would be at least one royal high fey to anticipate Saffron coming.

Two, if Taran valued his life.

52

THE BEGOTTEN

Saffron almost expected to be taken to the same ritual circle where he'd failed to perform the spell between himself and Cylvan, but the beannighe instead walked him all the way to the burned-out library. It smelled no different than the fire of Beantighe Village, acrid and thick with the scent of ancient wood devoured by flames.

Most of the ceiling had been burned away, allowing red moonlight to sink all the way to the blackened floor. Nearly every fairy fruit that once speckled the ground had been eaten by Asche's magic, and it was surreal to pass through the little that remained. Kicking up dust and soot, Saffron realized he witnessed the library as it once was. As it sat after Clymeus came and purged the students of their places of study. Empty, abandoned, echoing with ghosts and only hints of the magic that once floated there.

Approaching the singed veil carving in the floor, the air was thick with buzzing electricity, as if a thousand pink-tinged veil bees still hummed in a cloud around him. The markings existed as ghostly remnants beneath licking flames, but not all of Sunbeam's hard work had gone to waste, just like she assured him in Fern Room.

Kneeling down to touch the nearest line, he jerked his finger back again as the carving was unexpectedly sharp. It nicked his finger instantly, tasting him, before thrumming with a low heartbeat.

"There is only one way to initiate a veil oath without an opulent partner on the other side... and that is to take advantage of an already-open door. It will be dangerous, however. It might even kill you."

The beannighe's voice echoed between what remained of the shelves, bouncing off the charred walls and into the sky for the moon to take for itself. Her tone was thoughtful again, as if returning to the comforting air of the ruins cleansed her of the manic fury and bloodlust demonstrated in the burning village. Elluin's viscera remained on the bottom half of her face as she spoke.

"If you are willing to try, once I return to the earth, beseech the spirit inside for what you want."

"R-return to the earth?" Saffron asked in surprise, but the beannighe didn't say anything, just searched through the ash for tiny morsels of wild fruits that managed to evade destruction.

"I've lived a very long time, child, and have no more deliverance to offer this place. Perhaps I can thank the ashen wolf king for one thing—and that is the clarity I saw once he destroyed my circle of threads outside. I realized there is no one else here to protect... and I'm sorry I was not quick enough to save the hamlet, either."

The hamlet, Saffron recalled that word written on the old signpost at the end of the main road, realizing she referred to Beantighe Village. The cottages must have been dormitories for students attending the Kyteler school. His chest throbbed in heightened anger.

Saffron didn't say anything else, just followed the woman's eyes as they trailed over piles of bones turned black in the heat of the fire. They remained scattered where Saffron had once disturbed them, and he had to look away again.

"There is nothing left for me to do here," she repeated in a whisper, returning her eyes to the circle in the floor. "But I can pass on knowing I saw my oath to the end. I protected my students long enough to empty every shelf, and for as many of them as possible to flee to the other side."

Closing her eyes, she shook her head again, then approached the markings.

"I will beseech the veil first, by performing my half of the ritual in reverse. It is symbolic of acknowledging everything I have received and given. Once it takes me, you should make your choice and step inside, repeating the spell from beginning to end, opposite the way I do it. Please—do not take this decision lightly. There are few people who have ever survived making an oath without a counterbalance on the other side."

"Thank you," Saffron nodded. He'd already made his decision.

She offered him a few of the remaining fruits in her grasp, dusted black like pixie hands in drawing charcoal. Saffron closed his fingers around them, stepping back when she motioned for him to do so. Just before she spoke again, he straightened up one last time.

"Thank you," he said again. "For everything. I'm—I'm sure the students you protected feel that way, too. If there's anything else I can do for them... I'll make sure it's done."

She offered him a gentle smile, and Saffron witnessed pure humanity in it. No more wild washer woman, despite the blood drying on the bottom half of her face.

"If you ever find an oracle you trust... ask them to release every memory thread I've knotted in the trees. There has been too much anguish is these woods for too long; it's time to let the forest finally heal."

Saffron nodded. "I will."

The beannighe turned back toward the circle, breathing in a deep sigh. She then proceeded to undress herself, unbuttoning the shirt that was once part of her uniform, then the skirt, the bloomers underneath, even doing her best to pick leaves and twigs out of her hair. Without another moment of hesitation, she spoke.

"Until thine bones return to mud; call yourself, rowan blood."

Stepping into the circle, Saffron jumped backward when the lines in the floor suddenly illuminated red like the smoke-choked moon overhead.

"Exchanging a look, a hand, a kiss; whichever you choose, share in your bliss..."

She buried her teeth into an ash-coated strawberry, juices spilling down her chin and leaving trails in what remained of Elluin's blood.

"Devour the flesh, the root of the other; breath to breath, exchange your charter..." The beannighe found the exact center of the circle, kneeling to the floor.

With her back to him, Saffron stared as, carved into her back, there were wounds older than he was. Perhaps older than even Baba Yaga. *Impertinence. Impatience. Belligerence.*

But, above them, like a brand at the top of her spine, there was a circle with two lines drawn horizontally through the middle. Saffron knew that mark—it was one of the feda letters he'd memorized. Was that her mark of the oath, the one Elluin meant to find in the previous trial? Would he have one just like it by the time the sun rose?

"Into the mounds the way you came; stripped of your magic, both the same."

Sweat dripped down the side of his face, whole body trembling as, at first, nothing happened—before the buzzing in the air grew faster, heavier, and Saffron took his first nervous step back.

The light, the colors within the circle shifted, warping around the floor and undulating like ocean waves. The beannighe never moved, as if she felt none of it, as if she knelt peacefully and merely waited. It burned in Saffron's eyes, made his bones vibrate, but no matter how badly he wished to, he couldn't turn away.

Saffron clenched his fists against the sensation, tightening his jaw and watching as the old woman did exactly what she said in her spell. Giving her magic back to the veil, slowly crumbling into white ash as if the age of her body finally caught up with her.

It must have only taken a moment—but Saffron felt like he stood there for a century, sensing the weight of the woman's entire lifetime as she stalked the outer edge of the ruins, seeking spiritual memories to help guard the campus, to supplement her waning deliverance supporting the barrier, going mad with age and loneliness. In the last moment her chalky remains stood in once piece, all he could think was—he was glad she didn't have to pass for a final time all by herself.

53

THE OATH

When silence fell again, when the spinning center of the veil circle closed and the beannighe drifted away on the breeze, Saffron finally took a breath. His heart pounded harder than he knew possible, feeling it all the way in his hands.

Saffron didn't know fully what it meant to become rowan blooded, but if he could manipulate opulence to control it, to share the burden of Cylvan's vulnerabilities, to lay claim to magic devices like Proserpina's Silver, to deliver for giant barriers to protect the people he cared about—then he knew what he had to do. Even if he had no idea what he might be giving up, even if it might kill him, even if he didn't have an opulent partner to balance the strain—*damnit*, Saffron had to at least try. He had nothing else.

Squeezing his fists again, Saffron closed his eyes, then kicked off his shoes.

"Into the mounds the way you came; stripped of your magic, both the same..."

Pressing the fruits in his hand against his mouth, he buried his teeth into every charred pink thing he'd been given.

"Devour the flesh, the root of the other; breath to breath, exchange your charter..."

Undoing and stepping out of his pants, he threw them in a pile on the edge of the circle with his shoes. He stripped off his shirt and threw that down, next, but paused upon finding the amethyst pendant dangling around his neck. His breath caught, and he squeezed it, only for ice to respond.

Then—his fingers brushed down the center of his chest, and he found the markings left by his shared spell with Cylvan in the henge missing. Proof the spell hadn't worked, hadn't stayed. He raked nails down his skin in quiet apology, then clasped the pendant once more. His eyes lifted to the center of the circle.

He might not have an opulent partner on the other side of the veil to bridge with him—but he did have a partner, with whom they both wished to share one another's burdens. One another's vulnerabilities.

He thought, perhaps the veil would show him mercy if it knew that—and left the pendant dangling around his neck.

The fairy fruits sank into his blood, and Saffron passed through the carpet of ash at his feet. Meeting the edge of the circle, he closed his eyes—and stepped inside.

"Exchanging a look, a hand, a kiss; whichever you choose, share in your bliss."

Lowering to his knees, Saffron hadn't seen the beannighe do anything else in that moment—but he thought of exactly what he was missing in the ceremony; something he had, but was out of reach. An opulent partner, who was meant to form the other end of the bridge with him. With whom to exchange energy, breath, *bliss*—to become one, to become bound to one another, balancing the other's magic...

He squeezed the pendant firmly.

It wasn't unlike their shared spell in the henge. Reveling in an emotional peak of sexual, physical, metaphysical energy. Exchanging their spirits back and forth, until they stretched into a long, shared energy.

Saffron—thought of Cylvan. Cylvan's mouth, his hands, how it felt to be kissed by him, for a warm tongue to trail up the side of his neck. It made his body flush hot, slouching forward as, for a moment, he swore he felt hands drape down his back. Tracing the same scars across his shoulders, down his spine, just like Cylvan's hands and mouth had in Connacht.

Share in your bliss.

Cylvan. Cylvan. Cylvan, he begged the name, focusing on his breaths. His bliss. More intangible, familiar hands groped him, cupping his shoulders, sliding over his chest, teasing his nipples in the way Cylvan always did. Saffron's breath caught, shuddering before reclining on his back.

Arching his spine, he kept his eyes closed, kept his breaths relaxed, rhythmic, as the fairy fruits in his body churned and pounded and made him tingle all over.

Where is your partner across the bridge, witch?

A sudden voice braided itself through Saffron's ears, and his eyes snapped open—finding himself within the undulating colors, breathing the electric air like bee's wings. His heart raced, discoloring the edges of his vision.

"In danger," he responded, barely speaking the words into existence. His voice was loud compared to the one that beckoned first; theirs was different, as if speaking a different language. Still, when it responded, coaxing Saffron's uncertain hand down between his legs, Saffron didn't hesitate.

You'll die without a counterbalance, it giggled and cooed, but brushed over the pendant on Saffron's chest. *Even the Holt twins had each other.*

Saffron bit back a sensual gasp as his legs trembled beneath his own stimulating fingers, the thought of Cylvan's hands doing to him what he himself teased only making his blood pound harder.

"I don't... care," he pleaded. "I've—offered to die so many times for him, already."

Ah... why do you wish to die so badly?

Saffron's head bent backward as he inhaled sharply, more heat building between his hips, at the base of his stomach.

"I-I don't," he whimpered. "I only—know how it feels—to rather die than be without him."

Ooohh~ the voice hummed—and it was then, he realized, it was his own voice calling out to him. Teasing him, flirting with him. Another part of himself, loud and vocal, that had perhaps been locked away the moment he was locked in the attic of Danann House. Taken by the veil to be his own reckoning.

"Please," he begged. "I promised to keep him safe."

Someone as inexperienced as you will never survive an entirety of arid potential. Why do you think it is so important to have an opulent partner taking their oath opposite you? A bridge has two sides, after all.

"Let me try."

You'll never be able to practice arid magic on the human side. You haven't even prepared on this side to carry the burden...

"I don't care," Saffron gasped. "I don't care. That's not where he is. He's here, he's where I am—this is where he needs me."

More incorporeal fingers played with the amethyst kissing Saffron's skin.

You might kill him, as dead as he has almost left you.

"I won't." Overwhelmed tears filled Saffron's eyes as his insides teased climax, biting it back.

You are the first to beseech me in centuries, little witch. Will there be anyone at all who can help you recover?

"Please," he could only beg again, not wishing to lose himself in taunting. Silence circled around him, before a bone-chilling tone found his ear.

... Alright. But only if you can survive the inundation without a partner on the other side.

It combed affectionate fingers through Saffron's hair.

"I won't die," Saffron promised. "Not until—I know he's safe."

The veil giggled again.

And if I grant your wish, you will have to grant mine.

"What wish?"

Ah... I will give you what you want... but once you and your beloved prince come into power, if you do not heal the defiled veil within a year... it will devour every single living thing that has ever known your face.

"Wait—" Saffron attempted, before biting down on his tongue and gasping as every inch of heat rushed into his chest, and then spread. Washing through his blood, into every muscle, every bone, every limb, every piece of skin that had even been tasted by Prince Cylvan dé Tuatha dé Danann.

His being, replaced with fairy wine, his organs with sparkling fruits, his mind with drunken threads and every simpering enchantment that ever dominated him, all at once—before climaxing in his chest until bitter, rowan-rich, ironick blood spilled from his nose. Dripped from his eyes. Filled his mouth. It dribbled from his ears, pooling beneath him, until replaced with shocking ice that devoured every bone and left him limp on the charred floorboards.

Every inch of exposed skin flushed, and then shrieked as searing opulence clawed at the rowan in his blood. Smothering him within scorching flames before roots and soil of the mounds erupted through the boards beneath his back, encircling him, dominating him, burying into his mouth—and dragging him under the earth.

Knock, knock.

54

THE MOUNDS

Aridity thrashed like teeth; opulence pulsed like a searing heart.

Soil filled Saffron's mouth, tasting of copper and salt and bitter carrion.

That time, waking beneath the weight of the mounds didn't come on the heels of sweet exhaustion—it came with agonizing pain rippling through every inch of his body, suffocating and gasping at the same time. Every bone in his body suffocating and gasping; burned on a pyre that broke beneath him; charred into dust; formed into a single, saturated device of iron magic.

Saffron's limbs moved on their own. Raking through the earth that crushed him like stroking through heavy water in search of air. Clawing, digging, scraping, not knowing which way was up —until his hands broke through the thick, knotted carpet of grass and ferns overhead.

His limbs, his spine, his neck twisted in their wake—but tearing through the hardened dirt, Saffron's head followed, and he gasped for air on the surface. Finally knowing what it really meant to sink beneath the mounds. To nearly disappear into them, where no one would ever find him again.

Finally knowing what it really meant—to be buried alive.

That time, he emerged with boiling blood and rasping breaths. He emerged alone in the dark, with no handsome daemons to greet him with reassurances he was still alive. It meant he had to rely only on his own strength to dig himself the rest of the way back into a state of living.

The more he dug—the more he realized, there was actual soil burrowing between his fingernails, crunching between his teeth. It wasn't only a dream; he was wide awake, and partially entombed. If his body didn't ache so badly, he might have had the strength to panic in confusion. A part of him even felt like he ended up exactly where he was supposed to, and just continued to untangle himself.

Dredging the remainder of his body from the dirt, Saffron finally cried out between his teeth as his whole being screamed, as every bone bowed beneath the weight of his interred limbs. He pulled, he dragged, he strained until all of him was finally on the surface, only to collapse back to the forest floor and fight to catch his breath.

Saffron cracked his eyes open, lashes tangled together with dry blood and dirt, swollen and puffy. His lips were chapped and tasted of rust, throat like sandpaper. His ears rang, full of thick cotton. At least the earth beneath him was flat. At least the dark sky above him was familiar. Even the dark trees shifting in a light wind were a welcomed sight.

The air smelled slightly of burning wood. There were distant voices of living creatures. Nighttime crows warbled away with a melancholy song from the branches looming over him, as if welcoming him back to the land of the living.

He dragged hands over his stomach, finding himself fully dressed, except for his missing boots. He couldn't recall doing that. Hadn't he stripped naked at one point?

Groaning, he lifted his head, then forced himself to sit up and take better stock of where he was, let alone how he got there.

Blinking through the darkness, rubbing more dust from his eyes, he frowned at the hole in the ground next to where he sat.

He... really did crawl from a grave. It really wasn't a dream.

He smacked his cheek, just in case, only to groan as the pain emanated like ripples on a pond. Yes—definitely awake.

But it wasn't only soil in the pit—something glowed slightly pink between the clods. Saffron leaned over the edge to sift his fingers around the bottom in search of what it was, but found nothing. There was no tangible source, just... faint light.

He frowned, patting all around on his body again in confusion, before rising stiffly to his feet. He shook a cloud of dust from his hair, scowling at the strange glow in the earth again—before a similar shimmer caught his attention out of the corner of his eye, and he turned to look.

Partially buried beneath the overturned soil of Saffron's self-exhumation, a single wild fairy strawberry plant sprawled like a crushed spider. He recognized its pink color in an instant—but he'd never seen any of those in the Kyteler library glow that way. It wasn't unlike the light in the bottom of the hole...

The veil turns the berries pink.

"Oh—*fuck!*" Saffron squeaked upon realizing, leaping back in surprise.

He—must have passed through the veil after making his oath. Straight through Sunbeam's carved circle while it was still open, only to emerge on the other side of a random tear. Beneath the fucking earth, though? What a bitch. The veil was such a fucking—

He caught the sound of voices again, jumping and turning. But no matter which way he went, he saw nothing to hint at where they came from. His nerves heightened, suddenly worried he would have to make a run for it, recalling how there had been royal guards patrolling around Beantighe Village before Cylvan was taken.

Digging around in the hole for his boots, thinking they must have come off as he dragged himself out, Saffron found his red veil, first. He unearthed his shoes at the end of the open grave, next, tearing away a layer of grass and pulling them out like discovered artifacts.

Shoving his foot into the first one, then grabbing the second to do the same, he cried out as something bit him. Cursing and kicking, he turned the boot over to dump whatever creature had crawled inside—only for Proserpina's silver needle and quill to tumble out and poke into the grass.

He stared at them, racing thoughts falling silent in an instant. A shimmer of light surrounded them, too. The glow was whiter than that of the veil tear, though, making him wonder if it was something different, or...

Pressing a hand to his head as it throbbed, Saffron squeezed his eyes closed. Inhaling through his nose was nearly impossible with how much dried blood clogged his nostrils. His insides spun. He just—forced himself to reflect. To sew all of his scrambled memory threads back into place before continuing any further.

He'd watched the beannighe fade into white ash. He'd stripped naked and stepped inside the veil circle, kneeling in the center...

Saffron's eyes cracked open. He'd made an oath with the veil, just like the beannighe told him. He'd survived the inundation of magic. He was rowan blooded, just like he beseeched of it. And...

Glancing around himself again, he mentally reiterated how perhaps that rush of magic was powerful enough to open the veil all the way, sucking him through. It would explain how he ended up outside. Underground, even, right on top of the veil tear...

A bead of nervous sweat dripped down his spine when he realized—he didn't actually know how deep the veil went, let alone how far he tumbled. What if...?

He felt like he'd suddenly been kicked in the stomach. Frantically wrenching his opposite shoe back on, Saffron swept up the needle and quill and took off into the trees in a full-blown panic.

He chased those voices on the wind. The closer he grew—the more he felt it. That bone-deep ache, intense enough to make fresh blood drip from his nose. He just kept wiping it away, focusing only on one thing—confirming he was still in Alfidel. On the fey side of the veil. On the same side as Cylvan. On the side where Saffron could still find him, save him...!

Closer. More blood dripped from his nose. Closer; more blood surged up the back of his throat. Closer; more dripped from the corner of his eye. Still, he pushed ahead. It didn't matter how badly it hurt, he had to know where he'd crawled out of. If he—

If he was somehow on the human side—

He would simply race back to where he'd emerged, and bury himself all over again.

Finally locating the source of music, laughter, conversation, Saffron stopped short upon reaching the sudden edge of the trees. In front of him, the landscape opened across a wide, grassy courtyard, bigger than the entirety of Beantighe Village.

Directly across from where Saffron hovered, built with white stone, a shimmering palace stood illuminated in warm yellow light. Pinpricks of bright windows like gold coins adorned the side Saffron faced, with flaring cliffsides and mountains rising at its back. Towers and spires clawed at incoming clouds like bony fingers, nearly high enough to pierce the moon overhead.

Further decorating the massive courtyard, gaudily-dressed partygoers glowed strangely while wandering between hedges and walls of flowers, forming circles around golden fire pots brimming with warmth, dancing to string music with heels clacking against a jutting stone terrace from the palace wall. Just on the other side of the dancefloor, glass doors opened into what Saffron swore had to be a ballroom of some sort, internally lit as golden as the rest of the grand building.

Saffron's breath caught when he realized, the halos of light pinned behind the heads of the guests... were the same sort of white as that encircling the silver needle in his hand. On their chests, he swore he could even seen pinpricks of crimson—right where a high fey's true name would be.

It was then a pair of wandering guards came just close enough for Saffron to make out what was emblazoned on their pine-green tunics—recognizing a barn owl encircled by ferns and thorns.

Oh—

"Fuck!" Saffron hissed for a second time, buckling to his knees and taking cover behind the nearest bush. "Fuck, fuck, *fuck—!"*

He was—right outside the capitol palace in Avren.

How? How the fuck—Why—In what stroke of a divine hand—

Saffron's balance shifted as he thought he might puke more of the fucking blood rolling in his stomach, only for the amethyst pendant to tumble from beneath his shirt. He scrambled for it, gazing down at his purple-tinted reflection. He brushed a thumb over the shiny surface, before swallowing back the previous rush of confusion as he suddenly thought he understood.

Daurae Asche once said... they'd found Saffron locked in Kaelar's trunk by following Cylvan's matching pendant. *Two parts of a single bonded amethyst root... broken at midnight on an equinox... locked in their relationship to one another...*

Saffron croaked a laugh, running fingers back through his hair as he could hardly believe it, let alone make sense of it. He'd—passed through the veil, from the circle where he made his oath; it must have latched on to the companion of his silly little charmed pendant shared with Cylvan, and thrust him across Alfidel, to the nearest tear in the ground...

Was that—even possible? Was the veil so intelligent, so nuanced, that it could do something like that without being prompted...?

He recalled the way it mimicked his own voice while making their oath. The way it spoke like a real being, how it teased and made promises to him. Surely, something like that could pluck Saffron off Morrígan's campus and drop him outside of Avren. It had even dressed him on the way.

He gulped back another mouthful of blood summoned by the rush of opulence nearby. He wouldn't question it. He couldn't. There wasn't time. He would simply—accept the gift he was given.

Cylvan was within reach. Somewhere nearby, a raven prince was waiting for the spell Saffron once swore to give him. Saffron only had to find him. Find him, and find Taran, who controlled the prince with his name.

To control with a name...

Saffron pulled the silver needle and quill out from the back of his waistband, examining their white glow again. His heart pounded in his ears, thinking about... Taran. His bones. The wolf king's opulent silver.

Control it... no differently than how high fey can compel us.

"*Obey me,*" he breathed, recalling the few times he'd compelled Cylvan with his true name. The needle trembled, and Saffron grinned as the white halo surrounding the silver crested slightly brighter in response. He wiped his nose as fresh blood dripped against the swell of opulence in his hand.

This is why you must give names to opulent silver.

Saffron just had to give Taran's silver bones a name.

His heart thrummed, and then slammed hard inside his chest. He nearly burst out laughing.

55

THE WITCH

Saffron crossed the courtyard beneath his red veil. The closer he grew, the more it hurt—but the rowan in the chiffon acted as the slightest numbing boon to the pain. It did nothing to dull the brightness of every opulent fey he passed, though, blinded by the glow of white light in a circlet behind their heads, the flicker of bright red in the center of their chests. He was almost giddy every time he got close enough to read a true name. No fucking wonder Proserpina worked so hard to kill any and every rowan blooded witch she could find.

Approaching the stone terrace where fey guests danced, Saffron hovered just long enough to determine his prince wasn't amongst them. He did, however, recognize two other people he least expected—dancing arm and arm, though looking a little self-conscious, Professor Adelard and Professor Dullahan shared in quiet, affectionate conversation. Saffron bit back a smile, hurrying away before he was spotted. Adelard, of all people, would be the one to make a scene at the sight him.

Saffron peered into the glowing ballroom, next. He walked the length of the buffet tables both inside and out, even snagging a few bites to eat for himself. He smiled drunkenly with a mouth full of blood whenever anyone gazed at him too long, then made the mark of beseeching a Night Court just to watch the color drain from their faces.

Still with no sign of his raven prince, Saffron expanded his search into the less populated areas of the courtyard. He appreciated the warmth of the nearest golden fire pot, intrigued at how it glowed with white opulence, too; he plucked long strands of indigo-blue iris flowers to absentmindedly weave into a crown over his red-veiled head; he stood on his toes and peered into any low-standing windows of the palace, spotting dark corridors, rooms filled with books, others with fine furniture and canopied beds.

Then—he overheard a frenzied voice right before rounding a corner, and stepped back into the wall to listen. Biting down on his tongue, he recognized the owner of the words.

"Where is Lord mac Delbaith? Where is he? It's very important —I've seen witness of a rowan witch. He must know!"

Headmistress Elluin stumbled through a group of courtiers, all of whom wrinkled their noses and hurried away in disgust. Elluin just rushed to the next ones she could find, asking the same questions, making the same frantic demands. As she did, she held a messy bandage wrapped around her throat, stained bright red with blood. Her voice was hoarse and breathy, as if only one vocal cord remained after the beannighe's assault. She looked about as wild as Saffron did—and something about that made him bite back amusement.

From one group of fey to the next, the headmistress made her demands—until, finally, someone told her what she wanted to know.

"Lord mac Delbaith is already in the engagement clearing with the others. If you wish to speak to him, you will have to wait until they return at sunrise."

Saffron's eyes followed the same pointing finger the headmistress did, spotting a pathway on the opposite side of the wide lawn illuminated on both sides with lanterns. Protected at the entrance by two guards, the path disappeared into a thick grove of trees, and Saffron recognized a curl of smoke rising from the heart of it.

He stared longer than he should have, petrified by the sudden rush of adrenaline—and when he came back to his body, Elluin was already gone. At the last moment, he spotted exactly where she stepped into the treeline, right where the guards wouldn't spot her.

Saffron followed.

It didn't take long to catch up to her in the undergrowth. Elluin stumbled over roots and plants as if it was her first time navigating terrain so uneven. Something about it was satisfying to watch, and Saffron's thrill only heightened the moment she turned when he accidentally crunched a branch beneath his foot. She went pale in an instant, mouth dropping open, then quickened her stride. Saffron's heart fluttered, smiling to himself and picking up his own pace.

He kept just far enough behind her to maintain a sense of mystery. An amount of incorporeality. As far as Elluin knew—he was just a ghost. Just the ghost every high fey kept trying to make him. If that was what they wanted, Saffron would give it to them.

He smelled spiced wood of a bonfire before he saw its light in the darkness. He saw the dancing bodies in varying states of undress, haloed by rays of opulent light before he saw exactly how many people encircled the flames. He smelled the indulgent cakes and honey-glazed meats and sweet breads before he felt the heat of the fire. He saw the Ostara decorations intertwined between the trees, with strands upon strands of twigs and branches and gold-braided garlands interwoven overhead, coming to a central point in the center of the clearing where the highest points of the middle flames coalesced.

For a moment, Saffron thought he knew exactly what all the old myths referred to when they described the beauty and opulence of Tír na nÓg.

At the head of the clearing, two thrones woven from ancient branches were occupied by who Saffron recognized as Kings Ailir and Tross, dressed as magnificently as the rest of the party in the colors of spring and collars of fresh flowers. Next to them sat Daurae Asche, donning similar celebration clothing and looking a mix of stiff and uneasey. They were always so observant, spotting Saffron lingering just inside the trees before anyone else did, though clearly not knowing who hid beneath the red veil and iris crown. They would find out soon enough.

King Ailir chatted boisterously with someone Saffron didn't recognize, while to his right, King Tross leaned in close to someone with similar black hair and horns as Cylvan, as well as— Luvon. Saffron bit back his breath of surprise, quickly pulling his eyes away as if knowing his patron-master would be able to sense it. He likely already had.

Around the base of the bonfire, golden tangles of thorns shone bright, on the verge of melting from the heat. With every melted spike, a flower bloomed at the sodden base. By the end of the night, each sharp point would be whittled down into lovely spring symbolism, perhaps to be draped over a door, or offered to the trees in hopes of a fruitful first sowing.

Perhaps that was its traditional purpose, but Saffron understood its second symbolism the moment he found his raven amidst the clearing, standing opposite the flames where Saffron encroached just within the shadows.

Dressed as the horned god, donning black and decorated with gold, Prince Cylvan danced arm in arm with Taran. With makeup as dark as the rest of his outfit, Cylvan's amethyst eyes stood out brighter than ever, locked on his partner who wore a forest green tunic, adorned with gold beading and chains, eyes decorated with lavender shadow to represent the welcomed arrival of spring. Taran donned fresh flowers and crystals in his hair, clearly embodying the goddess of Ostara. Dancing hand in hand with the shadow of winter wearing a crown of gold thorns, as if to emphasize his own importance. The warmth and light that would tame the cold and the dark. Saffron's nails burrowed into the bark of a nearby tree, cracking down to the cuticle root as he fought to control himself.

There was only one thing to quell his heightening rage—and that was the distinct way Taran mac Delbaith lacked a red glow in the center of his chest. How he lacked a white halo of opulence behind his head.

Taran mac Delbaith may not have a true name of his own at the start of the party—but Saffron would remedy that by the end of it.

Stepping from the trees, Saffron helped himself to a flute of fairy wine right as Elluin stumbled from her own wandering path through the woods. Gasping for breath, she searched the crowd for the royal party at the head. Saffron followed every movement with his eyes over the rim of his glass, indulging in the pink drink that might no longer reduce him to soft and simpering as it would have one veil-oath previously. A red smear stained the rim of the flute when he pulled away, like a smudge of lipstick.

Elluin shoved her way through the dancing guests, straight for the visions of spring gods at the front. Saffron claimed another glass of wine, sipping it while appreciating the way Taran's face turned up in disgust at the sight of her.

Saffron's eyes returned and lingered on Cylvan. His Night Prince, watching the headmistress speak no differently from Taran—except that his expression was lifeless. There was no light in his eyes, not even a twitch of his mouth. He should have been smirking sarcastically. Rolling his eyes. But there was nothing, as if only a shell. Trapped behind a wall, imprisoned in his own body by the name Taran held him by.

Saffron finished his drink. Next to him, a fey guest scoffed, muttering something about how Saffron was filthy, stinking of dirt and iron. Saffron met their eyes and smiled; beneath the crushing opulence of the clearing, blood dripped thickly from his nose and one of his eyes. Before the fey could tuck behind their fan and scurry away, though, Saffron reached out to adjust their cravat. In the process—he read the markings on their chest.

"Myndol," he said calmly, and the courtier staggered backward in shock. Saffron claimed and sipped a third drink in consideration. *"Myndol, pour this glass of wine on Taran mac Delbaith."*

The fey's eyes glazed over. Nodding, they took the glass Saffron offered, then wobbled through the crowd of people catching sight and sound of Elluin's raving. Saffron watched with an elated smile as his compelled courtier circled around the fire to where Taran stood—and splashed the contents of the flute all over him.

Taran whirled and snarled, grabbing the courtier and nearly throwing them into the fire. He might have, had the entire party not suddenly been watching, had the fey not erupted into pleas for mercy.

"I'm sorry, your highness! I did not mean to—it was the red beantighe! The red beantighe compelled me—!"

Conspiratorial whispers swept across the clearing like water in a basin. Taran searched the crowd in tandem—and his eyes halted on Saffron's veil through the flames of the bonfire. Saffron raised another glass of wine in shared acknowledgement, before lifting the chiffon off his face and taking a sip.

Taran kept his gaze for just a moment longer, before his head snapped toward the nearest guard, demanding their attention. Saffron's smugness only faltered the moment he realized—the guard turned and walked straight for Luvon. They took him by the arm and dragged him toward Taran, gasps of confusion rising from the crowd. King Tross also leapt to his feet, but Ailir's hand grabbed him before he could exclaim anything. Saffron saw how the kings shared an intense look, exchanging words without speaking. Something about it made Saffron's stomach turn for more than one reason, as if it wasn't the first time one king had to stop the other from interrupting Taran's demands. Did Taran's family hold something over their heads, as well...?

"As much as I resent having to interrupt our engagement

party for something so uncouth..." Taran then announced over the gossip. Luvon was brought to his side, and Saffron was relieved when he at least wasn't shoved to his knees, or thrown into the fire like Taran almost did the first courtier. "There are some things more important than our celebrations—namely, ensuring the safety of every high Alvian, no matter the time or place."

Taran locked eyes with Saffron through the flames again, and all others turned to join him. Saffron felt the crushing burden of a forest-full of opulence strike him, but didn't flinch, even as new blood dripped from his nose, bubbled in the back of his throat. He just nodded in agreement. It clearly rubbed Taran the wrong way, demonstrated by how his jaw clenched. He lifted a hand to point, and Saffron smiled at everyone who looked his way.

"The Headmistress of Morrígan Academy has just informed me, she was in the process of trialing this beantighe for arid magic when it escaped with want to find Prince Cylvan. Apparently it has been killing beantighes on the campus using a magic wolf, and always intended on allowing Prince Cylvan to take the blame."

More mumbling, even from the kings near their thrones. Luvon kept his white eyes lowered, but shook his head with a slight frown of disbelief. Saffron tightened his grasp around the glass in his hand, but otherwise still didn't react.

"What do you have to say for your actions, beantighe?" Taran asked when Saffron didn't offer anything, himself. That time, Saffron smirked. He finished off the rest of his drink.

"I still have one more trial to perform," he answered, and Taran's smile twisted in annoyance. "I wish to do so in front of the entire court, if it so pleases his highness, the fiancé to be."

"What is his final trial, headmistress?" Taran asked flatly, and Elluin went pale. She stammered instead of answering, but jumped when Taran flashed her a look.

"Erm—that is—he must... he must summon a familiar, Lord mac Delbaith."

Taran scoffed in amusement—but it faltered when he saw the

reactionary grin on Saffron's face, too. How predictable, that the final arid trial would also be the thing Elluin wanted to see most of all. She must have planned it on purpose—and Saffron could have kissed her.

"Well, then," Saffron said, taking a step toward the fire. "May I approach, your highness? I want to make sure everyone gets a good view."

"You may," Taran answered with a stately nod, but it was held behind more restraint. Saffron knew Taran must secretly love the attention, if nothing else. He must love being addressed with such a royal title. "May Danu oversee this trial, and guide us with benevolence."

Saffron crossed within reach of the fire. He passed through the congregation of high fey courtiers, the highest of stature in Alfidel, the richest and noblest and most powerful people to gather in one place. And those rich, noble, powerful people— looked at Saffron in dismay and apprehension. He might as well have been caressed over every inch of his skin by Ériu's sky maid- ens, by how much he reveled in the feeling.

Approaching where Taran stood with Cylvan, Elluin, and Luvon, Saffron's eyes traveled to his prince, again. Cylvan watched him—but his face remained blank. Saffron wondered if he knew what was happening, if there was a part of him screaming behind those glazed-over eyes. Saffron smiled at him in promise, just in case.

"Luvon mag Shamhradháin is no longer my patron-master," Saffron reminded Taran as he took his place facing the fey lord, back to the fire and feeling its tendrils reach out to caress him. "He has nothing to do with me any longer."

"Your patronage was never formally exchanged," Taran returned a wry smile. "Should you be found guilty of arid magic, he will be the next one tried for conspiracy."

"So be it," Saffron said flatly. As they spoke, never once did Luvon even flinch. His blind eyes found Saffron amongst the flames, expression strong and handsome and never wavering.

Saffron wished he could know what his patron-father was thinking—but at the same time, it didn't matter.

Saffron would prove himself arid, but that would be far from what every witnessing fey recalled from the night, once he was finished.

"Then I will begin," he said, pulling Elluin's silver needle and quill from the back of his waistband. "You say I am expected to summon my familiar, correct? Gladly."

56

THE MERCY

Taking in a long breath, Saffron closed his eyes, grounding himself. He recalled what the beannighe once tried to show him about the silver cuffs and giving them a name. He was further emboldened when it was clear Taran didn't wear any silver ring or other token that controlled his own silver bones, either. No glow of a true name, no white glow of an opulent halo—only the subtlest shine surrounding his body. No, surrounding his *bones.* His bones without a name, so sure to think they would never need one. So sure Clymeus and Proserpina had wiped out any rowan witch who would be able to take advantage of such a glaring vulnerability. Saffron would prove that hubris to be Taran's own downfall.

Saffron lowered to the grass, balancing on his knees and the balls of his feet. He didn't have a rowan branch to use, specifically —but perhaps he didn't need one.

"There's this human myth about a father and son, who escape captivity by forming wings from feathers and wax," he regaled, setting the needle in the grass ahead of where he knelt, pointing it directly at Taran's feet. "The boy's father tells him to mind himself, to not fly too close to the sun, else the wings would melt and he would fall to his death."

Unbuttoning the cuff of his sleeve, Saffron rolled it up to the elbow. Around him, every high fey listened intently, while Taran just continued smirking.

The bonfire illuminated Saffron's skin in orange and crimson, and he saw how the veins in his forearm were dark from the strain of opulence in the air. He could practically see his heartbeat pounding through them, fighting against the weight of counter-magic in every direction. Just a moment longer.

Saffron claimed the quill in his dominant hand, and the needle in the grass shivered. Just like when the beannighe held it.

Taran's arrogant smile fluttered in surprise. Saffron just rubbed two fingers up and down the bare skin of his forearm, then met Taran's eyes again.

"Despite the warning, the boy thought quite highly of himself and his abilities. Thrilled to be free of captivity, he soared into the sky, wanting to be the only one who owned the air, wanting to be above everything and everyone he thought himself better than. But, just like his father warned—the heat of the sun melted the wax of his wings... and he plummeted to his death with no one to catch him. It's a story of opportunity, ruined by one thing..."

He met Taran's eyes again. Taran had gone still.

"Arrogance." Saffron grinned. The scars on his back tingled as rowan magic surged in his body.

"Do you know what his name was, my lord?"

Saffron buried the tip of the quill into his arm. Tasting his blood, filling the mouth of the nib.

"Obey me," he compelled the needle in the grass—then tore the tip of the quill down his forearm.

The needle rushed upward, curving around—and slamming into Taran's back. It sliced down the length of his spine, mimicking the first mark Saffron made on his arm, then the rest that followed.

Taran shrieked. He twisted, attempting to grab the assaulting tool before it could cut any farther, but the needle kept just out of his reach as Saffron commanded it.

Another line in Saffron's arm—another cut buried into Taran's back. Then another, and another, every stroke mimicked.

Courtiers shrieked and scattered, shoving past one another and racing for the woods. Elluin joined them, barely wheezing a cry before tripping backward over her own feet and tearing off into the darkness.

Guards attempted to swarm Saffron from both sides as Taran commanded them—but branches of bright flame suddenly raced from the roots of the bonfire, erupting high and wild like trees on either side of him. It sucked the oxygen from the air, and Saffron turned to witness Daurae Asche standing with their hands extended alongside King Ailir. Their face was twisted in fury—staring directly at Taran. Taking the first opportunity they could to assist Saffron, without question—as if they'd been waiting for their own moment to stand up and strike.

King Tross grabbed Luvon right before the corridor of fire closed them off. The stranger with horns and black hair grabbed Cylvan. Saffron and Taran were instantly contained within the sweltering hovel, just the two of them.

"*Sybil—!*" Taran shouted, but his following command was drowned out as Asche flooded the flames with increased strength, a tower of heat erupting into the sky before crashing back down again.

Another mark, and then another, Saffron spelled the name he intended to sew directly into the opulence of Taran's bones. One letter per vertebrae, just like the beannighe showed him on the cuffs.

Taran would never transform into the wolf again, unless Saffron compelled him to.

Even if someone knew the myth, even if they figured it out by Saffron's words—it wouldn't matter. The controlling token was carved into Saffron's arm. He was the silver hands-and-dagger ring, the silver quill, the owner of the magic in Taran's bones—and no one would be able to control them unless they controlled Saffron, first. Not even Taran, himself.

Icarus. ⸻

"Now, *do as I say—and reveal yourself.*"

Saffron rose to his feet, compelling with every ounce of his soul.

The needle tumbled to the grass. Taran's face twisted in rage—and every remaining courtier, the kings, Cylvan, Asche, Luvon, witnessed the ashen heir of Clymeus mac Dela tear through his own skin to wear the flesh of the wolf king.

Further screams erupted, but Saffron's attention stuck on a brief shimmer of gold falling to the grass. The fern ring, Taran's engagement ring, displaced in the transformation and nesting in the grass between Taran's swollen paws.

Approaching the beast, Saffron clamped one hand over its wrinkled snout with all the confidence of approaching a trained animal. He bent and retrieved the ring. Taran snarled beneath Saffron's grip, but didn't attack. There was no harming the master of one's own name.

"*Open your mouth,*" Saffron compelled as hot wind whipped hair around his eyes, raked through Taran's dark fur.

Taran resisted, but the command inevitably won out, forcing him to stretch his jaw open. Saffron drenched the fern ring in the blood dripping from his arm, then buried his fist between the wolf's teeth and down his throat. Taran snarled, reeling backward, but Saffron just barked a laugh and shoved his arm deeper.

"Remind you of the last time?" He grinned bitterly, referring to their confrontation on the road outside of Beantighe Village, when he buried rowan berries down the wolf's throat and made him vomit bloody foam. The rowan magic in his blood had the same effect, making Taran wretch, throat tightening around Saffron's arm—but he sank himself all the way to the shoulder, pressing it into Taran's teeth.

"I am Cylvan's divine mercy," Saffron declared viciously. "And the sun you flew too close to. Remember that—the next time you underestimate me."

Taran's silver teeth pricked Saffron's skin, stamping him with the same halo of pockmarks once healed-over beneath Magnin's hands.

"For as long as this ring is inside you," Saffron compelled through grit teeth, using the edge of the ring's fern leaves to slice into the fleshy insides of the base of Taran's throat. *"You will not speak Prince Cylvan's true name."*

Taran snarled again, thrashing backward and finally pulling himself free of Saffron's grip. Saffron nearly commanded him to his knees, last—but more shouts caught his attention. He turned just in time to watch Cylvan through the flames shove one of the armed guards into the grass, pulling the crossbow from their belt. Stumbling backward, Saffron thought he meant to shoot Taran—but then Taran rumbled with laughter.

Cylvan's empty eyes found Saffron's through the flames, glazed over with Taran's final shouted enchantment—and he pulled the trigger, launching a steel bolt straight into Saffron's chest.

57

THE SUN

Surrounding flames swelled in a plume, as if thinking they could deflect the shot—but the steel bolt sliced with ease, and collided with its mark. Into the center of Saffron's chest, burrowing nearly to the fletching made of owl feathers.

The world went silent as Saffron stumbled backward, illuminated from every direction, seen by every pair of eyes that remained—before a cry of terror ripped through the sky, and the fire vanished back into the earth. The heat rushed upward, reclaimed by the stars. Even the bonfire suffocated beneath a sudden oppressive wave, and the clearing plummeted into darkness.

Saffron attempted to remain upright amongst the sound of rushing feet, shouts, hurrying bodies in every direction—but as if the sky collapsed on top of him, he sank to one knee. Gasping, it was agony to inhale, blood invading his lungs with every attempt to catch his breath. His fingers frantically searched for the bolt, gripping the end still emerging from his chest, but it was too slippery. There wasn't enough to find purchase. He would—have to leave it.

"*Fuck,*" he gasped, and a pathetic sound trailed the end.

He couldn't stay on the ground—Taran was still nearby, the wolf was still nearby, Saffron had to make sure Cylvan was safe—

Rot. Blood. Hot breath scattered over him, and Saffron strained to see through the darkness.

"I would have been the kindest fate offered him," Taran rumbled in a low, gutteral voice. "Now, all of Cylvan's suffering— will be because of you."

Saffron whimpered as blood bubbled up the back of his throat—but it wasn't the blood of magic overwhelm, it was—his own body flooding. The bolt in his chest, splitting him open to spill across the ground.

"Help me," he attempted—but there was no response. The wolf no longer loomed over him, gone from the shadows, gone from Saffron's command. To escape so easily amongst the chaos, when Saffron finally owned him—Saffron could only laugh, and then shudder, and then sink heavier toward the grass, bracing himself on one hand as the rest of his body shook.

"Fuck..." he whispered again, head drooping forward. He nearly buckled to the grass—but someone caught him before he could slip.

Rough, grappling hands made Saffron cry out as he slumped beneath the weight of the sky, devolving into gasping sobs as more pain rocked through him.

"Saffron—! *Saffron!"* Cylvan pleaded, pulling Saffron into his chest. He frantically pushed hair from Saffron's eyes, but Saffron couldn't see anything except the stars overhead. His head rolled to the side as Cylvan fought to sit him back up again. *"Saffron!* Saffron, oh, gods—Saffron, please, say something, púca!"

There were only stars. Only stars, and warm breath, and gardenia and pine, and needles, and water, and wind. So much wind—wind Saffron knew to gust with agony, carrying those cries of horror through the floorboards whenever he lay on his back in the attic.

The hands that grappled him—pulled him closer.

Every part of him protected. Hidden from the needles that dug.

"Hold on, Saffron—it's going to be alright, you're going to be alright—"

Saffron managed a shaky smile, but sank deeper against Cylvan's stomach when he could no longer hold himself up. Exhaustion struck him faster than should have been possible. Perhaps—it was the relief. The plummeting of adrenaline. Saffron had done it, he'd—

"I... did it," he said weakly, pathetically. "I did it, Cylvan."

"Y-yes, you did, púca," Cylvan assured him, pulling Saffron upright again when he slipped beneath his own weight. "You did it."

"Are you impressed?" Saffron's smile stretched slightly, pulled harder into Cylvan's body as a face pressed into the side of his neck.

"Yes, yes, yes, Saffron—" Cylvan's voice wavered, before lifting his head and screaming for someone to help him. More bodies circled—though Saffron didn't know if they were the living or the dead.

"Saffron!" Luvon shouted, followed by the sound of two bodies tangling as he thrashed against someone holding him back. *"Let me go,* godsdamnit—that's my child! *Saffron!"*

Saffron let out a long breath, attempting to lift his head, not wanting anyone to worry—but he was still too heavy. His fingers were starting to tingle. He wasn't sure where his legs had gone.

"I'm so tired, Cylvan," he mumbled, eyelids drooping with the same weight as the rest of him.

"No—no, Saffron—keep your eyes open. Open your eyes, Saffron—Come on, tell me—tell me how you figured it out. I want to hear everything. You figured out the right spell to use— you're extraordinary. You're absolutely... P-please, Saffron, don't —don't go, púca—you promised me, remember? You promised to stay with me. So don't..." Cylvan's words caught in a tight throat, and he pulled Saffron close again, pressing his face against

Saffron's shoulder. "Don't leave me, Saffron, please—not again. I can't lose you again, Saffron, I can't..."

"It's alright, Cylvan..." Saffron sighed again, unable to think of anything except his own exhaustion. He just had to close his eyes for a moment, just to rest for a moment. "I'm just so... tired."

"No, Saffron—you can't sleep right now—No, please, stay awake! *Someone help him!*" Cylvan's voice cracked, growing louder, more desperate. "Saffron, you have to let me keep my side of the deal. Right? I'm going to give you an academic endorsement. You can read as many books as you like. We'll find more nymphs for you to draw. We'll dance together whenever you want. So just—stay with me. The healer will be here soon, so just —just keep your eyes open. Keep talking. Tell me about your magic, púca. Tell me—about your favorite myth. Do you remember seeing Derdriu up close in the library? Do you remember when I carried you to see her? Please, *please*, stay with me, Saffron—I just got you back, don't leave me again, please, gods, don't leave me..."

Adelard's was the last voice Saffron expected to hear—but he whispered Cylvan's name in greeting, then Saffron's. He touched a hand to Saffron's chest, and Saffron cried out, choking on a sob as every one of his nerves lit up like hot coals. Cylvan roughly shoved Adelard away, spitting curses and damning him to rot— but Adelard just whispered apologies.

"If we get the bolt out, I can help him," he went on with calm certainty.

"No—" Saffron pleaded groggily, the sound wavering as he sank into bloodless inebriation. He weakly shoved away the first set of hands to grope at his chest—only for someone else to pin them back. *"No... no...!"*

He shrieked as fingers dug into his chest, screaming so loud his throat cut him off.

The moment the white-hot pressure released, he slumped again, going numb, body limp in Cylvan's arms. Cylvan frantically pulled him back into place, touching his face and begging him to come back. *Wake up, wake up, púca, please, open your eyes—!*

Voices from every direction blurred together, emerging from one mouth, from a dozen, words twisting and tangling.

What will you do?

Heal him. Spell. Cinch the wound.

Blood—burning you, Cylvan.

Just do something!

Why isn't it working?

Saffron. It must be—Is he—

A vow... the veil.

Rowan blooded?

What does that...?

Professor?

How did you do this, Saffron?

Just help him!

I... can't.

Jostled. The sound of hissed threats and fists grabbing clothing, making feral demands followed by uncertain apologies.

... Saffron?

But—Saffron was sunken. Into the earth below, into the mounds where he always slept more peacefully than any night before. Always alongside Cylvan, always in his arms. Even that time, wrapped up against him, Saffron would sleep. And sleep. And sleep.

What remained of him on the surface—heard Cylvan scream. Felt him pull and claw Saffron into his body, wishing to wrench him back out of the earth like ripping a tree from the roots. A gale of wind tore out in every direction—before crashing inward again and leaving the world silent. Silent, except for the sound of Cylvan's gasping sobs as he held Saffron as close as he possibly could, cradling him back and forth, begging endlessly for Saffron to come back again.

"We have to go, your highness." Another unfamiliar voice spoke above the rest. Cylvan didn't respond, just tightened his

grasp on the human draped in his arms, fingers nearly digging down to the bones. *"Prince Cylvan—we have to go. Now."*

"I won't leave him, Saoirse—"

"It isn't safe. Come on, Cylvan—let Master Luvon take him, before anyone sees—"

Saffron searched for the candle meant to guide him to the other side. Perhaps he wouldn't get one, as dying in a court of high fey meant he would simply cease without a batting eye. But Cylvan would remember him. Even if it meant Saffron would wander forever in the darkness, not knowing which way to go to pass on, at least Cylvan would remember him.

Cylvan, who was always so warm. Who always tucked hair behind Saffron's ear, and kissed the tears off his cheeks.

Cylvan, who played the violin. Who controlled the wind and the sky. Who taught Saffron to love romantic myths—and then showed him what it was like to live in one, tragic ending and all.

Cylvan, the Night Prince, who promised again and again to show Saffron what it was like to live in the Day—never realizing he alone was all the sunlight Saffron ever needed.

"You can't be seen protecting the human who attacked—"

"I WILL NOT LEAVE HIM ALONE!" Cylvan erupted, cutting through the numbness laying claim to Saffron's thoughts. Like a stake driven into the mounds, rending it open for one last gasp of air to reach him.

Silence returned to the clearing, and Saffron's body shifted again. Arms wrapped around his shoulders, his lower back, pulling him chest-to-chest against Cylvan. The Night Prince trembled, muscles clenched—but no longer in fear, or desperation. Saffron felt it reverberate through the earth. The mounds reached farther, attempting to drag him down faster, fleeing from the rage of a coming Night King.

"This is the person I choose as my fiancé," Cylvan declared, tucking a piece of hair from Saffron's eyes. Saffron had never heard an answering silence as shocked, as heavy as the one that fell following those words. Cylvan spoke into it again, owning every presence, every ghost in that clearing. Forcing them to hear without question. "And should my future Harmonious King die before dawn..."

The mounds tugged Saffron deeper. Attempting to pull him from Cylvan's arms, as if knowing the warning that came. As if knowing the danger of what Cylvan would declare, knowing exactly what would happen if—

"... All of Alfidel will learn *exactly* what it means to despair beneath my Night Court."

58

THE GEIS

Crimson-stained cotton. Carrying Taran's sagging body, a few inches taller and wider than Saffron even when standing up straight. Heavy. Crushing. Reeking of flesh and rot, blood from gaping wounds sinking into Saffron's flayed skin, spreading through his veins. Kissing his fingertips. Flushing his heart. Staining his rowan blood black like ink, until his bones solidified, died, rusted into silver.

A tiny, flickering light beckoned to Saffron far out of his reach. Saffron focused on its little glow, knowing, surely, it would lead them out of the darkness.

"It's a heavy burden," Taran whispered. "Who are you to carry it?"

"What?" Saffron asked weakly, and Taran lifted a finger to point. Saffron focused on the light up ahead, realizing it belonged to one of the inch-tall funeral candles used for human burials—and it burned away faster than Saffron could chase it.

"No!" Saffron begged. No, no, no—he had to reach it before it snuffed. It was all he had, the only light he had to follow—

"Saffron," Taran's voice trembled, and Saffron nearly lost his footing, weighed down as Taran's legs gave out beneath him. "They'll eat you whole."

Saffron groaned beneath the fey lord's weight, practically dragging him, heaving with breath smelling of old blood, iron.

Only an hour. Only an hour to find the other side. Humans were hardly given any time at all to search for the afterlife. What would happen if Saffron didn't make it in time? What if Saffron was crushed beneath the weight of Taran mac Delbaith's expectations on his back—the darkness he swore to rid Alfidel of completely?

A flock of crows suddenly swept from the sky. Saffron stumbled, ducking, pulling Taran's limp body in close so the birds wouldn't scratch his face, pull out his hair. When the shadowy mass dissipated again, Saffron cracked open his eyes—but the path was blocked. Blood, rot. Wiry black hair, prickling on its shoulders. A snout furrowed, red eyes like drops of rubies in snow, ears flat back against its skull in threat.

Blood dripped from its mouth, teeth stained with more blood— matching the marks in Taran's arm. His chest. His throat. Ripping wounds Saffron hadn't noticed before then, but suddenly made him too heavy, too slippery to carry. Taran tumbled from Saffron's arms, collapsing limp across the path—flesh torn over every inch, until Saffron barely recognized him. Staining Saffron's hands in return, blending with his own blood, dripping from the wounds in his arms, the reopened halo of teeth around his shoulder.

It's a heavy burden.

Gasping for breath, Saffron turned back to the wolf in the path —only barely leaping out of the way as it lunged toward him, snapping teeth before landing crouched over Taran's motionless body on the road. Snarling, bearing its teeth, Saffron just threw his hands up—then watched in horror as the thick cloud of crows suddenly plummeted from the sky, surrounding the beast and tearing it apart. Ripping away fur, then skin, then flesh—leaving only silver bones. And when they were done—the birds turned to him, beaks still wet with viscera.

They'll eat you whole.

. . .

BURSTING THROUGH THE SOIL THAT FINALLY PINNED him in death, Saffron's lungs tore at the air in a horrific gasp. Jolting in his body, he slammed upward—only to be wrenched back against the pillows by bindings around his wrists.

A dream, it was only a dream—but Saffron's insides screamed against the eruption of pain in his chest, his forearm, every inch of his body flaring in torment. A shadow laying over the side of the bed lurched to its feet, throwing out its hands.

"Saffron! Púca—relax! Hey! Hey, it's alright!"

Cylvan's voice made Saffron's heart pound harder, eyes flashing wildly through the bright room to find him—and the moment he did, the moment he met Cylvan's amethyst eyes, once he felt the prince's hands gently caress his face and summon him to calm down—overwhelmed tears filled Saffron's eyes, but he blinked them away before they could drip. His breaths came hard, sinking into a different kind of panic as it was impossible to inhale all the way, wincing and gasping as he gazed down to find himself in unfamiliar clothes, in an unfamiliar bed.

Tied off to gold bars on either side of him, the room was bright, airy, windows open wide to let the breeze inside and play with the sheer curtains. Separated from the rest of the long room by a fabric privacy screen, Saffron heard other voices whispering to one another at a distance, could see how the rafters overhead extended past his limited view.

"Where—" He rasped, voice like someone emerging from beneath Lake Elatha. "Where am I?"

"You're in the family clinic—ah, the royal family clinic. You're safe here, Saffron, so just lay back—"

But Saffron strained against the bindings on his wrists again, grunting as his heart pounded harder. "Why—"

Cylvan took his face again, gently commanding Saffron to look at him. To meet his eyes. Saffron did—but it didn't ease how hard it was to breathe.

"Sit back... relax," Cylvan said gently. "I'll tell you everything, just, please, relax..."

Gulping, Saffron did as he was told, letting his clenched fists loosen into trembling fingers. He held back any more demands, any more rushes of emotion, just focusing on breathing. Every inhale was excruciating—each following exhale not any better—but being intentional about each movement helped. And as his heart rate slowed into a pace more manageable, it allowed him to take in more details of his surroundings.

Flowers. An ocean of them, covering nearly every surface of his end of the room. On the table directly alongside him was the simplest of them all in a wooden vase, and he recognized them as wildflowers from the Agate Wood. A scrap of paper sat propped up against the vase; in shaky, practicing letters, it read: *Hollow. Letty. Nimue. Baba Yaga. Fleece. Sunbeam.*

"What do you remember?" Cylvan asked in a gentle voice, touching Saffron's leg over the soft blankets covering him. Saffron's heart leapt at the question.

"T-Taran!" He gasped, wrists straining against the bindings again. "Taran, is he—!"

Before he could rile up further, Cylvan leaned forward—and took Saffron's face, placing a gentle kiss to his mouth. It brought Saffron's panic back down again, back to a steady thrum under his skin. His eyes remained closed, his chest breathless, even moments after Cylvan pulled away.

"You're safe, Saffron. Taran is gone."

"Gone?" Saffron asked weakly, eyes fluttering open again. "But—"

"We... don't know where he is," Cylvan clarified like it was meant to be a reassurance. It took everything in Saffron's willpower not to erupt into another panic. "Erm—his family has gone silent, too. I think you scared them, with your little trick... not to mention the scandal. Their most venerated son bearing the bones of the old king, that is... They're all acting like they had no idea, of course, as well as claiming they never knew their own magic silver contained bone ash from deceased Sídhe..."

Saffron suddenly felt faint. He closed his eyes, slumping back into the pillows, only for Cylvan's chair to jolt out from under him as he leapt to his feet and pleaded Saffron's name in a panic. Saffron's eyes snapped back open again, finding Cylvan pale, panicked, hanging over him.

On instinct, Saffron tried to reach out to him, only to be reminded of his tied wrists. He frowned at them, and Cylvan released a shuddering breath before shaking his head.

"Let me just..."

Cylvan patted around on his waist, and that was when Saffron saw what he wore. A stiff doublet lined with gold and jewelry, intricate beading lining the collar and down the front. His wrists jingled with bracelets, the rings on his fingers clearly for show and not building access. Even the knife he pulled out had a jeweled handle, not meant for much more than showing off.

"Is this because... everyone saw me perform magic?" Saffron's voice cracked. He knew what that would mean. He knew not even Cylvan would be able to protect him if people saw. Saffron would be executed, first, and then Luvon, and then Baba Yaga, and Beantighe Village, and Cylvan, himself—

"No," Cylvan reassured him in a whisper, cutting the cords and allowing Saffron to rub his sore wrists. Around one of them, Saffron found a bracelet of woven twigs, wondering if it was the reason he felt the slightest relief from the opulence in the air. It reminded him of the one Asche wore outside the ruins. "I was worried... you would try to run away, if you woke up alone."

Saffron wheezed a laugh. Oh—Cylvan was right about that. He probably would have, had the pain in his chest not been so fucking awful. He touched the spot at the thought, wincing, and Cylvan gently coaxed his hand away.

"No one in Avren has had to heal a rowan blooded witch in a very, very long time," he explained in a low whisper, eyes flickering to the curtain separating Saffron from the rest of the room before leaning in slightly more. "And... most writings about them were destroyed when Proserpina made it taboo. Apparently, anything much deeper than a scratch... becomes immune to opulent magic. Even Adelard couldn't do anything with his arid spells, since you've technically become more powerful than even him, as he explained it. Unfortunately, these are wounds you will have to heal on your own..."

Saffron curiously trailed his finger over the wound again, before regarding the gruesome mark on his forearm. Mostly scabbed over, he could already tell it was going to leave a scar.

"Of those who saw you perform arid magic, well..." Cylvan went on, then trailed off, then shook his head. He didn't meet Saffron's eyes again. "They... they think I killed you. When I fired that bolt into your chest... they all assumed you died, and that's the pervading rumor in Avren."

Saffron—smiled. He even laughed, though it hurt. Cylvan didn't respond, though. He even frowned slightly.

"Well... that's a good thing, isn't it?" Saffron tried to reassure him, touching his hand. "That everyone saw you kill me, I mean. Erm... saw you kill an arid witch, I mean. Won't that be good for your... your reputation?"

Cylvan still didn't say anything, but his brows furrowed like there was an entire library of thoughts he wished to.

"I... almost killed you," Cylvan finally said, barely a sound. His jaw clenched, flexing a muscle in his cheek. "Because of Taran's enchantment, I shot you, I had no choice—and you almost died in my arms, and—all of Alfidel is celebrating because they think you actually did..."

Saffron touched Cylvan's hand again, but Cylvan still wouldn't look at him. His mouth just dangled open slightly, at a loss.

"I'm... sorry," he said, before his face contorted in self-loathing. "*Fuck*—gods above, how do I ever—? How can I ever apologize in a way that isn't so—so fucking pathetic? How can I ever express how fucking awful it was—!"

Saffron was the one to grab Cylvan's collar, that time, pulling him in for a reassuring kiss. He let it linger for a long time, until Cylvan's clenched features finally relaxed.

"Remember when you wouldn't let me apologize for kissing you at the party in Connacht?" He asked softly. "This is no different, your highness."

"It's different—"

But Saffron kissed him again, cutting it off. He smiled between their lips.

"While you held me, you also said... you would endorse me, now," he teased in a soft voice. "And take me to see more nymphs. Did you mean that?"

Cylvan shuddered—then cupped a hand around the back of Saffron's head, kissing him harder. Saffron's breath caught, but he held Cylvan's face, slid his hands under his jaw, caressed every inch of him to keep the tension from returning.

"I meant all of it, Saffron," Cylvan promised breathlessly, refusing to pull their mouths apart. "Everything I said—every single word."

Saffron giggled. "Perhaps—almost every word."

Cylvan's jaw flexed under Saffron's hand. He pulled away with a look of confusion, edging on personal insult.

"What do you mean?" He asked. Saffron raised his eyebrows, then smiled awkwardly.

"You... erm, you declared me your Harmonious King. But... but only so that they would try and heal me, right? Otherwise they would have let me die... because I'm just a beantighe... right?"

Cylvan watched Saffron in silence for a long, long time, and Saffron finally huffed in annoyance.

"Stop looking at me like that!"

"I'm sorry, I just—I find you fascinating."

"Are you teasing me?"

Cylvan's hand found Saffron's again, holding it, then pulling it to his mouth to kiss.

"You and I both know high fey can't lie."

"You and I both know that's bullshit, actually…"

Cylvan smirked against the back of Saffron's hand. He just kept smiling. Kept smiling. Kept smiling—until heat flared in Saffron's cheeks, and something akin to a death rattle tumbled from his mouth.

"N-no!" He wheezed, and Cylvan grinned brighter. "No—*no! Cylvan! Damnit! I'm not—! I can't—!"

"Not what? Can't what?"

"I can't be *king!*" Saffron nearly shrieked, and Cylvan leapt to cover his mouth. Saffron just continued in a near-hysterical hiss. *"Is that even allowed!"*

"What, for me to choose?"

"I'm a *human!*"

"And a rowan witch."

"That's—!"

But Cylvan just leaned forward, pulling Saffron into another gentle kiss.

"I can do whatever I like," Cylvan whispered as they parted again. "I can marry whomever I like."

"But—there's never been a human Harmonious Partner before, has there?" Saffron asked in a tiny voice, face remaining tucked close to Cylvan's as another flicker of panic set in. "Every-one… they already think you're going to bring destruction… there was this gossip column Taran read to me on the train… and they called you *seelie prince* in Connacht… they said it made you the next Proserpina…!"

All just because of *rumors*. Those were only pranks, only students being bullies. But for Cylvan—to legitimately propose to a human? What then? There weren't *pranks* in real life. There wasn't *bullying*—there were death threats. And assassination attempts. And wars. And overthrowing the throne—!

"You can't!" Saffron took Cylvan's face, begging him. "You can't, Cylvan, not me—!"

"Only you," Cylvan insisted. "It's only ever been *you*, Saffron. Even from the beginning—you never took advantage of my true name, except when I deserved it. You saw the good in me, first. You showed me forgiveness. You risked everything to protect both myself and your friends. You're even kind to the forest pixies, and sprites that sleep in flowers, and probably even the dust motes in Danann House's vents. You almost died—for the sole reason of keeping Taran off the throne, because you knew he wouldn't allow the people you care about to live in peace..."

Pressing their foreheads together, Cylvan closed his eyes.

"You do not fear a Night Court—because you've lived your entire life in one. You know what the most vulnerable of all of us need. You understand how to help people—not just humans, but high fey, too. Wild fey, even. To lift another golden-spooned, over-educated, prissy bitch to the throne... would only mean another court of misery for the people who need help the most."

Cylvan cupped his hand behind Saffron's head, holding him.

"Please, Saffron... be my king. Be my Harmonious King. Bring the new perspective Alfidel needs, so that everyone, *everyone*, may know how it feels to live in the Day... not just us who were born into it."

Saffron stared down at their hands clasped together on the sheets. Cylvan's, soft and flawless; Saffron's, cracked and scarred. Two entirely different worlds. Two different lives. He almost refused again, wanting to shake his head, to pull away, to insist *"they'll hate me! They'll hate you! Who's to say they won't do whatever it takes to kill us both...?"*

But instead, he squeezed his eyes closed.

He thought about Hollow. And Letty. He thought about Nimue, whose human death was used for something as petty as ruining Cylvan's reputation. Nimue, who was *used* as an object to invite hate against Cylvan—when it was Taran's hands, glamoured, who really threw her into the waves.

"I don't... know anything," was Saffron's argument, instead. As if Cylvan had forgotten. But Cylvan just combed fingers through Saffron's hair, finally pulling away with a reassuring smile.

"You forget so quickly what I've already promised." He smirked. "I owe you an academic endorsement, *beantighe.*"

Saffron meant to laugh, but Cylvan's sincerity made him hesitate.

"You'll attend Mairwen Academy, as soon as it's safe," Cylvan went on, and Saffron's mouth dropped open. "As a formal student, right alongside me. Of course, there will be some precautions we'll take at first, like glamouring you to look like a fey, maybe... we won't tell anyone you're my fiancé right away, perhaps just a distant relative, or a friend of the family... But, Saffron, you'll enroll in classes. And sit in lectures. And you'll have dry, soul-sucking homework, and stay up all night studying for tests, and cheer for me at hurling matches, and spend all the time you could ever want in the library. You'll even be able to borrow books to take back to your dorm—*and* you can keep them for as long as you want. To read as many times as you want."

"I won't have to burn them," Saffron's voice wavered, knowing it was silly—but the sentiment made more hot tears flood his eyes. "Really?"

"Really."

"But—won't they know? They'll know I don't know anything—"

"King Tross is very good friends with some very good tutors—including Professor Adelard, who already knows about most of this. You'll spend the rest of spring preparing. You might have to spend some time at Morrígan until the gossip dies down here, but you'll do so learning. I've already sent builders to address Beantighe Village and make more repairs in our absence, too. Our dear headmistress has also already fled the country, and Tross has agreed to let me choose her replacement."

"But—how will I have time?"

"Time?"

"Between my chores, and—"

Cylvan burst out laughing, and Saffron punched his arm in

annoyance. But Cylvan just laughed more, mussing up Saffron's hair as he nearly broke down.

"Chores! Oh, perhaps this will be harder than I thought."

"Stop teasing me—Cylvan!"

"Your chores, from this moment forward—are to simply be as cunning and lovely as you are now. Can you do that?"

"... You're teasing me."

"I'm not."

Saffron wrung his fingers together, biting his lip as his mind raced. It was all too much to be told in one moment, so soon after the events of the night before. Or had it been longer than that? How long had he been asleep?

"Are my friends alright?" He asked, feeling a jolt of worry. He'd fallen through the veil immediately after making his rowan oath, he hadn't had any chance to make sure they were alright after the fire. Even if Cylvan already said he sent builders to repair Beantighe Village—"Hollow and Letty and Nimue, Sunbeam, Baba Yaga—and you said Adelard was still here? Is he alright? What about Luvon? And Asche?"

Cylvan pressed a reassuring hand to Saffron's mouth as the anxiety kicked his words into a race, and Saffron breathed in long and hard through his nose.

"Everyone who matters is absolutely fine," Cylvan reassured him, and Saffron wondered if he had heard news of Kaelar's death in the celebration field. "I've been told no humans were harmed in the fire at Beantighe Village, including your friends. I think you already saw their wildflower bouquet next to your bed, there. Adelard has been enjoying the sights of Avren with Professor Dullahan. Asche, I'm sure, is right on the other side of the clinic door waiting for permission to pounce. Luvon might be right alongside them; he also left me with quite a threat yesterday morning. Something about how, if you ever get hurt for my sake again, he'll stuff me full of frostapples and tie me up to one of his trees in the dead of winter, until my eyes pop out and he can squeeze them into wine... Oh, should I have told someone about that...?"

Saffron's anxiety snuffed when he couldn't hold back the uneasy laughter, holding his hand to his chest as it throbbed. He hooked a finger over Cylvan's collar, pulling him in for another quick kiss.

"Thank you," he said with a relieved smile. "Um, I want to write a letter to Baba Yaga and everyone else, letting them know I'm alright... Is that possible?"

"Of course." Cylvan nodded, kissing the back of Saffron's hand before rising to his feet. "I'll fetch some paper and a bird. I'll ask someone to bring you something to eat, as well. How does strawberry cake sound?"

"... Do you actually mean cake, or do you intend to eat me?"

Cylvan smirked. "Don't worry—we'll have plenty of time going forward to eat as much *strawberry cake* as we both want."

Saffron bit back the blush, wringing his hands together on the blanket while he and Cylvan just grinned at one another. Finally, Saffron broke the spell: "Let Asche and Luvon in, too, if you'd like."

"Oh—I wouldn't be able to stop them if I tried."

Cylvan pressed one last kiss to Saffron's forehead, before excusing himself around the partition separating Saffron from the rest of the room. Saffron listened to his voice as it spoke to someone on the other side, followed by his heels echoing into the distance.

Collapsing back into the pillows, Saffron stared up at the ceiling as his heart pounded in his throat. He fondled the woven bracelet around his wrist, recalling what Cylvan said about it acting like his citrine ring did for his own powers.

And—*school*. Saffron would go to *school*. And not just any school—Mairwen, in Avren, where Cylvan attended before Nimue was killed. Just like Cylvan said, Saffron would sit in classes, and have peers, and maybe even wear a uniform that wasn't for cleaning in. He would... eat in the dining hall, maybe.

And live in a dormitory. And have days off to explore the city, or to sit in the library and read for hours and hours and hours... and there would be no one to stop him.

"Oh..." he whispered as it struck him. Blinking back more emotion that burned his eyes, Saffron knew if he continued to cry, he would dry up like a pond on a hot day. But it was hard to keep the fluttering of his stomach under control.

"Close one, huh?"

Saffron bolted upright, surprised by the voice—but there was no one entering from the walkway. Instead, he spotted a stranger perched on the edge of the open window, as if they'd climbed through while Saffron wasn't looking. "Thank god the first rowan witch in centuries didn't die by crossbow, right? That would have been such a waste."

Saffron's instinct was to smile uncomfortably, wondering if the newcomer was some palace guard, or something—but then his eyes lingered on the stranger's ears, as round as Saffron's were. He sat up slightly more, memorizing the rest of the person's appearance, wondering why it was so familiar... before realizing, it reminded him of what Sunbeam wore in the ruins. Comfortable fabrics, clearly worn-in with use. A layered belt donning knives, a rope, a circlet of golden rings that jingled with every movement. His dirty blonde hair was pulled back into a messy ponytail at the base of his neck, and stubble darkened the bottom half of his sun-kissed face. He looked young, but weathered, as if he'd spent his whole life sailing the ocean. But perhaps the most intriguing was his accent, something Saffron had never heard before.

"... Who are you?" Saffron asked in uncertainty, jumping slightly when the stranger kicked his legs forward to get to his feet and approach. He sat on the edge of the bed, opposite where Cylvan had been.

"You know... that fiancé of yours is supposed to be bad news," the stranger said instead of answering. "Especially for humans like you and me."

"... How did you get in here?"

"Don't worry—I'll keep an eye on you. Can't have my newest rowan witch dying at the hands of a Night Court," he continued, as if Saffron didn't speak at all. Running fingers back through his hair, he offered Saffron a handsome smile that made his heart thrum slightly. "I'll let you have your romantic summer before you see me again. I have some things of my own to plan in the meantime, now that this is all in motion... But once everything's settled, once you realize none of these high fey are going to do anything to help you learn what it is you've made an oath to do... come find me in the Finnian ruins, yeah? Ah, and also—tell Sunbeam I already have Chandry waiting there for her, too. She's been, erm... *dying* to see her."

"Tell me your name," Saffron demanded, hating how the man smiled so smugly the moment he raised his voice.

"My name is Ryder Kyteler, your highness."

A surge of energy flooded the room, and Saffron threw his arm up against it. He could then only stare, wide-eyed, as Ryder Kyteler smiled at him, then lifted a hand to show the ring on his finger, like pixie wings pinned in gold.

The ground beneath him illuminated—and he vanished as quickly as he arrived, through an instantaneous veil tear ripping open beneath his feet.

Overwhelm flooded every inch of Saffron's body, splintering his blood, his soul, until the world spun and blood spilled from his nose, his mouth, his eyes, his ears—

Choking, Saffron hunched forward, clutching his chest. He attempted to wipe the blood away on the blankets, gagging on what flooded the back of his throat, coughing and gasping in an attempt to breathe. It made his chest flare, tears flooding his eyes and spilling over in agony.

The ground turned beneath him. He lost his balance, tumbling over the edge of the bed and hitting the wood floor with a miserable grunt as his chest bowed beneath his weight.

It echoed in Saffron's ears, a sound that thundered through

the clinic the moment the tear opened, loud enough that a dozen feet raced inside.

Cylvan was suddenly there, throwing his arms out to grapple for Saffron in shock and drenched in blood on the floor. Touching his face, his hair, Cylvan asked what happened—but Saffron just stared at the empty place where Ryder had vanished, ears ringing with the sound of the veil swallowing him.

Knock, knock.

ACKNOWLEDGMENTS

My partner, soulmate, and cover artist, Mo, who remains my biggest supporter, cheerleader, and the love of my fucking life. Your constant reassurances and shoulder to cry on are only a small part of all the reasons I love and appreciate you, but damn if they are some of the only reasons I keep going sometimes. This series and its success is as much yours as it is mine; I couldn't do it without you. I can't wait to continue to build our little worlds together forever, both what we show people and what we keep to ourselves. Point me where you want me, mon petit coeur noir.

artstation.com/morlevart;
Twitter: @morlevart

Arielle M. DeVito, my developmental editor and copy editor; your feedback is always so incredibly helpful, even though my requests and timelines can be a little wibbly-wobbly. I'm looking forward to working together on so many more project in the future!!

ariellemdevito.com/;
Twitter: @ariellemdevito

The Rowan Blood fandom—I truly never anticipated my debut novel to make such an impact, and your ongoing support, memes, art, and inspiration honestly means the entire world to me. I hope to continue providing characters and worlds that inspire and excite you in the future.

My beta readers, new and old, who provide such valuable insight into the plot and characters; I know every time I promise "I'm not gonna change much in the final version" but I have once again done exactly that and for that I apologize!!

The book reviewers who hooked onto POTS early on, and helped to share my debut with such a wide audience. Big or small, I appreciate you all so much—you're the reason indie dreams come true, and I will continue to shout it from the rooftops.

Ben Alderson, who offers so much constant support and friendship and vent-sessions and idea sharing chats—your friendship means SO MUCH to me, and I can't wait to climb all the way to the top with you and our gay books!

ABOUT THE AUTHOR

Kellen Graves (they/them) is a queer indie writer and artist from the Pacific Northwest, where they live with their partner, two cats, and crystal collection. They also enjoy digital illustration, photography, collecting planners, and disappearing into the ocean.

You can find more info about this release and upcoming releases, see their art, and connect by following Kellen on social media or checking out their website.

TWITTER: @SKELLYGRAVES
INSTAGRAM: @SKELLYGRAVES

SKELLYGRAVES.COM
SKELLYGRAVES.CARRD.CO

ALSO BY KELLEN GRAVES

ROWAN BLOOD

PRINCE OF THE SORROWS (VOLUME ONE)
LORD OF SILVER ASHES (VOLUME TWO)

VOLUME THREE (2023)

THE FOX AND THE DRYAD (2023)
A STANDALONE FANTASY-ROMANCE SET IN A MODERN-DAY ROWAN BLOOD UNIVERSE WITH NEW CHARACTERS, NEW PLOTS, NEW SETTINGS.

ALSO COMING 2023:

SOME ZEALOTS BELIEVED THE WORLD WOULD END IN FIRE-- BUT THE ALIENS WHO RAINED DOWN FROM THE SKY WERE ACTUALLY MADE OF ICE.

EVEN AS A FIG TREE

A SCI-FI ROMANCE FOR NEW ADULTS.